A Hawai'i Anthology

A HAWAI'I ANTHOLOGY

A Collection of Works by
Recipients of the
Hawai'i Award for Literature,
1974–1996

Edited by

JOSEPH STANTON

STATE FOUNDATION ON CULTURE AND THE ARTS
HONOLULU, HAWAI'I

Printed in the United States of America

97 98 99 00 01 02 5 4 3 2 1

ISBN 0-8248-1976-4 cloth   ISBN 0-8248-1977-2 paper

University of Hawai'i Press books are printed on
acid-free paper and meet the guidelines for permanence
and durability of the Council on Library Resources.

Distributed by
University of Hawai'i Press
2840 Kolowalu Street
Honolulu, Hawai'i 96822

Contents

❧

1. Growing Up in Hawai'i

2. Legend and Song

3. Historical Considerations

4. Growing Up Elsewhere

5. Being Where We Are

List of Art Selections

The art selections that appear in this volume and the water color painting that appears on the cover are all works included in the Art in Public Places Collection of the State Foundation on Culture and the Arts and have been reproduced with the permission of the artists.

Evening Light   FRONT COVER
Shizuko Mansho, 1996
watercolor on paper, 21″ × 28¾″

Hands of Children at Kilohana, Manaʻe   5
Richard A. Cooke, III, 1980
color photograph, 14″ × 19¾″

Young Koa, Mauna Loa   39
Boone M. Morrison, 1974
black and white photograph, 35½″ × 35½″

Kaukolo Nā Maka O Ka Makani I Ka Mālie-Nana, 1990   117
Anne Kapulani Landgraf, 1990
black and white photograph, 12¾″ × 9¼″

Hotel Window, Chicago   177
Francis Haar, 1957
black and white photograph, 19″ × 15¾″

Underwater #15   207
Wayne Allen Levin, 1984
black and white photograph, 12″ × 17¾″

Preface

The Hawai'i Award for Literature represents a tradition of recognizing outstanding literary achievements with relevance to Hawai'i and Hawai'i's people. Since 1974, the award has been presented annually by the State Foundation on Culture and the Arts and the Hawai'i Literary Arts Council in a public ceremony convened by the governor. Award recipients reflect the rich and diverse history and perspectives of our literary heritage; a heritage that touches the shores of many lands and traverses the hearts and imaginations of many peoples.

This anthology of literary contributions is a celebration of the creative spirit of Hawai'i. It is a valuable educational resource and a wonderful *ho'okupu* or gift offering of *aloha* by the writers honored with this award. The collection echoes the distinguished voices of Hawai'i's literary luminaries and their lasting words which nurture, heal, reveal, inspire, and shape our lives.

My hope is that through these selections the reader will be instilled with the spirit of these esteemed writers in keeping with a traditional Hawaiian saying: *"A 'ole pau ke 'ike i ka hālau ho'okāhi"* (One can enjoy learning from different knowledgeable sources).

WENDELL P. K. SILVA
Executive Director
State Foundation on Culture and the Arts

Acknowledgments

This volume has come into being primarily because of the enthusiasm, perseverance, patience, and hard work of Estelle Enoki of the State Foundation on Culture and the Arts. It was her idea in the first place, and she has all down the line provided the energy and support that has made the project possible. Wendell Silva, in his role as executive director of SFCA, was most helpful throughout the planning process. We are likewise grateful to the SFCA commissioners for their ongoing support. It should be noted, too, that the assistance of Ronald Yamakawa and the SFCA Art in Public Places Program enabled us to illustrate this book with award-winning visual works of art from the SFCA collection.

The SFCA should also be congratulated for continuing its support for the Hawai'i Award for Literature all these many years. Between the giving of the first award to O. A. Bushnell in 1974 and the most recent joint award to Eric Chock and Darrell Lum in 1996 lies over twenty years of annual declarations that literature matters. In this regard, the involvement of Hawai'i's various governors in the award decision has always been symbolically important.

It has been the responsibility of the Hawai'i Literary Arts Council to nominate writers for the award. The various HLAC presidents and board members who have kept the award going through their volunteer efforts deserve special thanks. HLAC's nonprofit endeavors have helped sustain Hawai'i's literary life for two decades.

Our thanks, too, to the various publishers, authors, and other copyright holders who have given us permission to reprint the works in this volume: Ku'Pa'a Publishing Inc. for "The Pool," Milton Murayama for "The Substitute"; Bamboo Ridge Press for "from 'No Mistaking,'" "The Mango Tree," "Termites," "Poem for My Father," "Papio," "Mānoa Cemetary," and "My First Walk with Ashley"; Bishop Museum Press for "from 'Within the Circle of the Sea,'" "The Shark Guardian," "The Punahou Spring," and "Can You Keep a Secret"; Rubellite Johnson for "from *Kumulipo: The Hawaiian Hymn of Creation*"; University of Hawai'i Press for "from *Nā Mele o Hawai'i Nei*", "Fire Chant for King Ka-lā-kaua," "August 22," "Morning," and "Inhabitant"; Mutual Publishing for "Liholiho and the Longnecks" and "The Marchers of the Night"; W. S. Merwin for "Kanaloa," "The Strangers from the Horizon," "Chord," "Hearing the Names of the Valleys," "Manini," "After Douglas," "Rain at Night," "The Last One," and "Anniversary on the Island"; Gavan Daws and Island Heritage Press for "Tides"; Victoria Kneubuhl for "from *The Conversion of Kaʻahumanu*"; O. A. Bushnell for "from *Kaʻaʻawa: A Novel about Hawaiʻi in the 1850s*"; Aldyth Morris for "from *Damien*"; Ruth Denney for "The Squire of Melford"; Leon Edel for "A Town in Saskatchewan"; Maxine Hong Kingston for "The Making of More Americans"; Marjorie Sinclair for "The Feather Lei," "Green Place," and "The Octopus"; Yoshiko Matsuda for "Selected Tanka"; Phyllis Hoge Thompson for "The Palms Transplanted," "Naupaka of the Mountain," "The First Heaven," "Wāimanalo," "The Word in the Water at Kaʻena," and "Blue Ginger: Déjà Vu"; Ian MacMillan for "The Rock,"; Hawaiʻi Literary Arts Council for "Volcano" and "State Symbol"; *Chaminade Literary Review* for "Oʻahu: Midday Concert in Orange Air"; and Cathy Song for "Easter: Wahiawā, 1959," "Lost Sister," "Untouched Photograph of Passenger," "Chinatown," "Mother on River Street," "Mooring," "Tangerines and Rain," and "Square Mile."

Introduction

❦

The Hawai'i Award for Literature is the most important literary award given in the State of Hawai'i. It is a recognition that a writer is a mature talent and an acknowledgment of the widespread appreciation the writer has earned in Hawai'i. Since 1974, when O. A. Bushnell was the first winner, the Hawai'i Award for Literature has become a primary opportunity for collaboration between the Hawai'i State Foundation on Culture and the Arts and the Hawai'i Literary Arts Council. The role played by Hawai'i's governor as the official presenter of the award and the celebration of the award occasion in the governor's office have underscored Hawai'i's desire to encourage excellence of literary endeavor.

The recipients of the award have been diverse, and their works as creative writers—and in some cases also as historians, linguists, folklorists, and practitioners of other disciplines of cultural study—have captured many important dimensions of the story of Hawai'i and of the many groups of people who have come to live here. The ways in which the works of the winners of the Hawai'i Award for Literature are reflective of Hawai'i have been carefully considered in the selection of works for this anthology. Although the first priority in the selection of pieces was the literary quality and individual strength of the writing, there has also been an effort to choose works that, in various general and specific ways, present an account of what Hawai'i is or has been.

This accidental fellowship of selections by recipients of the award cannot be expected to be inclusive of all aspects of Hawai'i as a physical and spiritual place; we cannot ask this collection to cover everyone and everything that is Hawai'i. This book cannot come close to completeness, but it is our hope that this gathering of well-wrought fragments from the desks of some of our best writers will point in interesting directions and stimulate our minds and imaginations so that we will be ready for the excellent works of the writer who will receive the award next year and the writer who will win the year after that, and so on, continuing into the next century. Hawai'i's literature will, of course, never be finished.

The plan of this volume has been developed in line with our desire to give the story of Hawai'i an interesting shape and to sequence the selections in such a way that the reader will find the individual works supplementing each other and building toward an enriched view. Ideally, this book would be as satisfying to reread as to read for the first time. Although we have tried to provide an arrangement with a coherent flow, we understand that many readers will want to pick their own sequence. Each section and each individual piece can stand alone.

Our first section, "Growing Up in Hawai'i," starts the book with powerful stories reflective of earlier eras. All three tales show us remarkable elders and give us compelling glimpses into matters of life and death. First, John Dominis Holt's story "The Pool" presents a young boy's view of a North Shore place and a Hawaiian elder who leads the boy to some important understandings and to some equally important inexplicable mysteries. Second, Milton Murayama's "The Substitute" gives us an unforgettable portrait of some intense family relationships in the Japanese camp of a Maui plantation. Lastly, Darrell Lum's "No Mistaking" gives us the distinctive voice of an elderly Chinese uncle reminiscing about his life.

The next cluster displays the rich tradition of story and song that resides in the heart of Hawaiian culture. Katharine Luomala gives us the sweep of the great Hawaiian epics. Rubellite Johnson renders one of the most important and beautiful of Hawaiian chants, The Kumulipo—a work that Johnson shows to be a blend of science and history as well as a celebration of the miracle of life. Samuel Elbert, Mary Pukui, and Alfons Korn give us further access to poetic and mythic dimensions of traditional materials. W. S. Merwin writes as a modern or postmodern singer of mysteries, who is in many respects in tune with older traditions of poetic thinking. Some of his poems here are mythical in their inclinations; others are historical. Merwin's poetically historical works help prepare us for the next section.

In the third chapter "Historical Considerations" are raised by Gavan Daws and A. Grove Day in elegantly essayistic pieces. O. A. Bushnell demonstrates what can be accomplished in the historical novel; and Victoria Kneubuhl and Aldyth Morris show us that dramatizations of history can enable us to experience events of long ago with intimate immediacy.

In "Growing Up Elsewhere" we are given three very different childhoods: Reuel Denney's in an Irish-American neighborhood in Brooklyn; Leon Edel's in a multiethnic village in Canada; and Maxine Hong Kingston's in a California Chinatown. It is worth noting that Denney's and Edel's pieces are relatively new works that are receiving their first widespread distribution through this anthology. These three pieces illustrate the diverse nature of the backgrounds of the people who live in the State of Hawai'i.

The last chapter, "Being Where We Are," showcases reflections upon what it means to be here in the beautiful and surprising place that is Hawai'i. We have fine stories here by Marjorie Sinclair and Ian MacMillan, but the dominant mode in this last section is poetic. Hawai'i's landscapes—both inner and outer—have inspired a wide range of lyrical musings. For many years now Hawai'i has had more than its share of fine poets. The poetic reflections of Marjorie Sinclair, Yoshiko Matsuda, Phyllis Thompson, Eric Chock, John Unterecker, and Cathy Song seem the best way to try to come to grips with the essential, elusive something that is Hawai'i. The verses collected in these concluding pages demonstrate that poetry here, as everywhere, is the news that stays news.

It is perhaps our greatest hope for this anthology that it will confirm that much can be done in Hawai'i in the literary field. It is our earnest desire for this collection that young writers of Hawai'i, or even those many of us who are no longer young, will find encouragement in this collection to keep working at the not-quite-hopeless task of striving to arrange the best words in the best order, so that twenty years from now there will be a second volume, continuing this collection, that will be just as good as the first.

I

GROWING UP IN HAWAI'I

John Dominis Holt

In one of his last books, *The Art of the Featherwork in Old Hawai'i*, John Dominis Holt carefully describes the crucial differences between the various kinds of feathers: "Even in color there is a difference. O'o feathers are pale yellow, the color of lemons. Mamo feathers are golden yellow, almost orange. . . . The 'e'e feathers give it the appearance of weightlessness—splashes of pale yellow sprouting from the more compact koto mamo feathers." The passionate precision of that passage says much about the importance of John Dominis Holt and his books. He wrote his way toward the truth of his various matters with evident desire to capture his subject in the best possible way.

There is no doubt that Holt was deeply concerned about his family's past. He has talked about his childhood desire to know what his elders knew. "I would sit at the edges of the inner circle of elders as they ruminated on past events. Old chiefs, kings, queens. . . . I absorbed the heat of this talk and greedily absorbed my heritage for they spoke of family members and their circle of friends, mostly people from royalist families, the Hawaiian and part-Hawaiian aristocracy during the last days of the Monarchy."

A descendant of Hawaiian and Tahitian chiefs, European nobility, and New England missionaries, he was proud that his blood mingled many far-flung peoples, and he felt an interest in the ironies and complications of those mixtures. Although the protagonists in his fictional works are usually aristocratic, as in the plays of Chekhov, the comforts of their furnishings solve nothing for Holt's inquiring characters. In fictions such as "The Pool" and *Waimea Summer*, his characters must face dangerous outer and inner landscapes—and face them well. Always the beauty of Holt's prose is primary to the finding of a saving grace.

Among Holt's major works are the novel *Waimea Summer*, the collection of stories *Princess of the Night Rides*, and the play *Kaulana na Pua—Famous Are the Flowers*. His numerous nonfiction books and the many publications of the publishing house he founded and nurtured are among the ways he continued, throughout his life, to listen along the edge of the family circle.

The Pool

It was perhaps as large as a good-sized house. It tended to be round in shape. At the far southern end of Kawela Bay, it sat open to the wind, the sun. Scattered clumps of coconut grew around it, splashing shade with the look of Rorschach ink blots here and there at the edges of the water.

Fresh water fed into it from underground arteries, blended with warmer water pushed in by the tide from the sea through a volcanic umbilical cord. "The lagoon," as we called it, had a definitive link to the sea, being joined as it was by virtue of this unique tubular connection.

We were always afraid of "the lagoon." For one thing it was alleged to be so deep as to be way beyond anyone's imagination like the idea of endless space to the universe or the unending possibilities of time. Its dark blue-green waters were testament to the fact of the pool being deep according to our elders. We accepted their calculation, but not entirely. It was deep to be sure, but not depthless.

Within "the lagoon," huge ulua, a local variety of pompano or crevalle, would suddenly appear in ravenous groups of three or four, chasing mullet in from the sea. Once in the confines of this small body of water the mullet were no match for the larger, carnivorous predators. Ulua could grow to the size of three or four feet and weigh nearly a hundred pounds. The mullet feasts by ulua in the lagoon were wild and unpleasant scenes. We would watch as children, both enthralled and frightened, as mullet leaped for their lives in glittering silvery schools of forty or fifty fish, some to fall with deadly precision into the jaws of the larger fish. The waters swirled then and sometimes became bloody. The old folks said this would attract sharks. They would wait at the opening of the tube in the ocean to prey on the ulua, whose bellies now were fat from feasting on mullet. These tumultuous invasions were not frequent, but they were reason enough to keep us from swimming in "the lagoon." Perhaps most fearful to us were the tales we heard offered by assorted adults that a goddess of ancient times inhabited these strange blue-green waters. Some knew her name and mentioned it. I have forgotten what it was. She was said to be a creature of unearthly beauty, a queen of the Polynesian spirit world, who revealed herself at times in the forms of great strands of limu, a special seaweed growing only in brackish water; her appearance depending on tides, the moon, winds, and certain cosmic manifestations we could not completely understand because they were mentioned in Hawaiian.

I wandered by the hour in the area of "the lagoon" and on the reefs nearby with an ancient, bearded sage who was our caretaker. His hut of clapboard and corrugated roofing sat near an old kūʻula, a fisherman's shrine, half-hidden under some hau bushes. His people had been fishermen from time immemorial. Some of his relatives lived a short distance down the coast toward Waimea Bay. Infrequent visits were made upon the old man by these ʻohana; usually three or four young men came to consult him about fishing. His knowledge of the north shore and its inhabitants in the sea was vast. Once or twice a year he paid a ritual visit to their little house standing in its tiny lawn surrounded by taro patches and sheltered at the front by clumps of coconut and lauhala trees. He spent hours explaining in Hawaiian, and in his own unique use of pidgin, the lore of the region, mentioning with distaste his wine-drinking nephews. I was only four or five years of age at the time. Much of his old-world ramblings is now lost to me.

But I do remember him mentioning that the sea entrance to "the lagoon" was too deep for him to take me to it. He was too old now to dive to those depths. He secretly led me to the kūʻula, a built-up rock shrine, round in shape, where we took small reef fish and crustacea we had speared. We would pray; the old man in Hawaiian, I in a mixture of the old native tongue and English. It was being impressed upon us how we must speak perfect English. The use of Hawaiian was discouraged. After prayers we would leave offerings on the kūʻula walls and walk to "the lagoon" where more prayers were said and the remaining bits of fish thrown into the pool as offerings to the beautiful goddess.

All of these activities fell within a definitive framework of time and circumstance. These were not helter-skelter rituals. I obeyed without question and I declared it untrue when confronted by my mother—whose father, a half-white, had lived for years as a recluse in the native style in ʻIao Valley—that the old man of Kawela was teaching me pagan ways.

In horror one day I heard the old man say "hemo ia oe kou lole—take off your clothes," which consisted of a pair of chopped-off dungarees.

"Hemo la oe kou lole e holo oe a iʻa i ka lua wai—take off your clothes and swim like a fish across the pool." My body froze and goose bumps formed everywhere on my skin.

"Awiwi—hurry."

I stood in sullen defiance, thinking: He is an old man, a servant. He cannot order me to do anything, anything.

"Au, keiki, Au! Swim, child, swim! Do not be afraid. They are with us."

I remained motionless.

"Auwe, heaha keia keiki kane? He kaika mahine puiwa paha?—What is this child, a frightened girl?"

Thoughts came to me of past fishing expeditions when I clung to the old man's back and he dove with me into holes filled with lobsters and certain crabs. He would choose as time allowed, pluck them from the coral walls, hand me two. Then, I could cling to him with only the use of my legs. In time I learned to rise to the surface alone, clinging with all my might to the two lobsters the old man had handed me. What excitement the first of these expeditions created! I leaped and danced around the crawling catch. We went down for a second take. Again two were brought up. On the reef above they were crushed, one then left as an offering on the kūʻula walls, the other fed to the akua in the pool. I was four or five then and wild with joy.

There were other days when he took me to great caverns swarming with fish of such brilliant colors you were nearly blinded by the reds, yellows, greens, blues and stripes. Above on the reef he would name them for me. Patiently he named them, these reef fish, aglow in cavern waters: the lauʻīpala; the manini; the uhu; the ʻalaʻihi; the kihikihi with its black, yellow and white stripes; the humuhumu with its blue patch on the throat and vibrant yellow and red fins.

On one very special day, a sacred day in his life and mine as well—for I was linked to the family gods, the ʻaumākua —he took me, clinging to his back, to the great sandy places under the sharp lava edges of Oʻahu's North Shore, to the places where the great sharks lazed in the light of day. Breaks in the lava walls sent shafts of light to sandy ocean floors and there we could see the sometimes-dreaded monsters rolling from side to side in harmless, peaceful rest. Shooting up to the surface, the old man would breathlessly tell me the names of this or that shark—names given them by his contemporaries.

"Why names?" I would ask wonderingly.

"Are they not our parents, our guardians—our ʻaumākua? Did you not see the old chief covered with limu and barnacles? He is the chief, the heir of Kamohoaliʻi. I used to feed him myself and clean the ʻaumākua from his eyes. Now a younger member of my clan does that."

I could not absorb these calm, reassuring concerns of denizens I had been taught to dread from early years.

But had I not been down in their resting place, close enough to see yellow eyes, to almost feel the roughness of their skin scraping like sandpaper across my arms?

My dreams were wild for several nights and my parents, worried, held several conferences with the old man. He was chastened, but at my insistence we went several times more to the holes under coral ledges to see the ʻaumākua lazing in the daytime hours.

And now, frozen at the edge of the green pool, I looked hatefully at this magnificent relic of a Hawai'i that was long vanished. I loved him. There was no question I loved him deeply. Ours was a special kind of love of a man for a child.

I was blond-haired. Exposed for weeks to the summer sun when we made long stays at Kawela, I became almost platinum blond.

The old man was bearded, tall and thin. Still muscular. He was pure Hawaiian. Blond though my hair might be and my skin fair, I was nonetheless three-eighths Hawaiian. I think this captured the old man's fancy—often he would say to me in pidgin, "You one haole boy, yet you one Hawaiian. I know you Hawaiian—you mama hapa-haole, you papa hapa-haole. How come you so white? You hair ke'oke'o?" He would laugh, draw me close to him and rub his scruffy beard against my face as though in doing this he would rub some of his brownness off and ink forever the dark rich tones of a calabash into my pale skin.

It was love that finally led me to loosen the buttons of my shorts and kick them off and race plunging into the green pool. I swam with all the speed I could and reached in what seemed a very long time the opposite side. When I turned around, the old man was bent over with laughter. I had never seen him laugh with such gustatory abandon.

"Look you mea li'i-li'i. All dry up. Like one laho poka'o ka'o—like an old man's balls and penis. No can see now." He pointed and made fun of my privates, shrivelled from a combination of cold water and fear. I turned away from him and raced home, naked.

Four days later I walked past the pool, across the sharp lava flats to the old man's hut. Flies buzzed in legion. The stench was unbearable. I opened the door. Lying face up and straight across his little bed, the old man lay in the first stages of putrefaction. Sometime during my absence the old man had died. At midday? In the cool of night? In the late afternoon, the time of lengthening shadows and the gathering of the brilliant array of gold-orange and red off the coast of Ka'ena to the south facing the sea of Kanaloa? When did the old man die? Why did he die? Tears began to stream down my cheeks.

I shut the door of the shack and went to sit in the shade of the hau branches near the kū'ula—my heart was pounding so I could hardly breathe. What should I do? Tears rolled in little salty rivulets down my cheeks. I enjoyed the taste when the moisture entered my mouth at the corners of my lips.

What should I do? Some instinct compelled me not to go home and tell my family of the death of the old man and the putrefaction that filled the cottage. Perhaps I was too stunned—perhaps it was perversity.

The family was gathering for a large weekend revel. Aunts, uncles, cousins—all the generations coming together. Usually I enjoyed these congregations of the family. There would be masses of food, music, games and the great lauhala mats spread on the lawn near the sandy beach. Someone would make a bonfire and the talk would begin. I would sit at the edges of the inner circle of elders as they ruminated on past events. Old chiefs, kings, queens, great house parties-scandals and gossip of one sort or another would billow up from the central core of adults and leap into the air like flames. I absorbed the heat of this talk and greedily absorbed my heritage for they spoke of family members and their circles of friends, mostly people from royalist families, the Hawaiian and part-Hawaiian aristocracy during the last days of the Monarchy. I heard of this carriage or that barouche or landau, this house or that garden, this beautiful woman in love with so-and-so, or that abiding "good and patient" soul whose handsome husband dashed about town in a splendid uniform, lavishing on his paramour a beautiful house, a carriage and team, and flowing silk holokūs fitted finely to her ample figure. O, the tales that steamed up from those gatherings on lauhala mats at Kawela's shores!

One of my great-aunts, an aberration of sorts, came once in a while for the weekend. She brought a paid companion and her Hawaiian maid. She looked like Ethel Barrymore and talked with an English accent. Her gossip was spicy, often vicious, and I loved it. She fascinated me as caged baboons fascinate some people who go to zoos.

She was also forbidding. I thought she had strange powers.

Often the old man had joined us during these family gatherings, and I would sit on his lap until I fell asleep.

There was something of great warmth and unforgettable charm in these gatherings. Even as the talk raged over romances, land dealings and money transactions long passed, I revelled in hearing about them and loved everyone there, particularly those who talked. There was an immense feeling of comfort and safety, of lovingness for me on those long nights of talk.

But now under the hau branches I scorned my family. I hated them. I held them responsible, for some unknown reason—a child's special reason I suppose; inexplicable and slightly irrational.

I decided not to tell them of the old man's death but to run down the path along the beach to the house where his relatives lived. I would tell them. They must rescue him from his rotting state; they must take him from the tomb of his stench-filled shack. I ran down along the beach, sometimes taking the path pressed into winding shape from human use in the middle of grass and pōhuehue vines.

The men were at home, mending fishing nets. This was a good sign. I ran to the rickety steps leading upward to the porch where they sat working at their nets.

"The old man is dead," I said forcefully.

One of the young men looked down at me.

"Make."

"Yes, he's make. His body is stink. He make long time." They put down their mending tools and came in a body to the top of the stairs.

"How you know?" one of them asked.

"We just came back from Punaluʻu. I went to the old man's house. I saw plenny flies. I open the door and see him covered with flies. It was steenk." I spoke partly in pidgin to give greater credibility to my message.

They fussed around, called into the house, held a brief conference, and faced me again.

"You wen' tell anybody?"

"No, nobody."

The four men took the path at a run. I was under the hau bushes, catching my breath, when they flew past me heading back to their house. I sat for what seemed like hours in the shade of hau.

My sister appeared at the side of the pool. I ran to fend her off. She caught the stench from the shack.

"Something stinks."

"The old man has fish drying outside his shack."

"Where is he?"

"Down on the reef fishing."

"When are you coming home?"

"Pretty soon."

"Mamma is looking for you—Uncle Willson is here with those brats." She referred to his adopted grandchildren. Uncle Willson was a grand old relic. Something quite unreal. He was brimming always with stories of the past.

"Aunt Emily has arrived with Miss Rhodes and that other one," my sister added, referring to the maid whom she hated.

The cottages would be bulging and perhaps tents would be set up for the servants.

My Sister swung around abruptly and took the path back to our cottage. She was always purposeful in her movements.

"Tell Mamma I'll be home soon and kiss Uncle Willson and Aunt Emily for me."

"Don't stay too long. You'll get sunburned."

I walked past the pool. It seemed purer in its color today. Deep blue, deep green. I was crying again. The stench filled the air with a stronger, punishing aroma as the sun rose high and began the afternoon descent beyond Kaʻena Point. I walked along the reef; the tide was rising. I peeked into holes the old man had shown me, watched idly the masses of fish swimming in joyous aimlessness it seemed.

What ruled their lives? There was life and death among them. They were continually in danger of being devoured by larger fish. Some grew old and died, I suppose, they died of old age.

Death. Such an angry, total thing. There was no escaping it.

I looked back at the shack and shook my fists. The old man's nephews had returned with gleaming cans. They poured the liquid which filled them all around the little house. I rushed backed to the hau bushes as two of them threw lighted torches of newspaper at different places around the shack. Soon it was in flames which leaped to the sky; as the dry wood caught fire, it crackled angrily. The flies buzzed at a distance from the blaze as though waiting for it to die down. The heat was intense. The smell of burning rotting flesh unbearable.

I ran from the hau bushes toward the pool. One of the men saw me and yelled, "Go home, boy. Go home."

"Git da hell outa heah, you goddam haole," another one shouted. I was angry and stunned in not being accepted as a Hawaiian by the old man's nephews.

I ran around the pool at the side we seldom crossed. My family was massing nearby to watch the fiery spectacle.

"What's happening, son?" my father asked with more than usual kindness.

I ran to my mother and hugged her thighs.

"The old man is dead. I found him. He was stinking. I ran down to tell his family."

"And now the bastards are burning him up," my father said. "It's against the law."

Aunt Emily had arrived on the arms of her companion and maid. Her handsome face pointed its powerful features to the center of the burning mass.

"What is happening?" she asked in Hawaiian.

"Our caretaker died. Been dead for several days. The boy found him."

"What are they doing?"

"It's illegal. They're cremating him without going through the usual procedures."

Aunt Emily blasted forth with a number of her original and unrepeatable castigations. Everyone listened. They were gems of Hawaiian metaphor.

Uncle Willson and his man servant arrived.

"The poor old bastard finally died. He was the best fisherman of these parts in his younger days. No one could beat him. As a boy he was chosen to go down to the caverns and select the shark to be taken to use for the making of drums. His family were fishermen. One branch was famed as kahunas. He was a marvel in his day."

"But Willy," Aunt Emily was saying in a commanding tone. "Those brutes are burning his body. The boy here says it was rotten. He'd been dead for several days. The whole thing's a matter for the Board of Health authorities. The police should be called."

"No, no!" I screamed.

"Emily dear," Great Uncle Willson intervened. "He is one of us. His 'ohana, those young men, are a part of us. Leave them alone. They are doing what they think best."

I had gone from my mother to my nurse Kulia, a round, happy, sweet-smelling Hawaiian woman.

"No cry, baby. No cry. We all gotta die sometime. Da ole man was real old."

"Not that old," I whimpered.

Aunt Emily cast one of her iciest looks at me.

"Stop that snivelling. Stop it this instant. What utter foolishness to cry that way over a dirty, bearded old drunk."

She turned to my mother,

"This child was allowed to be too much with that old brute. I think his attachment was quite unnatural—quite unnatural."

"Another one of your theories, Aunt Emily," my mother snapped.

"Not a thing but good common sense. Look at him clinging to Kulia and whimpering like a girl."

Kulia took me away. We walked on the beach.

How I hated Aunt Emily's Ethel Barrymore profile and her English accent.

Late that day, in the early evening, the old man's nephews came back and carried off his charred remains in the empty cans of kerosene. No one ever found out what they did with them.

When did the old man die? Why did he die? This I will never know. We called him Bobada, but I remember from something Great Uncle Willson said on the night the shack was burned that Bobada's real name was Pali Kapihe.

Milton Murayama

Writing about Milton Murayama's *All I Asking for Is My Body*, Arnold Hiura described it as "the only comprehensive literary treatment of the Hawai'i plantation experience, an experience which directly or indirectly affects a very large segment of Hawaii's population." Hiura points out Murayama's remarkable success at capturing "the real, human situation of the plantation."

Milton Murayama was born in Lahaina, Maui and grew up in Lahaina and in the nearby plantation camp, Pu'ukoli'i. Both localities would later serve as his subjects when he began to write fiction centered on life in Hawai'i in the 1930s. One of the provocative aspects of these stories was their implicit comparison of the authoritarian, hierarchical structure of the plantation system to similar structures in the Japanese family.

During World War II, Murayama trained at a Military Intelligence Language School and served with Army Intelligence in India. He received a B.A. in English and philosophy from the University of Hawai'i in 1947 and an M.A. in Chinese and Japanese from Columbia University in 1950. For many years Murayama worked at jobs that would allow him time and energy to write at night.

All I Asking for Is My Body is the manuscript that resulted from those late-night efforts. Meeting with resistance from commercial publishers to his innovative presentation of plantation voices, he eventually decided to publish the book himself in 1975. The University of Hawai'i Press republished it in 1988, after its many years of gathering fame. It has today the status of a classic and pioneering work of Asian-American writing that is especially admired by the many younger writers to which it offers inspiration and a potent example of what can be accomplished. To writers in Hawai'i, it has been a galvanizing demonstration that the local writer could look toward his or her own experiences and forms of language as sources for literary work.

The University of Hawai'i Press published Murayama's *Five Years on a Rock* in 1994. It is the story of the Oyama family in the years that precede the action of *All I Asking for Is My Body*. The sequel to the original novel is also in the works.

Murayama has adapted the story of the Oyama family for the stage in a much-praised drama produced by the Asian-American Theatre Company of San Francisco. Other plays by Murayama include the 1977 historical drama *Yoshitsune*.

The Substitute

Mother had always been weak and sickly but she got so sick I thought she was going to die. It was the end of January 1934 and we all had rotten teeth, but hers were the worst and she had them all pulled at Dr. Hamaguchi's and fainted and was rushed to Dr. Kawamura's. She stayed at Dr. Kawamura's three-bed hospital for a week and father had to stay home and cook and launder for us as he'd done a year ago for a couple of months. Tosh was a freshman in high school and he went directly to Aoki Store after school, and so I was number-one son and father told me to look after things when he decided to go out to sea. I told three-year-old Hanae to look in on mother every so often and come and get me at school if she fainted. Takako and Miwa were in school with me.

We always stopped home after grade school on our way to language school, and after a week mother was on her cushion on the floor, legs doubled under her, sewing a kimono.

"Why don't you rest some more?" I said.

"I'm all right."

"Why don't you sew something easy like a pants or a dress?"

"There's more money in a kimono."

"Why don't you sit on a chair or at the sewing machine where you can stretch your legs?"

"There's a proper way of doing everything."

Father's fishing was so bad, mother's sewing was the only money coming in lots of times. She'd taught herself to sew by watching Mr. Oshiro sew when we lived next door to his tailor shop on Dickenson Street. Both Tosh and I got hit by cars, and mother finally persuaded father that it was a bad-luck house, and we moved to Omiya Camp. Now she took more orders than she could handle.

A couple of weeks later I came home from Lili'uokalani School and shouted as usual, *"Tada ima!"* When she didn't answer, I ran into the house without washing my feet. She was sprawled on the floor. "Mother!" I shook her and touched her forehead. I got a futon from the bedroom and lifted her onto it and freed her legs from under her and covered her with another futon. Then

I flew out of the house shouting, "Hanae! Hanae!" and kept running. I met Takako and Miwa coming home from school. "Quick! Taka-chan, go get Mrs. Kanai! Mama's fainted! Miwa, you stay with Mama! Hurry! Run!" I didn't stop till I got to Dr. Kawamura's and my face felt puffed like a balloon fish. "Doctor, mother has fainted! I just found her! I don't know how long she's been unconscious!"

He grabbed his black bag and drove his car to Back Street and through the dirt road into Omiya Camp. He knelt beside mother and put something under her nose and she jerked back her head and opened her eyes. "I . . . I felt so dizzy," she said. "You'll be all right. Can you stand up? We'll take you to the hospital for a checkup." We lifted her and took her to his car. The three-bed hospital was empty, and mother said, "I'll take the same bed, it was lucky the last time," and we lowered her into it. Mrs. Kanai, the wife of the Methodist language school principal, bustled in with Takako. "What happened? How are you?" "I'm sorry to be such a nuisance," mother said. "You're not being a nuisance." She sat on a chair and held mother's hand. Then she went into the other room and talked to Dr. Kawamura and came out. "The doctor says you're going to be all right, your mother's going to be all right," turning to me and Takako. "Come, Taka-chan, I'll walk you back to school. Kiyo-chan will sit with her. You have to get well, *ne?* You have to want to get well, *ne?* It would be *zannen* to die in a strange place like Hawai'i, *ne?*"

Father was out at sea and was not due back till tomorrow night. When Takako came back from her one-hour language school class, I sent her to Aoki Store to get Tosh. "How you feeling?" Tosh said. "I'm all right now, I just overworked myself." "You shouldn't worry about the debt. Just take care of your body." When outside Tosh said, "How come you never been call me earlier?" "I would've if she was real bad." "You goin' stay with her?" "Yeah." "Good. When's Papa coming home?" "Tomorrow." "You know, he oughta quit fishing. There's no more fish left in the sea. All it does is we go deeper in the hole and Mama over-worries and overworks. And damn wahine, she too superstitious. She thinks she goin' die, she believe in it. She talk to you about it?" "No." "Yeah, she no can get it out of her head." "Why?" "They all like that. Bulaheads are crazy."

Mother did seem to have more superstitions than most people. She insisted that rice should always be scooped at least twice from the big bowl to the individual bowls even if the second scoop was a token one without any rice on the ladle. The double scooping protected the family from seeing a second mother, meaning your first mother would not die or run away. *Mama* in Japanese meant cooked rice or mother.

Then there was the bad-luck word *shi*. It could be the number "four" or "death" depending on the character. All through 1933 mother worried about father because he was forty-two years old and forty-two was bad luck because it was pronounced *shi-ni*, which had the same sound as *shi-ni-iku* (to go to die). Father laughed it off saying it was nothing but silly Chinese and Buddhist superstition, but sure enough he had two near fatal accidents at sea. Once his anchor rope got tangled around his propeller in a storm and he drifted a full day before he cut it loose. He tied a rope around his waist and dived beneath the boat and dived for his life every time the thirty-two-foot sampan reared up and slapped its stern over his head like a giant palm. The other fishermen had organized a search party by the time he came chugging home. He shrugged, "With the rope, they'd find my body at least." Later in the year a tsunami slammed his boat against a pile of rocks near the wharf. The boat was badly damaged, but he escaped without a scratch.

I went home to cook for the girls and went back to the small hospital room and sat there while mother slept. I skipped school the next day and stayed at the hospital. She was awake but didn't seem to get any better.

I sent Miwa to wait for father at the wharf the next day and he came directly to the hospital. "How are you?" "I'm just tired." Mother had a tall nose with a slight cleft at the end. She rubbed it with the tip of her finger like she was trying to rub it smooth, "In Japan they say people with these clefts die young." Don't talk like a fool, you'll outlive us all," father said.

She stayed at the hospital for three days and father stayed home and cooked and sat with her. When he decided to go out to sea after a week, I was assigned to cook and pack the school lunches and cook supper and build the fire for the bath. Hanae was to watch her and not run off to play as she'd done before. Takako was to help with the cooking and she and Miwa were to wash the dishes and clothes and do the ironing. Every night I cooked some rice gruel and crushed some fried fish with a spoon and tried to feed mother like she was a baby, but she hardly ate. Dr. Kawamura came every day with more pills and medicines in bottles, but they didn't seem to help her.

One day she looked so tired I stayed home from school and sat with her.

"We have a very large debt," she said weakly. "We owe Aoki Store about $2,000, then Chatani Fish Market, hmmm, maybe about the same, Tanabe Store about $400, Saito Store about $200, the rent to Kanagawa about $300, Dr. Hamaguchi the dentist $150, Dr. Kawamura about $300. Except for Aoki Store and Chatani Fish Market you have to pay them at least $5.00 a month to show them you're sincere. There're other smaller debts but I can't remember them now. They're in my record book in the sewing machine drawer. We've been in debt from the very day I came to Hawai'i. It's bad luck if you don't pay off your debts by New Year's. That's why maybe . . ."

"Don't worry. Toshi-chan and I shall be out of school soon and working and we'll pay off the debt in no time once we start working."

"It's too bad you're not the number-one son. You're wiser than Toshio so you have to see to it that he and father don't fight so much. He's so disrespectful, he says the first thing which comes into his mind and shouts so much he scares the girls. Takako and Miwa aren't as good in school, but Hanae is more like you and Toshio. It's better that way, boys should have better heads. Look after them, they like you, they—"

"Don't tire yourself, save your strength." I felt sick in my stomach.

A couple of days later she said, "You know, there's a saying, 'A bad wife is fifty years of bad crops.' They say fifty years because that's how long the average life was then. I'm thirty-seven now by Japanese age. I wasn't a bad wife, but a bad-luck wife. Funny thing is your father's family asked for me because my grandfather and your father's grandmother were brother and sister. In Japan you investigate the bride's family for insanity, leprosy, and other diseases. Being in Hawai'i, they couldn't investigate any picture bride so they asked for me whom they knew to be safe, being a relative. I cried when I left, 'Don't worry, father, mother, I'll be back in five years! I'll work hard for my husband's family for four years and everything I earn in the fifth year I'll save for you!' That was in 1915. After that it was all hardship. In 1922 grandfather finally saved enough money to repay his debts in Japan and open his store in Tokyo. The next year the earthquake wiped out everything. Twenty years of work in the cane fields for your grandfather, twelve years for your father, half of that maybe for his two younger brothers. Everything in the first seven years of our marriage was handed over to grandfather. Years of frugal living and saving wiped out in less than a day. That's fate. It can't be helped."

"Rest, don't tire yourself."

"I didn't know what work was till I came to Hawai'i. There were only two of us in the family, me and my sister, and father was so gentle. He wasn't any good at farming or business either and he sold his farm like grandfather and went into business and went bankrupt. He wrote me just before he died that he was overjoyed in a way when that letter came from Hawai'i in 1914 asking for my hand. He didn't have enough money to give me away in Japan and it had been worrying him how he was going to get me married off and the proposal from Hawai'i solved everything. He wasn't strong and he played the stock market and barely supported us, but he spoiled us both. Then he died suddenly of a stroke. No, it wasn't so suddenly. Your youngest uncle graduated from Wakayama University in June and in August he was dead from tuberculosis. He worked his way through college and strained his health. Your grandmother doted on him and she just wasted away and died of grief in November. Then on December 14 father died of a stroke. So it was happening all the time, it's still happening, it happens in cycles of fours. It must be some retribution. What did I do? I lie here and search and search my mind."

"We've never done anything that bad."

"No, but some close relative might've. We can get punished as the substitute."

You heard about Death, but you never saw it. It only happened to grandparents in faraway Japan. Nobody had grandparents in Hawai'i. *Obaban* or Granny in Kahana was an exception. She was grandfather's older sister. She was the oldest in the family, but grandfather was number-one son. "*Obaban* was black sheep," Tosh explained to me once. "They been kick her out of the family in Japan."

"Why?"

"Because she been elope with *Anshan's* father. Her father been die and she been elope with him before the forty-nine-day mourning period was over. Here you not supposed to even drink sake for forty-nine days, and she been run off and marry *Anshan's* father. So the family in Japan kicked her out for good, they cut her off and told her they considered her dead. Thass why she been come to Kahana. She was one of the first ones in Kahana. It was just dirt then, no trees, and she been born six kids with *Anshan's* father. Anshan was number six. Then she been ditch *Anshan's* father and marry Kitano. But *Obaban* was the only one who was kind to Mama when Mama been come from Japan. Everybody, especially Grandma, been treat Mama like dirt. Thass when *Obaban* been step in and save Mama's life. She was older than grandfather so she could tell him off. The Oyama men are kind of gutless and Grandma was a miser and a slavedriver."

"You been know her?"

"No."

"How you know?"

"*Anshan* been tell me. When he was drunk. Not only that, *Obaban* got hot pants. All the Oyamas got hot pants."

"What's 'hot pants'?"

"You doan know what's 'hot pants'?"

"No."

"Forget it then."

I stayed home the next day and about nine she said, "*Obaban* hasn't come to see me. I'd like to see her."

"Shall I go get her?"

"No, it costs too much to hire a taxi all the way to Kahana."

"I can go to Aoki Store and phone the plantation store in Kahana and ask them to ask *Obaban* to come."

"No, it'll just be more trouble."

"She doesn't know you're sick. You should've written her."

"I thought it'd just be a trifle."

"I'll go get her."

"No."

The neighbors and friends of the family had come bringing oranges and fruits in paper sacks, but *Obaban* in far-off Kahana hadn't heard anything. She wouldn't find out unless we told her. She'd been midwife for all of us and when Hanae was born, father woke me up at 4 A.M. to bring *Obaban* in the Mikami taxi. I got to Kahana before five and found *Obaban* in her plantation house packing the day's lunches for Mr. Kitano and *Anshan*. She dropped everything and we rushed back to Pepelau in the taxi. We got back to our house before six and Hanae was born at 8 A.M.

Now the more I thought about it the more nervous I got. It's silly to think money at a time like this. Besides, mother was always denying herself for us; she asked so little for herself it'd be terrible not to give her what little she asked when she did ask. About ten I went into the bedroom and said, "I'm getting the Mikami taxi to bring *Obaban*.

"You shouldn't. She'll come later."

"She doesn't know how sick you are—I mean, she doesn't know you're sick."

"You'll only trouble her."

"She'd be glad to come."

"Thank you," she said weakly.

I had visited *Obaban* for a week every summer. It gave me something new to write about when I went back to school in the fall. Otherwise "What I Did During Summer" would be the same old thing, spearing fish in the morning, surfing in the afternoon, then swimming at the old wharf till sunset. Tosh was working the last two summers so I went alone and I spent a lot of time with *Obaban*. She was real old, so old she could sit cross-legged with the men in the parlor and smoke her long pipe and tell the men off in her low voice. But she sighed a lot and didn't talk much.

She was in the kitchen when I ran in. "*Obaban*, mother is very sick and wants to see you."

"Oh, what happened?"

"She pulled out all her teeth a month ago and fainted and got worse. She can't eat anything. She said she wanted to see you but didn't want to trouble you. I told her the only reason you haven't come is because you didn't know. I got the Mikami taxi waiting. Can you come?"

"Of course. Why didn't somebody tell me?"

"We should've written."

"Where's your father?"

"He's out at sea. He stayed home for a week."

"Where's Toshio?"

"He's in high school. He goes directly to Aoki Store and works till late."

I'd forgotten how cool this mountain village was. Living in Pepelau, you figured every other place was having the same heat spell.

She put on a wide skirt which came to her ankles and a matching blue-grey jacket. She had square jaws and shoulders and wide hips and hobbled slightly. I helped her into the taxi and got into the back with her. "She shouldn't have so many children," she muttered as we rode down the hill toward the sea. "What?" "Nothing," she patted my hand. She always seemed like she was too tired, like it was a strain for her to talk. "Stop it," she'd say every time Mr. Kitano and *Anshan* argued back and forth too much. Even when she sat cross-legged with the men she didn't say much; even when they stopped and asked her opinion she'd say "Hmmm" in her deep voice. She had a black lacquer Buddhist altar on the parlor wall and higher up beside the doorway to the bedroom, a Shinto *kami-dana* shelf. She always burned incense at the Buddhist altar and had food offerings at both. "Why do you put out the food?" I asked her one day when she offered me a star fruit from the altar. "They're for my parents, your great grandparents." "Do they eat it?" "They eat the spirit of it." "What if you don't put it out?" "Then they get hurt and angry." "Are they ghosts?" "No, they're spirits." "What happens if they get hurt and angry?" "They're like living people, they can harm you like living people." "But what if they can't find you?" She laughed then, the only time I remember her laughing, "That's why we hang paper lanterns during *Bon*, so that they won't get lost."

Once you got back down to the sea the road followed the shoreline. The cane fields came down to the tar road, and on the other side of the road was the narrow strip of sand and the ocean. The island was a mountaintop, and the land sloped from the shore for about five miles to the foot of the bluish-green mountains. Sugarcane covered the entire slope, and the plantation spotted camps like Kahana in the light green fields to farm the fields around them. Kahana sat on the northern slope and it caught a lot of wind and rain. Things grew wild in Kahana, whereas there wasn't enough water in Pepelau even for a home garden. As Mr. Mikami curved in and out with the shoreline, I said in a low voice, "*Obaban*, do you believe in *bachi* (retribution)?"

"Why?" she said after a while.

"Mother thinks she's getting somebody else's *bachi*."

"Hmmm."

"She believes she's being punished as somebody else's substitute."

"Hmmm."

"Do you believe that?"

"It can work both ways," she said tiredly. "If she can find another substitute, then she'd be freed."

I watched her for a while fingering one of her amulets. She always carried several of them in her purse. "Can you give mother one of your amulets?"

"Well, all of mine have my name on them, but I can have one made for her at the temple."

"Does it really work?"

"Yes, if you believe it does."

Bachi was a punishment you got when you did something bad and got away with it. The scary part was it didn't have to happen to the wrongdoer himself, it could fall on his children or any substitute. Father pooh-poohed the whole thing. "If you wait long enough, some bad luck is bound to happen to everybody." Father had become a Methodist soon after he came to Hawai'i. In the old days there was nothing going on in Kahana on Sundays except at the Methodist Church, he said. When mother was sent for to be his bride, she became a Methodist too and we were all baptized. Father didn't believe in Christianity any more than he did in Buddhism, but mother had grown up in the country steeped in all the superstitions. Most of them had to do with warding off bad luck. Each New Year had to be started clean: all debts paid, all the food cutting and cooking done by midnight on New Year's Eve, there should be no cleaning or sweeping or cooking except rewarming on New Year's Day, and you bathed in the morning on New Year's Day. Then there were all the things having to do with death: if you stumbled on your way to a funeral somebody in your family would die, if you were sleepier than usual a relative would die, if you sliced a melon at night you would not be present when your parent died. I tried to laugh them off like father, but mother worried about them so much she made me worry.

When we walked into the bedroom mother sat up with outstretched arms and in a moment she was clasping *Obaban* and crying like a child. "Come." I took Hanae's hand and led her out. I told Mr. Mikami I'd come and get him at his stand when *Obaban* was ready to go home, and Hanae and I sat on the veranda. "Is Mama goin' die?" She asked. "No." Mother was always fixing fish some new way, saying eating a new dish made you live seventy-five days longer. There would be no more special eats and the kitchen would be cold forever. On nights when father was at sea mother always set the first bowl of rice at his place on the table and talked about all the fish he was catching and how tired he must be. We'd have an early supper at times and walk to the beach and watch the sunset and when it got dark, mother would say, "Good night, father," and we'd all say, "Good night, father," to the ocean. There was a low chanting from the bedroom, sounding at times like a hum. *Obaban* was praying. I'd heard the same kind of chanting when passing Buddhist temples. It was loudest during funerals.

Then she stopped and they were talking and I went in and said from the doorway, "I'll go get your taxi." *Obaban* nodded. "Sorry to cause you so much trouble," mother kept saying. "You'll be all right, I'll make an offering at our altar." I rode back with Mr. Mikami and asked him to charge the fare to the family. "You'll get the amulet for mother?" I said as I helped *Obaban* into the back seat. "Yes." "Thank you, *Obaban*." "You're a good boy," she patted the back of my hand. Nothing else had worked, none of my prayers, none of Dr. Kawamura's medicines.

Mother looked relaxed. "How about some gruel?"

"No, I'm not hungry."

"You're really fond of *Obaban*."

"She's my Hawaiian mother. I didn't even have a wedding ring when I got married. She made me one out of a gold coin. See?" It was the band she always wore.

"I understand grandmother was very mean to you."

"She couldn't help it. She had such a hard life herself."

"Why didn't father protect you?"

"How could he? He had to be a filial son first."

"Why do the Buddhists have a forty-nine day mourning period?"

"That's how long it takes the dead spirit to tidy up everything on earth."

"Where does it go then?"

"Depends, but most of them go to Amida's paradise."

"Why is it so bad for the relatives to act differently during the forty-nine days?"

"They shouldn't disturb the dead spirit while it's making its preparations to leave."

"Is that why they have *hi no tama* (fireballs)?" These were bluish fireballs the size of a softball, which hovered late at night around the eaves of a house in which there had been a death. Everybody talked about it, but nobody saw one.

"Hmmm, they say it's a sign of a disturbed spirit."

"Have you seen one?"

"No."

"Why don't you go to sleep?"

"Yes."

She slept for several hours and when she got up at about three, she said, "I had a marvelous dream. I was back in Japan and father was still alive and we all cuddled and cried. You know, I was sent for as your father's bride so that I could help grandmother with her housework. She'd been cooking, laundering, doing everything for your grandfather, your father, and your two uncles who all worked in the cane fields. She kept a dozen pigs, made beancake, and pushed her cart around camp to sell them, and she exhausted her body and just couldn't get well. When I got here, your aunt, Masako, who was only four then, said to grandmother, 'Mother, you can die now, elder sister has come from Japan to look after me.' Aren't children terrible?"

"You shouldn't talk so much, you'll tire yourself."

When father came home from sea at dusk I told him he should stay home the next few days. Mother had that look about her I'd taken for relaxation. It was more like *Obaban's* resigned look. She was putting everything in order, she'd said everything she had to say, she'd told you where she kept everything so that she wouldn't be a bother after she left. "She thinks she's been chosen for someone else's punishment," I said. "That's silly superstition," father said, but he stayed home and the next morning I went to school.

About eleven o'clock father showed up at the doorway of my sixth grade class and my heart started pounding like a fist against my chest. He never came except on parents' visiting day when he happened to be home! "Kiyoshi," Mrs. Mikimoto, our teacher, looked suddenly very sad. "There's been a . . . some sad news, you may be excused from class." "Please God, please God, please God, let her have a little breath left!" I was shaking all over and wobbling like a drunk as I walked to the head of the class where father waited. *"Baban chubu ni kakatta,"* he whispered, and suddenly I felt like jumping and shrieking like I hit a home run! I had to hold myself now to keep from dancing. *"Baban* had a stroke." "When?" "Ten this morning. They telephoned Aoki Store. I'm going ahead. She might still be alive. You get Takako, Miwa, and Toshio." "Yes." I grabbed his hand and pumped it and he looked at me like I was crazy.

I got Takako and Miwa from their classes and went home. Mother and Hanae were already dressed, and mother was packing some fresh clothes into the old suitcase. She was trembling.

"You shouldn't go, mother, you're still not well," I said.

"I'm all right. I'd insist on being carried if I couldn't walk."

When Mr. Mikami came back from Kahana, I rode with him to Pepelau High which sat a mile above the town and got Tosh. Tosh changed his clothes and we all got in the taxi.

"Don't stumble now," mother warned, and I carried the suitcase and made sure Hanae or Miwa didn't stumble. I felt so relieved I felt kind of guilty. But *Obaban* was the logical substitute, she was old and lived a full life, Mr. Kitano and *Anshan* who was about thirty wouldn't miss her that much. Mrs. Kanai once told us a story in language school of a famous poet who'd been invited to a Name Day and asked to compose a poem. He wrote, *"Jiji ga shine, oya ga shine, ko ga shine."* (The grandfather should die, then the father, and then the son.) His host shouted, "How dare you speak of death when we're celebrating birth!" The poet said, "It celebrates happiness. It's a happy household where death happens chronologically." Things will be looking up now that *Obaban's* put an end to the cycle of bad luck.

When we got to *Obaban's* house in the middle of Japanese Camp, she was already dead and everybody was mad at everybody else. *Anshan* wanted her cremated so that he could take her ashes with him. Mr. Kitano wanted her buried at the Kahana graveyard in the cane field. Father stepped in and told *Anshan* why didn't he agree with his stepfather for now and afterwards, meaning after Mr. Kitano died, he could dig up *Obaban's* bones and cremate them. Both agreed. Father was a good middleman, but he was angry too. Mr. Komai, the Shingon Buddhist priest, had shown up in his priest's robes as he did at nearly every death or near-death of a Buddhist. "What's he doing here? *Obaban* doesn't belong to his sect," father said. A neighbor said, "Let him pray as long as he's here." Reverend Komai had chanted over the unconscious *Obaban*. When he finished his prayers and clapped his hands, *Obaban* started. "There, she's getting better already," Reverend Komai said. "Fool!" father yelled at him as *Obaban* started to die. "Pay him the money and get him out of here! That's all he comes for anyway!" father said. It wasn't required, but it was understood that Reverend Komai got a ten-dollar bill in a white envelope for his prayers. I felt good that father was the way he was. I'd be a nervous wreck if he was like mother. Here I was acting worse than mother. I'd assumed *Obaban* was dead, I'd wanted her dead, just to be mother's substitute.

Whenever I visited *Obaban* I slept with *Anshan* on the futon on the wooden floor in the parlor, and the place always smelled of incense and *Anshan's* Stacomb. Now *Obaban* was laid on the bedroom floor where she and Mr. Kitano slept. She wore a white linen kimono folded left-handed and tied at the waist with a narrow white band. I'd expected to see the kimono on her inside out. "You're wearing your kimono dead-man's style!" mother would scold us whenever we put one on inside out by accident. She must've made that one up. It seemed so strange; here was she not full of life but very alive yesterday. I touched her hand when I thought nobody was looking and shivered at its coldness. This was the first time I was seeing a dead person. We sat on futons across the length of *Obaban*, Mr. Kitano and *Anshan* at her head, then father, Tosh, me, mother, Takako, Miwa, and Hanae at her feet. *Obaban* lay between us and the bedroom doorway for which there was no door, and the villagers came in one or two at a time and said the usual polite things, except for Mr. Takeshita who came about eight and really let go. "Why, oh, why did you leave us, Kitano-san? Why didn't you wait a little longer? Why didn't you give us a chance to repay you for all the wonderful things you've done for us? Kahana will never be the same without you!" He went on and on, crying real tears and rocking back and forth. He was real old too, and maybe he was thinking of himself. The parlor behind him was filling up with other guests when he finally stopped and wiped his tears and blew his nose like a loud horn, and backed out of the bedroom. I knew then it hadn't been for real. You couldn't turn it off just like that.

Mother sat to my right rocking back and forth, tears streaming down her sunken cheek. She'd try to choke her sobs and she'd gag and burst out crying. I kept looking sideways at her, hoping she'd stop. *Anshan* too was crying buckets. During the short moments when there was no visitor, he'd cry out unable to keep his voice from cracking, "Toshio, Kiyoshi, *Obaban's* gone! We can't visit with her anymore! She's left us!" I didn't feel any real grief but I felt pretty bad for having felt so happy. *Anshan or ani-san* (elder brother) was *Obaban's* youngest child by her first marriage. In a Japanese divorce all the children go with the father so as not to interfere with the mother's new marriage, and *Anshan's* father had taken them all back to Japan, but *Anshan* was the only one to come back to Hawai'i. He loved Johnnie Walker and remembered a lot when drunk: "Ooooooo," sounding like a distant train whistle, "you'll never know, Kiyoshi, how much I suffered. I was only ten and my father farmed me to a carpenter as an apprentice. Ooooo, he was harsh. If I was slow or made a mistake, kotsun! right on the head with his wooden plane. Feel this bump? Plantation work is nothing compared to what I went through. I lived and worked for ten years for this man for nothing, not even a cent. But he made me the best carpenter in Hawai'i. See this arm? It's crooked and broken at the elbow, but it can hang the best door in all Hawai'i. Oooooo, how I suffered. Your mother, too, oooooo, how she suffered! Your grandmother worked her like a slave, sunrise to way past sunset, seven days a week. But she didn't complain, she did everything she was asked to do when most women would've run away. You look all over Hawai'i and you'll not find a woman like your mother." "Why did you come back to Hawai'i?" I said. "I wanted to look after *Baban* especially after her death. I knew the worthless Kitano wouldn't do it."

We sat there till about ten, and mother and the girls went to the Nakamura's to spend the night, and Tosh and I went to sleep at another friend's. "*Anshan* taking it real hard, eh?" Tosh said. "Mama too." "It's the last time we goin' visit *Obaban's* house," Tosh said. "Yeah." Mr. Kitano would never invite us. Even *Anshan* would be leaving as soon as the forty-nine days of mourning were over. But I was numb and tired and didn't feel like talking.

The next day I put on a long-sleeve white shirt and tie, a pair of navy blue pants, and my Keds basketball shoes. There were over a dozen women in white aprons at *Obaban's* house, fixing all kinds of meatless eats for after the funeral. They seemed more energetic, brighter faced, less sunburned than the women in Pepelau. I took off my shoes and went into the parlor and peeked into the bedroom, half expecting to see *Obaban* sitting there on a straw mat, smoking her Japanese pipe, the tobacco box with its tin-can ashtray beside her.

Last night had been a dream, but now in the bright morning light she was nowhere, like she'd run off for good.

I went back into the yard. A light rain had fallen in the night and the trees danced in the wind. It was what I enjoyed most visiting *Obaban*, fooling around in the green-green yard early in the morning. I'd already be in the ocean with goggles and spear back in Pepelau. But here it was so cold I needed a sweatshirt. I used to climb the mango tree, pick avocados with the long bamboo pole, pick papaya, lime, soursop, starfruit, and pomegranate. I picked and ate a chili pepper on my first visit and went crying to *Obaban*. These were *Obaban's* trees and she watered them, fed them manure, and mumbled to them. But I wouldn't hesitate a second if it was a choice between her and mother. Children who lost a parent stuck closer together, but it was more like they were huddling closer waiting for it to strike again. They never got over that dread.

When mother and the girls showed up, I greeted them at the front gate.

"I'm so glad you went to get *Obaban*. We must've both known, something must've told us we wouldn't see her again. It would've been too much if she too died without my seeing her. Thank you, thank you." She held my hand in both of hers and bowed and bowed. Her bony face looked fresh like the air washed by rain.

"She was your substitute."

"I'm such a nobody and twice I've been saved."

She let go my hand and started up the slight hill to join the other women. She walked very slowly, but her steps seemed surer. She wasn't trembling. She paused and put her hand to her mouth, "I feel so ugly. It's been like losing all your old friends at once."

"You'll have to get some false teeth," I said.

"Yes."

Darrell H.Y. Lum

Many of Darrell Lum's works emphasize basic values, reminding us of the difficult importance of friendships and family bonds, yet Lum's gifts as a humorist are, more often than not, what carry the day. He is somehow able to achieve serious insights while making the reader laugh out loud.

Lum is often praised by commentators for his innovative use of the pidgin dialect of Hawai'i. His stories featuring pidgin-speaking first-person narrators are particularly renowned. Lum's deft use of local dialect has been a crucial influence for many younger writers in Hawai'i. His achievement in this regard should come as no surprise to students of American literature. Mark Twain accomplished something similar for the literature of the midwest with a novel called *Huckleberry Finn*.

The humor in Lum's work is usually tinged with poignant irony. His characters—often young or elderly—endeavor to make sense of the small and large absurdities of their marginalized situations. In every one of his pieces details of life in Hawai'i are vividly rendered. Lum's distinctive stories and plays and the works of many of the followers of his example provide considerable hope for the future of Hawai'i's fiction and drama.

Lum's two collections *Sun: Short Stories and Drama* (1980) and *Pass on No Pass Back* (1990) have both achieved wide readership in Hawai'i and, increasingly, on the mainland. His much-praised plays—which include *Oranges Are Lucky, Fighting Fire, A Little Bit Like You, My Home is Down the Street*, and *Magic Mango*—have been produced extensively by Kumu Kahua Theatre, Honolulu Theatre for Youth, and other theatrical groups.

As co-founder and co-editor (along with Eric Chock) of the literary magazine *Bamboo Ridge*, Lum has encouraged the further development of Hawai'i's literature. *Bamboo Ridge*, which began in 1978, is still going strong as the 1990s draw to a close.

from "No Mistaking"

"Dis morning, ho, erryting buckaloose. I thought I was gone wit da wind. Dey come massage me. Ho, da rough dey rub me. I donno how come dey so rough. And all kine doctors stand around my bed. Four doctors one time. My doctor ask me, 'Mr. Lee, you know who I am?'

"I tell, 'Of course. You my doctor. And dat my sister Florence and my brother-in-law Ed, and my brother Howard and Irene.' Get four doctors checking up on me and da man nurse rubbing me and massaging me rough. I donno why dey so rough. Dey push me all over.

"Chee, dey went call everybody to da hospital like dat, just like when my mother died. Chee . . . maybe I was little mo gone wit da wind, yeah? Otherwise dey no call up everybody like dat, yeah?

"Chee, maybe little mo gone wit da wind," he circled his hand in the air. I imagined the wind.

"But now I feel okay. But dis morning, gone with da wind. Huh, da Buddha, Kwan Yin, look aftah me. No come fo me yet.

"Thirty-five years I live by myself. Take care myself . . ." he trailed off and looked out the window. The view outside the hospital room was of exhaust pipes from the kitchen and the boiler room and across the way, windowless concrete walls. "But me," he continued, "I have self control . . . no have temptation."

"Plenty ladies like marry me, you know. Dey pinch my ear, pinch my cheek, pinch down there," he pointed toward his groin and grinned.

"But I no damn fool. If I marry now, I gotta give half da house to her. What fo, when I got em so dat da two girls, my two granddaughters, get da house when I die? I no need wife. Night time, I get lonely, I hug my blanket, hug my pillow, dat's all.

"Me, I like girls, you know. Boys, you tell dem someting dey say 'Yeah, yeah,' but in their mind, dey fight you.

"Well, I'm eighty-eight years old. At least I got to see my granddaughter get married. Japanee boy. Well, dat's okay you know. I took care of dem when dey were babies, you know. Later on they can have dis house. Good girls. Good to have girls.

"I think dis American food they give me better fo me, you know. One scoop rice only, little bit meat, vegetables. Me I like eat *hahm gnee*, salt fish, you know. Ho, dat buggah make you eat rice. . .

"Now no mo *hahm gnee*, no mo *hau see*, oysters, yeah. Heh, I used to steam da *hau see* and eat wit rice. Put oyster sauce, *hau yau*, on top. Ho da good dat. No good eat dat kine, too salty, bad for da high blood pressure, but I like eat dat, boy. Da social worker like me go inside one of dose homes, but I no can eat dat kine Filipino food. You know da Filipinos run da nursing homes nowdays . . . ho, I no can eat dat kine. I tell her, 'Yeah, yeah,' but I thinking, 'I not going to dat kine place, eat Filipino food.' They no can make me go dat kine place, yeah?

"Waste time sit around here. I told my doctor, 'What fo I stay in here only sit around. I can sit around at home. Same ting!' I went call up my sister Florence dis morning, tell her to bring my clothes and my wallet. Mo bettah I catch da cab go home! She told me I no can go until da doctor say I can go home. 'He said pretty soon,' I told her. Pretty soon."

At home, Uncle Kam Chong looked even thinner than when he was in the hospital. Pale and thin, just flesh hanging on a skeleton after almost being "gone with the wind." He had always been skinny. But now he was so thin, I couldn't imagine him anymore with one of those white paper caps serving up sodas and malts behind the fountain at Benson-Smith Drugstore downtown. It was one of those fountains with the tall swivel stools and the chrome gooseneck spigots: water, soda water, and Coke. I remembered barely being able to see over the counter waiting for my Coke float with an extra cherry and watching Uncle's ears. He had interesting ears, just right it seemed for holding up the paper cap, and long floppy lobes which years later explained the funny kinship I had always felt between my uncle and the Kwan Yin statue at the Academy of Arts. There always was a peaceful comfortableness about being around both of them.

And now, long after Benson-Smith and bussing dishes at a string of Chinese restaurants, those same ears held up a felt hat with a fancy feather hatband. In the summer, it was the cooler woven straw one. You could track his comings and goings in Chinatown by that hat. He was so short and stooped that you could only find him by his hat: walking the streets, stopping to look in store windows, to peer down alleys. Or by the cloud of pipe smoke in Wing Wah

Jade where he sat with the owner and thumbed the bas relief carvings on the new jade pieces.

"I used to catch da bus erryday to Chinatown. Walk around. Me, I no like stay home. Catch da bus, walk around. Chew da fat little while at da jewelry store. Den come home. Sundays, I catch bus go church. I gotta go around. No can stay home. No can now. Maybe I gotta stay home little while. Chee, I miss dat. Pretty soon maybe I can go again. Now no can.

"Now I'm alright. Maybe later I gotta go Palolo Old Man Home. But now I'm okay. Maybe one, two years from now. I donno. Ho boy, nine hundred bucks a month, you know. Dem pakes wanna cheat you, you see. Dey get anykine donations from errybody, but dey still wanna charge you nine hundred bucks a month. Ho boy."

We sat there, not looking at each other. We both looked out the window. The window screen needs cleaning, I thought. I scanned the coffee table pushed up against the corner of the living room. It was full of old photographs: his sons, his granddaughters. I found a picture of me and my brother. I must've been four or five, the "baby" of the family and had my hair slicked down and was sucking my left thumb. He complained about the weather and his arthritis.

"I'm eighty-eight years old last week. Eighty-nine, Chinese calendar. All my life I never had dis kine trouble. Now erry morning I take five pills. Damn pills cost me seventy bucks, you know. And dis damn weather ... my arthritis ... all sore ovah here in my shoulder and in my hands."

He stretched his fingers out wide, then closed his hand. I noticed his thumb: big and knobby and calloused still from tamping hot pipe tobacco. He wore two pieces of jade pinned to his undershirt and when we talked, he turned his good ear toward me. His earlobes bobbed and wobbled as he talked about his aches and he massaged the base of his thumb at the joint. The wind in the valley had picked up; he must've felt the rain coming. It was time to go.

It was two months later after a couple of false starts and, I imagined, quite a bit of grumbling, Uncle Kam Chong made the move a couple of miles up the road to the "old man home."

Palolo Chinese Home. It was at the back of the valley where the road began to curve around and started back out again. The place was clean, plain, and functional. It was strikingly Chinese: layers of blood red paint on the columns, dark green trim and light green and white walls. There were two dormitories with upturned eaves, men's and women's, separated by a cafeteria.

It was quiet when I drove up. The men ringed the outside of their building just sitting or smoking in chairs pushed up against the walls. It was a quiet bunch. No loud talking like in Chinatown or shouting like at the mah jong games or arguing like at the fish market. Mostly everyone was just sitting outside, two or three chairs apart or inside the lounge watching TV. It looked like I was the only visitor that day. Uncle Kam Chong was sitting right outside the front door, cane in his lap, unlit pipe in his hand. He didn't recognize me until I got closer and I called out, "*Kau Goong*, Uncle. How you?"

"Heh, I'm okay. I'm okay, now."

"How's this place? How's the food?"

"Not bad. Food not bad. I eat everything. Fresh air."

"Lousy," the man two seats down muttered to himself loud enough for us to hear. I looked at him and he looked away and lit a cigarette. "Same ole ting for six years," he offered to no one in particular.

Uncle Kam Chong ignored the interruption and continued, "I eat good, eat regular. Dey no need wash my dish, I eat um so clean! So far so good, I never relax like dis before, no need worry about cook, about wash dishes. They serve you."

Another resident shuffled up and smiled at me. He pointed his cane and introduced the old timer who didn't like the food, Mr. Chun, to me. Then he introduced himself, Mr. Tam.

"Yeah," Mr. Tam said. "This is a good place. Anything you want, they get for you. The ladies very helpful." He beamed at us.

"Come watch boxing on TV," he said. He jabbed the air with his cane in the direction of the lounge.

It had started to drizzle. A light mist. Mr. Tam urged us to sit inside the lounge, "Much more comfortable and don't get wet."

Uncle pointed out that we were under the eaves.

"No, thank you," I said. "It's dry out here."

Mr. Chun muttered, "Dis only mosquito rain, rain little bit and then pau. At's all."

Mr. Tam tugged at his knitted hockey cap and pulled it down securely over his ears. Except for the cap, everyone was dressed nearly the same: bundled up in long trousers and an aloha shirt topped by a collarless, button-up sweater. Mr. Chun was one of the few who was sweaterless. Just a white tee-shirt and trousers.

"You should wear one of these hats," Mr. Tam instructed Uncle. "Keep warm."

"Yeah, maybe later on I get one," Uncle said.

"No, no just ask the ladies. They bring fo you. Free." Mr. Tam tugged again at his cap to make his point. "Free."

Mr. Tam beamed a toothless grin at me. Reassuringly he said, "This place good. Everybody is nice. You come back learn Chinese," he added as he shuffled off.

Uncle fingered his pipe. It was unlit and empty.

"Hey, you need anything. You got enough tobacco?" I asked.

"Yeah, I need tobacco. I had one big can but I donno where I put um. And matches, I need matches. I used to have some place. I donno where I put um . . ."

"Next time I'll bring you some matches," I said.

"Yeah, one box nuff. Sometimes I forget nowadays. Ho, the other day I forget where I put my teeth. Come time to eat, I no can find um. Ho, I worry like hell. No mo teeth, no can eat, you know. Later on, somebody find um in da bathroom. Good ting. I no can remember where I left um. Drop inside da toilet, you know! Ho, da lady go soak um in solution fo me. One whole day she soak um. Otherwise, no can eat! Lucky."

"Lucky you found um," I repeated.

"Lady. Lady find um." It was Mr. Chun again. "Da lady janitor found um. Me too, sometimes forget things nowadays."

Uncle said, "One of the cafeteria ladies told me she hold my teeth for me. Whenever I need um, she bring um. 'Nah,' I told her. I no like bother."

"You gotta take care now. No lose um again. Maybe better to let the lady hold um fo you," I worried out loud.

"Hey, when you gonna take over the cafeteria?" I teased. "J'like the old days at Benson-Smith. You used to be manager or something, huh?"

"Manager, buyer, everything I was. Work there fo forty years. Start off at two dollars a week."

"A week?"

"A week. After the fourth grade, after my father died, I went work. Make some money. Help out the family. I no need too much. Only go movies now and then. Cowboy movies, Shucks.

"Pretty soon they let me run the lunch counter. Big place you know. Three hundred one time can sit down. They try anykine, you know. They bring in all kine guys, but they no can make money. Only I could. One time they bring in three *haole* guys from the mainland to watch me fo one month because they no believe my profit so high: seventy, seventy-two, seventy-four percent. At the end of the month they ask me, 'Lee, how you do it?' I says, 'I donno.' You think I gonna tell them? Baloney! How come they ask me!"

"So how you did it, Uncle?" I asked.

"You know, only three things you gotta watch: the girls no put too much, you know, when they make samwich they put two or three slice meat. Next, watch so they no eat too much. You know, sometimes they make two, three samwich for themself and they take one, two bite, then leave um alone. You see, how much waste, yeah? And den you watch sometimes they no charge their friends or they make something big and only charge little bit. Dat's all. Dat and at the end of the month, no good have too much inventory. You order heavy at the beginning and den cut down, cut down so by the end of the month you get almost nothing. Dat's all."

"You're all right, Uncle."

"Yeah, you watch the inventory. All my meat, one size. I regulate the machine to slice, you see. One pound ham supposed to get twelve slices. Huh. And they ask me, 'How you do it, Lee?' Dey no can get seventy percent profit. When you only get forty, fifty percent that no good, you know. Something wrong."

Uncle fingered his empty pipe.

"Let's go look for your tobacco," I said. "You can show me your room."

There were four beds in each room, each corner identical with a clothes locker and small table next to the bed. Looking for the tobacco was like looking through a locker at an elementary school. Little treasures mixed in with the necessities, all conspicuously marked. My mother must've done it when he moved in. I recognized her fat, round script on every handkerchief, shirt, pants, and pair of underwear. There weren't too many places to look. I stopped myself from suggesting that we go look in the community bathroom down the hall. Maybe the tobacco tin had ended up in the same place as his teeth. I found a brown paper sack full of boiled peanuts. Uncle Kam Chong offered them to me when I showed him the bag. I sniffed at it suspiciously.

"Where did you get these?" I asked.

"My friend gave me," he answered a little defensively. "One old guy. One Chinese guy. He say he know me. But I no can remember him. He know me. But I no recognize him. Ah . . ."

"When did he come?"

"Oh, couple days ago."

"Maybe you ought to give this to the kitchen. They can keep um in the ice-box for you. So it doesn't spoil." I sniffed the package again.

"It's all right. No sour."

I poured a handful out. Uncle cracked one open and chewed. We settled down in the chairs right outside his room.

"So what, get activities? Things to do?"

"Yeah, they get exercise class. One lady, I donno how she know my name, she tell me, 'Eh, Mr. Lee, let's go exercise.' I say, 'No thank you, I too old.'"

"But if you exercise you sleep good, you know," I suggested.

"Hah, next day you get up, you ache all over," he laughed.

"So what, that lady your new girlfriend now?"

"Naw, I don't believe those kine now. Girlfriend. Only mouth, girlfriend. They try to skin you, boy. Danger, you know. Some of dem smooth-talker, you know." He paused to reflect and chewed on a few more peanuts.

"Well, depend on the man," he continued. "You bite, you trapped already. One time one lady tell me, 'Eh, Lee, you funny kine of man. You funny kine of man.'"

"Why she call you funny kine?"

"I donno. Maybe because I no like marry her. Shucks. You tink I damn fool?"

"Not so funny kine den, Uncle. Smart."

I poured out another handful of peanuts for him. It was slimy and white with mold.

"Aw, this is no good, Uncle," I shouted, excited and worried about the ones he had already eaten.

"It's too old, Uncle, don't eat it," I said as I swept the rest off the table into the bag. He was quiet. Like a scolded child. I looked down at his feet and I recognized my mother's round script again, "Kam Chong Lee" written across both slippers in black felt pen. They reminded me of a boxful of little girl's slippers that I had just marked with my daughter's name in preparation for school. And it all finally seemed right somehow. All of it. Uncle Kam Chong and Palolo Home and his name written across his slippers and me writing Lisa's name on hers. And the long line of toothless Chinese men and women who lived here and those yet to come. I took my place in that line and glanced down at my slippers.

I left them just the way I found them. Uncle was sitting outside, cane in his lap. Mr. Chun was smoking. Mr. Tam was waving enthusiastically from the TV room. I waved back and grinned. I'd be back.

. . . .

2

LEGEND AND SONG

Katharine Luomala

An anthropologist and folklorist by profession, Katharine Luomala's reputation in her fields is considerable; in fact, in introducing her for the Hawai'i Award for Literature ceremony, Samuel Elbert pointed out that she had become one of the most famous folklorists in the world. Her work is, however, admired beyond its considerable importance as social scientific research. The literary excellence of her writing and her talent as a teller of tales make her the best possible recounter of legends. She manages especially well in her books for the general reader, most notably in *Voices on the Wind*, to provide access to the magical life of the heroic tales of Polynesia.

Although trained in the scientific approach to social science research by her mentors at UC Berkeley, Luomala always cares deeply about the divinities who figure in the stories she retells. Tahaki she calls "the perfect chief"; Hina and Tinirau "the handsomest and most romantic couple"; Rata "the irreverent vagabond." She feels special esteem for Lono, whom she refers to as "the essence of wisdom and other incomparable attributes." Respect for the beliefs of the cultures and attention to how the stories are told and performed in their original contexts are crucial to her approach.

Elbert summarized her output as "120 items published between 1933 and 1975, including 49 articles and essays, 44 book reviews, and nine books"; but for many readers her great work will always be her most beautiful book, *Voices on the Wind*, with its lyrical evocations of the oceanic universe and its glorious illustrations by Joseph Feher.

from "Within the Circle of the Sea"

I arrive where an unknown earth is under my feet.
I arrive where a new sky is above me.
I arrive at this land, a resting place for me.
Spirit of the Earth! The stranger humbly offers
his heart as food for thee.

This charm to appease the spirits of an alien land is said to have been recited more than twenty generations ago by a chief when he landed on The Long White Cloud (Te Aotearoa), now called New Zealand. Seeking a new home, he and his followers had sailed their great canoes from the old home, Hawaiki, an unidentified island somewhere to the northeast and perhaps nearly two thousand miles away.

As his people, the Maoris, express it, the chief "trod" the mountains, the valleys, the lakes, the rivers, and the meadows of his new land. When he discovered places that reminded him of Hawaiki, he named them in memory of home. Other names commemorate adventures, either heroic or trivial, that he and his followers had on that first tour of inspection. Still other places were named for parts of his body. Thus he united the past with the present, and both with his hopes for the future, when his descendants would fill the land.

Let anyone challenge the chief's identification with the land, or his descendants' rights on it, and the names and the adventures of the first exploratory trip are recited as evidence. Boys of later generations, as they trudge with their fathers and grandfathers over the land to set traps for edible wood rats and birds, are taught the names and the associated traditions. They are also told that when they travel inside or outside their boundaries and come to natural shrines—an unusual tree or stone or mound perhaps—they must recite their ancestor's charm and make a little offering, if only a wisp of grass. This will make them as safe as their ancestors were.

They need not fear, then, that they will be transformed into a mountain, which is what happened to a careless contemporary of their ancestor who neglected etiquette.

By such means the chief's descendants have orally preserved his potent charm and the story of his arrival in New Zealand. It is the same throughout Polynesia; all knowledge—whether of magic, religion, navigation, fishing, agriculture, or literature—was passed on by word of mouth or by example before Europeans introduced writing. The other charms, prayers, poems, and narratives to be presented here also represent the orally produced and maintained traditions of the Polynesians.

The charm that the chief recited is unusual in that it expresses the Polynesian newcomer's emotion upon arriving in a strange land. It is more in accord with native poetic convention for the voyager to look back longingly across the sea and to name and describe the beloved places of the old home. Or if a poem does mention arrival in a new land, it has been composed much later and uses the confident stereotypes of a settler who has already identified himself with the once unfamiliar landscape. Yet arrival as an apprehensive but hopeful alien who intends to settle on foreign soil is a theme often repeated in Polynesian history.

If he was like other Polynesian voyagers who have found a new home, the Maori chief who offered his heart so humbly to the spirit of the earth of The Long White Cloud soon lost it, and rejoiced in the loss. Whether it is a dry, barren atoll with broken and infertile coral glaring in the sunlight or a great and mountainous island with misted valleys and jagged green peaks, a Polynesian loves his home island and district and jealously defends them. One of the typical classes of poetry in this island area describes the beauties of nature and eulogizes the home island. Prose descriptions of landscape, on the other hand, are rare, although catalogs of place names, many with descriptive epithets, are very popular. When a patriotic eulogy seems called for in a narrative, the characters resort to chanting.

. . . .

One of the many reasons Polynesians set out on hazardous voyages to other islands is the restless desire to visit strange places, to go sightseeing. Often this is a reaction as much to an overwhelming boredom as to intellectual curiosity about the world beyond the home shores. Some wanderers never reach their destined ports but are lost at sea or make unscheduled landfalls. The custom of going sightseeing, to judge from a Society Islands tradition, goes back to the period immediately after the time of creation when the sky, which had hung suffocatingly low over the earth, had been pushed to its present height and people could move about more easily. According to this tradition, Ru, one of the company of divine heroes and gods who had helped raise the heavy blue stone vault of the sky, made the first world tour. This is not the same Ru who discovered Aitutaki, although narrators, either deliberately or through confusion, sometimes identify them as one. That Ru, who is the skypropper, set out to see the world in a canoe that bore the elegantly simple name of The Hull. He was accompanied only by his sister Hina, who acted as pilot while he paddled.

Ru could not have chosen a more satisfactory companion than his sister, for Hina's spirit of adventure and curiosity about the world was as great as his. She expressed it in her personal song, which has the refrain, "Let the farsighted who dwell on land, Arise and see!" Her song first invites listeners to look inland to the settled mountains; then to look far across the sea that belongs to The Lord of the Ocean; next to behold above Atea, who is the god of the limitless firmament; and finally to gaze below at Te Tumu, god of the solid earth, and there to look

> At the jungles and the rushing streams,
> At the fountains of the deep,
> At the fountains of the surface,
> At the waves of the East,
> At the waves of the West,
> At the stable nooks, at the burning nooks,
> At the great development extending over the eight directions.

No more is told of the itinerary of Ru and Hina, the two intrepid explorers who wanted to see all eight directions of the newly created world, than that they went southwestward to Te Aotearoa, or New Zealand, and then headed back to the Society Islands.

A sacred poem, known at first only to the priestly artisans who supervised the building of sacred canoes and later to navigators, tells of their return. As The Hull nears home, Hina calls Ru's attention to each landfall. This gives Ru an opportunity to identify the island and to recite phrases reminiscent of its landscape or history. For example, the naval success of Borabora Island, where the warriors muffled their paddles to surprise their enemies, is celebrated in the same breath with the pink leaves of the island. The poem is largely in the form of questions and answers. It begins:

> Astern was Te Aotearoa, ahead was the vast ocean!
> Astern was Ru, ahead was Hina!
> And thus Ru sang: . . .
> "I am drawing, drawing to land
> *The Hull, O The Hull!*
> I am drawing, drawing thee to land,
> Now hold steadily on to Maurua."

Then cried his sister Hina,
"Upon the foaming waves,
O Ru, land is looming up.
What land is it?"

"It is Maurua; let its watchword be,
Great Maurua forever."

Ru then sings again his refrain about magically drawing The Hull to land, but this time he orders Hina to hold steadily on to Borabora. When she sights land, she calls to Ru, in the same words as before, to identify it; and he replies,

"It is Borabora. Let its watchword be,
Borabora the great, the firstborn,
Borabora of the fleet that consumes two ways,
Borabora of the muffled paddle,
Borabora of the pink leaf,
Borabora, the destroyer of the fleets."

Next, Great Tahaa of the Peaceful Sky is sighted. Finally the voyagers see their home island, Havaii, now called Raiatea, where the priestly chanters of this song lived. The song concludes with an intense plea designed to inspirit any sacred new canoe so that, like The Hull, it will be successfully launched and navigated.

So insatiable is Hina's love of travel that later, on the night of a full moon, she sets out from Raiatea in her canoe to visit the sky. She likes it so well there that she pushes her canoe adrift and makes her home on the moon.

Travelers over whom she protectively watches, even today, can look up from their canoes and see her sitting under a great banyan tree whose bark she beats into tapa and whose large branches throw shadows across the face of the moon. Once a branch from which she was stripping the bark slipped out of her fingers and fell to earth. It took root near the god Oro's famed temple at Opoa in Raiatea, where, residents claim, it was still growing during the early European period. All the other banyans now growing on earth sprang from seeds that Hina's pet green pigeon scattered from a branch he carried down from the moon. In mid-air he was attacked by a giant man-of-war bird who was jealous of the little pigeon for being the one to introduce the banyan to the other islands. However, with Hina's magical aid the pigeon successfully fought off his attacker; but his banyan seeds were scattered far and wide.

The people of many Polynesian islands other than the Society Islands believe that there is a woman industriously beating tapa in the moon and that her name is Hina. The white clouds are the tapas she has set out to air on the blue stone floor of the sky. People say that she worked so energetically even when she lived on earth—an example to earthly women—that the gods got tired of the noise of her mallet. Once when the god Tangaroa was suffering from the effects of drinking too much kava he became so angry about the eternal pounding of Hina's mallet that he sent his messenger to order her to stop. Hina ignored the messenger, who came more than once to carry Tangaroa's order, and told him that she would not stop. She then named a long list of gods for whom she had to prepare tapa. Finally the messenger angrily seized the mallet and struck Hina on the head with it so hard that her spirit left her body. According to some versions of Hina's career, it was then that she decided to live in the moon, where she continues to beat tapa and to watch over the lonely voyagers on the ocean below.

. . . .

The most outstanding Polynesian journey of song through an archipelago is that of the girl goddess, Hi'iaka, who went on a mission for her oldest sister, the volcano goddess, Pele, and traveled from the southernmost to the northernmost of the Hawaiian Islands. For hundreds of years, this journey has inspired and continues to inspire the native poets and the dancers and the chanters who perform the songs. Hi'iaka is popularly regarded as the composer of the chants and dances because, in the course of her journey, she seems to compose spontaneously and because, in real life, the most notable composers and dancers are believed to be divinely chosen and inspired by the deities they serve; and Hi'iaka has inspired many. Hawaiians call poets haku mele. Mele means song or chant; haku means to sort out feathers, as for a feather cape. Composers sorted not feathers, but words for their songs. The names of few composers of poetry for the Pele and Hi'iaka cycle have been remembered, but perhaps this is a tribute to the haku mele for so beautifully sorting out words appropriate for the two goddesses and their companions to chant.

Hi'iaka's journey gives Hawaiian composers an unparalleled opportunity to pour into song their love of the islands and their keen observation of the changing weather and conditions of the landscape. Here, as everywhere in Polynesia, nature is believed to reflect the mood of the characters in the myths and traditions, as in real life; to communicate with them through omens; and to acknowledge the rank and beauty of highborn characters, male or female. Characters often communicate with each other through chants that outwardly describe the rain or the sun or the ocean but inwardly convey a personal message, usually intelligible only to the composer and to the object of his devotion. Other chants carry on the action of the plot and may conveniently refer to geographical places, to the state of the weather, or to the aspect of the sea. But in addition to these chants that have symbolic meaning, there are many that are intended only to portray nature. All this is true of the songs incorporated into Hiʻiaka's itinerary. Hiʻiaka, because of what countless unknown poets have given to her in her name, is the greatest of all artists known in Polynesian oral literature.

The Pele and Hiʻiaka cycle, to give a connected summary of events, begins with Pele and her seven younger sisters and other kin having to leave their home on Kuaihelani Island to seek some "unknown land below the horizon" because of the bitter jealousy between Pele and Namakaokahai, who was either her elder sister or her cousin. Although Kuaihelani Island had three decks, or levels, the two quarrelsome goddesses would not stay on their respective decks and out of each other's affairs, particularly out of each other's love affairs.

Kuaihelani is a beautiful and mysterious floating island that is often mentioned in Hawaiian narratives. Old accounts state that it floats about in the mythological region called Kahiki. However, in historic times it has apparently extended its route to float around the Hawaiian Islands, for a Hawaiian occasionally reports having seen it drift past his home at night, like a great ocean steamer. Because Kahiki is a dialectical variant of the name Tahiti, the floating island from which Pele and Hiʻiaka originally came is sometimes said, as in the poem given below, to have been in the Society Islands, in the neighborhood of Tahiti and Borabora (Polapola to the Hawaiian-speaking narrators).

This poem is a version of the first song in the Pele and Hiʻiaka cycle. It tells of the family group departing from Kahiki in a canoe which is manned by gods, some of whom are the brothers of Pele and Hiʻiaka. Kamohoaliʻi is the eldest brother. The canoe is once referred to as Kāne's canoe, a commonplace way to honor and to win the protection of the god Kāne, who has a very high position in the Hawaiian pantheon. Like any hula relating to Pele, this opening chant, which is accompanied by a dance, should be performed only on important occasions to honor highborn people; and it must be preceded by an offering to the goddess of salt crystals and a spinach made from a young unfurled taro leaf.

> From Kahiki, the woman Pele,
> From the land of Polapola,
> From the red billowing cloud of Kāne,
> From the cloud blazing in the heavens,
> From the fiery cloud-pile in Kahiki.

Eagerly desirous of Hawai'i, the woman Pele
Hewed the canoe *White Earth*,
Thy canoe, O Kamohoali'i.
They rushed to finish the work,
The lashings of the canoe of the god,
The canoe of Kāne, Hewer of the Earth.

The tide rises.
Over it dashes Pele of the Red Earth;
Over it dashes The Heavenly One, encircling the island;
Over it dashes The Myriad Gods.
Malau is seated
To bail out the bilge of the canoe.
Who shall sit astern, be captain, O royal companions?
Pele of the Red Earth!
The splash of the paddle dashes over the canoe.
Those two, Kū and Lono,
Disembark on solid land,
Alight on an island shoal.
Hi'iaka, Wise One, a goddess,
Stands, goes to stay at the house of Pele.
Thunderous belching in Kahiki!
Flashing lightning! O Pele!
O belch forth!

On reaching the Hawaiian Islands, the party tours the archipelago to find a suitable homesite for fiery Pele. During this search, Pele falls in love with Lohi'au, a handsome chief of Kaua'i Island, and when she finally selects the volcano Kīlauea in the district of Puna on Hawai'i as her home, she sends Hi'iaka, her favorite little sister, to fetch Lohi'au. Hi'iaka is the only one of her sisters whom Pele trusts for such a mission, and in return for Hi'iaka's loyalty she promises to protect the girl's beloved groves of red-blossomed lehua trees from fire.

On her journey to Kaua'i, the northernmost of the major islands in the archipelago, Hi'iaka travels through many sections of Hawai'i, Maui, Moloka'i, and O'ahu. Along the way she is often in great danger from evil magicians who assume many grotesque disguises to deceive her, but Hi'iaka, like many younger sisters in Polynesian narratives, is as able a magician as she is a composer and a dancer, and she successfully wards off the magical attacks upon her.

One of the most memorable of her adventures is her eerie meeting with a lonely dancing ghost on a beach on Maui. When Hi'iaka sees the ghost girl dancing merrily by herself, she tosses her a hala from a lei that she is wearing. The ghost catches the bright red and green fruit in her pitiful stumps, which are all that remain of her hands and arms, and she then sings and dances the "Song of the Lei," which dancers still chant today as they prepare wreaths to wear in a hula. The ghost sings about the little islets of Ka'ula and Ni'ihau, about the thirsty wind called Drink-water, and about the hala which is associated with the place called Naue, just as Puna and Kīlauea are places associated with Pele. Because Pele's name must not be casually mentioned, she is often spoken of merely as the woman, as in this chant. In its composition, the "Song of the Lei" illustrates, as does the chant above, the Hawaiian style of linking lines by repeating a key word. The English translation tries to maintain the style by repeating the words "calm," in the second and third lines, "drink," in the third and fourth lines, and "hala" and "Naue," in the fourth and fifth lines.

> Ka'ula wears the ocean as a lei.
> Ni'ihau glitters in the calm.
> After the calm blows Drink-water.
> Then the halas of Naue drink in the sea.
> From Naue, the hala; from Puna, the woman,
> From the Pit, from Kīlauea.

Wherever she goes and regardless of dangers and discomforts, Hi'iaka has time to make many careful observations of the weather and natural conditions. When she reaches O'ahu, she suffers intensely from the bad weather and from nostalgia for her groves of red-blossomed lehua and for her dearest friend on Hawai'i, a girl who can transform herself into a lehua tree. The rainy season is at its worst when Hi'iaka visits the windward, or Ko'olau, side of O'ahu. She notices the "lily-tufts of Ihukoko, Gnawed away by the water, Thrashed about by the wind, Beaten down by the rain," and, to judge from her famed chant about the Ko'olau rain, she herself is as beaten as the lilies. More than one version of her rain chant exists; and in one of them a poet, speaking for Hi'iaka, identifies her mood with that of the weather. The wild rain lashes her as fiercely, says the poet, as does the unhappiness that storms within her and makes her eyes "into a bundle of tears."

> Vile Ko'olau, vile Ko'olau,
> Eat and drink a belly full of Ko'olau rain,
> Raining at Mā'eli'eli,
> Guttering out at He'eia,
> Rain scooping forth into the sea.

The rain dances with joy, at ʻĀhuimanu,
The bended knee dance.
The rain sways hips in a dance,
Making the coral piles spin.
Rain surrounds houses at Place-of-burdens.
I am burdened, O burdened,
With eyes a bundle of tears
Pouring down.

Another poet's version of the same experience merely describes the rain, a favorite theme of Hawaiian composers, without mentioning Hiʻiaka's mood.

'Twas in Koʻolau I met with the rain.
It comes with lifting and tossing of dust,
Advancing in columns, dashing along.
The rain, it sighs in the forest;
The rain, it beats and whelms, like the surf;
It smites, it smites now the land.
Pasty the earth from the stamping rain;
Full run the streams, a rushing flood;
The mountain walls leap with the rain.
See the water chafing its bounds like a dog,
A raging dog, gnawing its way to pass out.

The thundering roar of the ocean at Waialua on Oʻahu inspires Hiʻiaka, or the composer who speaks for her, to play upon the syllable *wa*, and secondarily upon the letters *k* and *1*, to describe the sound.

O Waialua, kai leo nui,	Waialua, great-voiced sea,
Ua lono ka uka o Līhuʻe.	Resounds in the uplands of Līhuʻe.
Ke wa la Wāhiawa, e!	O it roars at Wāhiawa!
Kuli wale, kuli wale i ka leo;	Deafened, deafened by the voice;
He leo no ke kai, e!	O the voice of the sea!

The depression that has afflicted Hiʻiaka in the rainstorms on Oʻahu begins to alternate now with moods of intense sorrow and rage, for even as she prepares to leave Oʻahu and to cross over to Kauaʻi, she learns, through the power of her magic, that Pele has broken her promise and has covered the lehua groves with hot lava and, with them, Hiʻiaka's friend who can become a lehua. Pele behaves as she does because she is jealous, undisciplined, and violent-tempered. Not long after her little sister has left Hawaiʻi, Pele begins to wonder whether she has been wise to send a pretty young girl like Hiʻiaka to fetch handsome Lohiʻau. The more she thinks about it, the more convinced she is that Hiʻiaka and Lohiʻau will find each other irresistible. Finally certain that her suspicions represent the truth, even though Hiʻiaka has not yet reached Kauaʻi where Lohiʻau lives, Pele pours forth her red lava on the lehua trees and Hiʻiaka's friend.

Hiʻiaka, who is too loyal to break her part of the agreement, goes on sadly to Kauaʻi. She learns there that Lohiʻau is dead. However, her efficacious chants, knowledge of herbs, and magical ministrations restore Lohiʻau to life; and when she has nursed him back to health, they start the journey southward to Pele's Pit on Hawaiʻi. Most of Hiʻiaka's chants on the home-ward journey have a recurrent refrain of sorrow; many are wild laments for her dead friend and the trees. On reaching Hawaiʻi after many adventures and after having delivered Lohiʻau to the brink of the Pit, her emotions go out of control. The long dangerous journey to Kauaʻi and back, the sight of her fire-blackened groves, and the great love that has grown in her for Lohiʻau since their meeting on Kauaʻi convince her that she owes Pele no more loyalty and that she should take revenge. In her own quiet way, the young goddess is as passionate and determined as Pele herself, and far more sensitive. So, as she sits on the edge of the volcano, she passionately throws her arms around Lohiʻau.

Pele's rage is now directed at Lohiʻau, whom she feels is responsible for Hiʻiaka's astonishing behavior. She orders her other sisters to kill him, but they attack the handsome chief so halfheartedly that she orders the male gods to kill him. Those gods, who bear the family name of Kū, refuse. Pele there-upon exiles them, and they flee to the forests for protection from her fire and become vagabonds, guardians of travelers, and patrons of canoe-builders and foresters. Other gods obey Pele and kill Lohiʻau. It is the second time that he has died within a short time.

Lohiʻau's spirit now flies to his friend Paoa and tells him the story of Pele's treachery and baseless suspicion. Paoa goes to Pele, who is astonished to hear the truth, and declares that Lohiʻau shall be restored to life. However, once he is alive again, she no longer wants him, for meanwhile she has fallen in love with Paoa. Lohiʻau leaves Hawaiʻi, and soon after, Hiʻiaka, who is disgusted with Pele's capriciousness and infidelity, also leaves, intending to revisit Kauaʻi where she first met the handsome chief. On her way north she stops at Kou (a district in present-day Honolulu) to visit a famous hula school. Like other Hawaiian hula schools it is a gathering place for visiting performers and any footloose and distracted traveler who is eager for news and companionship. At this school is another wanderer as unhappy and as weary as Hiʻiaka. It is Lohiʻau. And with their meeting, at least this version of the Pele and Hiʻiaka cycle ends on a joyful note. It also ends the greatest journey of song in Polyne-sian oral literature.

Awake, O rain, O sun, O night,
O mists creeping inland,
O mists creeping seaward,
O masculine sea, feminine sea, mad sea,
Delirious sea, surrounding sea of Iku.
The islands are surrounded by the sea,
The frothy sea of small billows, of low-lying billows,
Of up-rearing billows that come hither from Kahiki.

Rubellite Kawena Johnson

Rubellite Kawena Johnson is best known for her scholarly work in the area of traditional Hawaiian literature and folklore. Her extensive research has addressed many important specific and general topics. For instance, she has engaged in linguistic analysis of Hawaiian place names and described the operation of thematic variations in Hawaiian folklore. Her study of traditional Hawaiian literature culminated in the 1981 publication of *Kumulipo: Hawaiian Hymn of Creation, Volume 1*, a major reinterpretation of a crucial example of Hawaiian oral poetry. This work of translation and scholarship is outstanding not simply for its importance as research, but also for its literary distinction. In addition to Johnson's long list of publications in such scholarly publications as *Pacific Studies, Journal of Oriental Literature*, and *Journal of Polynesian Society*, she has numerous creative publications to her credit. In her much admired rendition of the *Kumulipo* she shows what can be achieved in the translation of poetry when scholarly understanding and poetic voice unite to recapture the singing cadences of a traditional masterpiece.

Johnson was born and raised in the historic district of Kōloa on the island of Kaua'i. She attended the University of Hawai'i at Mānoa in the early 1950s, where Samuel Elbert first encouraged her interest in written Hawaiian tradition. After obtaining a B.A. in English in 1954, Johnson did graduate work in anthropology and folklore at the University of Indiana. Later, under the tutelage of Kenneth Emory, she conducted research on Hawaiian music and folklore at Bishop Museum. Specializing in the fields of folklore and advanced Hawaiian, she taught for many years as a professor in the Department of Indo-Pacific Languages at the University of Hawai'i at Mānoa. Now retired from the University, she continues to be in great demand as a lecturer and consultant on Hawaiian culture.

from *Kumulipo:*
The Hawaiian Hymn of Creation

(A Translation with Introduction)

The Kumulipo is a genealogical creation chant composed in Hawai'i for the chief, Ka-'Ī-i-mamao, around the eighteenth century. It attracted scientific attention in nineteenth-century Europe due to its rudimentary concept of evolution. Evolution as a theory of the biological origin of man had become the object of intense skepticism after the appearance of Charles Darwin's authority-shattering study, the *Origin of Species by Means of Natural Selection* in 1859. The possession of a similar concept of evolution by a neolithic people such as the Hawaiians with neither a system of writing nor an inductive method of scientific inquiry was a matter uniquely pertinent to the ensuing rivalry between science and theology over the soundness of church doctrine established on the biblical account of creation in Genesis. The Kumulipo did not take Europe by storm, as did the controversy that men may be descended from or closely related to apes, but those who were observers of the struggle encountered by Darwinian theory with church resistance were intrigued by Polynesian concepts that were the exception to the prevailing mystical notion of Divine Cause as the source of all life upon earth. The Kumulipo suggested not only that life evolved of itself upon the earth but also that the visible universe had been set into motion by the heating surfaces of celestial bodies. The rotation of the heavens could then be the means by which cosmic time could be measured and thereby the orderly structure of the universe understood.

It was not the intention of the Hawaiian priests who composed the Kumulipo, however, to explain the universe in scientific terms. Dictated by centuries of established Polynesian custom, their intent was simply to relate a newborn chief of high social rank to his ultimate origins in earth's very beginnings, at the point where all prehuman forms of nature and human life are but common kindred. Yet among origin myths in almost every known age and society, the Kumulipo is comparatively rational for its nonmystical treatment of biological relationships and cosmic time. As this study broadens and deepens into the interpretation of the chant's several themes, the Kumulipo will perhaps demonstrate on its own merits the close parallel between its evolutionary deductions and those arguments for evolution more convincingly reasoned in the inductive study of Charles Darwin.

When life appears in the Kumulipo, it is the product of active, *natural* forces. Supernatural forces are not excluded from that process, but a reading of the poem will confirm that the mythical appearance of deities who are mythologically personified forces of nature *follows* the formation of earth and life-forms already accomplished by spontaneous generation. The only assumption of a causative agent is the preexistent presence of dual energies, one abstracted as male and the other as female. To understand the role of that assumption in Hawaiian life and thought is to fully examine the symbolic core and antithetical style of the dualistic themes of the Kumulipo.

. . . .

Kāwaʻakahi

O ke au i kahuli wela ka honua
O ke au i kahuli lole ka lani
O ke au i kūkaʻiaka ka lā
E hoʻomālamalama i ka malama
O ke au o Makaliʻi ka pō
O ka walewale hoʻokumu honua ʻia
O ke kumu o ka lipo, i lipo ai
O ke kumu o ka pō, i pō ai
O ka lipolipo, o ka lipolipo
O ka lipo o ka lā, o ka lipo o ka pō
     Pō wale hoʻi
Hānau ka pō
Hānau Kumulipo i ka pō, he kāne
Hānau Poʻele i ka pō, he wahine

When space turned around, the earth heated
When space turned over, the sky reversed
When the sun appeared standing in shadows
To cause light to make bright the moon,
When the Pleiades are small eyes in the night,

From the source in the slime was the earth formed
From the source in the dark was darkness formed

From the source in the night was night formed
From the depths of the darkness, darkness so deep
Darkness of day, darkness of night
Of night alone

Did night give birth
Born was Kumulipo in the night, a male
Born was Poʻele in the night, a female

Hānau ka Uku-koʻakoʻa
Hānau kana, he ʻĀkoʻakoʻa, puka

    Born the coral polyp
    Born of him a coral colony emerged

Hānau ke Koʻe-ʻenuhe ʻeli hoʻopuʻu honua
Hānau kana he Koʻe, puka

    Born the *burrowing worm*, hilling the soil
    Born of him a *worm* emerged

Hanau ka Peʻa
Ka Peʻapeʻa kana keiki, puka

    Born the *starfish*
    The *small starfish* his child emerged

Hānau ka Weli
He Weliweli kana keiki, puka

    Born the *sea cucumber*
    A small *sea cucumber* his child emerged

Hānau ka ʻIna, ka ʻIna
Hānau kana, he Hālula, puka

    Born the *coral-dwelling sea urchin*
    Born of him a *short-spiked sea urchin* emerged

Hānau ka Hāwaʻe
O ka Wana-kū kana keiki, puka

    Born the *smooth-spined sea urchin*
    The *sharp-spiked sea urchin* his child emerged

Hānau ka Hāʻukeʻuke
O ka Uhalula kana keiki, puka

> Born the *unspiked sea urchin*
> The *thin-spiked sea urchin* his child emerged

Hānau ka Pīʻoe
O ka Pipi kana keiki, puka

> Born the *barnacle*
> The *reef oyster* his child emerged

Hānau ka Pāpaua
O ka ʻŌlepe kana keiki, puka

> Born the *large clam*
> The *hinged mollusk* his child emerged

Hānau ka Nahawele
O ka Unauna kana keiki, puka

> Born the *mussel*
> The *hermit crab* his child emerged

Hānau ka Makaiauli
O ka ʻOpihi kana keiki, puka

> Born the *dark-fleshed limpet*
> The *limpet* his child emerged

Hānau ka Leho
O ka Pūleholeho kana keiki, puka

> Born the *cowry*
> The *small cowry* his child emerged

Hānau ka Naka
O ke Kupekala kana keiki, puka

> Born the *naka* shell
> The *chama shell* his child emerged

Hānau ka Makaloa
O ka Pūpū'awa kana keiki, puka

    Born the *drupe*
    The *bitter drupe* his child emerged

Hānau ka 'Olē
O ka 'Olē'olē kana keiki, puka

    Born the *triton*
    The *small triton* his child emerged

Hānau ka Pipipi
O ke Kūpe'e kana keiki, puka

    Born the *nerita snail*
    The *large nerita* his child emerged

Hānau ka Wī
O ke Kīkī kana keiki, puka

    Born the *fresh-water snail*
    The *brackish-water snail* his child emerged

Hānau kāne iā Wai'ololī
O ka wahine iā Wai'ololā

    Born male for the narrow waters
    Female for the broad waters

Hānau ka 'Ēkaha noho i kai
Kia'i iā e ka 'Ēkahakaha noho i uka

    Born the *coralline seaweed* living in the sea
    Kept by the *bird's nest fern* living on land

He pō uhe'e i ka wawa
He nuku, he wai ka 'ai a ka la'au
O ke Akua ke komo, 'a'oe komo kanaka

O kāne iā Wai'ololī
O ka wahine iā Wai'ololā

It is a night gliding through the passage
Of an opening; a stream of water is the food of plants
It is the god who enters; not as a human does he enter

Male for the narrow waters
Female for the broad waters

Hānau ka 'Aki'Aki noho i kai
Kia'i iā e ka Mānienie-'aki'aki noho i uka

Born the *'aki'aki* seaweed living in the sea
Kept by the *manienie* shore grass living on land

He pō uhe'e i ka wawa
He nuku, he wai ka 'ai a ka la'au
O ke Akua ke komo, 'a'oe komo kanaka

O kāne iā Wai'oloī
O ka wahine iā Wai'ololā

It is a night gliding through the passage
Of an opening; a stream of water is the food of plants
It is the god who enters; not as a human does he enter

Male for the narrow waters
Female for the broad waters

Hānau ka 'A'ala-'ula noho i kai
Kia'i iā e ka 'Ala'ala-wai-nui noho i uka

Born the *fragrant red seaweed* living in the sea
Kept by the succulent *mint* living on land

He pō uhe'e i ka wawa
He nuku, he wai ka 'ai a ka la'au
O ke Akua ke komo, 'a'oe komo kanaka

O kāne iā Wai'oloī
O ka wahine iā Wai'ololā

It is a night gliding through the passage
Of an opening; a stream of water is the food of plants
It is the god who enters; not as a human does he enter

Male for the narrow waters
Female for the broad waters

Hānau ka Manauea noho i kai
Kiaʻi iā e ke Kalo-manauea noho i uka

    Born the *manauea* seaweed living in the sea
    Kept by the *manauea* taro living on land

He pō uheʻe i ka wawa
He nuku, he wai ka ʻai a ka laʻau
O ke Akua ke komo, ʻaoʻe komo kanaka

O kāne iā Waiʻololī
O ka wahine iā Waiʻololā

    It is a night gliding through the passage
    Of an opening; a stream of water is the food of plants
    It is the god who enters; not as a human does he enter

    Male for the narrow waters
    Female for the broad waters

Hānau ke Kōʻeleʻele noho i kai
Kiaʻi iā e ke ko Punapuna, kōʻeleʻele, noho i uka

    Born the *kōʻeleʻele* seaweed living in the sea
    Kept by the *jointed sugarcane* living on land

He pō uheʻe i ka wawa
He nuku, he wai ka ʻai a ka laʻau
O ke Akua ke komo, ʻaʻoe komo kanaka

O kāne iā Waiʻololī
O ka wahine iā Waiʻololā

    It is a night gliding through the passage
    Of an opening; a stream of water is the food of plants
    It is the god who enters; not as a human does he enter

    Male for the narrow waters
    Female for the broad waters

Hānau ka Puakī noho i kai
Kia'i iā e ka Lauaki noho i uka

> Born the *puakī* seaweed living in the sea
> Kept by the *lauaki* sugarcane living on land

He pō uhe'e i ka wawa
He nuku, he wai ka 'ai a ka la'au
O ke Akua ke komo, 'ao'e komo kanaka

O kāne iā Wai'ololī
O ka wahine iā Wai'ololā

> It is a night gliding through the passage
> Of an opening; a stream of water is the food of plants
> It is the god who enters; not as a human does he enter

> Male for the narrow waters
> Female for the broad waters

Hānau ke Kakalamoa noho i kai
Kia'i iā e ka Moamoa noho i uka

> Born the *kakalamoa* seaweed living in the sea
> Kept by the *moamoa* plant living on land

He pō uhe'e i ka wawa
He nuku, he wai ka 'ai a ka la'au
O ke Akua ke komo, 'a'oe komo kanaka

O kāne iā Wai'ololī
O ka wahine iā Wai'ololā

> It is a night gliding through the passage
> Of an opening; a stream of water is the food of plants
> It is the god who enters; not as a human does he enter

> Male for the narrow waters
> Female for the broad waters

Hānau ka limu Kele noho i kai
Kia'i iā e ka Ekele noho i uka

> Born the *kele* seaweed living in the sea
> Kept by the *ekele* taro living on land

He pō uheʻe i ka wawa
He nuku, he wai ka ʻai a ka laʻau
O ke Akua ke komo, ʻaoʻe komo kanaka

O kāne iā Waiʻololī
O ka wahine iā Waiʻololā

> It is a night gliding through the passage
> Of an opening; a stream of water is the food of plants
> It is the god who enters; not as a human does he enter

> Male for the narrow waters
> Female for the broad waters

Hānau ka limu Kala noho i kai
Kiaʻi iā e ka ʻĀkala noho i uka

> Born the *kala* seaweed living in the sea
> Kept by the *ʻākala* raspberry living on land

He pō uheʻe i ka wawa
He nuku, he wai ka ʻai a ka laʻau
O ke Akua ke komo, ʻaʻoe komo kanaka

O kāne iā Waiʻololī
O ka wahine iā Waiʻololā

> It is a night gliding through the passage
> Of an opening; a stream of water is the food of plants
> It is the god who enters; not as a human does he enter

> Male for the narrow waters
> Female for the broad waters

Hānau ka Līpuʻupuʻu noho i kai
Kiaʻi iā e ka Līpuʻu noho i uka

> Born the *līpuʻupuʻu* seaweed living in the sea
> Kept by the *līpuʻu* moss living on land

He pō uheʻe i ka wawa
He nuku, he wai ka ʻai a ka laʻau
O ke Akua ke komo, ʻaʻoe komo kanaka

O kāne iā Wai'ololī
O ka wahine iā Wai'ololā

> It is a night gliding through the passage
> Of an opening; a stream of water is the food of plants
> It is the god who enters; not as a human does he enter

> Male for the narrow waters
> Female for the broad waters

Hānau ka Loloa, noho i kai
Kia'i iā e ke Kalama loloa, noho i uka

> Born the *long seaweed* living in the sea
> Kept by the *tall ebony* living on land

He pō uhe'e i ka wawa
He nuku, he wai ka 'ai a ka la'au
O ke Akua ke komo, 'a'oe komo kanaka

O kāne iā Wai'ololī
O ka wahine iā Wai'ololā

> It is a night gliding through the passage
> Of an opening; a stream of water is the food of plants
> It is the god who enters; not as a human does he enter

> Male for the narrow waters
> Female for the broad waters

Hānau ka Nē, noho i kai
Kia'i iā e ka Neneleau noho i uka

> Born the *nē* seaweed living in the sea
> Kept by the *sumach* tree living on land

He pō uhe'e i ka wawa
He nuku, he wai ka 'ai a ka la'au
O ke Akua ke komo, 'a'oe komo kanaka

O kāne iā Wai'ololī
O ka wahine iā Wai'ololā

It is a night gliding through the passage
Of an opening; a stream of water is the food of plants
It is the god who enters; not as a human does he enter

Male for the narrow waters
Female for the broad waters

Hānau ka Huluwaena, noho i kai
Kia'i iā e ka Huluhulu-'ie'ie noho i uka

Born the *hairy seaweed* living in the sea
Kept by the *hairy pandanus* vine living on land

He pō uhe'e i ka wawa
He nuku, he wai ka 'ai a ka la'au
O ke Akua ke komo, 'a'oe komo kanaka

It is a night gliding through the passage
Of an opening, a stream of water is the food of plants
It is the god who enters; not as a human does he enter

O ke kāne huawai, Akua kena
O kalina a ka wai i ho'oulu ai
O ka huli ho'okawowo honua
O paia ('a) i ke auau ka manawa
O he'e au loloa ka po

The male gourd of water, that is the god
From whose flow the vines are made vigorous;
The plant top sprouts from the earth made flourishing
To frame the forest bower in the flow of time,
The flow of time gliding through the long night

O piha, o pihapiha
O piha-'ū, o piha-'ā
O piha-'ē, o piha-'ō

Filling, filling full
Filling, filling out
Filling, filling up

O ke ko'o honua pa'a ka lani
O lewa ke au, iā Kumulipo ka pō
Pō no.

Until the earth is a brace holding firm the sky
When space lifts through time in the night of Kumulipo
It is yet night.

Samuel Elbert

Samuel Elbert, a longtime professor of Pacific languages and linguistics at the University of Hawai'i, is the author of *Spoken Hawaiian, Pulawat Dictionary, Dictionary of the Languages of Rennell and Bellona,* and other books on Polynesian languages and cultures.

With Mary Kawena Pukui he co-authored *Hawaiian Dictionary* and *Hawaiian Grammar,* books that are often spoken of as essential to the understanding and teaching of the Hawaiian language. At the Hawai'i Award for Literature ceremony in 1976, Alfons Korn had high praise for the collaborative works of Pukui and Elbert. "The *Hawaiian Dictionary* is more than a book, more than a monument to Hawaiian literacy. Packed with quotations from *oli* and *mele,* abounding in folk-sayings and Hawaiian proverbial wisdom, 'Pukui-Elbert' is an extension in print—a spacious annex—of the ancient Polynesian oral legacy. It is most fitting today to think of the *Dictionary* as a treasure-filled storehouse, or *hale ho'āhu,* whose rafters will always ring with the language of Hawai'i's unwritten song."

Because of the efforts of Elbert, Pukui, Korn, and others, a great many Polynesian songs have not remained unwritten. The excerpt from Elbert's and Noelani Mahoe's *Na Mele o Hawai'i Nei* that is included in this anthology demonstrates Elbert's dedication to the preservation of the literary art of Hawaiian song. Elbert has been supportive of respect for poetic art in all the various parts of Polynesia he has studied. One of Elbert's best-known articles discusses "The Fate of Poetry in a Disappearing Culture"; and he has done much to promote the idea that poetry can be a saving grace in Polynesia and everywhere else.

from *Na Mele o Hawai'i Nei*

Symbolism, Indirection, and *Kaona*

The Hawaiian name for hidden meaning is *kaona*. The penchant for *kaona* or indirection is only partially explicable by the vagueness of the language occasioned in some parts by lack of sexual gender, verbs without subjects or objects, and verbless sentences, as indicated earlier. It may also be tied to the culture and to the value of pleasant interpersonal relationships, with an attendant failure to call a spade a spade, an adze an adze; and it may be linked with intellectual sprightliness and humor.

How prevalent is the *kaona* in Hawaiian songs? An extreme view was taken by Padraic Colum, the Irish poet who was hired by the Territorial Legislature in the early 1920s to compile a book of Hawaiian legends. He rewrote them in an Irish vein. He did not know the language, but saw hidden meanings everywhere, and he claimed that every Hawaiian poem had at least four meanings—an ostensible meaning, a vulgar meaning, a mythico-historical-topographical meaning, and a deeply hidden meaning. This hypothesis was sensibly answered by Mrs. Pukui: "There are but two meanings: the literal and the *kaona*, or inner meaning. The literal is like the body, and the inner meaning is like the spirit of the poem. . . . There are some poems that have no inner meaning, and to read such meanings into them is folly."

To say that every poem has a vulgar meaning sounds like a comment by some of the more extreme nineteenth-century missionaries.

One perusing even a few songs is impressed by the constant references to ferns, *lehuas*, pandanus, fragrance, winds, rains, and wetness. The ferns, flowers, and birds in love songs refer to sweethearts; the theory will be offered shortly that water and rain and soakings also refer to sweethearts. The more obvious meanings of water and rain are life, fertility, growth, grief, and hardships.

Hawaiians love the rain and know that the beauty of their islands is due to rain. This is expressed succinctly in the saying on the water fountain in front of the Board of Water Supply Building in Honolulu: *Uwē ka lani, ola ka honua* (the sky weeps, the land lives).

Grief may be expressed, too, by rain, but postmissionary songs do not portray grief. The great rains of Hanalei in the song "Hanohano Hanalei" represent the beauty of this valley, with romantic overtones, but do not indicate grief as they do in the saying *Luʻuluʻu Hanalei i ka ua nui, kaumaha i ka noe o Alakaʻi* (Hanalei is downcast with great rains, heavy with the mists of Alakaʻi).

In the chants, the rain, storms, and cold may be linked with hardship and trouble, as in the chant by a hula dancer who wants to be admitted to the hula school:

Eia ka puʻu nui o waho nei la,	Great trouble outside here,
He ua, he ʻino, he anu, he koʻekoʻe.	Rain, storm, cold, chill,
E kuʻu aloha e,	My beloved,
Maloko aku au (Emerson)	Let me in.

The only song in the present collection with such connotations is "Hole Wai-mea."

Hardship, like grief, is not discussed in the songs, which in general are happy and romantic, and the conclusion seems inescapable that—like the flowers—the rains, dews, waterfalls, wetness, soakings, winds, and coolness are romantically inspired. (This theory has been described by Elbert in a rather inaccessible publication.)

Even a glance at the songs in this collection will show that water, rain, sea spray, mist, coolness, and peace are nearly everywhere displayed. Here are some examples.

"Wet in fine and gentle rain,
Adornment of forest upland,
Bearer of sweetness
Coolness and palpitations."
    "Ka-ʻili-lau-o-ke-koa"

"Drenched by the dew
She and I are two,
Three with the rustle of sea spray."
    "Hanohano Hanalei"

"Wet in the creeping rain,
You and I are there
In the fragrant forest."
    "Pulupē nei ʻIli i ke Anu"

"Finally I have known
Twofold peace;
We two in peace
Liquid spattering on the cliff."
"Koni Au i ka Wai"

"We two in the spray,
Oh joy two together
Embracing tightly in the coolness,
Breathing deep of *palai* fern. . .
Oh such spray."
"Kāua i ka Huahuaʻi"

The Power of the Word

The early Hawaiians spoke no language other than their own, and may not have known of the existence of other languages. When they heard English they called it *namu* (gibberish). So, like the Stoic Greeks, they thought their names were universals with inherent nonarbitrary meanings. The meanings had power and explained the universe. In the section "Structure of the Hawaiian Language" we saw that the wrasse fish, ʻaʻawa, was believed genetically related to *Piper methysticum*, ʻawa, because of a resemblance in the sounds in their names. The word had power: *I ka ʻōlelo nō ke ola, i ka ʻōlelo nō ka make* (in the word is life, in the word is death).

This was especially true in the religious chants, and efforts were made to preserve them unchanged throughout the centuries. A mistaken syllable might change the word and the new word might have connotations distasteful to a god, who might then cause the chanter's death. Many of the chants were sacred to the gods, including the family gods, and to the family. For this reason they were not freely imparted to passing strangers. They, as priceless heirlooms, were passed down to rightful heirs. The songs, such as those in this collection, are no longer sacred, nor are they family heirlooms. But still the sense that they were not to be freely bestowed has persisted in the face of mass acculturation and commercialism. This may be a reason for the rarity of song collections. Just as one's family stories and chants were not to be shared in publication, so were not the songs. We, the compilers of this collection, believe that we are not betraying secrets or friendships. We hope not. We believe that these songs—unlike so many chants—are no longer sacred, and that there is no longer the need to ʻauʻa (hold back). And we hope that more people will be encouraged to sing Hawaiian songs more accurately and with greater understanding.

The word, however, is still powerful, and the composer even today must consider double meanings. Many composers avoid such words as *uli* (dark, foreboding) and *hala* (pandanus, pass away), but not all composers have these restrictions or we would not have so many songs about pandanus.

. . . .

Adios Ke Aloha

Adios, My Love

This song was composed by Prince Lele-iō-Hoku. Mexican cowboys at Wai-mea, Hawai'i, added Spanish words.

E ku'u belle o ka pō la 'ila'i,
Ka lawe mālie a ka mahina
Kōaniani mai nei e ke ahe
'Ahea 'oe ho'olono mai.

O my belle of the peaceful night,
Feel the calm moon
Breeze-cooled
Calling you to listen.

HUI

CHORUS

'Ahea ('oe), 'ahea ('oe),
'Oe ho'olono mai
I nei leo nahenahe.
Adios, adios ke aloha.

Calling you, calling you,
Listen
To this soft voice.
Adios, adios my love.

E ka hau'oli 'iniki pu'uwai,
E ke aloha e maliu mai 'oe,
Ke ho'olale mai nei e ke Kiu,
Ua anu ka wao i ka ua.

O joy tingling heart,
O love, turn here,
The Kiu wind implores,
The depths are cool with rain.

Ho'okahi kiss dew drops he ma'ū ia,
E ka belle o ka noe līhau,
Eia au la e ke aloha,
Ke huli ho'i nei me ka neo.

A single moist dewdrop kiss,
O belle of the cool mist,
Here am I, O love,
Coming back with nothing.

Ahi Wela

Hot Fire

The composer of the first of the two versions of this well-known song is not known. The composers of the second version (dated 1891) were Lizzie Doirin and Mary Beckley. Little girls sometimes sing and dance this hula. The words suggest that this is hardly an appropriate number for them.

Older Version

Ku'u pua i li'a ai	My flower desired
A'u i kui a lawa	For me to braid and bind
I lei ho'ohiehie	An elegant lei
Nō ke ano ahiahi.	For evening time.

HUI

CHORUS

Ahi wela mai nei loko	Hot fire here within
I ka hana a ke aloha	The act of love
E lalawe nei ku'u kino	Overpowers my body
Konikoni lua i ka pō nei.	Throbbing last night.

'Elua nō māua	Two of us
A i 'ike ia hana	Have felt the power
La'i ai ka nanea 'ana	Peaceful relaxing
Ho'oipo i ku'u kino.	Making love within my body.

Later Version

'Elua nō māua	Two of us
I 'ike ia hana,	Have felt the power,
La'i wale ke kaunu	Calm after passion
Ho'onipo i ka poli.	Making love within the heart.

HUI

CHORUS

Ahi wela mai nei loko	Hot fire is here within
I ka hana a ke aloha	The act of love
E lalawe nei ku'u kino	Overpowers my body
Konikoni lua i ka pu'uwai.	And my throbbing heart.

'Auhea wale ana 'oe,	Heed,
Ku'u pua i kui a lei,	O flower of mine strewn in a lei,
I lei ho'ohiehie	An elegant lei
Nō ke anu ahiahi.	In the coolness of the evening.

'Ahulili

This song has numerous versions. The one following was given to Mary Kawena Pukui and Eleanor Williamson at Kau-pō, Maui, by Mrs. Francis Marciel (née Violet Poepoe) on December 1, 1961. 'Ahulili is a prominent peak easily seen from the lanai of Mrs. Josephine Marciel's home at Kau-pō. The song was composed many years ago by Scott Ha'i, a Kau-pō resident. Note the pun on Mt. 'Ahulili and *lili* (jealous). An alternate last stanza is *Ha'ina mai ka puana* followed by the first three lines of the first stanza.

He aloha nō 'o 'Ahulili,	Love for 'Ahulili,
A he lili paha kō iala	Perhaps she's jealous
I ke kau mau 'ole 'ia	Because not always rests
E ka 'ohu kau kuahiwi.	Mist upon the mountain.
E'a iho nō e ka 'olu,	Here sweetness,
Ke 'ala kūpaoa	Heady fragrance
Lawa pono kou makemake	Enough for your desires
E manene ai kou kino.	And your tingling body.
'Ako aku au i ka pua	I have plucked the flower
Kui nō wau a lei,	Strung into a lei,
A i lei poina 'ole	A lei never forgotten
Nō nā kau a kau.	From one season to the next.
Pa'a 'ia iho a pa'a	Hold, hold fast to
Ka 'i'ini me ka 'ano'i,	Desire and yearning,
He 'ano'i nō ka 'ōpua,	Yearning for the cloud banks,
Ka beauty o Mauna-hape.	The beauty of Mount-Happy.
E ō 'ia ka lei,	Respond, lei,
Ke 'ala kūpaoa,	Heady fragrance,
Ka puana ho'i a ka moe,	The answer to dreams,
Ka beauty o Mauna-hape.	The beauty of Mount-Happy.

ʻĀina-Hau

ʻĀina-Hau (*hau*-tree land) was an estate near the site of the present Ka-ʻiu-lani Hotel in Waikīkī that had belonged to Princess Ruth Keʻeli-kō-lani, but which she gave to her godchild, Ka-ʻiu-lani, at her baptism in 1875. The estate was planned and supervised by Ka-ʻiu-lani's father, Archibald S. Cleghorn. The song was composed by Ka-ʻiu-lani's mother, Princess Likelike (sister of Ka-lā-kaua and Liliʻu-o-ka-lani). R. L. Stevenson was a frequent visitor at ʻĀina-Hau when Ka-ʻiu-lani was thirteen years old. Cleghorn inherited the property at Ka-ʻiu-lani's death in 1899, and upon his death in 1910 he left it to the Territory for a park. The Territorial legislature did not accept the gift.

*Nā ka wai lukini, wai anuhea
   o ka rose*
	Sweet water, cool water
	   of the rose

E hoʻopē nei i ka liko o nā pua.	Drenching flower buds.

*Nā ka manu pīkake manu hulu
   melemele*
	Peacocks and birds with
	   yellow feathers

Nā kāhiko ia o kuʻu home.	Adorn my home.

*Nā ka makani aheahe i pā
   mai makai*
	Wind blowing gently
	   from the sea

I lawe mai i ke onaona līpoa,	Brings the fragrance of *līpoa* seaweed,

*E hoʻoipo hoʻonipo me ke
   ʻala kuʻu home,*
	Love and delight and
	   perfume for my home,

Kuʻu home, kuʻu home i ka ʻiuʻiu.	My home, my home paradise.
HUI	CHORUS

*Nani wale kuʻu home ʻĀina-Hau
   i ka ʻiu,*
	So beautiful is my home ʻĀina-Hau
	   in a paradise,

I ka holunape a ka lau o ka niu,	Swaying leaves of coconuts,

*I ka uluwehiwehi i ke ʻala
   o nā pua,*
	Verdant beauty and fragrant
	   flowers,

Kuʻu home, kuʻu home i ka ʻiuʻiu.	My home, my home paradise.

A Kona Hema ʻO Ka Lani   The King At South Kona

The music for two versions of this chest-slapping *(paʻi umauma)* hula is given by Roberts, who stated that the song comes from Maui and is "an old stock hula tune for it was encountered again and again in different guises." The song honors Ka-lā-kaua but at the same time praises the Kona and Kohala districts of Hawaiʻi. Well-known places mentioned are Ka-ʻawa-loa, Ka-wai-hae, Māhu-kona, and Kohala, with their associated poetic epithets. *Lēʻī mai ʻo Kohala i ka nuku* (Kohala is crowded at the mouth) is part of a chant and a saying in the foolish intelligence report of Pūpū-kea to the Maui leader Kama-lālā-walu, that all the Kohala people had gone to the mouth *(nuku)*, probably the harbor mouth, leaving the island unprotected; Kama-lālā-walu then invaded the island and was disastrously defeated. Note in the song the linked terminals *ʻehu ʻehuehu; i ke kai, i ke kai; Ka-wai-hae, hae ana; naulu, uluulu; ka moana, ka moana.*

A Kona Hema ʻo ka lani	The king at South Kona
Nānā iā Ka-ʻawa-loa	Beholds Ka-ʻawaʻloa
ʻIke i ka laʻi o ʻEhu.	And senses the peace of ʻEhu.
Ehuehu ʻoe, e ka lani,	The power of your majesty,
Ka helena aʻo Hawaiʻi la	Face of Hawaiʻi
Mālamalama nā moku,	Islands radiant,
Ahuwale nā kualono,	Ridges erect,
ʻIke ʻia ka pae ʻōpua	Cloud banks seen.
E kukū ana i ke kai,	Rising in the sea,
I ke kai hāwanawana,	In the whispering sea,
ʻŌlelo o Ka-wai-hae.	Voice of Ka-wai-hae.
Hae ana, e ka naulu.	O showers, pour forth.
Ka makani hele uluulu,	Wind mounts to gales,
Kū ka ʻeʻa i ka moana,	Spray seethes in the sea,
Ka moana o Māhu-kona,	The sea of Māhu-kona,
Ka makani ʻĀpaʻapaʻa.	And the wind ʻĀpaʻapaʻa.
Lēʻī mai ʻo Kohala	Kohala is crowded
I ka nuku nā huapala.	To the very mouth with handsome ones.
Haʻina ʻia mai ka puana	Tell the story
Ka lani Ka-lā-kaua.	Of his majesty, Ka-lā-kaua.

Alekoki

This is an example of the storytelling qualities of the old songs. Songs were pronounced clearly, the hearers listened carefully to the story being told, and the more stanzas the better. The monotony of the tune was counterbalanced by the interest in the words.

The hula "Alekoki" is sometimes attributed to Ka-lā-kaua, with music by Lizzie Alohikea, but N. B. Emerson stated that the song was composed in about 1850 by Prince Luna-lilo and refers to his disappointment in not being able to marry Victoria Ka-māmalu, the sister of Lot Kamehameha and Liho-liho.

Alekoki is the name of Nuʻu-anu Stream seaward of Kapena Falls. Maʻemaʻe is the hill above the juncture of Nuʻu-anu and Pauoa streets. Māmala is Honolulu harbor. The spray flurries refer to opposition to the marriage. The wind carrying news is perhaps scandal. The singer finally finds other flowers—but does he sound happy?

Today Hawaiian words as exotics embellish English songs; formerly English words as exotics embellished Hawaiian songs; *piliwi* (believe) in the first verse was substituted for an earlier *manaʻo*.

ʻAʻole i piliwi ʻiā	Unbelievable
Kahi wai aʻo Alekoki	Waters of Alekoki
Ua hoʻokohu ka ua i uka	Like the rains of the uplands
Noho maila i Nuʻu-anu.	In Nuʻu-anu.
Anuanu makehewa au	Cold forsaken me
Ke kali ana i laila	Waiting there
Kainō paha ua paʻa	Believing certain
Kou manaʻo i ʻaneʻi.	Your thoughts were of me.
Iō i ʻaneʻi au	Here I am
Ka piʻina aʻo Maʻemaʻe	At Maʻemaʻe Hill
He ʻala onaona kou	Where your sweet fragrance
Ka i hiki mai i ʻaneʻi.	Has come to me.
Ua malu neia kino	This body is captive
Mamuli o kō leo,	To your voice,
Kau nui aku ka manaʻo	Thoughts linger
Kahi wai aʻo Kapena	At the waters of Kapena.
Pani a paʻa ʻia mai	Blocked
Nā mana wai aʻo uka,	Upland streams,
Maluna aʻe nō au	And I am above
Ma nā lumi liʻiliʻi.	In little rooms.

Mawaho a'o Māmala	Outside Māmala
Hao mai nei ehuehu	Spray flurries
Pulu au i ka hunakai	And I am wet with foam
Kai he'ehe'e i ka 'ili.	And sea slippery to the skin.
Ho'okahi nō koa nui	One brave man
Nāna e alo ia 'ino,	Faces the storm,
'Ino'ino mai nei luna	The storms above
I ka hao a ka makani.	And the blustering wind.
He makani 'aha'ilono	A wind bringing news
Lohe ka luna i Pelekane.	That the king of England hears.
A 'oia pō uli nui	This deep black night
Mea 'ole i ku'u mana'o.	Cannot worry me.
E kilohi au i ka nani	I behold beauty
Nā pua o Mauna-'ala.	And the flowers of Mauna-'ala.
Ha'ina mai ka puāna:	Tell the refrain:
Kahi wai a'o Alekoki.	Waters of Alekoki.

'Ālika   *The Arctic*

Kamakau mentions the ship *Arctic* landing at Kaua'i between 1787 and Vancouver's arrival in 1792. An editor's note on the same page gives the first four verses. The song was later printed in Smith. This hula illustrates the Hawaiian fondness for place-names (rather imaginary here) and veiled risqué meanings. It is sometimes credited to Charles Ka'apa.

Aia i 'Ālika	There in the *Arctic*
Ka ihu o ka moku.	The prow of the ship.
Ua hao o pa'ihi,	Set firmly,
Nā pe'a i ka makani.	Sails in the wind.
Ke liolio nei	Taut
Ke kaulu likini,	Rigging lines,
'Alu'alu 'ole iho,	Not slack,
Nā pe'a i ka makani.	Sails in the wind.
'A'ole i kau pono,	Not fixed,
Ka newa i ka piko.	The needle in the north.
Ka'a 'ē ka huila	The wheel turns
E niniu i ka makani.	Spinning in the wind.
Ke kau a'e nei	Placed
Ka ihu o Macao	The prow of the *Macao*
Ke iho a'e nei	Down
E komo 'Asia.	To go to Asia.
Me ke Kai Melemele,	The Yellow Sea,
Ke kōwa o Pelina,	Bering Straits,
Nani wale ka 'ikena,	A lovely view,
Nā pua i Sarona.	Flowers of Sharon.
I noho ka ihu	The prow sets
I ka piko i Himela,	Towards the Himalaya summit,
Ka hale lau pama	A palm-leafed house
Ho'omaha i ke kula.	For the rest on the plains.
Ha'ina 'ia mai	Tell
Ana ka puana:	The refrain:
Aia i 'Ālika	There in the *Arctic*
Ka ihu o ka moku.	The prow of the ship.

. . . .

Aloha ʻOe   *Farewell To You*

This most famous of all Hawaiian songs was for decades sung for every departing and arriving steamer. A rather ambiguous statement in *Hawaiʻi's Story by Hawaiʻi's Queen* (Liliʻuokalani) suggests that the song was composed while the queen was imprisoned in ʻIo-lani Palace, but on a copy of the song in her own handwriting in the State Archives are the place and date: Mauna-wili, 1877. According to popular belief, and according to an account by Helen Caldwell, "the inspiration for the words and music of this composition was furnished by the fond parting embrace of two lovers, whom the queen discovered when returning over the pali from a horseback party on the other side of the island." Hawaiians say, but this has not been seen in print, that one of the lovers was Likelike, Liliʻu's sister, who later married A. S. Cleghorn.

Liliʻu once heard "Aloha ʻOe" sung at the funeral of a missionary friend. She was shocked. "This is a love song," she said afterwards, but was told that the song would live forever as a song of farewell.

The *lehua ʻāhihi* in the song are a kind of *ʻōhiʻa* that on the rugged pali slopes suggest Japanese bonsai trees.

In the queen's notebook, the next to the last line is *I laila hiaʻai nā manu*, with the same meaning as given below.

Haʻaheo ʻē ka ua i nā pāli	Proudly the rain on the cliffs
Ke nihi aʻela i ka nahele	Creeps into the forest
E uhai ana paha i ka liko	Seeking the buds
Pu a ʻāhihi lehua o uka.	And miniature *lehua* flowers of the uplands.

HUI	CHORUS
Aloha ʻoe, aloha ʻoe,	Farewell to you, farewell to you,
E ke onaona noho i ka lipo.	O fragrance in the blue depths.
One fond embrace, a hoʻi aʻe au	One fond embrace and I leave
A hui hou aku.	To meet again.

ʻO ka haliʻa aloha ka i hiki mai	Sweet memories come
Ke hone aʻe nei i kuʻu manawa.	Sound softly in my heart.
ʻO ʻoe nō kaʻu ipo aloha	You are my beloved sweetheart
A loko e hana nei.	Felt within.

Maopopo kuʻu ʻike i ka nani	I understand the beauty
Nā pua rose o Mauna-wili.	Of rose blossoms at Mauna-wili.
I laila hoʻohie nā manu,	There the birds delight,
Mikiʻala i ka nani o ia pua.	Alert the beauty of this flower.

Mary Kawena Pukui

Mary Kawena Pukui was renowned for the depth and breadth of her knowledge of Hawaiian culture. She served as a precious bridge between Hawai'i's still living cultural forms and a modern society that too often turned its back on the riches of Hawaiian language, literature, dance, music, religion, and crafts.

Until the age of six Pukui lived with her grandmother in the remote Ka'ū district and spoke only Hawaiian. Momi Naughton has explained the importance of Pukui's continuous use of the Hawaiian language. "Because her first language was Hawaiian and her mother continued to enhance her understanding of the language, Kawena was not only fluent in Hawaiian, but was also able to appreciate its subtle nuances and poetics. She was a naturally gifted writer and by fifteen she was already collecting and translating folklore and historical tales."

Mrs. Pukui was proud of her European as well as her Hawaiian ancestry. Her mother descended from a long line of medical kahunas and her father from the seventeenth-century Massachusetts family that included the poet Anne Bradstreet.

As a poet, she recorded and translated numerous songs and chants and also composed new songs of her own. Her collections of Hawaiian proverbs are among the best places to observe her mastery of the Hawaiian language and its subtle tendencies toward double meanings. Naughton points out that "many of these ingenious proverbs and some of the clever intricacies of the Hawaiian language would have been lost to the world had Pukui not written them down at the point in time she did."

Perhaps best known to the widest audiences are Pukui's many collections of tales. Some of the stories were told to her, others she found in Hawaiian newspapers or other sources. Her feeling was always that "this is not my work but the work of my people." Her tales are some of the most familiar, but they are familiar largely because Pukui has retold them so well.

The Marchers of the Night

Every Hawaiian has heard of the "Marchers of the Night," *Ka huaka'i o ka Pō*. A few have seen the procession. It is said that such sight is fatal unless one had a relative among the dead to intercede for him. If a man is found stricken by the roadside, a white doctor will pronounce the cause as heart failure, but a Hawaiian will think at once of the fatal night march.

The time for the march is between half after seven when the sun has actually set and about two in the morning before the dawn breaks. It may occur on one of the four nights of the gods, on Kū, Akua, Lono, Kāne, or on the nights of Kāloa. Those who took part in the march were the chiefs and warriors who had died, the *'aumākua*, and the gods, each of whom had their own march.

That of the chiefs was conducted according to the tastes of the chief for whom the march was made. If he had enjoyed silence in this life his march would be silent save for the creaking of the food calabashes suspended from the carryingsticks, or of the litter, called *mānele*, if he had not been fond of walking. If a chief had been fond of music, the sound of the drum, nose flute and other instruments was heard as they marched. Sometimes there were no lights borne; at other times there were torches but not so bright as for the gods and demigods. A chief whose face had been sacred, called an *alo kapu*, so that no man, beast, or bird could pass before him without being killed, must lead the march; even his own warriors might not precede him. If on the contrary his back had been sacred, *akua kapu*, he must follow in the rear of the procession. A chief who had been well protected in life and who had no rigid tabu upon face or back would march between his warriors.

On the marches of the chief, a few *'aumākua* would march with them in order to protect their living progeny who might chance to meet them on the road. Sometimes the parade came when a chief lay dying or just dead. It paused before the door for a brief time and then passed on. The family might not notice it, but a neighbor might see it pass and know that the chief had gone with his ancestors who had come for him.

In the march of the *'aumākua* of each district, there was music and chanting. The marchers carried candlenut torches which burned brightly even on a rainy night. They might be seen even in broad daylight and were followed by whirlwinds such as come one after another in columns. They cried *"Kapu o moe!"* as a warning to stragglers to get out of the way or to prostrate themselves with closed eyes until the marchers passed. Like the chiefs, they too sometimes came to a dying descendant and took him away with them.

The march of the gods was much longer, more brilliantly lighted, and more sacred than that of the chiefs or of the demigods. The torches were brighter and shone red. At the head, at three points within the line, and at the rear were carried bigger torches, five being the complete number among Hawaiians, the *ku a lima*. The gods with the torches walked six abreast, three males and three females. One of the three at the end of the line was Hi'iaka-i-ka-poli-o-Pele, youngest sister of the volcano goddess. The first torch could be seen burning up at Kahuku when the last of the five torches was at Nonuapo. The only music to be heard on the marches of the gods was the chanting of their names and mighty deeds. The sign that accompanied them was a heavy downpour of rain, with mist, thunder and lightning, or heavy seas. Their route the next day would be strewn with broken boughs or leaves, for the heads of the gods were sacred and nothing should be suspended above them.

If a living person met these marchers, it behooved him to get out of the way as quickly as possible. Otherwise he might be killed, unless he had an ancestor or an *'aumākua* in the procession to plead for his life. If he met a procession of chiefs and had no time to get out of the way, he might take off his clothes and lie face upward, breathing as little as possible. He would hear them cry "Shame!" as they passed. One would say, "He is dead!" Another would cry, "No, he is alive, but what a shame for him to lie uncovered!" If he had no time to strip he must sit perfectly still, close his eyes, and take his chance. He was likely to be killed by the guard at the front or at the rear of the line unless saved by one of his ancestors or by an *'aumākua*. If he met a procession of gods he must take off all his clothes but his loincloth and sit still with his eyes tightly closed, because no man might look on a god, although he might listen to their talk. He would hear the command to strike; then, if he was beloved by one of the gods as a favorite child or namesake, he would hear someone say, "No! he is mine!" and he would be spared by the guards.

Many Hawaiians living today have seen or heard the ghostly marchers. Mrs. Wiggin, Mrs. Pukui's mother, never got in their way but she has watched them pass from the door of her own mother's house and has heard the Ka'ū people tell of the precautions that must be taken to escape death if one chances to be in their path.

A young man of Kona, Hawai'i tells the following experience. One night just after nightfall, about seven or eight in the evening, he was on his way when of a sudden he saw a long line of marchers in the distance coming toward him. He climbed over a stone wall and sat very still. As they drew near he saw that they walked four abreast and were about seven feet tall, nor did their feet touch the ground. One of the marchers stepped out of the line and ran back and forth on the other side of the wall behind which he crouched as if to protect him from the others. As each file passed he heard voices call out "Strike!" and his protector answered, "No! no! he is mine!" No other sounds were to be heard except the call to strike and the creak of a *mānele*. He was not afraid and watched the marchers closely. There were both men and women in the procession. After a long line of marchers four abreast had passed, there came the *mānele* bearers, two before and two behind. On the litter sat a very big man whom he guessed at once to be a chief. Following the litter were other marchers walking four abreast. After all had passed his protector joined his fellows.

A month later the same young man went to call on some friends and was returning home late at night. Not far from the spot where he had met the marchers before was a level flat of ground, and drawing near to the spot he heard the sound of an *ipu* drum and of chanting. He came close enough to see and recognize many of the men and women whom he had seen on the previous march as he had sat behind the stone wall. He was delighted with the chanting and drumming, with the dancing of the *'āla'apapa* by the women and the *mokomoko* wrestling and other games of the past by the men. As he sat watching he heard someone say, "There is the grandson of Kekuanoi!" "Never mind! We do not mind him!" said another. This was the name of a grandfather of his who lived on the beach and he knew that he himself was being discussed. For a couple of hours he sat watching before he went home. His grandfather at home had seen it all; he said, "I know that you have been with our people of the night; I saw you sitting by watching the sports." Then he related to his grandfather what he had seen on the two nights when he met the chiefs and warriors of old.

In old days these marchers were common in Ka'ū district, but folk of today know little about them. They used to march and play games practically on the same ground as in life. Hence each island and each district had its own parade and playground along which the dead would march and at which they would assemble.

Mrs. Emma Akana Olmsted tells me that when she was told as a child about the marchers of the night she was afraid, but now that she is older and can herself actually hear them she is no longer terrified. She hears beautiful loud chanting of voices, the high notes of the flute and drumming so loud that it seems beaten upon the side of the house beside her bed. The voices are so distinct that if she could write music she would be able to set down the notes they sang.

The Shark Guardian*

This is a story of the days when Mary Kawena Pukui was a little girl in Ka'ū on Hawai'i. One very rainy day she got to thinking of a certain kind of fish. "I want nenue fish, " she said.

"Hush, child," her mother answered. "We have none."

"But I am hungry for nenue fish!" the little girl repeated and began to cry.

"Stop your crying!" said another woman crossly. "Don't you see we can't go fishing today? Just look out at the pouring rain. No one can get you nenue fish. Keep still!"

The little girl went off into a corner and cried softly so that no one should hear, "I do want nenue fish! Why can't someone get it for me?"

Her aunt came in out of the rain. It was Kawena's merry young aunt who was always ready for adventure. "What is the matter with the child?" she was asking. "The skies are shedding tears enough, Kawena. Why do you add more?"

"I want nenue fish," the little girl whispered.

"Then you shall have some. The rain is growing less. We will go to my uncle."

In a moment the little girl had put on her raincoat, and the two were walking through the lessening rain. It was fun to be out with this merry aunt, fun to slip on wet rock, and shake the drops from dripping bushes. At last they reached the uncle's cave. "Aloha!" the old man called. "What brings you two this rainy morning?"

"The grandchild is hungry for nenue fish," Kawena's aunt replied.

"And nenue fish she shall have," said the old man. Net in hand he climbed the rocks above his cave home. Kawena and her aunt watched him as he stood looking out over the bay. He stood there like a man of wood until the little girl grew tired watching. The rain had stopped and sunlight touched the silent figure. Why didn't he do something? Why didn't he get her fish? Why did he stand there so long—so long?

Suddenly he moved. With quick leaps he made his way to the beach and waded out. Kawena and her aunt hurried after him and saw him draw his net about some fish and lift them from the water. Just as the girl and woman reached the beach the old man held up a fish. "The first for you, old one," he said and threw the fish into the bay. A shark rose from the water to seize it. "These for the grandchild," the old man added. He was still speaking to the shark as he gave four fish to Kawena.

The little girl took her fish, but her wondering eyes were following the shark as he swam away.

"That is our guardian," the uncle said. He too was watching the shark until it disappeared.

"Tell her about our guardian," said the aunt. "Kawena ought to know that story."

The uncle led them back to his cave. There, dry and comfortable, they sat looking down at beach and bay. "It was from those rocks that I first saw him," the uncle began, his eyes on rocks below.

"One day, many years ago, I found my older brother lying on the sand. For a moment I thought that he was dead. Then he opened his eyes and saw me. 'Bring 'awa and bananas,' he whispered. I stood looking at him, not understanding his strange words. After a bit he opened his eyes again and saw me still beside him. ' 'Awa and bananas!' he repeated. 'Get them quickly.'

"As I started away I saw him pull himself to his feet, holding onto a rock. He looked out over the bay and called, 'Wait, O my guardian! The boy has gone for food.' Then he sank back upon the sand. I looked out into the bay, but saw no one.

"I got 'awa drink and ripe bananas and brought them to my brother. He pulled himself weakly to his feet once more and out onto those rocks, motioning me to bring the food. He called again and his voice was stronger. 'O my guardian, come! Here is 'awa drink! Here are bananas! Come and eat.'

"Suddenly a large shark appeared just below the rocks on which we stood. As my brother raised the wooden bowl of 'awa, the great fish opened his mouth. Carefully my brother poured the drink into that open mouth till all was gone. Then he peeled the bananas one by one and tossed them to the shark, until the great fish was satisfied. 'I thank you, O my guardian!' Brother said. 'Today you saved my life. Come here when you are hungry.' The shark turned and swam away.

"While my brother rested on the sand he told me his adventure. His canoe had been caught in a squall and overturned. He was blinded by rain and waves and could not find the canoe. It must have drifted away. The waves broke over him and he thought the end had come.

"Then he felt himself on something firm. 'A rock!' he thought and clung to it. Suddenly he felt himself moving through the waves and knew that he was riding on the back of a great shark and clinging to his fin. He was frightened, but kept his hold.

"The storm passed on, and my brother saw the beach. The shark swam into shallow water, and Brother stumbled up the sand. It was there I found him.

"He never forgot that shark. Often I have seen him standing on the rocks above this cave with 'awa and bananas ready. Sometimes he called. Sometimes he waited quietly until the shark saw him and came. Sometimes the shark drove a small school of fish into the bay as you saw just now. My brother caught some and shared them with the shark.

"The time came when my brother was very sick. Before he died he beckoned to me. 'My guardian,' he whispered. 'You must give food to the one that saved my life.'

"I have not forgotten, and the shark does not forget. I feed him 'awa and bananas, and he sometimes drives fish into my net. Today he wanted nenue fish and put the thought of them into your mind. Always remember our guardian, Kawena."

Kawena Pukui is a woman now, but she has never forgotten the shark guardian.

The Punahou Spring*

There was a dry time on O'ahu. No rain fell, streams dried, and many springs ceased to flow. It was a hungry time, for gardens too were dry.

In Mānoa Valley at the foot of Rocky Hill lived an old couple. This dry time was very hard for these old folks. Mukaka, the husband, must walk far up the valley to get ti roots and ferns for food. Kealoha, his wife, must walk each day to Ka-Mo'ili'ili where a spring still flowed. There she must fill her water gourds and carry them up the long rough trail back to her home.

One day the way seemed more long and hard than ever. Kealoha rested on a rock. "I can't go on!" she thought. "I can't carry the water all that way." But then she thought, "I must! We must have water." She rose and lifted her carrying pole. Wind swept about her, filling her eyes with dust. It almost blew her off her feet, yet she struggled on.

When she reached home she found Mukaka there before her preparing food. But Kealoha was too tired to eat. She lay upon her mats and cried with weariness. At last she slept and dreamed. In her dream a man stood beside her mats. "Why do you cry?" he asked her.

"Because I am so weary," she replied. "Each day I walk to Ka-Mo'ili'ili and fill my water gourds. The trail is hot, dusty, and long. I am too tired!"

"You need not go again," answered the man. "Close to your home, under the hala tree, there is a spring. There fill your gourds." The man was gone.

When morning came Kealoha told her dream, but her husband hardly listened. "An empty dream," he said, "that came to you because of thirst." He started for the upland.

She watched him, thinking, "He is bent and feeble. Why does he not listen to my words, pull up the hala, and open our own spring?" But when she went to look at the tree, she doubted. Under it the ground was dry and hard. Surely there was no water there. It was an empty dream!

That night Mukaka dreamed. A man stood by his mats and spoke to him. "There is a spring," he said, "under the hala which grows beside your home. You must pull up that tree. Go catch red fish, wrap it in ti leaves, heat the imu, and cook your fish. Make offering and pray for strength to uproot the tree. Then you will find the spring."

Mukaka sat up in the early dawn. "The same dream!" he thought. "It came to Kealoha, now to me. The god of the spring has come to help us in our need. I must obey him."

In the cool of the morning Mukaka and a friend went to Waikīkī for fish. The fish came quickly to their hooks, and some of them were red. "The god is with us," said Mukaka and hurried home to heat the imu. When the food was cooked he made offering and prayed. After they had eaten he said to his friend, "My wife and I each had a dream. Two nights ago Kealoha dreamed, and last night the same dream came to me. A god stood by my mats and said, 'A spring is here. Pull up that hala tree which grows beside your home, and water will flow.' O my friend, I have offered red fish to that god and prayed for strength. We both are strong with food. Now help me pull."

The two men grasped the hala tree. Their muscles strained, and sweat poured down their bodies. They stopped for breath, then pulled again, but still the tree stood firm. The friend looked at the dry earth. "No water here!" he said. "You dreamed of water because of your great thirst."

"The dream was true!" Mukaka answered. "Twice the god stood by our mats. He spoke to Kealoha and to me. His words were true." The old man prayed again. "Let us try once more," he said. "This time we shall succeed."

Once more they struggled with the tree. "It moves!" they shouted and pulled again with more strength than before. The tree came from the ground, and they saw water moistening the earth—a little water. Mukaka ran for his digging stick and cleared away earth and stones. A tiny stream gushed out.

For a moment the three stared in wonder. Then Kealoha shouted, "*Ka punahou!* The new spring!"

Now there was water for all that neighborhood. No more long walks to the Ka-Mo'ili'ili spring! Water flowed steadily. Men dug and let the water soak the ground. They built walls and planted taro. Through these taro patches the springwater flowed, and fish were brought to flourish there. Fish and taro grew, and so the spring gave food as well as water. The people thanked the gods that now their life was good.

Long afterward a school was built beside that spring. It bears the name that Kealoha gave in her glad cry, and its seal is a hala tree. "This school shall be a spring of wisdom," said its founders. "As the hala tree stands firm through wind or storm, so shall the children of this school stand strong and brave through joy and sorrow. As the hala has many uses, so shall these children be useful to Hawai'i."

Can You Keep a Secret?*

Poko was fishing with Grandfather. They had come out at dawn, and the boy had watched the daylight grow. Ocean and sky were pink like a pearl shell, all but one low gray cloud—a low gray cloud that rested on the waves.

They paddled toward the cloud, and it rose slowly, uncovering an island. This island was more green and beautiful than anything the boy had ever seen, and it was filled with growing things. Tall coco palms were heavy with ripe nuts, bananas shone like the sun itself, plants, vines, and trees were large and very green. Suddenly a cock crowed, and the cloud settled down once more upon the island.

"Grandfather!" the boy whispered. "What is that land? Let us go there!"

"It is one of the hidden islands of Kāne, and we cannot go to it."

"Why not, Grandfather? Didn't you see how green and beautiful it is? I want to go there. I want to see it all. Come, Grandfather, let us go."

"Grandson," the old man answered solemnly, "this I have heard: If the gods move that land close to the homes of men, then one can reach it in an hour. But often the land is hidden, and one may sail the ocean until he is gray-headed and never find it. Today the gods gave us sight of that fair land, and then they hid it. It is gone from us forever." The boy said no more, but his heart was filled with longing.

Poko became a man, married, and had a fine family whom he loved. Still the thought of that beautiful green island stayed with him. Still he longed to go there.

Today he and his family were in Puna visiting relatives. His wife and her cousins talked together of kapamaking and other women's matters. Tired of listening, Poko wandered off along the beach. He found a shady spot and sat down to rest. He leaned against a rock and dreamily watched a log rolling in the surf. Up the beach it came, pushed by the waves, then down again. As he watched, Poko thought again of the hidden island. If only he might go there! Perhaps he slept.

Suddenly he was roused by a hand upon his shoulder. He sprang up and looked into the face of a woman he had never seen before. Her pā'ū was of dark seaweed, her lei and bracelets were of shells. "You dream of the hidden island of Kāne," she said, and her voice was like the song of pebbles washed by the waves. "I am the daughter of Kāne. I will take you to that hidden land. Come with me."

The young man followed the stranger down the beach. He saw her touch the rolling log. It became a canoe, and they stepped in. The woman paddled.

The canoe slipped through the waves as swiftly as a fish and as quietly. Poko's heart was full of joy. He did not know whether they paddled a short distance or far when, just ahead, he saw the low-lying cloud. It lifted, and underneath he saw the good green land he had seen long ago.

The canoe scraped on the beach. The two jumped out, carried the canoe up on the sand and looked about them. It was as the young man remembered only more beautiful. Strange trees dropped ripe fruit. Strange birds sang. Here was a garden where sugarcane reached far above his head. Sweet potatoes burst from the rich earth. Ripe bananas and breadfruit dropped from plant and tree. A fat pig waddled through the garden, so well fed it only sniffed the fruit. A fat dog lay sleeping in the sun. Farther on, he saw a hen sitting on eggs among the grasses. Another called softly to her chicks. It was a homelike land—only there were no people and no homes.

The young man turned to the woman who still walked at his side. "I want to stay!" he said. "Oh, let me live here always!"

"You may stay," she answered.

Suddenly, with the eyes of his mind, Poko saw his wife. He saw the white flowers about her head, her hand resting lovingly on the fat baby. And he saw his girl and boy. Turning to the daughter of Kāne he said, "I cannot stay alone. I want my wife and children."

"Can you keep a secret?" the woman asked.

The young man looked at her in wonder. "Yes," he answered.

"Then you and your family may live here all your lives."

The two launched the canoe and paddled back to Puna. As they stepped out, their canoe became once more a log rolled by the waves.

The daughter of Kāne spoke earnestly to Poko. "Keep your secret well. Do not tell anyone where you have been. Do not tell anyone where you are going. When six days have passed bring your family to this beach. If you have kept your secret I will come for you, and you shall live upon the hidden island." Then she was gone.

The young man hurried home in great excitement. His wife saw his excitement and his joy. "What has happened?" she asked.

He smiled. "I cannot tell you," he answered. "In six days go with me to the beach, you and the children. Then you shall know."

Others were about. There was talk and laughter, and the wife said no more, but that night when they were alone she asked again. "I cannot tell," he repeated.

"If you love me you must tell," she begged.

He tried to put her off, but still she begged. At last he asked her, "Can you keep a secret?"

She looked at him surprised and answered, "Yes, I can."

Then he told her, "Today I visited the hidden land of Kāne. Six days must pass. Then we can all go there to live—you and the children and I. Only remember: No one must know. We must keep the secret." They talked long that night. He told her of the beauty of that land, of its fruit and vegetables, its pigs and chickens. They were so excited they could hardly sleep.

Next morning the children noticed the excitement and the joy. "What is it, Mother?" they asked. "What is going to happen?"

"I cannot tell," the mother answered. "It is a secret. When six days have passed your father will take us all to the beach over there. Then you will know."

"We want to know now!"

"What is it, Mother? We can keep a secret."

At last she told. "Remember," she whispered, "no one must know."

Six days is a long time to wait. The little daughter whispered to her friend, "Can you keep a secret?" Then she told her that the whole family were going to do what no family had ever done. The daughter of Kāne would take them to a hidden land.

"Can you keep a secret?" the boy asked the friend who surfed with him. "We are going to an island where is the best surfing in the world," and he too told.

The day came. Before the sun had risen father, mother, and children had reached the beach. But they were not alone! The news had spread. Quietly the neighbors gathered. All the village had come to see them off.

There was the log rolling up the beach and down, washed by the waves, but the daughter of Kāne did not come. The log did not change to a canoe. Poko looked longingly over the ocean. "I did not keep the secret," he said sadly.

His wife picked up her baby and looked about happily at her friends. "I think we should have been very lonely in that hidden land," she whispered.

*"The Shark Guardian," "The Punahou Spring," and "Can You Keep a Secret?" were co-authored with Caroline Curtis.

Alfons Korn

Marjorie Sinclair has described Alfons Korn as one of the "most quietly distinguished members of Hawai'i's literary scene." He was a writer and teacher "concerned deeply with literature, sensitive to a resonant use of the English language and involved in the history and life of Hawai'i."

Born in Iowa, he came to Hawai'i just after World War II to teach in the University of Hawai'i's English Department. One of his best known books, *The Victorian Visitors*, presents documents relating to the visit to Hawai'i by two English women as well as to the return visit Hawai'i's Queen Emma paid to these women in England. This complex of materials captures the nature and details of a kind of transoceanic encounter that has often been oversimplified and misunderstood. In *News from Moloka'i*, Korn edits and comments on the correspondance between the leper Peter Kaeo and his cousin Queen Emma.

Toward the end of his life Korn translated several manuscripts from the French that provide surprising and vivid accounts of Hawai'i and add significantly to our understanding of cultural matters not previously apparent in English language sources.

Korn worked for many years with Mary Kawena Pukui on the translations of Hawaiian chants and poems with scholarly notes that were published in the book *The Echo of Our Song*. Korn's contributions to this volume combine his deeply felt respect for Hawaiian culture and his delight in the potentialities of poetic language.

Fire Chant for King Ka-lā-kaua

(A Translation with Notes)

Oʻahu, 1874

In pre-Christian Hawaiʻi the burning of torches by day was kapu, a sanction, possessed only by certain royal chiefs. According to tradition, the fireburning kapu originated with a high chief of the island of Hawaiʻi during the sixteenth century. This semilegendary ruler, Iwi-kau-i-ka-ua, was a great-great-grandson of the famous King ʻUmi. Later rulers of the Ka-mehameha and Ka-lā-kaua families regarded Iwi-kau-i-ka-ua as the ancestor through whom they inherited the right to burn torches by day. Iwi-kau-i-ka-ua's wife, a woman of the highest rank, detested equally her husband's mother and his daughter born to him by a union with his sister. When Iwi-kau-i-ka-ua learned that his wife had brought about the murder of his mother and daughter, he deserted her and set out with his retinue on a tour of Hawaiʻi, keeping his funeral torches alight both night and day. As a result of his grief-stricken journey of revenge—"burning, burning, by day and by night," the right to burn torches by day became a sacred kapu of his descendants.

During the opening decades of the nineteenth century, the fire-burning kapu was one of the rights handed down from ruler to ruler among the Hawaiian kings descended from Ka-mehameha I and his ancestors. Later, when David Ka-lā-kaua was elected king of Hawaiʻi in 1874, he wanted especially to strengthen the belief that his claim to the throne rested on more than man-made agencies and mere constitutional procedures. To burn torches by day became under Ka-lā-kaua again a highly significant symbolic act expressive of the king's sacred power, his *mana*.

This was not the only royal kapu belonging to Ka-lā-kaua's line. He could also claim the hereditary power to compel subjects, including lesser chiefs, "to bow down full on the ground," in other words, to prostrate themselves at his feet. By 1874, however, the feasibility of glorifying a Hawaiian monarch by invoking the humiliating prostration kapu was definitely out of the question. This was not so with the fire-burning kapu, a spectacular custom that easily lent itself to the pageantry and excitement of political demonstrations even under a constitutional monarchy. There is no doubt that the organized burning of torches in Hawai'i under Ka-lā-kaua was in part a revivification of ancient Hawaiian practice; but it was also in imitation of the prevailing Western taste for staging sensational torchlight processions to arouse political enthusiasm, as in American presidential campaigns.

The *Fire Chant for King Ka-lā-kaua* was one of the first chants composed expressly in honor of David Ka-lā-kaua about the time of his succession to the throne in 1874. Though he had been elected to serve as king by a sizable majority of the Hawaiian Legislature, his political position at the outset of his reign was far from secure. On the very day of his triumph, several hundred supporters of the rival candidate, the Dowager Queen Emma, rioted at the scene of the election, both inside and outside the courthouse. Because of this disturbance, Ka-lā-kaua and his friends hastily decided to forestall further risks of civil disorder. Indeed, there would be no showy celebration of his accession to the throne until well after the new king had been sworn into office in some quietly safe and unobtrusive way.

After conferring with his leading advisors (several of them now members of his first cabinet), Ka-lā-kaua came to the conclusion that a royal progress through the kingdom would be the best device for allowing the dust to settle in the capital while consolidating grassroots support for his new dynasty. Ka-lā-kaua's first royal tour through his kingdom began in the second half of March, with a visit to Kaua'i as stately prelude, and continued through a good part of April, culminating in ever more and more popular visits to rural O'ahu. He was loyally welcomed on all three main outlying islands with the customary speech making in Hawaiian and English, hymn singing, traditional chanting, presenting of leis and other offerings, interspersed with frequent feasts and bouts of liquid refreshment. (The visit to the leper settlement at Ka-lau-papa on Moloka'i had important political overtones, but it was not made a festal occasion.) A marked feature of several of the public demonstrations, especially on Maui, was an elaborate fireworks display, not only in the familiar form of rockets and Roman candles, but enhanced by grand bonfires blazing simultaneously from beach and headland and by torches burning both night and day.

The *Pacific Commercial Advertiser,* on April 4, pronounced that the water-and-fire pageantry at La-haina, Maui, had been stupendous.

> A little before three o'clock in the morning, as soon as the Kilauea became visible, a large number of bonfires were lighted along the shore, from Shaw's Point in Kaanapali, to Ukumehame beach, while high up the mountain, overlooking the landscape, was the largest bonfire of all,

which shone like a perfect gem set in the mountainside, say 3,000 feet above the sea. . . . Meanwhile, the Court House was illuminated and a line of burning torches, held by willing and eager hands, arranged in close order along the beach from the near residence of His Excellency P[aul] Nahaolelua to the point beyond the lighthouse. Next came a procession of boats, nearly thirty in number, each illuminated by from four to ten torches, moving in single file out of the harbor to meet the steamer. As soon as the latter had anchored, the boats formed a circle around the ship and, after a couple of Hawaiian airs had been sung by chosen singers, three cheers were given for the King.

The *Fire Chant for King Ka-lā-kaua* commemorates the civic welcome given Ka-lā-kaua by his people on Oʻahu upon the *Kīlauea's* return to Honolulu on April 14. The chant was doubtless performed on later occasions during his torch-lit reign. The original text of the chant, published in Honolulu on April 21, was composed by a young supporter of Ka-lā-kaua, who was employed as assistant editor of *Nuhou (The News)*, a bilingual newspaper edited and owned by Walter Murray Gibson. With Ka-lā-kaua safely elected, Gibson almost immediately abandoned publication of his newspaper, which had successfully achieved one of its main purposes. Gibson eventually became King Ka-lā-kaua's premier and cabinet factotum in his government.

Gibson's editorial assistant, one of whose last journalistic productions for *Nuhou* was the *Fire Chant*, also began to play a more overt and active role in the party politics of the new dynasty. His name was David Malo and he was a relative (very probably a nephew) of *the* David Malo, the erudite Christianized native who under missionary sponsorship compiled *Hawaiian Antiquities (Moolelo Hawaii)*, a valuable source book on pre-Christian Hawaiian beliefs and customs. David Malo II accompanied Ka-lā-kaua on the royal tour round the islands. His chant appears to have been composed and sent to the press within a period of hours after the king landed at Honolulu.

While Ka-lā-kaua on Maui and Hawaiʻi was presenting his ideas about Hawaiʻi's future to the local population, the king's party and its well-wishers on Oʻahu meanwhile outdid themselves to assure a right royal welcome at home. According to newspaper announcements, Major William Luther Moehonua, formerly court chamberlain under the Ka-mehameha kings and a chanter and poet of note, had been in charge of organizing pyrotechnic displays (with the help of the royal militia) and encouraging interest in public manifestations of loyalty. The various bonfires and spectacular fireworks on Punchbowl hill identified in the chant are for the most part described from the point of view of an eyewitness stationed aboard the *Kīlauea* and approaching the windward coast of Oʻahu around nightfall. After landing at Honolulu harbor, the royal party and its guests proceeded by carriage or on foot from the wharf to King Street and into the palace grounds.

After Malo composed his chant for Ka-lā-kaua, it became under Hawaiian custom a personal possession of the monarch and his descendants, and its historic authorship was ignored or forgotten. That the chant exists today is not simply a consequence of its publication and survival in print. Court chanters by their performances during Ka-lā-kaua's reign kept their versions of the text alive as part of a deeply rooted oral tradition that continues to exist in Hawai'i today, though on a greatly diminished scale, almost a century after David Malo the younger wrote down his original composition as part of his "copy" for *Nuhou*. Indeed, in the early autumn of 1969, the well-known Hawaiian chanter Kaupena Wong of Honolulu recited a portion of the *Fire Chant for King Ka-lā-kaua* during a "lighting up" ceremony at 'Io-lani Palace, in joint celebration of that enduring symbol of the vanished Hawaiian Kingdom and the dedication of the handsome modern state capitol of Hawai'i Nei.

He Inoa Ahi nō Ka-lā-kaua

Lamalama i Maka-pu'u ke ahi o Hilo.
Hanohano molale ke ahi o Ka-wai-hoa.
'Oaka 'ōni'o 'ula kāo'o ke ahi i Wai-'alae.
Ho'oluehu iluna ke ahi o Lē-'ahi.
Ho'onohonoho i muliwa'a ke ahi o Ka-imu-kī.
Me he uahi koai'e la ke ahi o Wa'ahila.
Noho hiehie ke ahi i pu'u o Mānoa.
Oni e kele i luna ke ahi o 'Uala-ka'a.

A me he 'ahi la ke ahi o Kalu'-āhole.
Me he maka-ihu-wa'a la ke ahi o Helu-moa.
Me he moa-lawakea la ke ahi o Kālia.
Me he pāpahi lei la ke ahi o Ka-wai-a-Ha'o.

'O mai ke 'Li'i nona ia inoa ahi!

Kauluwela i Pū-o-waina ke ahi hō'ike inoa,
Uluwehiwehi ke ahi ho'okele Hawai'i.
Heaha la ia ka pāni'o o ke ahi? O ka Helu 'Elua.
Pū-'ulu hōku-lani ke ahi o Mālia-ka-malu.
A ma'amau pinepine ke ahi o Kawa.
'Alua 'ole ke ahi o Moana-lua.

I puʻupuʻua ke ahi ka mauʻu nēnē.
Kaʻi haʻaheo ke ahi puoko ʻula i ka moana.
ʻĀnuenue pipiʻo lua i ka lewa ke ahi o ke kaona.

ʻO mai ke ʼLiʻi nona ia inoa ahi!

Me he papa-kōnane la ke ahi o Alanui Pāpū.
Ahu kīnohinohi ke ahi i Alanui Aliʻi.
Me he pōnaha mahina la ke ahi o Hale Aliʻi.
Ku me he ʻanuʻu la ke ahi o ka pahu hae.
Wela kuʻu ʻāina i ke ahi o ʼIhi-kapu-lani.

ʻO mai ke ʼLiʻi nona ia inoa ahi!

Fire Chant for King Ka-lā-kaua

Torchlight of Hilo lighted his way to Maka-puʻu.
Now Ka-wai-hoa's royal fire burns clear in the Oʻahu night.
A throng of red flashing fires of Wai-ʻalae swirl in the air.
Lēʻahi's fire scatters to the stars.
Coals banked at sterns of canoes glow in Ka-imu-kī's dusky fires.
Smoky fire of Waʻahila rises like scent of acacia, aroma of love.
A chieftain pillar of proud fire stands on a Mānoa hillside.
Springing fire of ʻUala-kaʻa embraces the sky.
Gleam of *ʻahi*, fish of yellow flame, shines in the fire of Kaluʻ-āhole.
Fire of Helu-moa shows phosphorescent, a mirage at sea.
White cock, head of white cock lifted in darkness, is fire of Kālia.
A great Aliʻi, fire of Ka-wai-a-Haʻo, stands wreathed in purest light.

> Answer us, O Chief, whose fire chant we sing!

Intense fire spells out his name on Punchbowl Hill.
He is the Helmsman—*Ka Mōʻī*—revealed in flame and rockets' glare.
What is that portal of friendly lamplight? Fire Company Number Two.
Blessed fires of Mary of Peace shine like a congregation of stars.
Fire of constancy is the fire of Kawa, unwavering fire.
Bonfires of Moana-lua burn unmatched for wild display.
Banks of *nēnē*-grass one after another burst into blaze.
So proud warriors tread by torchlight, their marching mirrored in the sea.
That double rainbow arching the sky is the reflected fire of the town.

> Answer us, O Chief, whose fire chant we sing!

A checkered *kōnane*-board is Fort Street on fire.
Gay calico prints are the fires decorating King.
The fire at the Palace shines in a circle, a full moon.
Like a tower atop an ancient temple is the fire-ringed flagpole.
So lives my land heated everywhere by the sacred kapu-fire of
    'Ihi-kapu-lani.

    Answer us, O Chief, whose fire chant we sing!

NOTES

Maka-pu'u: Rugged point on coast of O'ahu east of Honolulu. The name (lit-
    erally, "hill beginning") also suggests "bulging eye," said to be the name
    of an image found in a cave in the cliff face. The image represented a leg-
    endary woman called Maka-pu'u who, with her sister, came in ancient
    times to O'ahu—"where we can see the cloud drifts of Kahiki."
Ka-wai-hoa: Point beyond Portlock Road east of Honolulu, literally, 'the
    companion's water'; in early times much used as a place of anchorage.
Wai-'alae: Approximately the same as the present Wai'alae-Kahala section of
    Honolulu, but originally the name of an *ahupua'a*, land division extend-
    ing from the uplands to the sea. The name (literally, "mudhen water")
    refers to a spring or springs and their streams flowing from various ele-
    vations, especially the summits of Wai-'alae-nui and Wai-'alae-iki. In
    the 1870s, despite introduced diseases and epidemics, the region was
    still well populated with Hawaiian farmers and fisherfolk, though not so
    densely as in the eighteenth century.
Lē'ahi: Variant of Lae-'ahi, old name for Diamond Head. The profile was
    compared by Hi'i-aka to the brow *(lae)* of the *'ahi*, yellowfin tuna.
Ka-imu-kī: Roughly the same as the section of Honolulu now so known,
    originally an *ahupua'a*. The name (literally, 'the ti oven') carried associ-
    ations with the Menehune, the legendary race of small people who built
    ovens by night.
Wa'ahila: Section between Mānoa and Nu'u-anu valleys; also name for a gen-
    tle wind and rain. Said to be named for a chiefess who became famous
    for her alluring dance of the same name.
Koai'e, in the Hawaiian text, is a native acacia with a particularly pleasant fra-
    grance. Allusions to *koai'e* in poetry sometimes refer to love: "a euphe-
    mism," according to N. B. Emerson, "for the delicate parts".
Mānoa hillside: In the Hawaiian text this is given as *pu'u o Mānoa*, and refers
    to the present Rocky Hill, part of ancient Mānoa-ali'i ('chief's Mānoa'),

a land division on the western side of a line running from Moloka'i Hill (Pu'u-luahine) at the end of Mānoa Valley down to Rocky Hill.

'Uala-ka'a: Early name for Round Top Hill; literally 'rolling sweet potato,' alluding to a legend in which a rat bit a sweet potato causing it to roll down the hill, where it sprouted. Ka-mehameha I owned extensive lands on the steeps where the sweet potatoes persisted in rolling away.

'ahi: In the Hawaiian the chant indulges in wordplay involving the nearly identical sounds of ahi, 'fire', and 'ahi, yellowfin tuna. The colors of fire and those of the yellowfinned silvery fish lend themselves to magical notions of the fiery spirits present in both.

Kalu'-āhole (for Kalua-āhole): A fishing spot along the shore of Diamond Head famous for its aholehole (Kuhlia sandvicensis).

Helu-moa: Old land division in Wai-kīkī in vicinity of present Royal Hawaiian Hotel; once the site of an important heiau near a favorite residence of Queen Ka-'ahumanu. The name (literally, 'chicken scratch') refers to a supernatural rooster who sometimes appeared there.

phosphorescent: From maka-iha-wa'a in the Hawaiian text. Light seen in the water at night that is produced by luminescent organisms.

head of white cock: A free translation of moa-lawakea, 'white cock,' but the emphasis on the primitive image serves to heighten the contrast in the next line with the light-garlanded (me he pāpahi lei) steeple of Ka-wai-a-Ha'o Church.

Kālia: Section of Honolulu in the vicinity of the present Ala Wai Canal and adjacent yacht harbor; in early times this was a region of fishponds, gardens, and well-beaten trails.

Ka-wai-a-Ha'o: The historic Congregational church and meetinghouse in central Honolulu at the intersection of King and Punchbowl streets, designed by Hiram Bingham, pastor, erected by royal authority, and dedicated on July 21, 1842. In early days it was often called the "Stone Church," because it was built of coral blocks from the harbor, replacing its four grass-thatched predecessors (the earliest was erected in 1822). The native name, 'the fresh water pool of Ha'o,' was derived from the church's site, adjacent to an area where in ancient times were ponds and a kapu stone. Certain highest chiefs were allowed to bathe in the upper pool or drink where water flowed over a sacred stone; commoners were permitted to drink only from below. In 1927 the kapu stone was moved from its commercial surroundings and deposited within the walls of Ka-wai-a-Ha'o Church.

Punchbowl Hill: The old name of this volcanic hill and extinct crater about five hundred feet above sea level and overlooking central Honolulu was Pū-o-waina. A cannon battery was maintained there for saluting vessels, honoring royalty on birthdays, solemnizing funerals, and so forth. The hill was long used as a post and training ground for the Hawaiian militia, both infantry and cavalry. The Hawaiian name (literally, 'hill of placing') referred to its ancient use as an amphitheater for human sacrifices, rituals in which victims were burned to death. Now it is the site of the National Memorial Cemetery of the Pacific.

Helmsman: This is given in the Hawaiian text as ho'okele, 'steersman', one who heads affairs. An observer aboard the Kīlauea representing the Pacific Commercial Advertiser, April 18, 1874, noted that "Looming high above and away at the rear, was Punchbowl, its highest peak surmounted with a blazing crown, forty feet from the ground, beneath which in letters of fire were the words Ka Mo'i ['The King']."

Fire Company Number Two: The building was the headquarters of Engine Company Number Two, one of several stations housing equipment of the Honolulu Fire Department. At the time of his election Ka-lā-kaua had been a member of Engine Company Number Four for about thirteen years.

Mary of Peace: Our Lady of Peace, the present Roman Catholic cathedral on Fort Street, a stone church erected from 1840–1843, following the arrival of a small band of Catholic missionary priests in 1840. Religious toleration had been first positively adopted as a policy of the Hawaiian Government in 1839.

Kawa: The bonfires at Kawa in the harbor area were the tribute of His Majesty's loyal prisoners at Iwilei Prison.

Moana-lua: Land division and stream west of Honolulu in vicinity of present Fort Shafter.

nēnē-grass: Piles of 'ai-a-ka-nēnē (Coprosma ernodeoides), a native, woody, trailing plant, became blazing mounds, easily replenished by the prisoners.

kōnane-board: Papa-kōnane in the Hawaiian text, a checkerboard. Kōnane was an ancient game similar to checkers, played with pebbles on a lined stone or board.

calico prints: This is given in the Hawaiian text as kinohinohi 'decorated,' 'printed, as calico'. The Hawaiian text suggests the profusion of commercial goods (ahu 'heap,' compare ho'āhu 'storehouse') characteristic of the business quarter.

the Palace: Not the present 'Io-lani Palace constructed during Ka-lā-kaua's reign (dedicated 1879) as a symbol of the majesty and elegance of his dynasty, but the "Old Palace," a modest one-story affair in bungalow style, built of coral blocks with a lookout on top. Governor Ke-kūana-ō'a built the house for his daughter, Victoria Ka-māmalu, in the 1840s. After 1843, when Ka-mehameha III moved the seat of government from

La-haina, Maui, to Honolulu, the house became the official royal residence (Hale Aliʻi) of the Ka-mehameha kings, used especially for diplomatic audiences, state receptions, and formal dinners.

circle, a full moon: A spacious circular drive faced the "Old Palace" on its King Street side. The comparison of the fires with the full moon (*ponaha mahina*, 'round moon') probably refers to an arrangement of kukui torches bordering the drive.

ʻIhi-kapu-lani: Name of a former house on the palace grounds, near the old banyan tree and present Archives of Hawaiʻi. King Ka-lā-kaua and Queen Ka-piʻo-lani took up residence, somewhat ostentatiously in the eyes of their critics, in the house shortly after their election. The name of the house, 'hallowed royal kapu,' associates the house with the fire-burning kapu, as does the mention in *Kuokoa*, April 18, of its appearance on the night of the royal party's arrival by carriage after landing from the tour: "Before the door of ʻIhi-kapu-lani house were lights in the form of a crown and above that were decorations used in ancient times. Upon a roof was a fire container kept burning by a handsome youth."

W. S. Merwin

W. S. Merwin was born in New York City and grew up in New Jersey and Pennsylvania. In the early years of his career he lived in France, Portugal, and Majorca. For a time, he earned most of his income from his translations from French, Spanish, Latin, and Portuguese. His many books of poems, stories, and essays have earned him numerous awards, including the Pulitzer Prize for *The Carrier of Ladders*. His other books of poems include *The Drunk in the Furnace, The Moving Target, The Lice, Writings to an Unfinished Accompaniment, The Compass Flower, Opening the Hand*, and *The Rain in the Trees*. Since the late 1970s, he has spent much of his time at his home on the island of Maui.

Several of the Hawai'i-based Merwin poems included in this collection are mythlike works that make powerful statements concerning the endangerment of cultural and natural worlds. Merwin worries about both the loss of physical habitats and the loss of the original, and thus primary, names of those habitats. "The Last One" has a generalized setting that exists in the everywhere or anywhere of mythic incantation. This powerful chantlike "re-creation" tale is one of Merwin's most famous poems, and its harrowing and darkly humorous environmental theme has particular resonance for Hawai'i where so many plants and animals are endangered "last ones."

Two of the Merwin poems in this anthology are historical pieces set in Hawai'i. "After Douglas" and "Manini" both appeared in Merwin's 1993 collection *Travels*. In "Writing Lives," a poem in that volume dedicated to Leon Edel, Merwin makes a statement that could be taken as a definition of the biographical approach he uses in many of the poems he has published in the 1990s: "to us it is clear/ that if a single moment could be seen/ complete it would disclose the whole." Merwin's poems of this kind reveal key dimensions of certain historical figures by giving the reader a glimpse into a crucial fragment of the subject's consciousness. In one of his biographical poems he gives us David Douglas, for whom the Douglas fir is named, in the form of a ghostly consciousness that speaks from the heart of the moment after his tragic death—killed by a bull trapped in a pit he fell into on the slopes of Mauna Kea. In the other biographical poem included here, he lets us overhear the musings of the eccentric early European transplant to Hawai'i, Don Francisco de Paula Marin, whose thoughts give us sideways glances into a long lost Kingdom of Hawai'i.

Kanaloa

When he woke his mind was the west
and he could not remember waking

wherever he looked the sun was coming toward him
the moon was coming toward him

month after month the wind was coming toward him
behind the day the night was coming toward him

all the stars all the comets all the depth of the sea
all the darkness in the earth all the silence all the cold

all the heights were coming toward him
no one had been on the earth before him

all the stories were coming toward him
over the mountain

over the red water the black water
the moonlight

he had imagined the first mistake
all the humans are coming toward him with numbers

they are coming from the beginning to look for him
each of them finds him and he is different

they do not believe him at first
but he houses the ghosts of the trees

the ghosts of the animals
of the whales and the insects

he rises in dust he is burning he is smoke
behind him is nothing

he is the one who is already gone
he is fire flowing downward over the edge

he is the last he is the coming home
he might never have wakened

The Strangers from the Horizon

Early one year
two ships came in to the foot of the mountain
from the sea in the first light of morning

we knew they were coming
though we had never seen them
they were black and bigger than houses

with teeth along the sides
and it is true
they had many arms

and cloaks filled with wind
clouds moving past us but they were not clouds
trees stopping before us but they were not trees

without having ever seen them we knew
without having ever seen us they knew
and we knew they knew each other

in another place they came from
and they knew that we knew
that they were not gods

they had a power for death that we wanted
and we went out to them taking things of ours
that they would surely need

Chord

While Keats wrote they were cutting down the sandalwood forests
while he listened to the nightingale they heard their own axes
    echoing through the forests
while he sat in the walled garden on the hill outside the city they
    thought of their gardens dying far away on the mountain
while the sound of the words clawed at him they thought of their wives
while the tip of his pen traveled the iron they had coveted was
    hateful to them
while he thought of the Grecian woods they bled under red flowers
while he dreamed of wine the trees were falling from the trees
while he felt his heart they were hungry and their faith was sick
while the song broke over him they were in a secret place and they
    were cutting it forever
while he coughed they carried the trunks to the hole in the forest
    the size of a foreign ship
while he groaned on the voyage to Italy they fell on the trails and
    were broken
when he lay with the odes behind him the wood was sold for cannons
when he lay watching the window they came home and lay down
and an age arrived when everything was explained in another language

Hearing the Names of the Valleys

Finally the old man is telling
the forgotten names
and the names of the stones they came from
for a long time I asked him the names
and when he says them at last
I hear no meaning
and cannot remember the sounds

I have lived without knowing
the names for the water
from one rock
and the water from another
and behind the names that I do not have

the color of water flows all day and all night
the old man tells me the name for it
and as he says it I forget it

there are names for the water
between here and there
between places now gone
except in the porcelain faces
on the tombstones
and places still here

and I ask him again
the name for the color of water
wanting to be able to say it
as though I had known it all my life
without giving it a thought

Manini

I Don Francisco de Paula Marin
saved the best for the lost pages
the light in the room where I was born
the first faces and what they said to me
late in the day I look southeast to the sea
over the green smoke of the world
where I have my garden

who did I leave behind at the beginning
nobody there would know me now
I was still a boy
when I sailed all the way to the rivers of ice
and saw the flat furs carried out of the forest
already far from their bodies
at night when the last eyes had gone from the fires
I heard wet bodies walking in the air
no longer knowing what they were looking for
even of their language I remember something
by day I watched the furs going to the islands
came the day when I left with the furs for the islands
it would always be said that I had killed my man

I still carry a sword
I wear my own uniform as the chiefs do
I remember the islands in the morning
clouds with blue shadows on the mountains
from the boat coming in I watched the women
watching us from under the trees
those days I met the first of my wives
we made the first of the children
I was led into the presence of the chief
whom the Europeans already called the king

we found what each of us
needed from the other
for me protection and for him
the tongues and meanings of foreigners
a readiness which he kept testing
a way with simples and ailments
that I had come to along my way
I learned names for leaves that were new to me
and for ills that are everywhere the same

the king was the king but I was still a sailor
not done with my voyages
until I had been to both sides of the ocean
and other islands that rise from it
many as stars in the southern sky
I watched hands wherever there were hands
and eyes and mouths and I came to speak
the syllables for what they treasured
but sailed home again to my household and the king

since we have no furs here
he sent the men into the mountains
with axes for the fragrant sandalwood
it was carried out on their flayed backs
and sold for what they had never needed
all in the end for nothing and I directed it
with the wood a fragrance departed
that never came back to the mountains
all down the trails it clung to the raw backs
as the furs clung to the limbs of the fur-bearers

that fragrance had been youth itself and when it was gone
even I could not believe it had ever been ours

and when the king was dead and his gods were cast down
I saw the missionaries come
with their pewter eyes and their dank righteousness
yet I welcomed them
as my life had taught me to do
to my house under the trees by the harbor
where they stared with disgust
at the images of the faith of my childhood
at my wives at the petals our children
at the wine they were offered and the naked
grapes ripening outside in the sunlight
as we are told they once ripened in Canaan

I know these same guests will have me carried
by converts when my time comes
and will hail over me the winter of their words
it is true enough my spirit
would claim no place in their hereafter
having clung as I see now
like furs and fragrance to the long summer
that tastes of skin and running juice

I wanted the whole valley for a garden
and the fruits of all the earth growing there
I sent for olive and laurel endives and rosemary
the slopes above the stream nodded with oranges
lemons rolled among the red sugar cane
my vineyard girt about with pineapples
and bananas gave me two harvests a year
and I had herbs for healing since this is not heaven
as each day reminded me and I longed still for a place
like somewhere I thought I had come from

the wharf reaches farther and farther
into the harbor this year and the vessels
come laden from Canton and Guayaquil
I nurse the dying queens and the dropsical minister
I look with late astonishment at all my children
in the afternoon pearls from the inland sea

are brought to revolve one by one between my fingers
I hold each of them up to the day as I
have done for so long and there are the colors
once more and the veiled light I am looking for
warm in my touch again and still evading me

After Douglas

I could not have believed how my life would stop
all at once and slowly like some leaf in air
and still go on neither turning nor
        falling any more

nor changing even as it must have been
all the while it seemed to be moving
away whatever we called it chiefly
        to have something

to call it as people of the trees call
me Grass Man Grass Man Grass Man having heard that
from me and I neither turn nor am stirred
        but go on

after a sound of big stones to which I
woke as they opened under the hammer
my father and now they always lie open
        with the sound going

out from them everywhere before me like
the bell not yet heard announcing me once
for the one time but not as a name unless
        perhaps as my

name speaks of trees and trees do not know it
standing together with my brothers
and sisters my five senses in all their
        different ages

I see in the eyes of my first birds
where I am coming along this path
in the garden among glass houses
        transparent

walls and now my eyes are perfect finally
I think I must see China but
it is still the New World as I have heard
 there is the mouth

of the wide river that I know as
the Amazon there are tall bitter seas
sharp stones on the ocean the green pelt
 of the northern

continent sinuous to the shore line
and so deep that I reach out my hand to touch it
and feel that I am air moving along
 the black mosses

only now I am in haste no more
anger has vanished like a lantern in daytime
I cannot remember who was carrying it
 but each dried

form that was lost in the wide river is
growing undiscovered here in shadows
the mown rye continues to stand breathless
 in long summer light

gulls flash above sea cliffs albatross
bleats as a goat I see that the lives one by one
are the guides and know me yes and I
 recognize

each life until I come to where I forget
and there I am forgetting the shoes
that I put on and the mountain
 that I have climbed before

there I go on alone without waiting and
my name is forgotten already into
trees and there is McGurney's house that I
 have forgotten

and McGurney telling me of the dug
pits on the mountain and there unchanged
is the forgotten bull standing on whatever
 I had been

Rain at Night

This is what I have heard

at last the wind in December
lashing the old trees with rain
unseen rain racing along the tiles
under the moon
wind rising and falling
wind with many clouds
trees in the night wind

after an age of leaves and feathers
someone dead
thought of this mountain as money
and cut the trees
that were here in the wind
in the rain at night
it is hard to say it
but they cut the sacred 'ōhi'as then
the sacred koas then
the sandalwood and the halas
holding aloft their green fires
and somebody dead turned cattle loose
among the stumps until killing time

but the trees have risen one more time
and the night wind makes them sound
like the sea that is yet unknown
the black clouds race over the moon
the rain is falling on the last place

The Last One

Well they'd made up their minds to be everywhere because why not,
Everywhere was theirs because they thought so.
They with two leaves they whom the birds despise.
In the middle of stones they made up their minds.
They started to cut.

Well they cut everything because why not.
Everything was theirs because they thought so.
It fell into its shadows and they took both away.
Some to have some for burning.

Well cutting everything they came to the water.
They came to the end of the day there was one left standing.
They would cut tomorrow they went away.
The night gathered in the last branches.
The shadow of the night gathered in the shadow on the water.
The night and the shadow put on the same head.
And it said Now.

Well in the morning they cut the last one.
Like the others the last one fell into its shadow.
It fell into its shadow on the water.
They took it away its shadow stayed on the water.

Well they shrugged they started trying to get the shadow away.
They cut right to the ground the shadow stayed whole.
They laid boards on it the shadow came out on top.
They shone lights on it the shadow got blacker and clearer.
They exploded the water the shadow rocked.
They built a huge fire on the roots.
They sent up black smoke between the shadow and the sun.
The new shadow flowed without changing the old one.
They shrugged they went away to get stones.

They came back the shadow was growing.
They started setting up stones it was growing.
They looked the other way it went on growing.
They decided they would make a stone out of it.
They took stones to the water they poured them into the shadow.
They poured them in they poured them in the stones vanished.
The shadow was not filled it went on growing.
That was one day.

The next day was just the same it went on growing.
They did all the same things it was just the same.
They decided to take its water from it.
They took away water they took it away the water went down.
The shadow stayed where it was before.
It went on growing it grew onto the land.
They started to scrape the shadow with machines.
When it touched the machines it stayed on them.
They started to beat the shadow with sticks.
Where it touched the sticks it stayed on them.
They started to beat the shadow with hands.
Where it touched the hands it stayed on them.
That was another day.

Well the next day started about the same it went on growing.
They pushed lights into the shadow.
Where the shadow got onto them they went out.
They began to stomp on the edge it got their feet.
And when it got their feet they fell down.
It got into eyes the eyes went blind.
The ones that fell down it grew over and they vanished.
The ones that went blind and walked into it vanished.
The ones that could see and stood still
It swallowed their shadows.
Then it swallowed them too and they vanished.
Well the others ran.

The ones that were left went away to live if it would let them.
They went as far as they could.
The lucky ones with their shadows.

Anniversary on the Island

The long waves glide in through the afternoon
while we watch from the island
from the cool shadow under the trees where the long ridge
a fold in the skirt of the mountain
runs down to the end of the headland

day after day we wake to the island
the light rises through the drops on the leaves
and we remember like birds where we are
night after night we touch the dark island
that once we set out for
and lie still at last with the island in our arms
hearing the leaves and the breathing shore
there are no years any more
only the one mountain
and on all sides the sea that brought us

3

HISTORICAL CONSIDERATIONS

Gavan Daws

It has been said in praise of Gavan Daws' work that it has been his "remarkable achievement . . . to free Hawaiian history from the dust of history." Daws has explained that many of his insights are the result of careful attention to the voices of those who lived during the various periods of time he was investigating. "The deeper I went into the documentary sources on Honolulu, this strange town—a capital city without self-government, a Western port in a native society, geographically isolated in mid-Pacific but tied inextricably to Europe and America—the more it seemed to me that the writings of Honolulans themselves suggested the proper emphasis and tone for my work and at the same time offered me a kind of truth to which the making of comparisons and application of general theories added relatively little."

Daws, who was born in Australia, taught history for many years at the University of Hawai'i at Mānoa and at the Australian National University. In 1989 he retired from his position in Australia and moved back to Honolulu to devote himself full-time to his writing.

His books include *The Hawaiians, The Shoal of Time, Holy Man: Father Damien of Molokai, Land and Power in Hawai'i, A Dream of Islands,* and *Prisoners of the Japanese.*

Tides

By the time Kamehameha the Great died in 1819, there were not many Hawaiians alive who knew what the world had been like before Cook. Where the haole came from and what he really wanted—these things were not clear. But it was obvious that the Hawaiian gods had not much to say about the comings and goings of foreigners. The haole did not respect the kapu days of gods, the kapu grounds of chiefs. And he did not seem to suffer for it. He was rich, powerful, the possessor of magic the Hawaiian could hardly begin to comprehend: metalworking, gunpowder, circumnavigation, writing. He was no god, but he could do things that made the Hawaiian gods look small.

The idea that man can snap his fingers at the gods has a horrible fascination. The haole, just by the fact of his existence, led the Hawaiian to try it. The haole seemed a free man; the Hawaiian came to think of himself as prisoner of the kapus. The chains began to chafe.

As long as Kamehameha was alive, things changed only as he allowed them to. He commanded gods and haoles both—a great man. That he was great and that he was a man—both were important after his death. His son and heir, Liholiho, was less of a man. And Kamehameha, with a score of wives to match his powers and his passions, left some formidable widows.

For female chiefs, the kapus were especially confining. They enjoyed the privileges of their rank and paid the penalties of their sex. The loftiest, with the power of life and death over commoners, could not even eat a meal with their men. Every day, every week, every month, they were reminded that the kapus cursed them with inferiority.

It was the women who challenged the gods. Keopuolani was the mother of the new king. Ka'ahumanu was the favorite wife of the old king; full-fleshed, robust, imperious, uncontrollable, a natural force. These two were Eves of great appetite. They wanted the experience and the knowledge of godbaiting. They did not offer an apple in secret. They set a feast of foods forbidden to women, and called the king to eat with them, in public.

Liholiho could hardly tell whether this was a feast of death or a feast of life, whether the earth would open and swallow everyone, or merely shift and give the Hawaiians a new, secure place to stand. He went back and forth, back and forth, oppressed by the weight of the past, appalled at the void of the future. Then at last he ate. And killed the gods.

The temples did not heave; the graves did not open; the islands did not sink into the sea. A few traditionalists protested. They were put to flight with the guns so sensibly amassed by Kamehameha. So it was not so much after all—a meal, the rout of some malcontents. Yet the Hawaiians had done something so singular that there does not seem to be a parallel anywhere in the civilized world. They had given up their religion in favor of nothing, nothing at all. And so they went on into the nineteenth century, without divinity to sustain them, haunted at every turn by ghosts from the past and omens of alienation.

. . . .

One other creature of the spirit—the Noble Savage—ought to have fallen with the kapus and died with the gods, killed at long last by experience. Yet he refused to die. Civilized men willed him to go on living because they needed him. The latecomer searching for the Savage was really on a journey to the interior. His destination was an island of the mind, and it would be his good fortune to find a Noble Savage in himself.

But most voyages to the islands after Kamehameha's death were made by another kind of men, nineteenth-century "improvers" of one sort or another, men certain of themselves, bringing demonstration kits of a better world. The program had begun with Cook.

"Being desirous of helping these poor people," Cook left the Hawaiians goats and pigs. George Vancouver left cattle, and Kamehameha put a kapu on them so they could breed and become established. Richard Cleveland brought horses from California in 1803. The rest of the Western menagerie followed, chewing its way remorselessly from the seashore to the highlands.

Cattle got to the top of Mānoa Valley behind Honolulu and came back down again to nibble the house gardens of the town. The natives were set to work in 1831 building a six-foot fence to keep them out. The beasts blighted the uplands of East Maui. They ran wild in scores of thousands on the slopes of Mauna Kea until well into this century, and now there are square miles of useless country, where the grass is gone and the topsoil is washed away. The wild sheep stand on their hind legs and stretch their necks to get at the leaves of the māmane tree.

On the small island of Kahoʻolawe, off Maui, all the cover was long ago eaten and the soil pounded into dust by the hooves of goats. The water has dried up, no men have lived there for years, and the Navy uses the place for a bombing range. Shell-shocked goats browse neurotically in straggling dry grass. People on the beach at Mākena opposite Kahoʻolawe will every so often see a puff of red dust spring up as a beast bites into a butterfly mine and shreds himself.

Away along the chain to leeward, on uninhabited Laysan, guano diggers gutted the island. Feather hunters in a single strike early this century killed more than 200,000 birds, mostly albatrosses. Rabbits and hares, brought in by some low-level visionary who said he wanted to start a cannery, ate every blade of grass and all the small bushes and drove most of the birds out of their nesting places. The island started to blow away. Scientists there in 1923 saw the last three birds of one native species killed in a sandstorm.

When Cook came, those interesting Hawaiian honeycreepers were everywhere, from the mountain slopes down to the trees along the shore. Then in 1826 a ship in from Mexico dumped a barrel of bad water on shore at Maui. The water contained mosquitoes, and the mosquitoes carried a kind of malaria that would kill the honeycreeper. These days the mosquitoes own the air up to about 2,800 feet above sea level. The honeycreepers do not come below that line.

This has been the story all along: the advance of introduced species, the retreat of the native. The Hawaiians brought one kind of rat with them. Westerners brought other kinds, then the mongoose to keep down the rat. But the mongoose, it turns out, does not care this way or that about the rat. The two pests—one on his way home, the other on his way to work—nod politely to each other, and the mongoose goes off to eat the eggs of native birds, and in sunstruck moments gnashes at golf balls forsaken in the rough.

The mynah bird, imported a century ago to control cutworm in the cane fields, immediately sent raiding parties to the city. He has become a delinquent, sharp-eyed and impudent, quite without social conscience, congregating in thousands to waste time in the banyans at dusk, unsettling people for hundreds of yards around with his top-of-the-lungs brainless shouting.

A good many other bird cries are now not heard at all. In the Red Book of Rare and Endangered Fish and Wildlife of the United States, almost half the species listed are Hawaiian. Of all the birds in the world that have gone extinct in modern times, about 15 percent are Hawaiian. The state bird, the nēnē, the Hawaiian goose, has been brought back from the edge of extinction by the most laborious effort over the last decade or so. But every time a mangrove swamp is filled, a Hawaiian fish pond drained and dredged for a marina, a housing subdivision, a golf course—every time a military road is cut through an upland forest and half-tracks grind a habitat to pieces, it becomes just so much harder to be a Hawaiian plant or bird or animal.

. . . .

The change began when a white man found a harbor on the south coast of Oʻahu, "a small but commodious basin with regular soundings from 7 to 3 fathoms, clear and good bottom, where a few vessels may ride with the greatest safety." In a good year for the whaling fleet, more than 150 ships crowded together there, and a man could walk a mile from deck to deck and never get his feet wet. Until the age of deep-draft steamers the harbor needed no dredging. There was no other anchorage like it in the islands, nor in the Pacific for thousands of miles in any direction.

The harbor made the nondescript native village of Honolulu a capital city in just over half a century, though the first haole to take a ship inside the reef there got no thanks. William Brown was a Britisher, one of those enterprising, risk-taking merchant captains who sailed in the fur trade between the northwest coast of America and the market city of Canton. He dropped down in the winter months to refit and refresh at the islands and peddle guns to the chiefs. Brown christened his harbor Fair Haven, mixed in the native politics of Oʻahu, and died of it on New Year's Day, 1795, when his Hawaiian allies stole his ships, murdered him, and carried off his body.

Honolulu grew up a seagoing city, smelling of bilge-water, sandalwood, sperm oil, manila cordage, oakum, molasses, and spilt rum. After dark the loudest sounds were ships' bells by the score telling the watches of the night and the oaths of liberty men pitching out of taverns on their heads in Fid Street. The first seamen's chaplain of the town used to scull about the moorings in a little boat handing up temperance tracts to larboard, for the sailors to throw promptly over the side to starboard. It was the whalerman's joy to drink his earnings, put as much extra grog as he could on the credit slate, and steal away with the tide, paying his debts at the foremast, as the saying went.

Now and then, others left who should not have. Keep your eye out, said a rueful advertisement in the Honolulu *Polynesian* in 1847, for James F. Lewis of the National Hotel, American, thirty-five years old, six feet tall, stout and well-built, swarthy, with black eyes and hair and a roman nose, wearing small gold earrings, and carrying $9,000 in specie and bills of exchange belonging to his employer. Reward $500.

People kept dropping off ships and back on, into the life of the town and out again. They stayed to be cured of scurvy at the consular hospital, or to die of consumption, enriching the doctors who padded their government accounts and kept patients on the books long after the bodies were signed out for burial in the seamen's plot at Nuʻuanu. There were ladies all over town pacing widow's walks on the rooftops and hanging lanterns in the windows against a husband's return. Bully Hayes the pirate left his woman, Stormbird Emma, ashore at Honolulu and never came back. She grew old and blind as a seamstress for King Kalākaua, and fell about the streets soaked in gin and self-pity, hiccuping out her pious song, "Count Your Many Blessings."

Some could afford to, at that. Honolulu's oldest business house began with two young sailors, James Robinson and Robert Lawrence, who arrived in 1822 on a schooner pieced together from the wreckage of their ship, broken up on Pearl and Hermes Reef hundreds of miles to leeward of Hawai'i. They took four months in the lagoon there to build the schooner and another ten weeks to make O'ahu, with nothing but a battered quadrant and a pinchbeck watch to guide them and just three gallons of fresh water left when they let go anchor. They built the first wharves at Honolulu, started a shipyard at Pākākā Point, and made a fortune.

Robinson and Co. ran itself like a ship for half a century. The main office had a wooden figurehead, bells rang in the works every fifteen minutes, and just before noon all hands downed tools to splice the mainbrace. Bobby Lawrence, who left the Point infrequently, O'ahu only once, and the islands never, always kept a bit of tarred rope in his pocket. When later on one of the Robinsons went to live at Frog Lane away from the harbor, he built a house with no electricity or other modern gadgets, no nails, everything wood-joined, to look like a ship.

The harbor made the town, and the town made the islands. Hawai'i has always turned its money around at Honolulu, with sandalwood for China in the early days, whale oil and bone brought in later from the northern Pacific for transshipment to the east coast of the United States, sugar for a century after that, pineapples in quantity for the last fifty years or so, and now the newest, most lucrative harvests of all, soldiers and tourists. One way or another, it has been enough to go ahead on.

Look up Queen Street as far as the customhouse, said the newspapers in the optimistic 1850s, and the salty part of the town is like one of the great marts of the world, teeming with merchants, ship chandlers, brokers, pilots, boardinghouse keepers, porters and reporters, car men, boat boys and natives. All the business of the waterfront goes on everywhere nonstop.

The wigwag telegraph on Diamond Head signals a ship offshore. The town loafers pile onto the lookout above the post office, straining to get a glimpse of a great clipper out beyond the reef, scudding by in a cloud of canvas, all sails set for China. A sidewheel steamer comes nervously inside through the narrow channel, pushed and shoved along by the belching harbor tug (named, inevitably, *Pele*). And aground in a tavern, a brine-pickled old whalerman delivers himself of some judgments on steamer captains: a race of silk-stockinged, pomatum-anointed, white-gloved, musk-scented gentlemen, better suited to play Miss Nancy than command a ship. What do they know? Well, for one thing, says the paper, they know how to get a cargo from Honolulu to Boston or New York in a hurry.

Go into the counting houses along Merchant Street, and see what Honolulu is really up to. You will see how dirty work makes clean money, what part whale blubber, oil, bone, and ambergris play in the political economy of man and woman—"how many extremes meet in that ultimate relation which connects the ambrosial beauty of Fifth Avenue with that floating manufactory of perfumes, that singular compound of horsepieces, bilge-water and cockroaches, the whaleship."

. . . .

The real difficulty with the blubbery trade, and sandalwood before it, was that they could not be depended upon. Sandalwood fever ran high for several years until the mid-1820s. When the demand was hottest, the commoners spent more time in the mountains with axes than they did keeping up their taro patches. The chiefs made sure of that. On credit, they were buying Western fancies—pleasure schooners, billiard tables, crystalware, big houses built in Boston and knocked down for shipment round the Horn. Then, suddenly, the huge stands of trees were all cut out. The chiefs were depleted, left with debts to be paid in wood that just was not there to be harvested any more.

In the whaling business the only certainty was that one year in five was apt to be a disaster. Once, in those same optimistic 1850s, the kingdom's treasury got down to $453.24. And in the best of times, whaling was still seasonal. Commerce at Honolulu, said the papers, was a hibernating animal that had got things mixed up, gorging itself through the fall and spring whaling seasons, dozing and licking its paws in the summer. For weeks after the first ships of the northern Pacific fleet made port and offloaded their barreled oil, arrival and departure times were of the first importance. But if in July or August the big public clock on Kawaiahaʻo Church tower ran down, it did not matter much. Three merchants playing cards all the drowsy afternoon in a doorway could have the entire Chamber of Commerce for an audience. The biggest financial gamble of the summer might concern the chances of one trader being able to wheel another home half a mile in a barrow for a bet.

It took a blithe attitude toward debit and credit to get through times like that. Even substantial men might crack. One pious merchant who convinced himself that he had not done conscientiously by his shareholders spent his last years barricaded in his bathhouse, praying and endlessly scrubbing his hands. Another, after thirty years of recording in his diary the business ups and downs of the port, the $500,000 spring and fall whaling seasons along Merchant Street, and the $2.30 summer Thursday afternoons at his store, lapsed at last into the strange perceptive poetry of the insane: "These days run uphill—other days run back again. . . . We touch the verge of the lamplighter. . . . It is strong ungovernable was very ungovernable."

So it was, so it was, and never more than when the whaling industry passed away in the 1860s and 1870s, dead of the Civil War, of disasters in the Arctic ice and oil wells dug on the American mainland. But the toughminded and adaptable survived. The smart, enterprising money went into plantations. Sugar, heaps of it, hundreds and then thousands of tons, poured into the troughs and valleys of the financial year. In 1869, for the first time, Hawai'i managed a favorable balance of trade, and for the better part of a century after that, it was sugar all the way.

Hawai'i's natural market was the United States, of course, and the men in Hawai'i who did best commercially were, as often as not, Americans. All the nations of man passed through the islands and the thing was to make common coin of heterogeneity. The quickest to learn the trick, according to a somewhat disdainful Englishman, was the "rapid, intelligent, all-sided" kind of man that "the social hotbed of the United States produces so quickly and in such numbers—a man, who if his practice as a surgeon fell off, would become a merchant; if he failed at that, would become an editor; or, meeting with disappointment in the last vocation, would without hesitation climb the steps of the rostrum as a preacher; and even at a pinch would offer himself as a candidate for the presidentship."

Such men, believing they could do anything and be right whatever they did, were apt to take over the running of affairs. There was a gold corner in Honolulu the same year as one in New York. The organizers were among those who pushed to have the Hawaiian kingdom joined to the United States by a treaty of commercial reciprocity in the 1870s, for the sake of the sugar market. ("Except sugar and dollars," wrote Isabella Bird Bishop, "one rarely hears any subject spoken about with general interest.") In the 1890s, for the sake of good government and good business, the improvers were for annexation. To turn the islands into American soil was the greatest improvement, the greatest victory. It was won in 1898.

Where there are winners, there are losers. If the harbor made Honolulu, and Honolulu made the islands for the haole, the effect on the Hawaiians was something else again. Quite unaware, every ship that hove to off Honolulu and fired a cannon for a pilot was declaring biological war. The natives who went out laughing on the reef with hawsers, to warp merchant ships and whalers to safe mooring, hauled in death hand over hand.

Measles or influenza or scarlet fever would kill a Hawaiian just as readily as typhoid, cholera, smallpox, leprosy, or plague. All these came in at the ports, and so did venereal diseases. Cook's men left syphilis on Ni'ihau. Coming back to Maui and Hawai'i at the other end of the chain less than a year later, they found the sickness there ahead of them—it had traveled the islands at the rate of a mile a day.

When Captain Cook came, the Hawaiians numbered something like 300,000. A century later there were no more than 50,000.

Twice a year, the Hawaiians made a new makahiki on sailors' money. They came to the ports to greet the whaling fleet, and there was no keeping them away. There was dancing in the taverns of Fid Street, a great tousling of blankets in the brothels of Cow Bay near Iwilei on the bad side of Honolulu and along Rotten Row in Lahaina. And in the back streets one of the briskest businesses was the making of plain coffins.

. . . .

Nothing was more clear than that the city, the haoles' world, was bad for Hawaiians and was likely to kill them, no matter how much they enjoyed living there. Native land and native people wasted away together at Honolulu, as the separate rational private plans of white men compounded themselves into public irrationality. By the 1870s, the watershed of Nuʻuanu was in ecological anarchy. The hillsides were denuded, and every time it rained heavily, millions of gallons of water sluiced straight to the sea. Floods and freshets began to assault the town. Lakes formed at street corners, houses sprang leaks, adobe walls crumbled, and down Nuʻuanu Valley, borne on rushing waters, came big logs from timber yards, flimsy laundries and bathing houses from the banks of the stream, spars, abutments, even complete wooden bridges. Occasional drowned animals went by, feet up and bloated, and here and there the coffins of Hawaiians, washed loose by the storm.

The sad thing was that the country offered no certain refuge either, at least of the old kind, because the city was pulling the country out of shape as well. Young women went to town to dance and make love and a little money. They might come home; they might stay and keep house for a foreigner. Young men shipped out from Honolulu or Lahaina on whalers. They might wind up beached somewhere else in the Pacific. The big plantations getting started after mid-century were owned and run from the city, for profit. The soil disappeared and the ʻohana, the family rooted in the soil, was pulled up by the roots.

Somewhere along the line, the saddest of balances was tipped. The Hawaiians came to think of themselves as doomed. The haole could count himself lucky. The land had not been made for him, but he had succeeded in making it his. For the Hawaiian, the old song was ending. To the kings and queens who succeeded Kamehameha the Great in the nineteenth century, only the merest handful of children were born, not enough to perpetuate the dynasty. The Kalākauas who followed were barren too. More often than seemed natural, the chiefs died young. Time and again, the heavy funeral processions set out at a slow march with flaring torches and doleful chants from the churches of Honolulu to the mausoleum in Nuʻuanu. And the commoners—the commoners spent more on funerals than on weddings.

. . . .

Hawaiian society was disintegrating, and hardly anybody would have been interested to put it together again, even if they had known how. Only the Protestant missionaries had a plan: God's plan, they were certain, but very much a New England plan too. These good smalltown men and their tidy wives were more of those same rapid, intelligent, all-sided Americans—but with a conscience.

In civilized Hawaiʻi, conscience was far to seek. The merchant mariner coming into the Pacific hung his on Cape Horn, to be reclaimed on his way home. If the Hawaiian had trouble counting and measuring and figuring percentages, and would cut more sandalwood than a contract called for, well and good, even if commoners cutting for months under the lash of a greedy chief lost their health and their ordinary taro-patch livelihood. If a Hawaiian seaman would work harder than a white man for less money, well and good again. The white man was a kōlea bird. All he wanted to do was roost at the islands, fill his belly, and leave, heavy with prosperity. What did he owe the native that concerned him half so much as what he owed his creditors in the United States or Europe?

The Calvinists approached Hawaiʻi another way. They came freighted negligibly with everything except piety. Conscience was their cargo. And learning. And industry. They were God's handymen: farmers, carpenters, printers, doctors. Lacking wealth, they overflowed with plans for making something out of nothing, and not only for themselves, but for the Hawaiians—stone meeting houses and wooden sugar mills, village industries and yeoman farms, textbooks and testaments, and land reform schemes and constitutions.

They were a new sort of improver, then, improving occasions as well as freeholds finding lessons everywhere, though they were rather better at teaching than learning. There were things about the islands that they never got over. They came from hand-hewn houses on flinty New England farms, where in winter cattle trembled in the snow and potatoes were rock-hard. They had a tendency to see Hawaiʻi in black and white rather than body-brown or the primary colors of nature. One of the first missionaries prepared himself for the islands by religiously eating bananas on the ship. He never did get to like them, any more than native Christians could bring themselves to eat baked beans with good grace. Then there was the little missionary boy who at his first glimpse of the palm trees of Waikīkī burst into terrified tears. And then, of course, there was so much blithely visible flesh to be abhorred, gay flowers in the hair to be reprehended, frivolous pastimes and impractical good humor to be schooled to sobriety, so much to do to translate Hawai'i into the sound terms of New England. Civilization is inhibition.

The Protestant missionaries numbered only a dozen or so to begin with, husbands and wives, and at the height of their influence never more than a hundred, in a population of some score thousand. There was holy presumptuousness in their proposal to save Hawai'i. Still, American Puritanism has always been famous for this. Calvinism is strong medicine, and those who thrive on it are likely to go about congratulating themselves on their special personal rigor, making others uncomfortable in their antiseptic presence. Whole societies have been known to prefer the sickness to the cure. Considering the particular sweet ailment of the gentle Hawaiian nature, the Protestants had great successes.

Half their ideas did not work, half did: an excellent average in a blundering world. They were here so early, from the 1820s on, and they had so many ideas, that the genuinely civilized institutional part of Hawai'i—the part having to do with schools and churches and representative government—can be said to have been mainly their idea. All this is no mean monument.

. . . .

The Hawaiian David Malo lived in himself the history of his people, in their contact with the merchant and the missionary. Dead a hundred years and more now, Malo was a remarkable man, far and away the most piercing intelligence among the natives of his day. He was more acute, for that matter, than all but a very few haoles, and those few only because they had learned the ways of the large world earlier than he. No one ever worked harder to come to terms with what was happening between brown men and white men.

He was a favorite of the chiefs. He knew their songs, dances, and amusements, and he learned their genealogies, their traditions, and the intricate workings of the kapu system. For years he had the reputation of knowing more than anyone else about what Hawai'i was like before Christianity.

This walking wellspring of pagan authority was converted in 1828. No mission ever made a more perfect Calvinist: severe of temper, harsh of judgement, strong of passion and prejudice (so ran his obituary, written by a missionary), yet, "allowing for all imperfections . . . an extraordinary example, of the wonder-working power of the Gospel, together with the accompanying appliances of education, upon natives of these Islands." Consumed by a pious lust for useful knowledge, Malo enrolled in his thirties at Lahainaluna School. He helped form the kingdom's first constitution, sat in the first national legislature, and was the first superintendent of schools. He composed dirges for dead chiefs and wrote the classic description of Hawaiian antiquities.

He grew his own cotton, spun it into thread and wove the thread into cloth, cut his own suits, and wore them with "conscious satisfaction." He made good molasses and bad marriages. He was married three times and widowed twice. His third wife was much younger than he, and did not take life seriously. Malo prayed, and she went to the bad with sailors at Lahaina. He beat her with a "small stick" and held onto the haole faith. He helped translate the Bible into Hawaiian, reproved native backslides, was licensed to preach the Gospel, and ended his days an ordained minister of God.

Malo was a man of great accomplishment and greater promise. Inside the resourceful young Hawaiian, it would seem, was one of those rapid, intelligent, all-sided Americans just waiting for the nineteenth century to let him loose.

And yet it is not as simple as that: Hawai'i is never simple. Malo might lament that when the commoner was released from servitude to the chiefs, he turned into an indolent layabout. But at the same time he hated the thought that haole industriousness would eventually make the islands haole altogether. The older he grew the more he found himself in his heart of hearts to be Hawaiian.

He never did bring himself to speak English, and that alone says a lot about him. He started too old, said the obituary: "His vocal chords were too stiff and unmanageable to allow him to utter English sounds." But that was not it, really. Whatever others may have thought was the reason, he did not want to foul the pure native sources of his expressive identity. When it came to the point, he choked on the noises haoles made.

One of Malo's missionary friends used to say of him that he was "fifty years before every one in the islands." This meant that Malo could not help but be an unhappy man. He could see what was coming for his people. Dying in 1853, he asked to be buried above the tide of civilization. His grave is high on the slopes of Mount Ball beyond Lahaina. It can be reached, but you must go on foot. There is no road. . . .

O. A. Bushnell

O. A. Bushnell has said that the tools of a historical novelist's trade include "imagination, understanding of peoples and cultures, research, and respect for versimilitude." The seamless interweaving of the historical and the imagined has been Bushnell's ongoing mission as a novelist. He feels strongly that, because the present is the product of the past, there is a special value to finding the living heart of historical subjects. He advocates getting the words right as a means to finding the truth and to achieving novels readers will want to read.

Bushnell is Hawai'i born and raised. He is a third-generation descendant of Portuguese and other European immigrants. As a boy, he often went with his father to meetings of the Camoëns Society, which is named after the six-teenth-century Portuguese poet whose epic *The Lusiads* is a classic instance of the mixing of history and fiction. Like Camoëns, Bushnell has endeavored to tell the monumental stories of his society's past.

Bushnell's novels include *The Return of Lono, Molokai, Ka'a'awa,* and *Stone of Kannon.* Each of his novels is an attempt to do justice to a complex and prob-lematic historical situation and, at the same time, to tell a good story.

An interest in getting the past right is inherent in Bushnell's other profes-sion. As a long-time professor of microbiology and medical history at the University of Hawai'i at Mānoa, he has endeavored to understand and recount the history of infectious diseases and their impacts on the peoples of Hawai'i. His ironically named 1993 nonfiction work *The Gifts of Civilization: Germs and Genocide in Hawai'i* provides the fullest exposition of Bushnell's views on the terrible consequences of imported diseases.

from *Ka'a'awa: A Novel about Hawaii in the 1850s*

Chapter 1. In Which a Man Rather Too Curious Is Called to Serve His King

The messenger came in secret, in the shadows of the evening, without runners to cry the way or guards to show who sent him. Quietly, as a friend or neighbor might, he rode into the yard of my country house at Makiki, in the hills above Honolulu, where we had fled from the sickness which was afflicting the people in the town.

We were sitting on the front verandah, my wife and I, with our daughters and sons. The cooking-fires had been put out, the lamps were not yet lighted, and we were talking of little things while we watched the colors changing in the sky above, upon the earth, and the sea below. Red the sky had been, from its eastern arch beyond Diamond Head to its western arch beyond the mountains of Wai'anae, red the color of blood, the color sacred to the great gods of old. Yet even as we exclaimed over the beauty of the heavens we gave no thought to the ancient gods or to the Jehovah who has taken their place. In our Christian household, we did not abide in fear either of the gods of our ancestors or of Him whose power is proclaimed in the glory of the firmament.

No. We were happy then, laughing at the game Daniel, our youngest son, was playing for our pleasure. Like a ship's captain he stood at the porch railing, holding a long curved piece of sugarcane to his eye as a mariner holds a telescope. "Red at night, sailor's delight," he was telling us with a big voice, in words learned from his father, "red in the morning, sailors take warning." And we were laughing because the little fellow was so comical, with his telescope pointing to the ground rather than to the horizon, and because of our contentment each with the other, when Palikū came into the yard.

I did not know it was he, for my eyes are somewhat weak with aging, and the sky's brightness did not help them to see clearly. But, as is proper with a hospitable man, I went at once to greet him.

"Good evening," I called in English, thinking he was a foreigner coming up from town to see me on business. The error was a natural one. He was dressed in a black suit, he had a tall hat upon his head and black boots upon his feet. Furthermore, evening is the time when foreigners make their visits, whereas Hawaiians come early in the day, the earlier the better, so they can partake of at least two meals as guests before they must go home again—if they go home. This is but one of the many differences between natives and foreigners. Some say that it is the difference between an open hand and a closed purse, but I do not think this is the reason, for I have found most foreigners to be generous enough in other ways.

"Good evening," he answered in our native speech as he dismounted. "Palikū is here, Palikū of 'Ewa."

While my mind wondered what this stranger could want with me, my tongue did its duty, my arm invited him to the house. "Welcome, Palikū of 'Ewa. Come in, come in. You have traveled far to find me."

"No," he said firmly, "we will talk here. This place is safer." Coming close, he showed me the back of his left hand. Written in black ink upon the brown skin were three words: Kauikeaouli, Ka Mōʻī: Kauikeaouli, the King.

"You understand?" asked Palikū.

Not for two years had I seen His Majesty, not for five years had he spoken a word to me. For five years I had thought I was out of grace with him, no longer of use to him. And now, suddenly, as fast as a shark appears beside a wounded swimmer, did he rise up out of the past to worry me. A man has the right to tremble when he sees the gape of a shark.

"He wishes to talk with you. Tonight. He is at 'Āinahau in Waikīkī. I will take you to him." Even as he spoke the King's messenger was removing the sacred writing from his skin, with spit and sweat and the rubbing of fingers. In the days of the great Kamehameha, father to Kauikeaouli, I was thinking, this herald would have been killed for such an act. So upset had he made me, so stupid for the moment, that I did not remember how, in those days before the missionaries came from America, neither Kamehameha nor any man of our race could put his name down in writing.

I am not a warrior, alas, not a man of bravery. I do not think I am entirely a coward, but no matter. I am indeed a man of great imagination: at that moment I could almost feel this shark's teeth scraping against my rib cage, where the heart is, and the liver. "Now?" I asked, trying to make my voice sound like a grown man's. "Alas, alas! And what have I done, that he calls me to meet him in the dark of night?" Like a sailor in a foreign port when constables approach, I strove to remember what crime I might have committed, what offense against the King or his laws. No crimes could I recall, and only the paltriest of sins. And these were committed so seldom, with Maria in our house in Pālama! Surely he wasn't calling me to account for her?

The summoners of kings must learn very early how they deliver fright along with their messages. Palikū of ʻEwa, a just man at heart if not an affable one, quieted me. "Would he tell me this?—But do not fear. Your friend is with him: the Prince Liholiho."

"Alex is there?—Ahh, then I have no fear." Palikū knew what everyone in Hawaiʻi Nei must know: that Alex is like a firstborn son to me, who attended him during the years of his childhood. And like a foster-father does he regard me. How, then, could I remain afraid? I ceased to tremble, my voice box was no longer tight around the sounds it made. "Come in, and rest a while. My wife will fix you a cup of tea, while I change my clothes." And now, entering into my mind, pushing fear aside, came curiosity. What does the King want with me?

"No," said Palikū, this man of stubbornness. "I shall wait here. Tell no one where you go. And do not put on the clothes you would wear to the Palace."

I heard him in amazement. "You talk like a man who has no wife! How can I just go away from here—like a wisp of black smoke drifting in a dark night?"

He waved my problem away impatiently. "Tell your wife what all husbands tell their wives when they must go from home in the night. Tell her that you are called away on business. Tell her that you are needed at a meeting. Tell her that you are called to the bedside of a friend who is sick."

"Chah!" I grumbled as I hurried back to the house. It is easy for him to talk so smoothly. But no other man can have a wife like mine. A mountain of suspicion is she, this green-eyed woman to whom I am wed. How can I tell her such a story, even if it is the truth? The last time I was late for supper she tracked me to the house in Kewalo where I thought I was dallying safely with Abigail Moepono. Such a screaming of women, such a rending of clothing and shattering of furniture I never want to hear again. And my crooked arm: in cold weather it still pains me where the bones were not set aright. "Next time I will break your head," she said grimly, as she took me in her carriage to Dr. Newcomb, for him to fix my arm. But he, poor man, to fortify himself against his awe of her, drank so much of the whiskey which was meant to sustain me, that neither of us noticed how ill-set the bones were.

There they waited, all of them, sitting, standing, reclining, hanging from the porch rail, expecting me to explain this mysterious visitor: four daughters, five sons, and one wife, the bosom of my family. Ten pairs of eyes turned upon me, questioning as judges in a courthouse. Ten pairs of big ears, pricked up like the ears of jackasses. I loved my family, as a good father should, but they were too much with me, up there in the hills of Makiki. Once again I wished I were still a carefree sailor, drunk in a faraway port, not yet a bounden husband, not yet the parent of so many inquisitive children. *Niele, niele* they were, every one of them, I fretted, not willing to admit that they came by this talent naturally.

. . . .

Chapter 2. In Which a Loyal Servant Is Severely Tried and Sorely Tested

Soft and gray was the light of evening when Palikū and I left my family, calling their goodbyes to me. At the gate, after I put up the wooden poles which shut out roaming cows and horses from our yard, he turned to the east, toward Punahou, not to the south, toward Kakaʻako. At Kakaʻako the long causeway begins that leads across the swamps between Honolulu and Waikīkī.

"Ho, Palikū," I called, checking my mount. "Here is the way to Kakaʻako." I had in mind not only the best road to Waikīkī but also the pretense of going to Noah Mahoe's house, which is not reached by riding toward Punahou.

"And do I not know this?" he said. "Tonight we take a shorter way."

"Through the swamps?" I cried, not wanting to believe him.

"Be quiet!" he barked. "And hurry!"

Never, since I have become a grown man, has anyone spoken to me so rudely. When I drew up beside him he growled, "Would you tell the whole city where we are going?"

Inasmuch as my house sits half a furlong inside its yard, and my nearest neighbors are half a mile away, I thought Palikū was being more officious than reasonable. Nonetheless, I kept my peace, not being a man who holds grievances. Who am I to know where big ears may be listening and big eyes may be watching? And besides, I remembered the lesson every Hawaiian learns when he is very young: "Kick down, not up," our elders teach us, which is to say, do not question a chief or the servant of a chief who has a higher rank than your own. My excitable father, alas, did not heed these wise words. Because he questioned in anger the right of Kahanaumaikaʻi, tax collector of the great Kamehameha, to take away our biggest sow, he died a young man, before I could know him—offered up in sacrifice he was, along with the sow, that time Kamehameha with his mighty army and vast fleet of canoes was gathering for the second time on Oʻahu to invade Kauaʻi. I, who have ever been soft with my answers, I hope to die a very old man, in my very own bed.

With Palikū, also, meekness softened wrath. "Do you not worry," he said after a few minutes. "I know the way, even in the dark of night." These were the last words he spoke during that terrible ride. No doubt he was a troubled man, as servants of kings often are.

Out of regard for my brittle bones, he set our mounts an easy pace. For a while I tried to enjoy the last traces of the evening's loveliness, the excitement of my adventure, putting off in these my worries about Mō'ili'ili's swamps and the King's intentions. To our left the valley of wide Mānoa opened up, the high tops of its mountains hung with clouds. "As springs in the sky are the clouds of Mānoa," says an old chant, and I believe it. Almost never does sunlight touch the uplands in that place of rains and waterfalls. People cannot live there, because of the lung fever such wetness causes; and wild cattle, the learned say, have grown webbed feet, like ducks, to keep them from sinking in the mud.

At the mouth of the valley, still distant from us across the plain, like stars lying upon the ground, twinkled the lights of the American missionaries' children's school at Punahou. Only there, with water flowing forth from the precious spring, or along the banks of streams issuing from the valleys, or in Mō'ili'ili's swamps, can people live, can they make Honolulu's earth yield them food for their bellies. Everywhere else upon this long plain of Kona, from Punchbowl to Koko Head, is only dust or sparse grass, cropped by horses and cattle which find no other forage. If trees grew here once upon a time, they were cut down for firewood long ago, by adzes of stone or by axes of steel.

And then the darkness was complete. But Palikū knew the way. After we had cantered for about half an hour, he slowed to a walk. We came to clumps of bushes, small shrubs, more like shadows standing up than things of stems and leaves. This sharp-eyed Palikū: his spirit-guardian must be 'Iole the rat. In a place I could not have found at midday he turned to the right, toward the distant seashore. My obedient horse followed, deaf to my moans. Trusting to him, I let the reins fall loose, thanking first Jehovah, then Kāne, Kū, Lono, and Kanaloa, the four great gods, and the forty lesser gods, and the four hundred, the four thousand, the forty thousand, the four hundred thousand little gods, that my Spanish saddle had a pommel I could clutch in my tight hands. From either side came the sounds of water, of flowing, gurgling, sighing water, yearning to embrace me when, with a single misstep, my horse and I would be thrown into the swamp, to sink in its mud and drown. Frogs croaked, night birds screeched, my stomach burned, my teeth chattered, and on we plodded in the dark. Miserable, dizzy, I clung to my pommel like a shipwrecked sailor to a spar, calling on all the spirit-guardians in my family's line to help me in this journeying through the ink sack of a squid.

How could they not hear the clamor I raised? In their mercy they sent Mahina to comfort me. Out from behind the wall of Mānoa's clouds she came forth for a long moment. Not yet in her full glory, she was like a pale cowry shell, or a China bowl, tipped in the heavens, to pour the rains of Ka'ele upon Mānoa below. But the moment was enough.

Just before the clouds covered her kind face again, she revealed to me a gift from the greatest gods: there, growing out of the earth beside the path, was a whole clump of *kī* plants. Swiftly I reached out and pulled from their stalk a handful of the long cool leaves. According to custom I should have tucked one of these leaves into my trousers, to protect the sacred organs of generation wherein lies my *mana* and that of my line. But I did not have time to follow the ancient law, and I hoped that Kāne would not mind if I thrust the leaf under the bosom of my shirt. From other leaves I fashioned wreaths to place around my wrists, forehead, and shoulders. The last two leaves I tied together, to make a *lei* for the horse. With such protection, the evil spirits, the demons in mud and water, those malicious beings from the other world who bring accident and sickness and sudden death, could not touch me or cause me harm. Nor could the great gods punish me for being a proudful traveler when I bore the amulets which asked their favor. Ahh, it is a good thing for a man to have about him the things of old, to give him comfort in times of jeopardy.

As I became more confident in the care of the gods, the ordinary things of earth, with which the gods do not bother themselves, began to afflict me. I itched, where the underdrawers we must wear these days were all bunched up, where the horse's flanks rubbed against the woolen trousers covering my legs. And the mosquitoes! A new kind of demon are they, another present from our generous foreigners. In my youth we did not have mosquitoes in Hawai'i Nei, nor scorpions, centipedes, cockroaches, or frogs. But now they are everywhere, like foreigners, poking their long noses or their sharp tails into every place, making their loud noises, beyond chasing out because they are so many. Sour as David Malo used to be, when he protested against foreigners at the Council of the Chiefs, I rode along, wishing I struck at foreigners as I slapped at mosquitoes.

And another thing!—Oh, how the anger in me swelled.—Why am I riding like this, through the swamps of Mō'ili'ili, in the dark of night? In peril to my health, if not to my very life? Were I at home now, comfortable in my parlor, I would be reading a good book, or dozing in a soft chair, thinking of a softer bed. In the dining room, seated around the big table beneath the bright whale-oil lamps, my children would be studying their schoolbooks, my wife would be sewing while she kept them at their lessons. As I thought of them, my four pretty daughters, my five handsome sons, my good and devoted wife—ahh, I longed to be with them again, I vowed I would be a better father and husband when I returned.

If I returned.—Ah, ah, I sighed again. What does the King want of me? This was the greatest worry. I skirted about it, running around it as a hunting dog runs around on a mountainside, sniffing for the scent of boar.—And why is His Majesty staying out there in Waikīkī, when he has a fine palace in Honolulu to do business in? Why doesn't he—

"No, no, I take that back," I mumbled, touching my *kī* leaves as a Papist would finger his beads. *Kick down, not up.*—Needing a safer target, I found it in something utterly useless: "What is this Waikīkī?" I addressed the air, full of swamp stinks and harmful vapors. "A sandspit bestuck with coconut palms and bedaubed with bird dung. A shoal of coral, caught between the vomit of the sea and the muck of Mōʻiliʻili."

Really, the gods are very patient, long-suffering indeed. There I was, tongue clacking inside my head, hands waving in the dark, thinking mean thoughts about everything and everyone, yet expecting only the kindest of treatment from both gods and men. A little breeze, perchance the very least of the littlest gods, was sent to warn me: lifting a bit of the frayed *lei* upon my shoulders, it tickled my ear. All right, I yielded. I understand, I shall be careful.

No doubt at one time, when Honolulu did not exist, before these foreigners came in their sailing ships and found the harbor of Kou for an anchorage, perhaps then this Waikīkī was an important place, the home of Oʻahu's kings. But now, with half of Oʻahu's people dead in their graves, with almost all the surviving half clustered around the wharves and warehouses, the grogshops and whorehouses of Honolulu, Waikīkī too is dead. It will never amount to anything. A breeding place for mosquitoes and frogs and rats it may be, but of no use to people. They do not come here anymore, to swim or to ride their long boards in the waters of the sea, as we did when I was a youth. Forbidden by the missionaries are these disportings in the sea because they are heathen pastimes, and, because the nakedness of swimmers is an invitation to sins of the flesh, is an anathema. Alas, alas! Such narrow minds, such dirty thoughts, those Christians have. I cannot remember being more lustful when I swam naked than I have been since I was girded about with clothing and armored with commandments. And what is sin, anyway?—

Cha! As peevish as a man trapped in an outhouse without leaf, shirttail, or piece of paper, I endured, swatting at mosquitoes, snapping at stinging thoughts. What a marvel is a man, that he should survive despite the gods' annoyance! Perhaps he lives because the gods hope that, with time, he will learn to be forbearing. Just as, in their patience, they have tried to teach me to be forbearing. Not wisdom do they ask, certainly not silence.—I should choke to death if they did.—Only kindness, from a man to other men, from a man to his gods: this is all they wish.

As we moved farther from the mountains the clouds were left behind, and Mahina lighted up the rest of our way. To the left, a dark battlement, rose Diamond Head. The narrow path underfoot widened to become a muddy road. The wild bulrushes, the swamp weeds, fell behind and watery plantations of taro took their place. On little islands raised above the level of the mud, clusters of thatched huts, domes of trees, barking dogs, gave proof that we were coming again into the world of people. Straight ahead the glow of fires showed, a beacon in the desert of night. Soon I could see the flickering torches, the plumed crowns of palms in the coconut grove where kings reside when they wish to be undisturbed. Mingling with the sweet scent of burning candlenuts came the stronger smells of seaweed, of the salty ocean.

With a suddenness that surprised not only me, we reached the end of our journey. A startled guard, naked as a farmer in his taro patch, ran toward us, shouting "Stand!—Who comes here?" From behind the stakes topped with globes of white *kapa* which mark the boundaries of a royal *kapu*, other guards appeared. Some were naked, some wore the loincloth, none was clad in the uniform all are forced to wear in town. In the shadows under the trees, upon outspread mats, women sat up to see who interrupted their pleasures of love.—O you of the worrying mind, I smiled to myself. It has not changed, this Waikīkī . . .

Palikū stopped his horse, lifted a hand to halt mine. "Be easy, he called to the sentry, "Palikū of ʻEwa is here. Returning as I departed, by the quiet path of Mōʻiliʻili."

"Ah, it is you," said the guard, beckoning him in. "Then welcome back from your little ride. You were not gone for long." As we moved forward into the light he burst out laughing. A most unsoldierly man is he, I was thinking, and is this the proper manner for a guard to the King? "Wait a moment," he bawled. "And who is this kahuna coming here with you? Have you plucked him from out of the swamp, perhaps?" Then I knew why he laughed. The loud-mouthed gossipmonger! May his stones shrivel in their bag, may moths be his seed! Many of the soldiers, who only a moment before were returning to their mats, gathered around, teeth and eyes flashing, fingers pointing at me, at the leafy *lei* I had forgotten to remove. "*Ē!* He is a jungle on horseback," said one. "Nah, nah, a parrot is he," said another, "a bird of many colors." "A *kahuna ʻanāʻanā*, beyond doubt," jeered still another. "Old man, what sorcery do you make tonight?" "*Ē*, womanless one," shouted a fourth at a companion, thereby changing his laughter to frowns, "ask him to make a love potion for to end your lonely days and nights."

A *kahuna*, indeed! They knew as well as I did, how the law of this Christian land forbids the practice of the evil arts of sorcery and even the kinder rites of magic for the sake of love. Feeling like a fool, I could do nothing but scowl at them, miserable as only an older man can be when he is taunted by the young. Something is wrong with the young men and women of today. When I was a youth, we had more respect for our elders. Never would we have mocked an old man or an old woman, never would we have dared to laugh at a *kahuna* 'ana'ana. But the young folk of today: alas for them. No wonder the nation is wasting away, no wonder we are beset with troubles from far and near.

Keeping my peace, I strove to keep my dignity. I intended nothing else, but I could mark the instant when dread entered among my tormenters. "*Auwē!*" wailed one, as he backed away, no longer laughing. "Forgive," murmured others, "forgive us." In the flick of a fly whisk they were gone, slinking away to the darkness under the trees. All of them went save one, the womanless youth who was in need of a love-potion. "Great is your *mana*," he proclaimed loudly, taking the bridle reins from my hand. Somewhat pleased with this effect—I think it must be the first reward for silence I have ever won—I looked toward Palikū, to share a little smile with him. But he did not see it, he was hurrying forward to help me from my horse.

"Now will we go to the house of the King," he said, when I stood upon the ground. While we walked along the path I removed the *kī* leaves. Not daring to throw them into the bushes, I tucked them into my shirt, where the other one lay warm against my belly. Cool they were, for a few moments, soothing against the place where my heart was beginning to quicken. The same dread which had quieted the jeering soldiers was stirring now in me. For greatest of all among the gods on earth are the Kamehameha. Very great is their *mana*, burning is their *kapu*. And deep, profound, was my fear of the King.

A. Grove Day

A. Grove Day once declared that "I can't remember a time when I didn't know I was going to become a writer of books," and, except for his heavy labors as a teacher, his life was entirely dedicated to producing one book after another. Prolific as both an author and an anthologist, Day's name is closely associated with the ocean-adventure genre. His love of tales sometimes involved him in writing his own fictions, but more often he retold historical and biographical stories or collected the fictions of others into his numerous widely read anthologies. Toward the end of Day's life, many of his books found new life in an attractive paperback republication series brought out by Mutual Publishing.

Day was born in Philadelphia but spent much of his boyhood in Mexico and Texas. His experiences in Sonoro, Mexico provided material that became his first book. After some nineteen years on the campus of Stanford University, first as a student and later as a teacher, he was persuaded by his friend Carl Stroven to join the then tiny English Department of the University of Hawai'i. He arrived in Honolulu in August of 1941 "after a twelve-day passage on a cattle boat, zigzagging each hour to avoid submarines."

He often collaborated with colleagues such as Stroven and a then up-and-coming novelist named James Michener. His Pacific anthologies include *The Spell of the Pacific, True Tales of the South Seas, The Spell of Hawai'i,* and *Horror in Paradise.* His best-known historical and literary-historical works are those he wrote with a broad, general audience in mind. *Rascals in Paradise, Hawai'i and Its People,* and *Mad about Islands* are three of his most popular studies.

Liholiho and the Longnecks

The first white women ever seen in the Sandwich Islands (except for wives of sea captains) were objects of high curiosity when they landed at the port of Honolulu in 1820.

The town was a far cry from their own remembered villages. Along the waterfront lay ship-chandlers' shops, adobe storehouses, and one tavern after another. The rest of the settlement was "a mass of brown huts, looking precisely like so many haystacks in the country; not one white cottage, no church spire, not a garden or a tree to be seen save the grove of coconuts." Through this scene walked the women, while a growing throng of natives ran to peer beneath their poke bonnets and exclaim to each other: "Their faces are small and set far back, and they have long necks!"

Thereafter the Longnecks were a cynosure. Day and night, large-eyed Hawaiians stared through the doors and windows of the mission quarters, and audibly wondered why these foreigners had come to the kingdom. Suspicions that the new arrivals might be bent on conquest were set at rest by the query: "Would a war-party bring women and children with them?" To the child-loving Hawaiians, the Chamberlain family made such questions absurd.

The lady missionaries served their cause not only by teaching in the schools they set up, but also by their needlework. The mountainous chieftainesses demanded dresses made in the latest haole style; the ladies turned out yards of cambric Mother Hubbards, and made shirts and suits for the chiefs as well. The king put in his order for a dozen ruffled shirts and a broadcloth coat.

Life in Missionary Row demanded great exertions. Six months of laundry work had piled up, for there had been no chance to wash clothes on the *Thaddeus*. The dirt-floored houses had to be made into homes, with the aid of gifts from friendly Honolulu merchants. In such a grass house was born, on July 16, 1820, Levi Sartwell Loomis, first white child to see the light in the Sandwich Islands.

The frame house sent from Boston finally arrived on December 25 on the *Tartar*—a very welcome Christmas gift. This was not the first frame house to be erected in the islands, for several of the chiefs had purchased such dwellings from the traders; but it was the most impressive. The visitor can walk through the rooms of that house today, for it still stands on King Street in Honolulu.

The missionary band sought to teach the meaning of Christianity in their schools before engaging in wholesale conversions. The rulers said from the first: "If *the palapala*—the written word—is good, we wish to possess it first ourselves; if it is bad, we do not intend our subjects to know the evil of it." Thus the first pupils were of chief's rank. "The king forbids our teaching any but the blood royal," wrote Mrs. Holman. The strategy of starting with the more important personages appealed likewise to the missionaries, still in the islands on sufferance.

By the end of the year of trial, the various mission schools had about a hundred pupils of both sexes and all ages, but mainly adults and mainly of the chieftain class. In spite of some opposition from rum sellers and impious sea captains, the missionaries had made themselves a familiar part of island life, and Liholiho granted permission for them to stay indefinitely.

Soon after the landing in Honolulu, Brothers Whitney and Ruggles had been deputed to return to his home the wandering son of the king of Kaua'i. Kaumuali'i gave an affecting welcome to his long-lost George, and rewarded Captain Blanchard with a load of sandalwood worth a thousand dollars. Kaumuali'i had an interpreter—a traveled native who had once been the dinner guest of George Washington in New York—but the king himself knew enough English to express his gratitude and to ask that a mission station be set up at Waimea.

Kaumuali'i nowadays stood out among his subjects for his noble Roman face, his taciturnity, and his fondness for fine European dress. He soon forsook the gin bottle and acted like an exemplary Christian. So religious did he become that when he went swimming, he paddled around with one hand and with the other held the Bible before his eyes. He placed his son George second in command only to himself, and smiled when that son displayed his accomplishments—attractive manners, easy English, and the ability to accompany hymn-singing sessions by playing on a treasured bass viol. But this idyl could not last.

Liholiho had not forgotten that Kaumuali'i had once promised that, when he died, he would yield the sovereignty of Kaua'i to the heir of his old enemy, Kamehameha I. Deciding to obtain a renewal of that pledge in person, Liholiho impulsively set out with Boki on July 21, 1821, to sail to Kaua'i, which he had never seen in his life. All the objections of his terrified followers he put aside—a hundred miles of rough channel to be crossed in a small open boat crowded with thirty persons, the lack of food or water, the possibility that Kaumuali'i would prove hostile. The need for a compass he supplied merely by pointing with his finger. When the boat was twice nearly capsized, he replied: "Bail out the water and sail on; if you return with the boat, I will jump overboard and swim to Kaua'i!" Through a day and a night Liholiho, with a courage verging on foolhardiness, urged them on.

Liholiho survived the sea and was welcomed by Kaumuali'i. High pledges of trust were made on both sides; but at the end of a pleasant visit, the king of Kaua'i was decoyed aboard the royal vessel *Cleopatra's Barge* and brought to O'ahu as a virtual hostage. Good behavior was assured when the unlucky monarch was married to Ka'ahumanu, the powerful *kuhina nui;* it made no difference that he had left a queen, Kapule, behind on Kaua'i. To make assurance doubly sure, Ka'ahumanu also married her husband's son Keali'iahonui, the young heir apparent. Kapule, the deposed queen, took the name of "Deborah" and cheerfully began operating an inn at Wailua that for many years was the most celebrated stopping place between Līhu'e and Hanalei.

George P. Kaumuali'i, prince returned from exile, now began backsliding. From playing the bass viol he went on to more violent diversions. Merely because a certain Captain Masters denied the young man a bottle of gin, George set fire to the captain's dwelling houses on Kaua'i and destroyed property worth $2,500. The fact that the old king indemnified the loss at the request of John Coffin Jones, American agent in the islands, did not mollify Jones, who referred to Mr. George as "one of the most finished rascals the islands offer."

Meanwhile the missionaries had been busy. The first Christian church in the islands was dedicated September 15, 1821, on the site of the present Kawaiaha'o Church. The printing press ran off, on January 7, 1822, the first sheet of what were to be millions of pages of reading matter. The first Christian marriage in the islands, celebrated August 11, 1822, united Thomas Hopu, Cornwall boy and friend of Opukahaia, with his bride Delia. The first chiefs to be married were Hoapili and his second wife, Kalakua, one of the widows of Kamehameha; the ceremony was performed October 19, 1823.

The weekly preaching had been helped by the arrival on the cutter *Mermaid,* in April, 1822, of a party of visitors from the London Missionary Society that included Daniel Tyerman, George Bennett, and William Ellis. Ellis, who knew the language of Tahiti and soon learned that of Hawai'i, was the first person to preach a sermon in Hawaiian. He was liked so well that he agreed to return and make his home in the Islands the following year. The missionary contingent was further reinforced on April 27, 1823, with the arrival of the "Second Company" on the ship *Thames.* By the end of that year, the Kailua station, abandoned when the king moved his capital to Honolulu, was again running; and a busy station was opened at the port of Lahaina on Maui. Another station on Hawai'i was started in 1824, at Hilo.

The missionaries preached every Sunday, but baptism into the church was not easily earned. The queen mother, Keopuolani, was baptized only an hour before her death on September 16, 1823; but the next baptism did not come until July 10, 1825, when a celebrated blind convert, Pua'aiki or "Bartimeus," was taken into the Lahaina congregation. On December 5, eight Hawaiians—most of them of high rank—were baptized in Honolulu. Long before that time, Liholiho had made a decision that would prove fatal.

Remembering his father's words to Captain Vancouver, Liholiho considered himself and his kingdom to be under the aegis of Great Britain. This allegiance had been strengthened in the spring of 1822 by the gift from the British government of a six-gun schooner, the *Prince Regent*, built in Australia. Hence, in the fall of 1823, he decided to visit England, fountainhead of the new civilization opening before him. He wanted to exchange ideas with his fellow monarch King George.

Liholiho and his party—including his favorite wife Kamāmalu, Governor Boki of O'ahu and his wife Liliha and the king's secretary, the Frenchman John Rives—embarked on the English whaleship *L'Aigle* on November 27, 1823. The royal party arrived at Portsmouth the following May, and were settled in a luxurious London hotel. They purchased and donned clothing of the latest mode. Before the program of regal entertainment had well begun, however, the king and queen, and several others in the party, were stricken with a disease that, in spite of every care, was to prove quickly lethal. It was the measles. Kamāmalu succumbed on July 8, 1824, and Liholiho, stricken with grief, lasted only until July 14.

Before his departure Liholiho, who with five wives had no child, had named his nine-year-old brother as his heir. The kingdom was really run by the dowager queen Ka'ahumanu as regent, and her attitude was to be of most influence upon the conversion of the islanders.

Ka'ahumanu (her name means "feather cloak") was indeed an imposing figure. She was six feet tall and weighed over three hundred pounds, but she was well formed and Vancouver had testified that she was attractive in the eyes of white men. Eldest daughter of Ke'eaumoku, she had been the favorite queen of Kamehameha I. The great king had been deeply in love with her and so jealous that, although she was entitled by her rank to have an extra husband of her own choice, Kamehameha refused her this privilege.

As regent, Ka'ahumanu was the virtual head of the kingdom. She was now the wife of Kaumuali'i, the unlucky king of Kaua'i, but by no means allowed that fact to prejudice the interests of the absent Liholiho. The royal captive from Kaua'i survived until May 26, 1824. His will fulfilled his promise that at his death the kingdom to the northwest would be bestowed upon the heir of Kamehameha.

George P. Kaumuali'i felt that he had been disinherited. He confided to Bingham his belief that "the old gentleman was poisoned," and feared for his own life. Persuaded by a group of malcontent chiefs, George led an attack on Sunday, August 8, against the old Russian fort at Waimea, Kaua'i, manned by a handful of Liholiho's soldiers. In spite of the leadership of the young veteran of the War of 1812, the attack failed bloodily and Billy Pitt soon put down the rebellion. George, who had been hiding in the mountains with his wife Betty, daughter of Isaac Davis, was taken in honorable captivity to Honolulu. (His child, born during the brief civil war, always bore the name of Wahine Kipi—"rebel woman.") There, on May 3, 1826, a prisoner of Ka'ahumanu, died the prince in whom the missionaries of the *Thaddeus* had placed so many high hopes.

Although Queen Ka'ahumanu had taken the lead in overthrowing the idols, her attitude toward the missionaries had at first been quite offhanded. She thought little of coming to call on them right after bathing in the ocean, wearing only the dress of Eden and dripping sea water on the floor of their sitting room. Her pride was so great that she had haughtily extended her little finger to them instead of a hearty handshake, but gradually her interest in the new teachings became so strong that she interrupted her card games to puzzle out the letters in a spelling book. Solving the mystery of the vowels, she exclaimed to her women: "*Ua loa'a i'au*—I have got it!" About 1824 she took the lead in promoting the Christianization of the realm. Often she attended the preachings, drawn by six servitors pulling a little American-built wagon.

Another amazon of high rank, Kapi'olani, sensationally testified her faith in December, 1824. She conceived the idea of helping the Hilo mission by defying the fire goddess Pele at the very lip of the bubbling crater that was the dwelling place of this most revered Hawaiian deity.

Kapi'olani led a hundred-mile march from Kona, through tropical undergrowth and across knife-edged lava flows, to the smoky pit of Kīlauea on the slopes of massive Mauna Loa. About noon on December 21, the party arrived to find Joseph Goodrich of the mission waiting for them. Together they gazed down upon the spouting billows of molten rock four hundred feet below.

That night, in a grass hut built for her among the giant tree ferns on the ledge above the crater, several members of the old faith tried to dissuade her and predicted her death. She replied: "I should not die by your god. That fire was kindled by my God." Next morning, on the way to the rim, a priestess again attempted to dissuade her by waving a piece of kapa which was supposed to be a *palapala*, or scroll, from Pele. "I too have a *palapala*," responded Kapi'olani. She then read from a Hawaiian book of hymns and a missionary spelling book.

At the edge of the fiery pit Kapi'olani broke an old ritual. A visitor was always supposed to tear off a branch of berry-bearing 'ōhelo, throw half of it into the crater, and proclaim: "Pele, here are your 'ōhelos; I offer some to you, some I also eat." Kapi'olani broke a branch but ate all the berries, pointedly refusing to share with the goddess. Then, above the roaring flames and the smoke of cinder cones, she uttered her famous challenge: "Jehovah is my God. I fear not Pele. Should I perish by her anger, then you may fear her powers. But if Jehovah saves me, then you must fear and serve Jehovah." A hymn was sung and a prayer uttered, and the party withdrew without being overwhelmed by fire from an enraged heaven.

Kapi'olani had flouted the old *kapu*, and was to live to tell the tale for seventeen years. Alfred Lord Tennyson, who heard in England about her feat, wrote a poem in her praise. Brother Goodrich found that the act of defiance was of immediate aid to the Hilo mission, where Kapi'olani spent the Christmas season. "We have reason to think that Kapi'olani did as much good by her visit here of ten or twelve days as we have done in nearly a year," he wrote, "for since her departure we have upwards of ninety scholars."

Victoria Nalani Kneubuhl

Victoria Kneubuhl has spoken eloquently about the importance of her form of art. "Theatre is a conduit into our everyday world through which mystery and magic may still enter. At the same time, theatre can serve as a powerful platform for examining the social and political issues of our time. I am extremely proud to be part of a craft that is forceful yet transitory and fragile. I love theatre which is above all theatrical, multi-dimensional, lively, and risky. . . . I am a playwright because I believe the theatre provides the possibility of a communal experience which is at once both artistic and intensely human."

Kneubuhl was born in Honolulu and is of Samoan, Hawaiian, and Caucasian ancestry. She feels her work is "inextricably woven together" with her experiences of island life and that she has "been fortunate as an artist to have this rich wellspring from which to draw." One of her productions was as much a community event as it was a dramatic presentation. In 1993 she wrote *January 1893*, a script for a festival of events commemorating the 100th anniversary of the overthrow of the Hawaiian monarchy. The production was staged as a historical reenactment in many of the actual Honolulu sites where the events originally took place.

At the time she received the Hawai'i Award for Literature in 1995, seven of her plays had been presented in Hawai'i, primarily by Kumu Kahua Theatre and the Honolulu Theatre for Youth, and several more plays had already been scheduled or projected for the near future. Her work has also received national and international recognition. *The Conversion of Ka'ahumanu* and *Ka'iulani* (which she co-authored) were performed at Edinburgh (Scotland), Washington, D.C., and Los Angeles. Her children's play *Tofa Samoa* was an invited production at the Okinawa International Children's Theatre Festival. Both the experimental ghostly play *Ola Na Iwi* and the children's play *Paniolo Spurs* were going into production in the year of her award.

Kneubuhl has degrees from Antioch University and the University of Hawai'i at Mānoa. As a UH graduate student, she won the award for excellence in playwriting. She worked for many years with the interpretative programs at the Mission Houses Museum and the Judiciary History Center. She was honored in 1994 with the Keeper of the Past Award from the Hawai'i Heritage Center for her contributions toward the cause of preserving and sharing Hawai'i's unique heritage.

from *The Conversion of Kaʻahumanu*

The Cast of Characters

Sybil Mosely Bingham (30s Caucasian)
Lucy Goodale Thurston (30s Caucasian)
Kaʻahumanu (40s Hawaiian)
Hannah Grimes (20s hapa haole,[Hawaiian/Caucasian])
Pali (20s Hawaiian)

ACT I, Scene I

Spot to Sybil in the playing area.

SYBIL: In 1815, I, Sybil Mosely, felt the calling of our Lord and Saviour Jesus Christ. I confessed my faith before the congregation and now cling to the bosom of the church. Though I am a sinner, I now have hope that God will call me his own and receive me at his right hand.

Spot to Lucy in the playing area.

LUCY: In 1815, I, Lucy Goodale, was washed in the blood of our Lord Jesus. My family rejoiced in my pious calling. I do now truly believe and trust that dear Redeemer who tasted death for us all.

SYBIL: In 1819, I am of low spirits. A kindred spirit to whom I was dearly attached has now departed from my life to serve God in another part of the world. I know not where my life is going or what the Lord would have me do. I feel many days of loneliness and sorrow. The joy I once felt at teaching these young girls slowly drains away, and I feel heavy with a weight I can neither understand nor overcome. I read of women who do mission work among the heathen peoples of this earth. I envy them; that they have a purpose and service to God. I pray that one day I might find such a purpose.

LUCY: In 1819, my mother died. My dear sister, Persis, was married and left our father's home. My mother, gone! Persis, gone! Wonder not when I say, that I more than ever felt myself an orphan. My solitary chamber witnesses my grief as I walk from side to side. My pillow is watered with tears. I apply to the fountain of all grace and consolation for support. I devote my life to the will of the Supreme.

SYBIL: My prayers were heard! Today I go to Goshen, Connecticut to meet one who is perhaps of the same heart and mind as I. A young man about to embark on a life of mission work in the Sandwich Islands seeks a companion for this noble cause. God will guide me.

LUCY: My cousin William visited me today. He gave me information that a mission to the Sandwich Islands was to sail in four to six weeks. He dwelt upon it with interest and feeling. Imagine my surprise to hear him say "will Lucy, by becoming connected with a missionary, now an entire stranger, attach herself to this small band of pilgrims and bring the word of the gospel to a land of darkness?" Now I feel the need of guidance! Oh, that my sister were here!

Sybil and Lucy move together.

SYBIL: On October 11, 1819, I was joined in Holy Matrimony to the Reverend Hiram Bingham.

LUCY: On October 12, 1819, I was joined in Holy Matrimony to the Reverend Asa Thurston.

SYBIL: On October 23, 1819, we set sail as members of a pioneer company of missionaries to the Sandwich Islands.

LUCY: Like Rebecca, we have said, "I will go."

Sybil and Lucy wave goodbye as if on a ship. The lights dim and Lucy steps out of the light.

Scene 2

A spot to Kaʻahumanu in the playing area.

KAʻAHUMANU: Here is why I, Kaʻahumanu, Kuhina nui and widow of Kamehameha, have done these things. For many years now we have seen these haole, these foreign men among us. We know that they break the kapu laws of the kahuna. Do the Gods come to punish them? No! Some of the women have gone to the ships and have eaten with these haole men. Do the Gods come to punish them? No! So why should it be that they will come to punish us at all? I think these beliefs are nothing, false. And here is another thing. We know where the punishment comes from. It does not come from

Gods. It comes from men. It comes from the priests who grow greedy for power. And who is it who hates most this kapu law of eating? We, women of the ali'i. We do not want a lowly place any more, and the men of the priesthood will see this! *(She laughs)* You should have seen the fear in their faces when we sat to eat. Hewahewa made a great prayer to the Gods. Liholiho, the king, approached the women's table. Many of the faces in the crowd became as white as the full moon. Liholiho sat with us to eat. He ate and the people waited in silence, waited for the terrible wrath of the Gods . . . which never came! Then a great cry rose from the women. " 'Ai noa, 'ai noa!" The kapu laws are ended! The Gods are false.

Blackout

Scene 3

The sound of a rough sea. Sybil enters.

SYBIL: What can I say to you my sisters this morning? I can tell you. Could your eye glance across the great water and catch this little bark ascending and descending the mountainous waves which contain your dear sister, your hands would be involuntarily extended for her relief, and your cry would be to save her. The sea runs very high, while the wind runs through the naked riggings as you may have heard it on a November's day, through the leafless trees of a majestic forest. The dashing of the waves on deck, the frequent falling of something below, the violent motion of the vessel, going up and then down, would seem to conspire to terrify and distress. Yet I feel my mind calm as if by a winter's fire in my own land. Is this not the mercy of God?

Lucy moves into the light. She is somewhat nervous.

SYBIL: Lucy, what are you doing out here?
LUCY: I felt so sick shut up in there!
SYBIL: It's very rough.
LUCY: How long have we been at sea?
SYBIL: About sixty days.
LUCY: And still not halfway there.
SYBIL: Lucy, are you all right?
LUCY: I'm frightened by the sea today.
SYBIL: *(placing her arm around her)* You are safe.
LUCY: What do you think will really happen to us, Sybil?

SYBIL: I don't know, Lucy.

LUCY: *(building)* You know anything, anything could happen to us out here in the sea, in the middle of nowhere. No one would know and no one would care. Why did I come here?

SYBIL: God called you.

LUCY: Suppose they don't want us in their islands? Suppose they aren't friendly? The sailors say,

SYBIL: Don't listen to what the sailors say!

LUCY: I hate the ocean and I hate this ship! *(she sinks down)*

SYBIL: Now we must lean on Him. Give all your thoughts and all your fears to Him.

LUCY: I'm trying.

SYBIL: And think on the poor heathen, Lucy, whose immortal souls languish in darkness. Who will give them the Bible and tell them of the Saviour if not us? Think of the Hawaiian people who will enjoy that grace because someone such as Lucy Thurston was willing to say "I will go."

Blackout

Scene 4

Lights to HH. Hannah sits playing with a ribbon.
Pali enters from the playing area.

PALI: Hannah, Hannah, have you heard?

HANNAH: What?

PALI: A war!

HANNAH: What are you talking about?

PALI: On Hawai'i.

HANNAH: Get in here and be quiet.

PALI: Why?

HANNAH: My father is drinking with some haole men. When they get drunk, they might come looking for me.

PALI: I'm glad my father isn't a haole.

HANNAH: Hah! You don't even know who your father is.

PALI: I do so!

HANNAH: Who then, who? . . . See? You don't know.

PALI: Well, at least I'm not chased around by haole men.

HANNAH: Because you aren't as pretty as me.

PALI: No, because I'm not hapa haole. I don't look like them.

PALI: Are haole men better than a kanaka?

HANNAH: I never went with a kanaka. My father would beat me until I couldn't walk. Besides, now I'm Davis' woman.

PALI: Will you have another baby with him?

HANNAH: Shut up, Pali. You're nothing but a chicken, clucking gossip all over the village. Now, tell me of this battle.

PALI: No, you told me to shut up. You think I'm stupid?

HANNAH: All right, I'm sorry. Tell me.

PALI: No!

HANNAH: Come on, Pali. Look, I'll give you this pretty ribbon, see? Everyone will envy you.

PALI: What should I do with it?

HANNAH: Tie it up in your hair. See how pretty it is?

PALI: Where did you get this?

HANNAH: I have a lot of them.

PALI: You're lucky.

HANNAH: Now tell me.

PALI: It's because of the free eating and the defying of the kapu. The chief Kekuaokalani and his followers don't like the old gods going. He doesn't like the way Ka'ahumanu has begun to burn the images in the temples. He will fight with Ka'ahumanu and Liholiho.

HANNAH: My father said this would happen.

PALI: What do you think of the kapu?

HANNAH: Lies!

PALI: How do you know?

HANNAH: I know! There are no such foolish beliefs in other places. I have heard the talk of foreigners.

PALI: And there is never any punishment?

HANNAH: No! And be quiet! I told you, I don't want them to hear us.

PALI: Blood will be spilled.

HANNAH: It's a foolish war. A fight over nothing.

PALI: Everyone knows Ka'ahumanu will win.

HANNAH: I don't care, my life won't change.

Lights down

Scene 5

Lights to KH. Ka'ahumanu sits on her mats.

KA'AHUMANU: I knew our lives would change forever. I knew that when I did this thing. There was blood spilled. Turmoil rose among the people. Kekuaokalani moved his forces out of Ka'awaloa. We met them at Kuamo'o. We had guns, that is why we won. From Kamehameha, I learned to strike swiftly and with strength. But my heart weeps for the death of Kekuaokalani and his faithful woman Manono, who fought by his side. Now the old Gods have lost their power, and will go. *(Pause)* Have I done right? Or have I done great evil? I took down what I knew to be false, but will I, Ka'ahumanu, be able to guide these islands, be able to guide the people? The people now have no Gods, only the ali'i. How will I steer the canoe?

Enter Pali

PALI: My Ali'i.
KA'AHUMANU: Ah, Pali, my pua. You are well?
PALI: Yes, thank you. *(Pause)* A ship has come.
KA'AHUMANU: *(sighs)* Many ships come. Too many.
PALI: This one brings white men and,
KA'AHUMANU: They all bring white men.
PALI: And haole women! And they say they are bringing a new God!
KA'AHUMANU: Women?
PALI: *(excited)* 'Ae!
KA'AHUMANU: This is a new sight. Perhaps I will come to see them, after I go fishing. You will come fishing with me?
PALI: Well, if it is your wish.
KA'AHUMANU: No, I can see your mind is filled with wondering about these haole women, go and satisfy this longing.
PALI: Oh, thank you, thank you, I will tell you everything that I see.

Lights down on KH. Lights up on the playing area.

Scene 6

Lights to Sybil and Lucy in the playing area.

SYBIL: Lucy! Come, you can see them!
LUCY: There are hundreds, maybe thousands of them.
SYBIL: They look so dark. It's hard to see in this blinding light.
LUCY: They'll be closer in a minute.
SYBIL: How beautiful the mountains are!
LUCY: My feet won't know how to walk on solid ground again.
SYBIL: Look! Now they're closer. I see a man waving to us.
LUCY: Where?

SYBIL: In that canoe. Next to the woman holding coconuts.

LUCY: Where? Oh, there! *(Pause)* Oh Sybil, those are not coconuts!

SYBIL: No? Oh, my, no.

LUCY: Look at them!

SYBIL: Hundreds of them,

LUCY: All of them,

SYBIL & LUCY: Naked!

LUCY: *(terribly nervous)* What shall we do?

SYBIL: *(also nervous)* Compose ourselves. We must compose ourselves.

LUCY: What? They're getting closer.

SYBIL: Now, we must try to act naturally.

LUCY: Naturally? Yes, we must. But it's disgusting. Even the men.

SYBIL: Well, don't look! There I mean.

LUCY: Where? Where shall we look?

SYBIL: Lower your eyes and wave politely.

> *Lucy and Sybil lower their eyes and wave politely. Lucy speaks straight to audience.*

LUCY: I had never conceived in my life that I would ever see such a sight. To describe the dress and demeanor of these creatures I would have to make use of uncouth and indelicate language. To the civilized eye their covering is revoltingly scanty to say the least. I have never felt such shame or embarrassment as when I first beheld these children of nature.

SYBIL: I saw them first as a swarming mass of dark savages, and even as I looked into their eyes I asked myself, can they be human? But the answer came to me: Yes! God made these people, they have immortal souls, yes they are human and can be brought to know and love our Saviour.

LUCY: Some of the women are grotesquely large.

SYBIL: Mountainous!

LUCY: Some chiefesses have western cloth wrapped about them.

SYBIL: In something which resembles a roman toga.

LUCY: But is thoroughly immodest.

SYBIL & LUCY *(holding hands)*:   Here we will begin God's work.

> *Lucy and Sybil freeze. Hannah and Pali enter. They walk around the women as if examining objects. Lucy and Sybil remain frozen.*

HANNAH: Look how they cover up their bodies so!

PALI: Auwē!

HANNAH: Look at this white hand.

PALI: What puny bodies! What sickly pink skin!

HANNAH: *(lifting up a dress)* Their legs are like sticks.

PALI: They look all pinched up in the middle.

HANNAH: And wide at the top.

PALI: Their eyes are so small.

HANNAH: They have no smiles.

PALI: I'm sure it's because they are so thin and sickly.

HANNAH: Maybe they would improve with bathing in the sea, and lying about in the sun. *(She takes Pali aside)* Now we have learned something. This is just why many haole men who come to these islands go so crazy over our women. It is because haole women are so revoltingly ugly. How could a man find any desire for such a creature? Auwē! It must be so hard for them to get children. I pity them, poor things. I will send them some food.

Sybil and Lucy come to life. They approach Hannah and Pali, offering them their hands.

SYBIL: Aloha.

PALI: *(shaking hands)* Aloha.

LUCY (TO HANNAH) AND SYBIL (TO PALI): Aloha.

PALI AND HANNAH: Aloha.

LUCY: Aloha.

HANNAH: Aloha.

Ka'ahumanu enters regally, with an air of disdain.
Sybil and Lucy timidly approach her.

SYBIL: *(offering her hand)* Aloha, your majesty.

Ka'ahumanu haughtily extends her baby finger.

LUCY: *(stepping back, afraid)* Aloha . . .

SYBIL: *(haltingly)* Your, um, majesty, we bring a message of hope.

KA'AHUMANU: Oh?

LUCY: Of Jesus.

SYBIL: The one true God, the blessed Jehovah,

KA'AHUMANU: *(insistent)* We don't need a new god. Why do you wear so much clothes?

SYBIL: This is the way ladies of America dress.

LUCY: Proper ladies.

KA'AHUMANU: *(fingering their clothes)* I wish to try such clothes. You will make one for me.

SYBIL: Yes, I think we could.

KAʻAHUMANU: I will send you cloth.

LUCY: Perhaps you yourself would like to learn to sew.

KAʻAHUMANU: Sew?

SYBIL: Yes, it is how we make clothes.

KAʻAHUMANU: No! I want *you* to make it for me.

LUCY: *(flustered)* Oh! Yes! We know, I mean, I only thought that,

KAʻAHUMANU: Why do you come to these islands? What do you want?

LUCY: Want?

KAʻAHUMANU: Yes. Is it sandalwood? Whale oil? Your men come for women? What do you want?

SYBIL: *(quickly)* We don't want anything like that.

LUCY: Oh, no.

SYBIL: We want to bring you the good news of our Lord and Saviour Jesus Christ.

KAʻAHUMANU: The news of Jesus Christ?

LUCY: Yes.

KAʻAHUMANU: Why should I care for news of someone I don't even know?

SYBIL: Well, he is God. The blessed Son of—

KAʻAHUMANU: I do not wish to hear of a God! We have finished with Gods. Pau! I have destroyed many images, burned many heiau. I have forbidden the worship in the old temples. And the king has spoken these things to the people: We want no Gods. The Gods brought only sorrow and unhappiness to our people. We will not have that again. Let us speak of other things.

A SILENCE

LUCY: Our God is different. He,

Kaʻahumanu glares at Lucy.

SYBIL: *(loud whisper)* Lucy, please!

KAʻAHUMANU: I want clothes which are yellow. I will send yellow cloth.

SYBIL: Yes, we will be happy to do this. You must also come so that we can measure you.

KAʻAHUMANU: Measure?

LUCY: So we can cut.

KAʻAHUMANU: Cut?

SYBIL: To make your clothes.

KAʻAHUMANU: Yes, then I will come. *(to Sybil)* You have a kind face, but very sad.

SYBIL: *(shyly)* Thank you. When you come, perhaps we will talk a little more.

KAʻAHUMANU: Paha (perhaps).

SYBIL: So we may come to know each other's ways.

KAʻAHUMANU: Paha.

Exit the Hawaiian women. Lucy and Sybil join hands.

LUCY & SYBIL: Here we will begin God's work. . .

. . . .

ACT II, Scene 3

Lights to Kaʻahumanu and Hannah at KH.

KAʻAHUMANU: Many chiefs have accepted this new God.

HANNAH: Yes.

KAʻAHUMANU: Kaumualiʻi wished I would believe; also Keopuolani.

HANNAH: Why don't you?

KAʻAHUMANU: Some things I like. I think it is good that with this god, women may speak to him. In the old days, only the kahuna spoke to God at the heiau. And I like to see that women may teach things about this god, such as Mrs. Bingham teaches. But some things I don't like. I'm afraid that this god would have too much power. That too many things would change. There is something about the mikanele that I do not trust, something which I can't name.

HANNAH: They have been kind teachers to us.

KAʻAHUMANU: And they seem to care for the people.

HANNAH: They do many things for us.

KAʻAHUMANU: *(bewildered)* Yes. *(pause)* You know, Hannah, when I was younger, I felt so strong. That is the good thing about youth, to feel strong in body and purpose. I was not afraid. I saw something to do, and I did it. But everything is changed with the coming of foreigners. Their wealth, ships, guns, these things change everything. They have made the power of the chiefs weak. I make a law against the sale of rum. A ship comes full of men eager for drink. If the captain does not like the kapu he says "sell us rum or we'll fire our cannon on your town. "Or perhaps he sends an angry mob to fight and make trouble. What am I to do? Keep the law and have destruction? If we engage him in battle more and more ships with guns will come from his country. Should I relent and give him rum, this makes the chiefs look weak. What will I do? In former days, I did not hesitate to act. My mind did not trouble me. The way was clear. I was not afraid to do away with what I knew to be false or to take up what I wished. But now . . .

HANNAH: Everything has changed so much. I know.

KAʻAHUMANU: ʻAe, the chiefs pass. All the old ones, my counselors and friends, Keopoulani, gone. My own Kaumualiʻi, gone! Kalanimoku grows so old. His strength fades. Our people die. I feel as if I am surrounded by darkness. . .

The lights go very soft to a spot on Kaʻahumanu alone. She chants a kanikau, *a mourning chant.*

KAʻAHUMANU: Elua no wahi e mehana ai
O ke ahi lalaku i ke hale
O ka hua o ke ahi
O ka lua kapa
I ka lua poli o ka hoa e mehanaʻi e
Eia la
Aia la
Eia la e

She lies on the mat. Hannah covers her with a quilt and exits. Voices speak from the darkness rising to confusion and chaos.

VOICE 1: Why did you destroy the old ones?
VOICE 2: Why?
VOICE 3: Why?
VOICE 4: Why?
VOICE 1: Your people are dying!
VOICE 2: Why?
VOICE 3: Do something!
VOICE 4: Can't you do anything?
VOICE 1: Too many haole.
VOICE 2: Another warship.
VOICE 3: Another government.
VOICE 4: Give us sandalwood.
VOICE 1: Women. Where are the women!
VOICE 2: And rum, more rum.
VOICE 3: Call for a warship. These chiefs can't tell us what to do.
VOICE 4: I'll do what I like. This isn't America.
VOICE 1: England.
VOICE 2: France.
VOICE 3: These aren't civilized human beings.
VOICE 4: Take care of your own people.
VOICE 1: Take care!
VOICE 2: Can't you do anything?

VOICE 3: There's too much sickness.

VOICE 4: I need some land.

VOICE 1: Send for a warship. I want to be paid!

VOICE 2: These are only native chiefs.

VOICE 3: Stupid savages!

KAʻAHUMANU: Why is it so hot?

VOICE 4: There aren't enough children anymore.

VOICE 1: Why did you leave the old gods?

VOICE 2: Can't you do something?

KAʻAHUMANU: It's too hot.

VOICE 3: What does every sin deserve?

VOICE 4: Everyone will die!

VOICE 1: Die!

VOICE 2: It's too hot!

VOICE 3: Why can't you do anything??

VOICE 4: Why?

ALL VOICES: We're Dying!! We're all dying. Do something.

Scene 4

Enter Lucy and Sybil. They begin to bathe Kaʻahumanu's face with damp cloths and tend her as if she is ill.

LUCY: Is she improved?

SYBIL: Not much, her fever is still very high.

LUCY: You should rest.

SYBIL: I'm fine. It's you I worry over.

LUCY: You've been here all day. You could become ill yourself.

SYBIL: I've had a little sleep.

Pali has softly entered.

PALI: Will she die?

SYBIL: *(frightened)* No, she won't die!

PALI: Put her in the stream.

SYBIL: No, Pali, it could make her much worse.

PALI: She'll burn up inside.

LUCY: Such a stupid belief.

Exit Pali, quickly

SYBIL: Sister Thurston.

LUCY: I know, I spoke too sharply.

SYBIL: People listen to those whom they feel to be kind hearted.

LUCY: It always happens when I feel tired.

SYBIL: *(urgently)* Perhaps you should go back to the mission and get Rev. Bingham and the doctor.

LUCY: Is she going?

SYBIL: I don't know. I can't tell if the fever is breaking or if she's falling into a worse state.

LUCY: I'll hurry.

Exit Lucy

KA'AHUMANU: *(mumbling)* No, no. I'm too hot. Go! Go! Go away . . . I won't go there . . . No . . . no . . . *(she opens her eyes slowly and looks at Sybil)* Binamuwahine!

SYBIL: *(smiling)* Yes, I'm here.

KA'AHUMANU: I'm very sick?

SYBIL: Yes.

KA'AHUMANU: I had a terrible dream. I saw that place.

SYBIL: What place?

KA'AHUMANU: The place of fires. *(She tries to sit up)*

SYBIL: You must lie down.

KA'AHUMANU: It was a terrible place. I saw my people burning. It was so hot, great rivers of lava.

SYBIL: It's all right. You're here now.

KA'AHUMANU: You're so kind to bring me back from that place.

SYBIL: It is the love of Jesus that has brought me here.

KA'AHUMANU: It is Jesus who saves us from this place?

SYBIL: He is the Light of the World. It is only through Him that we are saved.

KA'AHUMANU: Perhaps now, Binamuwahine, I will try one of these prayers to Jesus.

SYBIL: Now?

KA'AHUMANU: Yes, now, hurry.

SYBIL: Rev. Bingham will be here soon. Maybe you wish to pray with him.

KA'AHUMANU: No, it's you I wish to share my first prayer with.

SYBIL: *(touched)* Very well, we will pray as Jesus taught us to pray, saying: Our Father which art in heaven . . .

KA'AHUMANU: Our Father which art in heaven . . .

The Lights fade as they continue the Lord's Prayer.

Aldyth Morris

Aldyth Morris was living in Honolulu in 1936 when the body of Flemish priest, Father Damien de Veuster, was exhumed from its grave at the Leper Settlement on Moloka'i and transported back to the priest's native land of Belgium. Forty years later she was inspired to turn her thoughts about that exhumation into the best known of her plays. A reviewer for *Booklist* declared that Aldyth Morris's *Damien* "evokes the strength and spirituality of this complex man of God whose life of service was assailed by detractors and by his own inherently self-doubting nature." *Damien* has been translated into Flemish, French, Japanese, and Spanish. After its first performance in Honolulu, it was produced in numerous American theatres as well as in Japan, Canada, and Scotland. It was also mounted for public television to great acclaim, winning the Peabody award and receiving widespead viewership through its various broadcasts and rebroadcasts. The public television production has also been made available on videotape.

Altogether Morris has written eight full-length plays. Her plays on Captain James Cook, Robert Lewis Stevenson, and Queen Lili'uokalani resemble *Damien* in their compelling use of one-actor stagings and in their focus on strong protagonists whose lives were involved in important events in the history of Hawai'i.

Aldyth Morris was born in the Rocky Mountain town of Logan, Utah, and, after living and working in San Francisco and New York, made her home in Honolulu for sixty years. For many years she was the managing editor of the University of Hawai'i Press.

from *Damien*

The action of the play takes place during a journey from the Hawaiian island of Moloka'i to Louvain, Belgium, in 1936.

ACT I

The curtain is always up. As the house lights go down the offstage sound of a Hawaiian chant is heard. As the chant comes to an end the stage lights dim almost to darkness and the voice of Father Damien is heard.

DAMIEN: This is the time of day I always hear them. Dusk. When the sun's gone down but there's still light enough to recognize a face. Lepers—forty or fifty of them at a time—marched between armed guards, from Kalihi-kai down King to Bishop, and on down Bishop to the waterfront, where small boats wait to take them to that larger boat anchored farther out—the leper boat. It always leaves at dusk on Monday, and travels in the dark to dump its human cargo before the sun comes up. This is the time of day I hear their muffled step, the mourning sounds that follow after, the haunting farewell chant, the anguished cries of separation, then the shrill whistle as the leper boat moves off across the water.

(Stage lights up slowly to reveal Father Damien in priestly hat and cassock. He half stumbles downstage center. To the audience)

DAMIEN: My feet have always been a problem. Since I came to the Islands, that is. Oh, not when I was a boy in Belgium. I was as good on my feet as anyone in those days, running about the countryside, helping on the farm, driving the cows home at night, skating on the river Dyle. Why, the night before I left home for good I walked fourteen miles to meet my mother at the shrine of Our Lady, to say good-bye. Twelve years, I promised her. I didn't keep my promise.

Actually the trouble with my feet started in Puna, my first mission field, on the Big Island, where I'd walk miles over still-warm lava flows, in search of my stray sheep—in those ill-fitting boots. They'd itch and ache and burn—my feet, I mean—and I couldn't get to sleep at night unless I soaked them. After that I had trouble till the day I died.

(Moving to his quarters at the Settlement)

DAMIEN: The day I died—Monday of Holy Week, 1889. Palm Sunday night, around 11:45, Brother James lights the lantern, wakes up Father Conrardy, the priest who's come to take my place here at the Leper Settlement, and together they go to the church next door. Soon I hear them coming back, Brother James ringing the little altar bell as he walks ahead of Father Conrardy in the dark. Up they come to my room. Brother James holds the napkin under my chin, Father Conrardy says in a sleepy voice, "The body and blood of Christ," and I receive my last communion.

Then Father Conrardy asks if he can have my cassock— threadbare and full of leprosy. What would he do with it? Better I be buried in it.

Next thing I know my roosters are crowing and it's getting light. It's hard to breathe, so Brother James helps me to sit up, and while he's holding me I breathe for the last time. As Brother James bends over to close my eyes, the farewell chant begins outside my door and spreads throughout the Settlement, till every leper knows that Kamiano's spirit has departed.

Brother James brings the basin, washes my body, dresses it in my old cassock, and

(Moving into the neutral area midstage center)

carries it into the church. He puts it in a plain redwood box, and the rest of the day I lie in state. The choir sings my favorite hymns. The lepers file in to say good-bye. This time I have no ointment for their sores, no little jokes to raise their spirits.

By afternoon my sores have crusted over with black scabs. The sickness has consumed me. It has nothing left to feed upon. Toward evening, Father Conrardy helps Brother James dress me in my vestments. They light the candles and tiptoe out. I am alone. Everything is quiet—except the pounding of the surf and the everlasting whine of Mr. Clifford's barrel organ. That kind man brought it all the way from London, hoping it would amuse us. It has—beyond all expectations. The children wind it up and let it go and are eternally surprised when it makes music of itself. After a while it stops and there is nothing but the surf.

The Requiem Mass next day—with Father Conrardy at the altar—is much the same as those I've celebrated for other lepers, almost three thousand of them. Comforting the mourners, interceding for the dead, the choir pleading: "Eternal rest give unto them, O Lord, and let perpetual light shine upon them. May they rest in peace."

At last eight lepers lift the coffin to their shoulders and Blind Petero's fife and drum corps lead the procession to the cemetery. You know, sorrow at a leper's passing is tempered with gratitude for his release, so Petero's music is anything but sad—actually more like picnic music—as we move to the new grave under the hala tree where I spent my first night at the Settlement.

Young boys from the orphanage stand four deep around the open grave. One suddenly breaks ranks and climbs into the tree. Then the first shovelful of dirt.

For sixteen years I've been sole keeper of this city of the dead. The cemetery, church, and rectory form one enclosure, and it has been my habit to come here after dark to say my beads. Now I have come to rest.

And so I do—for almost half a century. Then, one February day, the black marble stone is rolled away, the ground dug up, the coffin lifted to the surface. A stranger's hands tear away the rotted lid. Lepers I have never known break spontaneously into Hawaiian chants and funeral songs for their dead heroes. And someone cries, "The body is intact, praise God!"

So it is. My hair has grown a little—and my beard. My skin's a deeper bronze, perhaps; the silver rosary is tarnished; the vestments are moldy and the gold embroidery dull. But there are no signs of leprosy. Except for my poor feet, from which a toe or two are missing, the body is intact.

(Coming downstage)

DAMIEN: It had been my wish and my intention to stay here with my lepers. Together we would await the resurrection. Apparently my wish has been forgotten. My body—still in its decaying coffin—is put into a packing case while the priest explains that Father Damien is leaving Kalawao. An airplane waits down at the landing. Why doesn't someone speak up for me? Insist I be allowed to stay?

Fifteen minutes to fly the channel. In my day it took all night, by boat, and whether you were a passenger on deck or a leper in the hold, seasickness was part of it.

The plane puts down in Honolulu; the packing box, draped with the Belgian flag, is transferred to an army caisson. With military escort it moves slowly to its destination: the Fort Street Cathedral.

(Moving upstage to the cathedral area)

DAMIEN: Four days I lie in state—in a koa casket—you know, the kind usually reserved to Hawaiian royalty.

This is my cathedral. The confessionals know my sins, the pews my penances. I was ordained in this cathedral. Here I renewed my vows of poverty, chastity, obedience. Right here, in this sanctuary, I lay under the funeral pall, dying to the world to live in Christ. These hands that have milked cows and curried horses, taken newborn calves, pitched hay, shoveled manure and barnyard waste—these hands were consecrated here. Bishop Maigret took me, a farm boy with only four years religious training—the minimum for priests is ten or more—took me and made a priest of me. "If they won't send me priests," he said, "I'll have to make my own."

When I turned from that altar and saw them at the railing—Hawaiians who only yesterday were worshiping their ancient gods, Kāne, Kū, and Lono, when I saw them waiting to receive from me the body and the blood of Christ, my hands trembled, my heart melted like wax, and I knew happiness beyond belief. From that moment I was their servant and their priest.

I attended my first island Mass in this cathedral. We missionaries came straight here from the boat to give thanksgiving for our safe arrival, bedazzled by the sunshine, the flowers, the friendly people chattering in English or Hawaiian, neither of which I then spoke or understood, and a grand cathedral like this where we'd expected none at all.

(Indicating an area just offstage)

DAMIEN: There, in the Bishop's office, I had my first interview with His Excellency. I approached in fear and trembling because of something that had happened at the boat. You see, we've been five months at sea and here we are, starting down the gangplank in Honolulu—six Brothers all in black and ten Sisters all in white. Our feet touch ground. But somehow we can't get our land legs, and the sight of us—sixteen religious staggering like drunken sailors toward our venerable Bishop—is too much. I howl with laughter. The boat-day crowds roar back, press up against the ropes, throw flower garlands round my neck. The Bishop, as I come close, is careful not to let his eyes meet mine.

But later, in his office, he laughs. "Nobody threw garlands round my neck when I arrived," he says. "They just deported me. But I came back—aboard a French warship which threatened to shell the city unless freedom of religion were guaranteed and I was allowed to stay. That was thirty years ago. It's still enemy territory, you might say, but that laugh of yours, my boy, helped more than you can realize."

(Back to the neutral area)

DAMIEN: Before the oil of ordination is dry, he ships me off to the Big Island for a few months in Puna, where they hadn't seen a priest in years. Then eight years in Kohala, a parish so large it took two weeks to cover—by canoe, on the back of my poor mule Kapakahi, or on foot. No wonder I started having trouble with my feet.

There were other meetings in the Bishop's office, usually with me begging for money to build chapels and His Excellency grumbling at the cost.

(To the Bishop)

DAMIEN: Yes, Your Excellency, I did send the Mother Superior two hundred pounds of potatoes we have raised. . . . Of course I sent a bill. . . . No, she didn't exactly order them, but everybody needs potatoes and next month when the whalers come the price will double in the market. She got a bargain. . . . For the chapels. . . . Because we need money for a paint bill coming due. . . . Of course chapels don't grow like mushrooms. I've built enough to know. . . . But the chapel's beautiful, Your Excellency. We've made a crucifix six feet high, all decorated with Hawaiian carving. You'll see when you come over for the consecration. . . . Yes, I understand, Your Excellency is busy. . . . Yes, yes, I'm leaving—

(Starts to leave, then turns back)

DAMIEN: You wouldn't be needing any tobacco here at the Mission, would you? Our second crop is coming on. It's beautiful. . . . Yes, yes, I understand. No more shipments of any kind to anybody without a written order. . . . Thank you very much, Your Excellency. Thank you.

(Coming downstage. To the audience)

DAMIEN: I wrote my parents from Kohala:

(Reading from a letter)

DAMIEN: Here I am on an island of volcanoes, one of which, so the Hawaiians believe, is the home of Pele, goddess of eternal fire. They worship her and, whenever there's an eruption, rush to propitiate her. One man just came by on his way to offer sacrifice, so I seized the opportunity to give him a sermon on the fires of hell. He listened politely, as though he knew more about the fires of hell than I did. There are times when I am tongue-tied before them. I could know all the theology books by heart and still not know what to say. But they like me—call me Kamiano—their way of saying Damien. I keep my body in good shape—and servitude—by spading the vegetables and caring for the lambs, which you will be interested to know, Father, I bought for only two and a half francs apiece. At last I have enough chapels and animals and fields so this year I can spend more time studying and visiting the sick—

(Looking up from the letter)

DAMIEN: I didn't mention the yellow flags. But they were there—on trees and fence posts and even on my chapel door: "All lepers and leper suspects are hereby ordered to report to government health authorities within fourteen days on pain of arrest."

Occasionally I'd see the sheriff's men, with guns and dogs, sniffing about the caves and valleys of my parish. Sometimes I'd hear a distant shot.

One day I came home to find a husband barricaded in my quarters, ready to shoot whoever tried to take his sick wife from him.

One night in the confessional a young boy coughed, hemorrhaged, and covered me with blood.

(Coming even farther downstage.)

DAMIEN: Later, in Honolulu, I saw that boy in one of those processions of lepers, down King to Bishop, down Bishop to the waterfront. I saw him torn from his parents' arms and forced into the little boat. I can still hear the father's sobs, see him crouching on the pier, straining for a last glimpse of the little boy he will never see again. I can still hear his mother's farewell chant. All this against an evening sky that seems to mock us with its beauty. What could I do to comfort them but promise that one day I would go to Moloka'i and see their son?

(Returning to the cathedral area)

DAMIEN: There came a time, much later, when I wasn't welcome in this cathedral. After the new Bishop took over. Not only because I had become a leper—that I could understand, but because—Oh, well, never mind. It's over now. Sixty years have passed and here I am—back in my cathedral, and obviously once more in favor. All kinds of dignitaries are filing past the koa casket. A solemn Pontifical Mass is being celebrated, and the Bishop is saying extravagant things about me and reading a message from the Vatican. Now I understand what this is all about: it seems my native country, Belgium, wants me to come home.

(Making the sign of the Cross)

DAMIEN: Go. The Mass is ended.

(Coming downstage right. To the audience)

DAMIEN: The koa casket is carried from the cathedral. The army caisson is loaded and the military procession moves down Bishop Street to King, across King and on down Bishop to the pier where a white ship waits to receive me into her hold. The military band begins its dirge, but I—I hear the anguished farewell chant, the cries of lepers as small boats ferry them to a vessel farther out, waiting—as my boat waits—to receive them into her hold, to carry them to Moloka'i.

(Looking out over the audience)

DAMIEN: Moloka'i. Usually it's no trick at all to see her silhouette on the horizon. Today the light's not right. Never mind. In a little while we'll pass quite close enough to see her clearly.

(To the audience)

DAMIEN: The first time I saw Moloka'i—the Grey Island as the lepers called it—was from the railing of the ship that brought me to the islands. St. Patrick's Day, 1864, the *R. M. Wood*, five months out of Bremerhaven, entering Hawaiian waters under full sail, sweeps past the other islands till it comes close enough to Moloka'i that I can see a part of it distinctly. A narrow, sour tongue of land sticks out into the sea—the loneliest, most useless piece of land you can imagine. Barren, rockstrewn, wind-whipped—I still find it unbelievable that I could pass so close without some premonition of what it would become: a place of horror, a dumping ground for lepers, the saddest spot on earth.

Of course I had no way of knowing that, while we were still two months at sea, a doctor in Honolulu had declared: "I take this opportunity to bring before the public a subject of great importance. I mean, of course, the rapid spread of that new disease called by the natives *ma'i Pākē*. It is, ladies and gentlemen, true Oriental leprosy, and it will be the duty of the next legislature to take some measures—effective but humane—by which may be accomplished the segregation of all those afflicted."

(Pause)

DAMIEN: From opposite directions, we—leprosy and I—had come to the Sandwich Islands. Contemporaries, you might say, although leprosy was old as time when it arrived and I was barely twenty-four.

(Pause)

DAMIEN: The military dirge comes to an end. A farewell chant starts softly, then fills the air.

Am I remembering? Or hearing it again?

Is it for lepers long ago? Is it for me? But I am out of time—the chants, the boats, the two processions merge, become the same forever. One could not be without the other.

The chant comes to an end. Airplanes cut the sky to ribbons. The koa casket goes aboard. The whistle blows. The white ship, impatient to be off, pulls from her slip and moves out into the channel.

Along the shore, off to the left, half hidden in a grove of palm trees, is the government building that housed the agency entrusted with taking measures—effective but humane—toward segregation of the lepers: The Board of Health.

(Moving downstage left, to the Board of Health area)

DAMIEN: In all good faith they made those yellow flags and nailed them up throughout the kingdom, on trees and posts and sides of buildings—even on the chapel doors of my Kohala Mission.

In all good faith, I'm sure, they bought that sour tongue of land I first saw from the ship. That natural prison, surrounded on three sides by vicious surf and on the fourth by sheer black cliffs that stopped prevailing winds and made them dump their rain; that shut out the sun at noon so the land lay half a day in shadow. "The place without a sunset," the lepers called it.

In all good faith that government body rounded up the lepers—at gunpoint when necessary—and shipped them off with a pair of pants or a cotton dress and a promise of daily rations to supplement what it was hoped the lepers themselves would produce.

In all good faith they called an empty wooden building a hospital and promised to staff it and stock it with supplies.

Effective? Yes. It got the lepers out of circulation so the foreign population could relax.

Humane? No! It was a barbarous method of isolation. That tongue of land became a living graveyard. Can you imagine hundreds—sometimes as many as a thousand—lepers, crowded six, eight, ten, into stinking one-room windowless shacks? Can you imagine a community of the living dead, without a doctor or a nurse? No resident police, no law, no work, no comfort, and no hope. As for the hospital—an empty building where the sickest ones lay on the bare floor in their own filth and waited. But no one came—except the flies by day and the rats by night to feast upon their sores.

Some of the more able-bodied lepers, determined to wrest the last bit of pleasure from their lives, gathered in a separate place, dubbed the Village of the Fools, brewed liquor from the roots of plants and spent their days and nights drinking, gambling, whoring, and boasting, " 'A'ole kānāwai ma kēia wahi"—in this place there is no law! And raiding the rest of the Settlement—stealing little girls and boys to use as slaveys or to satisfy their lust.

(Moving downstage center, pointing)

DAMIEN: There—off to the right—that's Moloka'i, its harborless coast, its steep black cliffs that plunge straight down into the sea.

The *second* time I saw Moloka'i was the day before Easter,
1873. A cattle boat en route from Maui to Honolulu, Bishop
Maigret and I aboard, stops long enough to land some lepers and
fifty head of cattle in its hold. Lepers from the Settlement crowd
the landing.

(Moving down the runway , looking upward)

DAMIEN: Look at them! Not one or two or three, but hundreds! In varying
stages of corruption, as if the grave has given up its dead. Walking, limping, crawling; they even come in wheelbarrows.
Maimed and twisted bodies, sunken faces, missing limbs, mag-
got-bloated sores. How, dear God, can such things be? I cannot
bear to look at them and yet I cannot tear my eyes away as they
reach out their rotting arms to welcome new lepers to this place
of horror. And they are singing—singing!
Leprosy and I are face-to-face at last.

(Turning to the neutral area, midstage left)

DAMIEN: The Catholic lepers are gathered round the Bishop, begging him
to send a priest—not four on a rotating basis as His Excellency
proposes—but one to live among them, to call them by their
names, to be a father to them. And he is telling them he cannot
ask that sacrifice of anyone. And still they beg.

(To the Bishop)

DAMIEN: They are right, Your Excellency. They must have one priest who
belongs to them. To prove to them that God has not forgotten
them. I suffer if I go a week without confession. They must go
months—years—without confession and the Mass. They must
face death without the sacraments. . . . You don't have to ask,
Your Excellency. I want to be their priest. I beg to stay.

(To the audience)

DAMIEN: Impetuosity, the Bishop says. Unbalanced generosity. Overreac-
tion to so much brutal suffering. If it had been right, and practical, he'd have sent someone long ago. He would have come
himself. Others, before me, have volunteered, but they have been
denied. No one, no one, he says, can put aside all human considerations and live—the one clean man—among a thousand lepers.
I don't seem to hear what he is saying. I only see their need and
know what I must do.

You see, a man enters the religious life in answer to a "call." Later, if he is lucky, he receives a "call within a call," he finds the niche that he was meant to fill.

This is my niche. This is what I was meant to do. This is why I was born.

So, like the stubborn Fleming that I am, I stick to my guns until His Excellency finally says—God help us both—that if I promise to be prudent I may stay as long as my devotion dictates. That's all I ask—to stay as long as my devotion dictates.

(Calling out to the lepers)

DAMIEN: You have your priest! Do you hear? I am to be your priest. My name is Kamiano. Confessions this afternoon, all night if necessary. And Easter Mass at sunrise!

(To the audience)

DAMIEN: Next morning, while it is still dark, the little church starts filling up with—God forgive me—creatures from a nightmare, limping, shuffling, coughing, spitting, touching with the fingers they have left the rosaries hung round their necks. They keep on coming till the church is filled, up to the railing. They crowd the windowsills, the doorways; they fill the church to overflowing, not only with their corrupting bodies, not only with the stench, but with a sadness so unbearable I stand there dumb. The vomit rises in my throat. I choke it back. They kneel and wait, and finally, in a voice I have never heard before, I say the words: *In nomine Patris, et Filii, et Spiritus Sancti. Amen.*

I still remember that first Sunday. I remember going from shack to flimsy shack, visiting people too sick to leave their mats, appalled at so much concentrated misery. I remember wondering how a few leaves from the castor oil plant, tied together with tough grass and anchored to a crumbling stone wall, could provide as much shelter as they did.

I remember someone showing me the shack where Hua, the kahuna, lived. While we were there she came outside and pointed to a formation in the clouds—like a calabash mouth downward—and said it meant the king would die and Emma would be queen and she would let the lepers all go home.

And I remember a young woman in a dirty bathrobe sort of garment telling me she's cold, then opening up her bathrobe to show me she has nothing underneath.

Then there is the man who comes from one of the shacks, carrying a large bundle of dirty rags. He puts the bundle in the wheelbarrow, pushes it to the empty jail house, and shakes it till the dirty rags roll out. I see the bundle move; I hear it groan; I watch it pull itself into the doorway, and lie face down to die.

Later two lepers come, roll the bundle over, tie it to a pole— hands and feet like a luau pig—then take it to the cemetery and bury it in a shallow grave.

And I remember my first night, under the tree there in the cemetery, with rats and scorpions and centipedes to share my vigil, and the sound of wild pigs at that shallow grave, eating their fill.

It was three whole days before I could look at some of the lepers without revulsion. Weeks before I could endure the graveyard smell.

A visiting doctor or agent of the Board of Health would always put a piece of camphor in a handkerchief and tie it round his neck, and every now and then he'd spray himself with camphor liquid. I chose a pipe. And strong black coffee.

The first few weeks I camped outdoors.

(Moving to his quarters)

DAMIEN: Eventually we built my quarters—the more able-bodied lepers and I. Ambrose made that window frame. He'd never touched a tool before. Now they feel the place is theirs somehow. They come here in the evenings, go out there on the lanai with their guitars and sing and play, and in the dark forget that they are lepers.

There was no water at the Settlement. We had to carry it long distances in dirty oil cans and let it stand for days. I couldn't wash my hands or soak my feet without robbing someone of his drinking water. So I roamed the hills for days until I found a place where we could build a reservoir. Some of the lepers helped me lay the pipes and we had running water!

The day my quarters were finished three women, Malia, Philomela, and Elikapeka, said they wanted to keep house for me. Their leper husbands were dead. They themselves were clean. When I hesitated, Philomela laughed. *"Manuahi*, Kamiano. Like you—we work for free." How could I refuse? I can still hear them laughing at me.

I can hear their scornful laughter, too, when my enemies started peddling scandalous stories about me.

(Crossing over to speak to the Bishop)

DAMIEN: Yes, Your Excellency, I do leave my door open and the light burning all night. . . . Because a priest can do no less. . . . Yes, I leave
it open to women as well as men—they get sick and frightened,
too. . . . Whoever comes to me comes as Christ, Your Excellency
knows that. . . . What do I care what the gossips say? . . . Yes, I
rub ointment on their sores with my bare hands. . . . What would
Your Excellency have me do? Attend only to the men and boys?
Leave the medicine on the gatepost as visiting doctors do? Talk
to my lepers through closed windows? Exhort them from the
pulpit but never chat with them in private? I'm not an agent of
the Board of Health, Your Excellency. I am their priest. Their
father in Christ. I'm there to comfort them, to win their hearts
and souls. . . .

Yes, I did promise to be prudent, and in my own way I am prudent. Since I am there to comfort Christ in them I am prudent
never to let even a shadow of fear or disgust come between us;
never to let there be anything but love. . . . Your Excellency, I
don't quarrel with other people's ideas of prudence; let no one
quarrel with mine. . . .

Yes, I do share my pipe with them. When we're together of an
evening, and I light my pipe, and one of them wants a puff or two,
can I refuse? Can I, Your Excellency? . . . Yes, I've thought of
that. . . . If it is God's will, I am prepared. . . .

By remembering that those worm-infested ulcers are the
wounds of Christ—that's how I manage to go on from day to
day. . . . If that's the way Your Excellency sees it, then I suppose I
am a fool.

(He kneels abruptly to kiss the ring, turns to go, then turns back)

DAMIEN: Yes, Your Excellency?

(Kneeling once more to kiss the ring)

DAMIEN: Thank you, Your Excellency. Thank you very much.

(To the audience)

DAMIEN: His Excellency said he meant I was a fool for Christ.

Intermission

4

GROWING UP ELSEWHERE

Reuel Denney

Reuel Denney is perhaps best known as the co-author of one of the most famous books of social analysis In America—*The Lonely Crowd: A Study of the Changing American Character*, written with David Reisman and Nathan Glazer. The book added the terms *inner-directed* and *other-directed* to our language, along with the familiar title phrase, thereby performing the most elemental and near-magical function of poetic language: the naming of things, in this case naming types of social character. In such a collaborative work it might be difficult to ascertain precisely who wrote what. However, it was rumored among Reuel's students at the University of Chicago that whenever *The Lonely Crowd* got poetic, that was Reuel Denney's part.

Denney's uniqueness as a poet and scholar derives partially from the enormous range of his intellectual interests and the originality of his thinking and publishing in so many diverse fields of knowledge. His innovative 1957 study of popular culture, *The Astonished Muse*, helped legitimize serious study of the artifacts and constructs of popular media such as movies, comics, sports, radio, and television.

Throughout his career, which included stints as writer and contributing editor for *Time* magazine, and writer and associate editor for *Fortune*, Denney found himself returning to teaching. After his years at the University of Chicago, he joined the faculties of the University of Hawai'i and the East-West Center in 1961. He remained with UH for the remainder of his career and retired as an Emeritus Professor of American Studies. Visiting professorships and fellowships also took him to Harvard, Kyoto, India, Puerto Rico, and California.

Always his major interest was poetry. His first collection of poems, *The Connecticut River and Other Poems*, won the Yale Series of Younger Poets award in 1939, selected by Stephen Vincent Benet. Other volumes of poetry include *In Praise of Adam* (1961) and the book-length poem *The Portfolio of Benjamin Latrobe* (1984).

At the time of his death in 1995 Denney was working on a number of projects, including a novel, a book of collected poems, and a gathering of essays. "The Squire of Melford," the piece included in this anthology, is a lyrical reflection on his boyhood in an Irish family in Brooklyn, part of an extended memoir-in-progress.

BY TONY QUAGLIANO*

*This introductory note is based on an article that was originally published in *Poetry Pilot* in 1988.

The Squire of Melford

It was World War I and then the years just after the Armistice. A good place to grow up at that time was a street in Brooklyn close to Gravesend Bay. At least Rick thought so.

In the wintertime the sunshine grew pale with afternoon and was suddenly replaced by a rush of darkness. Down the street came a man on a bicycle carrying a torch on a long pole. He stopped at the streetlamp near the house, turned on the gas and applied the torch. The yellow light rallied and bloomed and a man next door put on the phonograph an aria that sang whatever the lamplighter was thinking, in a voice that was supplied by Enrico Caruso.

"*E lucevan le stelle . . .*"

In the summertime, the darkness and the lamplighting came much later, of course, and Rick had to plead that he was in the middle of reading a chapter in order to stay up late enough to see the lighter at his magical task—and watch the drunken old yachtsman who lived across the street totter home from his club.

The war did wonders for the street. The Hoffmans who lived at the corner prospered with their dye plant and the children of the house were well supplied with sample powder bags of the finest analine hues. Noble, their shepherd dog, never had to appear in public in his ordinary coat—he was often purple from ears to shoulder and lemon yellow in the hindquarters. He made a fine sight following the Hoffman boys to a game of cat-and-stick in the street or tennis on the broken-down deserted court at the other corner of the block. Noble's colors were the moving advertisement for the main tennis court exhibition of the summer afternoon. This took place when his master, fourteen-year-old Alexander Hoffman, opened his fly.

"Show me a hard-on bigger than that," he said.

No boy was then of an age to be up to the challenge. Rick and the tennis crowd soon returned to the normal activity of the tournament—rescuing the single tennis ball from the slavering jaws of the court-wise Noble.

The biggest punchball team on the block was fielded by the sons and daughters of the rabbi who lived opposite the Hoffmans in a house that was small for that family of ten. Naomi was a beautifully built, long-legged girl whose place at third base was flagged by the large birthmark on the left side of her face. One of the best players, she never cried out in pain. When short of players, the team of the rabbi's family accepted all comers to their ranks. But their custom was clear: no recruit was assigned as anything but an outfielder.

"If they stick around, they get a chance at shortstop or second base," said Nathan, the oldest.

But one season a torrent of red leaves from the maple trees carpeted the street, the World Series loomed, and streetball players went back to school, and Rick was still only an outfielder.

School days or vacation days, the neighborhood centered in the little house where Rick and his mother lived with his grandparents while his father was away at war or just back from war and away looking for a job. The house was warm and the food was acceptable. At one time Rick had been driven to protest the meals. In a fairy tale that was read to him, a tiny tailor was trapped in a castle to make clothes for his captor and he wrote a message on the portals: "Too much turnips and not enough meat." Rick was inspired to write in chalk on the tiles of the entrance walk "too much potatoes and not enough meat." Grandmother accepted this with a prophecy that Rick would become a Tammany lawyer and turned her talk back to the subject of grandfather, who was known to her as "Himself."

Himself was the one who sometimes roused from the great rocker in which he read books from the Brooklyn Public Library—*Kenilworth* and *Coniston*— and put on his old felt hat and pushed his wheelbarrow to the beach. There he collected timbers washed in from barges and freighters and brought them home for kindling wood. Bucksaw and sawhorse enabled him to cut the logs into lengths and then he axed them along the grain on his chopping block. The wood smelled of pine, tar, iodine, and bilge and was a great help in starting the furnace and the kitchen stove. That is, until the furnace was converted for coal and the kitchen stove for gas.

"What a grace a kitchen gas stove is."

This was no great change as far as Rick was concerned. But he was accustomed to going to the store to buy a gaslight mantle which, when fitted over the gaslamp and lighted, took on a wonderful white incandescence. One summer all gaslights vanished, replaced by the fierce inhuman glare of electric bulbs.

"A new hat."

It was rumored around the house that Himself, grandfather, had voiced these words. To whom? It was not clear. Grandmother denied that he had said them in their hearing. The same with his son, his daughter, his son-in-law, and his grandson Rick. Yet Rick was familiar with his grandfather's habit of suddenly saying a phrase and then retreating into his book and pipe smoke. "His

Honor Mayor John F. Hylan!" or "Teddy the Ready Roosevelt!" or "Brian Boru" or "Coxey's Army!" or "Remember The Maine!" or "John L. Sullivan!" He did not seem to expect an answer to these inscriptions on the air.

What then about a new hat—if he had really said it? What did it mean? Morning and night the adult members of the family discussed this question.

As if for clues, observations were made of grandfather's old hat on the rack in the hall. It was characterized in various ways by various members of the family. Grandmother: "Worse than the curse of Cromwell." In her sounds, this came out as "Worse than the curse of Crummel." The mother: "Mouldy." The son: "Vaudeville." The article under scrutiny was a grey homburg that had turned old-hat green since its purchase twenty years earlier for a trip to Killarney, Ireland.

It was gradually concluded that the old man wanted to buy a new hat. For what? Another trip to Killarney? Or a visit to the old firehouse? This had to be investigated. Rick's mother was given the assignment of interviewing the old man to find out exactly what her father's intentions were.

Listening to the kitchen conversation of the grown-ups, but particularly the endless exchanges of information and opinion about the hat between his mother and his grandmother, Rick got some ideas of what was troubling the family about the hat. The wearing of the homburg by grandfather was associated in the family memory of the grown-ups not only with the famous trip to Killarney but also his preretirement jaunts into rural Connecticut.

Reading novels about American country folk, especially Yankees, had awakened a certain ambition in the man. He had learned his trade of handling horses as the groom and then the chief coachman of an English estate in southern Ireland. The idea of becoming a landowning squire on a small place in Connecticut, after he retired, struck him as a grand notion. Many a weekend he boarded a train at Grand Central with a round-trip ticket to a Connecticut town in hand. Arriving, he walked circling miles from the station, looking for farms that were for sale and noting their location and points. Then back to town, where he noted the name and address of the town's most imposing bank, a source of mortgage money, before taking his train back to New York.

As complex as all this was, it could be generally understood by a boy as young as Rick because it was told vividly and repeatedly in the kitchen conferences of his mother and his grandmother.

The old man evidently made no secret of his dreams about coming into a modest landed estate.

The old woman said: " 'Tis no strange thing that Himself would have had a craving for a country place, like a dog for a marrow bone. Wasn't he brought up on the easy side? A favored groom on a rich estate and, when he was head coachman, keeping a fine room over the barns and a servant to kindle his fire for him. He thought the country life was all show and shooting."

The old woman had been trained as a dairy maid, with a day starting four-thirty in the summer and ending not till candlelight.

"All show and shooting and going to the fair. Well, I thought, he can emigrate to Connecticut and welcome be the riddance of him, thinking that I would come up there and run out in the farmyard just to pump a pitcher of water and have a bathroom in the fields and no light in the house but a dirty oil lamp making smoke that penetrates the house and even poisons the pillowslips!"

All that was time past. The old woman's resistance to a country move had been successful.

Rick's mother soon established that the old man was not planning a trip to his realtor or his banker and indeed had no travel plan at all. But before she could learn more, the day approached for the hat-buying trip.

A family tradition of frugality required that men's new hats be purchased from a "Reject Shop" where one of the great hat manufacturers sold off the glamorous models of its assembly line that had not passed the inspector. It had been years since the last visit to the shop, and careful scheduling and planning for the trip were necessary—everyone wanted to go along in the automobile for the excursion, so the timing of the event had to fit everyone. While all this consulting went on, Rick tried to distract himself from his keen impatience for the trip by organizing campfires to cook potatoes in the empty lot opposite the tennis court and activating the rabbi's son Moishe to arrange for their acceptance as hangers-on at weddings in the synagogue so that they could help themselves to cake and fruit at the banquet table.

They were on their way back from the second of these raids when the day darkened on the parkway and thunder broke loose directly over them. It ripped its way through the sky and let down a rain heavier than any they had ever seen before. They were already wet, if not soaked to the skin, as they scrambled into the small entrance lobby of an apartment house. As they watched, the rain grew heavier, the sky exploded, and a stroke of lightning landed with a crash and a flash in an evergreen tree on the opposite side of the parkway. It split the trunk and skinned half of it and left a strange turpentiny electrical smell in the air. Moishe remarked that an angry god might be searching them out in vengeance for their repeated misrepresentations of themselves as bona fide guests at the weddings. Then he decided not.

"My father says he is too busy to bother with small offenders."

The day came when the expedition beyond the neighborhood to find the hat warehouse set out in the uncle's Chevrolet. The car was pointed along one of the avenues that would bring them to industrial Brooklyn, and the changes of route on the way were hotly discussed as they rolled along.

"No! No! Atlantic Avenue is that way!"

Tree-shaded avenues gave way to long rows of apartment buildings and a maze of factories and warehouses, buildings sometimes marked with large signs showing their place in the coffee, sugar, chemical, or paper trades, sometimes with blank faces that gave no hint at all of their occupations. The smoke and steam escaping from various stacks and vents at all levels of the great structures at first suggested that they were busy producing salt, steel, cardboard boxes, and filing cases without the assistance of human hands. But a certain moving and loading and unloading of green Mack trucks by men in resolute action was a dramatic reminder that human beings were involved. The car passed through narrow streets and wide ones and over viaducts and under railroad bridges and arrived at the place of hats.

It was a shockingly modest establishment. The corner of a factory had been architecturally modeled into a shop that stood on the intersection of an industrial street and a driveway that paralleled a railway cut. It jutted small and triangular at the corner, and the door of the shop stood up on three steps in the center of the blunted point of the triangle. There were no display cases, only a few windows for illumination. The name of the hat manufacturer on the arch over the door was so small that it was almost as if the company was trying to hide the fact that its inspectors sometimes spotted a defect that landed a new hat in this limbo. And with not a living soul in sight in any direction, it appeared that they might have succeeded.

Rick had no interest in the hat collection and agreed to sit in the car while his uncle and his mother accompanied the old man into the shop. He all too quickly read through the funny-paper book that he had acquired during a stop on the way. Soon his sense of time seemed to go off duty and he could not tell for sure whether he had been waiting five minutes or twenty. Restless, he got out of the car and walked over to the high cyclone fence that bordered the drop of the railway cut.

At first sight this was a vantage on another desert—a long, slightly curving pair of railroad lines sweeping into a perspective point in the black depths of a tunnel a block or two away. Fortunately for the sake of a young boy overcome by ennui, there was a small locomotive on one of the tracks, idling between jobs. It gave off a self-satisfied breathing of boilers and flues as it sent up a small spiral of smoke and displayed spurs of steam at its foretruck. After a few minutes it slowly heaved itself forward for a few yards and then began an officious run backwards toward the tunnel in the distance. In contrast to the brick and concrete emptiness of the surroundings, it gave a sudden spurt of vitality to the region. Then it vanished into the tunnel.

Waiting for it to come back again, perhaps with some loaded flat cars in couple, seemed no great burden. But minutes passed and the locomotive did not reappear. Perhaps by this time it was miles off and on a different spur, plying some unknown errand that would take it the rest of the day—or eternity for that matter. The tunnel into which it had vanished seemed to suggest that both tunnel and locomotive would grow smaller and smaller as they proceeded until there was so little left of them that they passed by necessity into another world—an opposing universe containing an opposing hat store, an antithetical railway cut, and a mirror-image Rick.

By now the line of time itself seemed so stretched out by some invisible force that the sun and the shadows stood still and the hands on the time clock in the factories, like those of the bewitched clock of a fairy story, became stuck on the clock face and could not move forward.

Rick was challenged by the idea that under certain circumstances the activities of everyday life—such as an expedition to buy a hat—necessarily led out of the neighborhood into a nonneighborhood that hypnotized and paralyzed by its blandness and indifference. Even the one sound of life, the engine, had been removed. There was no story in anything. Everything was like a stalled car.

Had the hat led then to another world, a zone of danger?

Had the adults, failing to come back out of the store, actually been deceived by the false storefront into walking straight into a trapdoor that dropped them into a pit? Would they ever surface again?

What was the Hat up to?

The voices of the shopping party could be heard coming out of the store and the child turned to see them heading to the car. His uncle was carrying a cylindrical box.

"Are you satisfied now?" asked Rick's uncle as he started the car.

The old man grunted and said "William Howard Taft!" His expression did not make clear whether he approved or disapproved of that personage, whoever he was.

On the way back, they were held up by a line of cars departing slowly, behind a hearse, from the funeral parlor on the right side of their route. The hearse was heavily decorated with flowers and the cortege was classy—Cadillac and Lincoln limousines moving like black mirrors in the pale sunlight.

"It's Frankie Yale," said Rick's uncle. "What they call a difference in the Family."

Having passed through the zone of gangster funerals, they reached home in time to find the punchball team of the rabbi's children still at play. Rick became so involved with the game that when it ended and he came back into the house he had forgotten about the hat. He was surprised to see that the hatbox, looking as if it were still unopened, stood on the little table in the front parlor. He secretly hefted it and the weight of the hat was still inside it. He figured that the grandfather had checked out the article and intended to come back to it later.

And this is what must have happened because the hat itself turned up on the hat rack sometime during the next week or so. It was a handsome thing, quite equal to those that had been worn by the male mourners at the funeral of the late gangster Frankie Yale.

Days after its enthronement on the hat rack, it was still there.

One day when Rick came home from school he was surprised to see the old man standing in front of the hat rack mirror. He was adjusting the fit of the new homburg and completely absorbed in the look of it.

But he never really used it, and there was no sign that he intended to. The maple trees sent off their winged seeds and their leaves curled in the street, getting in the way of steel ball bearings employed in the boys' game of chase-and-touch along the gutters. Soon even the fallen leaves were gone, raked up by the street-sweeper men. Their fires burned until lamplighter time.

Leon Edel

Leon Edel is esteemed as the definitive biographer and foremost editor and scholar of Henry James. Edel's biographical method depends upon careful attention to detail, a novelistic command of narrative flow, and an interest in the psychological dimensions of the artistic mind. The second volume in his five-volume study of James won both the Pulitzer Prize and the National Book Award. Other volumes were met with similar acclaim and critical enthusiasm. His biography of the Bloomsbury group is comparable to the James series in the intricacy and psychological delicacy of the interwoven stories it tells. His other works include biographies of Henry Thoreau, James Joyce, and Willa Cather; as well as distinguished works on the theory of biography and of the psychological novel.

After a long career as a teacher and scholar in New York City, Edel moved to Honolulu in the early 1970s to become the first permanently appointed Citizen's Professor of English at the University of Hawai'i at Mānoa. On the occasion of his retirement from the University of Hawai'i, he remarked on his vigorous second literary career in Honolulu. "I have a feeling today of what the French call *déjà vu*, I retired in 1971 from New York University and now I am retiring all over again. The last time, I told my students and colleagues that if they had a notion I would spend the rest of my days sauntering with a mai tai in my hand on the Hawaiian beaches talking to mermaids and dolphins, they could forget it. I was going to continue to write and teach. What shall I say today? I recall when I arrived here I told you that I would not allow the Citizen's Chair to become a rocking chair. Looking back I ask myself why was I such a drudge? There's a lot to be said for rocking chairs. . . . I will let Shakespeare speak for me: 'Men must endure their going hence, even as their coming hither. Ripeness is all.' "

"A Town in Saskatchewan," the excerpt from Edel's memoirs included in this anthology, makes its first appearance here. Professor Edel, still not resorting to the rocking chair, continues work on his extensive memoirs as this anthology goes to press.

A Town in Saskatchewan

My early years, those of discovery and recognition, were spent in a town called Yorkton in the Canadian province of Saskatchewan. The very linking of the Anglo name to the multisyllabled Saskatchewan showed a promising recognition of the Indian presence, but if you studied the map you found almost everywhere an emanation of the British Isles, at least in the names bestowed on the little would-be towns, handiwork of a railroad that had united Canada but then had to find passengers and freight in order to go on existing. The towns were named before they acquired buildings and habitations. The province's Indian name was actually Kisiskatchewan and it meant "swift current." It belonged to the thousand-mile river that sprang out of the Rocky Mountains skirting southwest Alberta, then crossed land-locked Saskatchewan and entered Manitoba, pouring its waters into Lake Winnipeg. The Anglo names—Worcester, Yorkton itself, Melville, Bedfordville, Churchbridge, Blackwood, and many more like these—had no relation to the terrain of the prairies that would ultimately be filled with golden wheat; nor with the immigrants that the railway drew with offers of land and a future, Russians, Ukrainians, Jews, Poles, Germans, Swedes, Lithuanians, Czechs, and other Europeans who sought, like the Puritans, an escape from old tyrannies. They faced new tyrannies, frozen winters and scorching summers, pioneering in the days when the Model T was yet to come. Radio and later TV were not even dreams, and the iceman delivered to homes the frozen residues of Canadian lakes and rivers. There were scatterings of other names, a few Indian, some French. The railroad towns often remained one-street affairs, a store, perhaps a post office and a bank, sometimes a church. It was a lonely land. I should add that in all my young years in Yorkton, I never saw an Indian.

My father, Simon Edel, was 23 when he fled Russia. There were massacres of Jews, pogroms. He had seen Canadian Pacific advertisements that promised land and a future and freedom from racial torment. The train set him down in Winnipeg, where he worked first on the railroad, then found odd jobs. He felt he should find a craft or trade, and was told he could learn about the clothing industry in Pittsburgh, in the United States. He crossed the Canadian border, marveling that no passport was required. In Pittsburgh he learned English and worked for a tailor. In due course he earned enough to send for his childhood love to join him in America. She came; they were married and in 1907, I was born. A second son followed; suddenly Simon was supporting a small family on $18 a week.

I must have been about three when my father lost his job during one of America's chronic recessions. My mother, Fannie Malamud, who was considered a "brainy" woman, urged him to remain in the United States and ride out the depression. But father's sister and her husband urged him to join them in blossoming Saskatchewan. His brother-in-law had obtained some of the available land and was prospering. He had begun opening stores in little empty towns to serve the immigrant farmers who were breaking the prairie land. Simon was offered management of one of these in a northern town. It was a solitary trading post with perhaps five or six houses. Fannie spent a frozen winter and experienced the loneliness of being a "pioneering" woman. In the spring she announced that her father had sent money for travel. Like Nora in Ibsen's *A Doll's House*, she was taking the children to her parents. She would visit until Simon could find some more urban place to live and work, and perhaps independence from his brother-in-law. From age four to five I found myself in a Russian *shtetel*, a part of the city of Rovno, near Kiev. My languages became Russian and Yiddish. Then after thirteen months my maternal grandfather told Fannie there would soon be a war in Europe and she had better return to Canada. We retraced our journey across the Atlantic and this time went to Yorkton—population 2,000.

By the time the war came we were settled, first in a house without plumbing, behind the rough wooden store Simon managed for his brother-in-law. We had a pump and an outhouse; mother bathed me every morning in a big washtub in water heated on a woodburning stove. I don't know the rest of that part of our story, but during 1913–1914 Simon set up his own trading post in Betts Avenue that the Anglos called "Jew-street," for the Jewish immigrants had created a little Canadian ghetto and built a synagogue in Yorkton.

We now lived in a sunny house with plumbing, and a barn with horses in it. Family friends were always coming to see us; for example, a short, twinkly, mustached man, the town barber, a lanky, tall, and cheerful man named Lazar who ran a livery stable, and the Kreissers, a couple from Willowbrook fifteen miles away that didn't have the railroad. They usually came for weekends in Yorkton to get away from the isolated half-dozen houses and their store.

One of the distractions of our parents and these friends was to walk to the end of Betts Avenue where the handsome red-brick Yorkton Collegiate Institute stood, with its rows of shining windows and its turreted portico that architecturally went back to Victorian pseudo-Roman. The raised entrance had two wooden Corinthian columns on either side. The approach was on curved cement sidewalks bordered by curved formal flower beds properly laid out in group plantings, a delightful mass of yellows, reds, blues, and in-between colors splashed against the edges of the scrupulously mowed lawns that stretched on either side into the surrounding prairie—an imposing build-ing set into a wilderness. My childhood eyes ignored the columns. They saw an effect of great neatness and order. Mother pointed to the signs: "keep off the grass," no touching, no picking. Soft, squatting, velvety purple and yel-lowy petalled flowers were identified as pansies. One of our elders explained that in Saskatchewan you planted hardy perennials. What I saw on these occa-sions, I later learned, were asters, phlox, columbines, marigolds, and tiny for-get-me-nots; also violets and geraniums. I have never forgotten the trimness; it reminded me of my father who insisted on absolute neatness in his new store at the other end of the avenue. I later learned the school building was just two years old. It had been a town extravagance of $54,000. We started school in this collegiate institute, which had special kindergarten rooms for youngsters. I think my parents and their friends liked the school, for it was Yorkton's one significant European-like building, unless you included the old Hudson's Bay store built of stone, which had two stories on the main street. Aside from a couple of banks, a big hardware store, and a drugstore that sold many other things beside pills, Yorkton was built of wood on small lots with small houses to withstand temperatures of fifty below zero.

I remember also picking wildflowers on the wide prairie that stretched beyond Yorkton's few streets. We would drive out in one of Lazar's horse bug-gies and picnic next to wheatfields and wild rose bushes. We gathered the pale pink petals, put them into big paper bags, and Mother made rose jelly from them. Being an intellectual, Mother approached the act of smelling as if it were a duty. "One should smell roses," she said. We obeyed. They had a faint pleasurable odor. I would discover richer-smelling bright red roses later and Yorkton's intoxicating June lilacs.

A sign proclaimed "S. Edel, General Store," but in reality Father's store came closer to being another trading post. The basic business of the little establish-ment was barter. Farmers from the area brought their produce and left with groceries, clothing, and other necessities. Simon arranged his small store neatly and efficiently. He knew exactly where everything belonged—the bags of dried chickpeas and other beans were up front; there was candy on the counter and a small scale for weighing everything he sold. To the rear a sepa-rate counter was devoted to dry goods and ready-made clothing. Father oiled the floor, as was the custom, and had some old fashioned gaslights, little white hoods that spread a glaring light. My brother and I were allowed to visit on Saturday nights when it was kept open till 10 P.M. However, we were confined in the late twilights of summer to the broad planked sidewalk, thick boards with space between each board so you could see occasionally the glitter of dimes and nickels people sometimes lost: the coins were unreachable save by poking a stick with some chewing gum attached. The brawny farmers, most of them from Central Europe, liked the store. My parents could speak their languages and Father was gentle, modest, and helpful. Mother, on her side, when she was able to help, ran a kind of social agency to the rear of the store for the wives whose big breasts sagged and who wore *babushkas* as a head covering, knotted under their chins. They seemed billowed in fat. Mother created a center of advice on feminine hygiene, and, as I later learned, pregnancies. She told the women which doctors to see and had other practical counsel to a population that was wholly unlettered. Fannie used to talk about their ignorance; Father took a different view: they were finding in Canada freedom from Europe's iniquities, as he did. Yorkton, when I think of it today, reminds me of movie Westerns I have seen; those wooden sidewalks, the hitching posts, the big market place—where the farmers tied up their strong dray horses and big wagons when they came at the weekend. However, Yorkton differed from the Hollywood Westerns. It had no cowboys, no gunplay, no gambling, no bars, no loose women. It was a prohibition town. The Women's Christian Temperance Union, to which Fannie belonged, was a force in the town; also the Travelers' Aid, designed to help young women traveling alone in the Wild West. There was a big pool room near the railroad station and the town's hotel, The Balmoral—a "royal" name—where rumor had it that liquor was sold under the counter. When I reached more mature years I heard there had been a brothel in Betts Avenue. I considered this apocryphal. It wasn't in the tone of the town. But then we must remember, my observations belong to my childhood.

None of the Yorkton streets were paved. We lived through high snowdrifts, fifty-below winters, and periods of deep mud in torrid summer weather when the wheat fields turned bright yellow. Our Saturday nights at the store, when we played on the edges of the wooden walks, usually began around 7 P.M. with the weekly visit of the Salvation Army, which conducted a street prayer meeting in front of our hitching posts. There were young women with big bonnets who sang and men in uniforms with brass buttons who played a trumpet, a trombone, and banged a large drum. We listened not knowing what the word Salvation meant, but we heard an ex-drunk describe how he found Jesus and how his sins were washed away. I used to enjoy this little Saturday prelude, at the end of which the leader placed the drum on the edge of the walk and people dropped nickels, dimes, and quarters on it. Father always gave me a quarter to contribute and mother always said a dime would have been sufficient. When the little "Army" marched their round of stores singing military-like hymns, we renewed our search for stray coins below the sidewalk.

The farmers arrived with big tubs of creamy or bright yellow butter. They had boxes of fresh eggs as well as esoteric products, such as brown senega root in small white bags. Drug companies used this root to make expectorants. They had also piles of muskrat furs. There were specific laws for the weight and measure of the barter, and Father adhered to them, except that he often tended to give the farmers something additional to what he owed them.

Some time between 9 and 10 our lively evenings came to an end. The broad-shouldered farmers and their bulky wives drifted away, and Father began to close up. In good weather I liked to stand on the sidewalk's outer edge and look at the intense gaslight inside. Insects buzzed through it. The dark closed in as the light illuminated the heavy features of the lingering customers.

There were lights in adjoining stores and houses, but this was the hour when the heavens took over and great spreads of stars seemed very close to us. Best of all I liked the autumn evenings, when the air acquired a bracing chill, a foretaste of our winters. I used to sniff it as if I were a hound. It delighted me; it swept away the smell of the crowd and the store. I was awed by the dazzle and glitter of the skies. Various persons had shown me some of the constellations and I looked first for the big dipper, or Ursa Major, as I had been told it was named in Latin when people seemed to think the dipper looked more like a Great Bear. Sometimes a big moon lit up the sky as if in competition with the stars.

Above all, my memory calls up evenings when the sky startingly offered me a parade of Northern Lights—shimmering curtains of illumination, blown, as it seemed, by cosmic winds from side to side, cascades of yellow and white, steely verticals tumbling over one another, becoming suddenly diaphanous and then thickening and resembling giants on parade, great armies. The formations changed, constantly folding into the sky and shattering the blackness. I remember the Northern Lights nearly always in association with Simon's store and its human congregation. There were now few passersby on the walks and I felt myself alone and tiny before the heavenly panoply. I can only grope for language to describe what the small boy couldn't describe then: for him it was simply a great mysterious visual series of wonders, and somehow the lights seemed to crackle with ethereal sounds. This was the greatest drama Yorkton could offer me during my childhood years.

Maxine Hong Kingston

Highly acclaimed for several multifaceted books that combine autobiographical material with legendary and fictional elements, Maxine Hong Kingston's breakthrough as a writer came with the 1976 publication of *The Woman Warrior*, a work that was widely praised and received the National Book Critics Circle Award for nonfiction and several other distinguished recognitions.

The selection included in this anthology is taken from her second book, *China Men*. Among the remarkable features of this work is Kingston's gallery of fathers, grandfathers, and uncles whose strange adventures in the American "gold mountain" add up to a chronicle of the difficult and exciting lives experienced by the first several waves of male Chinese immigrants to America. The multipleness of her elder figures allows Kingston to develop the story of her roots in every which way she can report or invent. Was her father a severe Confucian scholar who passed the last Imperial Examination, stabbing himself in the thigh to stay awake for the entirety of the grueling test? Did he lament his unmotivated students? Did his activities in New York City include dancing like Fred Astaire down Fifth Avenue? Did she have a great-grandfather in Hawai'i who rebelled against the plantation by coughing out curses in Chinese in such a way that his fellow workers could understand but his white-demon foreman could not? Did she have a grandfather who helped to build the railroad through the unyielding granite of the Rocky Mountains? Ultimately, it does not matter which of these stories, if any, are specifically ancestral for Kingston. The important thing is that her versions of ancestors are, as one critic called them, "instinctively genuine" anecdotes that strike "emotional truth."

Kingston grew up in Stockton, California, but she lived in Hawai'i for many years, working as a teacher at both high school and university levels. She has a degree from UC Berkeley and has spent considerable time in the San Francisco area, a location that is important to her third book, *Tripmaster Monkey*.

The Making of More Americans

To visit grandfathers, we walked over three sets of railroad tracks, then on sidewalks cracked by grass and tree roots, then on a gray dirt path. The roadside weeds waved tall overhead, netting the sunlight and wildflowers. I wore important white shoes for walking to the grandfathers' house.

The black dirt in their yard set off my dazzling shoes—two chunks of white light that encased my feet. "Look. Look," said Say Goong, Fourth Grandfather, my railroad grandfather's youngest brother. "A field chicken." It was not a chicken at all but a toad with alert round eyes that looked out from under the white cabbage leaves. It hopped ahead of my shoes, dived into the leaves, and disappeared, reappeared, maybe another toad. It was a clod that had detached itself from the living earth; the earth had formed into a toad and hopped. "A field chicken," said Say Goong. He cupped his hands, walked quietly with wide steps and caught it. On his brown hand sat a toad with perfect haunches, eyelids, veins, and wrinkles—the details of it, the neatness and completeness of it, swallowing and blinking. "A field chicken?" I repeated. "Field chicken," he said. "Sky chicken. Sky toad. Heavenly toad. Field toad." It was a pun and the words the same except for the low tone of *field* and the high tone of *heaven* or *sky*. He put the toad in my hands—it breathed, and its heart beat, every part of it alive—and I felt its dryness and warmth and hind feet as it sprang off. How odd that a toad could be both of the field and of the sky. It was very funny. Say Goong and I laughed. "Heavenly chicken," I called, chasing the toad. I carefully ran between the rows of vegetables, where many toads, giants and miniatures, hopped everywhere. Which one was the toad in my hand? Then suddenly they were all gone. But they clucked. So it isn't because toads look or taste like chickens that they are called chickens; they cluck alike! Dragonflies held still in the air, suddenly darted. Butterflies in pairs flew far away from their partners, then together again. I stepped into a green hallway in the corn and sat in a tepee grown of vines over lattices; from ceilings and walls hung gourds, beans, tomatoes, grapes, and peas, winter melons like fat green prickly piglets, and bitter melons like green mice with tails. But the real marvel was the black dirt, which was clean and not dirty at all.

In one corner of the yard was a pile of horse manure taller than an adult human being. "Aiya! Aiya!" our parents, grandfathers, and neighbors exclaimed, eyes open in wonder as they stood around the pile, neighbors and friends invited especially to view it. "Come here! Come look! Oh, just look at it!"—I could tell that the adults felt what I felt, that I did not feel it alone, but truly. This pile hummed, and it was the fuel for the ground, the toads, the vegetables, the house, the two grandfathers. The flies, which were green and turquoise-black and silvery blue, swirling into various lights, hummed too, like excess sparks. The grandfathers boxed the horse manure, presents for us and their good friends to take home. They also bagged it in burlap. It smelled good.

Say Goong took my hand and led me to a cavernous shed black from the sun in my eyes. He pointed into the dark, which seemed solid and alive, heavy, moving, breathing. There were waves of dark skin over a hot and massive something that was snorting and stomping—the living night. In the day, here was where the night lived. Say Goong pointed up at a wide brown eye as high as the roof. I was ready to be terrified but for his delight. "Horse," he said. "Horse." He contained the thing in a word—*horse*, a magical and earthly sound. A horse was a black creature so immense I could not see the outlines. Grasping Say Goong's finger, I dared to walk past the horse, and then he pointed again. "Horse." There was a partition, and on the other side of it—another horse. There were two such enormities in the world. Again and again I looked inside the stalls to solve the mystery of what a horse was. On the out-side of the shed was horse shit, on the inside, the source of horse shit.

What I could see in its entirety because it was inanimate was the vegetable wagon, which was really a stagecoach. I climbed up a wheel and into the seat. I opened the compartments, drawers, and the many screened doors. A scale hung in back, and in front were reins and two long prongs.

When I heard hooves clippity-clopping down our street, I ran to the upstairs window and saw two grandfathers and the two horses, which were contained between the prongs. They had blinders cupping their eyes. I had discovered the daily shape of horses. My mother opened the window, and she and I made up a song about grandfathers and horses; we sang it to them in the interplaying rhythm of hooves on the street:

> Third Grandfather and Fourth Grandfather,
> Where are you going?
> Hooves clippity-clopping four by four,
> Where are you going?

"We're going to the north side to sell lettuce," they said. Or, the horses fac-ing another direction, "We're going to the feed store," or "We're going home." "We're going on our route of demonesses." The grandfathers could understand demon talk; they told us how the white ladies praised the tomatoes all the same size. "Allee sem," said the demonesses.

Sometimes under our very windows, the grandfathers fitted nosebags of oats over the horses' muzzles. The water for the horses had run into two buckets from a block of ice that sat melting in the middle of the wagon. The grandfathers sprinkled the vegetables with a watering can while the horses drank. Neighbors who had waited until late in the day for bargains circled the wagon. Through the screens they looked shrewdly at the red, yellow, and green vegetables. The god with the gourd had a gourd like the ones the grandfathers sold. At New Year's, tangerines hung by the branch from the roof, and in the fall persimmons. In summer, the grandfathers sold watermelons, which grew in China too, only there the meat was light pink and nobody we knew had ever tasted it. A railing along the top of the stagecoach kept the sacks of potatoes and yams from rolling off. Our family got what remained for free.

One time I went to the shed to have a look at the horses, and they were gone. "Where are the horses?" I asked. "They're gone," said both my parents with no surprise or emphasis. Not satisfied with the answer, I asked them again and again. Such vastness could not possibly have disappeared so completely. But they said, "They've been gone a long time." I walked inside each bare stall. "Where are the horses? Where are they?" "No more horses." "What happened to them?" "They've been gone for a long time." No explanation. Did they trot away down the street without the stagecoach and the grandfathers? Time must have gone by, then, since I'd last come to visit them, though the visits seemed like the same time, no time at all, time just one time, but it must have been later, a last time. I looked inside the first stall, looked again in the other one but found no aliveness there, bright now and not dark with horses. I could see boards and into corners, no vestige of horses, no hay spilling over the troughs, not a single yellow straw sticking out of a crack, the floor not covered with straw and horse shit, everything swept clean. Manure pile gone. I looked for proof of horses, and found it in the family album, which has photographs of horses with blinders, though the men standing in front of the wagons are not the grandfathers but the uncles, the same ones who later had their pictures taken with cars and trucks.

The stagecoach was still there. I sat in the seat, shook the reins, and looked in the distance for Indians and bison.

One day, Sahm Goong, Third Grandfather, came to our house alone, and he said to my mother, "Say Goong is standing in the stable."

"No." said my mother. "He's dead."

"He's in the stable. I saw him. I left him there just now, standing by the wall near the door."

"What was he doing?"

"Just standing there. Not working."

"You know he's dead, don't you?"

"Yes. It must be his ghost standing there. He comes to visit me every day."

"What does he have to say?" she asked.

"Nothing. I talk to him, but he doesn't answer."

"You tell him to go home," said my mother. "Scold him. 'Go home!' Loud. Like that. 'Go home, Say Goong!' " They both called him that name, even though he was my fourth grandfather, not theirs.

Sahm Goong walked back home. He sat on a crate in the empty stable, the gray floorboards awash with afternoon sun. There in the shade beside the door stood his brother.

"How nice of you to visit me again," said Sahm Goong.

Say Goong did not reply. He was wearing his good clothes, his new bib overalls, a white shirt, a tie, his cardigan, and his cloth cap, which he had worn when working in the yard or driving the stagecoach.

"Sit down," invited Sahm Goong, but his brother did not want to. He certainly could not be seen through, and he was not floating; he had his feet on the floor. The high work shoes were polished.

Third Grandfather stood up and walked over to Fourth Grandfather, the two of them the same size. They did not touch each other. "I am very well, you know," the live grandfather said. "My health is good. Yes, the rest of the family is fine, too. Though there are a lot girls. We're all well." Say Goong did not say a thing. Sahm Goong walked sideways and examined him in profile; he certainly looked as usual. Then Sahm Goong sat down again, looking a moment into the garden. When he looked back, his brother was still there— no shimmering, no wavering, just as solid and real as ever before. The two brothers stayed with each other until suppertime. Then Sahm Goong went in the house to cook and eat.

After dinner he took his flashlight and went again into the shed. He shone it into the place where the ghost had been. He was still there. He turned off the flashlight so as not to glare it in his face and sat in the dark with his brother. When he felt sleepy, he said, "Good night," and went back up to bed.

The next morning he ate breakfast, then watered the yard, and left the hose trickling. He went into the stable and did not see his brother, but the next time he checked, there he was again. Again he sat with him for a while. Then he got up and looked into the familiar old face. They were alike, two wispy old men, two wispy old brothers.

"Do you need to say something to me?" Sahm Goong asked.

The ghost did not answer.

"You don't have something to tell me, then? No message?" Sahm Goong paced about. "What are you doing here?" he asked. "What do you want? You don't have something to tell me? No message? Why are you here?" He waited for a reply. "What do you want?"

But Say Goong's ghost said nothing,

"It's time to go home, then," said Sahm Goong. He said it louder. "Go home! It's time for you to go home now. What's the use of staying here anymore? You don't belong here. There's nothing for you to do here. Go home. Go back to China. Go."

There did seem to be a flickering then. All was still, no sound of bird or toad, no aroused insect, only the humming that could have been the new refrigerator. "Go home," Sahm Goong said sternly. "Go back to China. Go now. To China." His voice was loud in the bare shed.

Say Goong disappeared, as if the vehement voice had filled the space he had been using, He had been startled away, reminded of something. He did not come back again. Later Sahm Goong couldn't say whether he had been looking directly at his brother at the moment of disappearance. He might have looked aside for a second, and when he looked again, Say Goong was gone. A slant of light still came in at the door.

Then Third Grandfather too disappeared, perhaps going back to China, perhaps dead here like his brother. When in later years their descendants came to visit us from Canada and Boston, we took them to the place where two of our four grandfathers had had their house, stable, and garden. My father pointed out where each thing had stood: "They had two horses, which lived in a stable here. Their house stood over there." The aunts and uncles exclaimed, "Their horses were here, then," and said it again in English to their children. "And their house over there." They took pictures with a delayed-shutter camera, everyone standing together where the house had been. The relatives kept saying, "This is the ancestral ground," their eyes filling with tears over a vacant lot in Stockton.

Third Grandfather had a grandson whom we called Sao Elder Brother to his face, but for a while behind his back, Mad Sao, which rhymes in our dialect. Sao firmly established his American citizenship by serving in the U.S. Army in World War II and then sent for a wife from China. We were amazed at how lovely and kind she was, even though picked sight unseen. The new couple, young and modern (mo-dang), bought a ranch house and car, wore fashionable clothes, spoke English, and seemed more American than us.

But Sao's mother sent him letters to come home to China. "I'm growing old," she said or the hired letter writer said. "If you don't come home now you'll never see me again. I remember you, my baby. Don't wait until you're old before coming back. I can't bear seeing you old like me." She did not know how American he had looked in his army uniform. "All you're doing is having fun, aren't you?" she asked. "You're spending all the money, aren't you? This is your own mother who rocked you to sleep and took care of you when you were sick. Do you remember your mother's face? We used to pretend our rocker was a boat like a pea pod, and we were peas at sea. Remember? Remember? But now you send paper boats into my dreams. Sail back to me." But he was having his own American babies yearly—three girls and a boy. "Who will bury me if you don't come back?" his mother asked.

And if she wasn't nagging him to return, she was asking for money. When he sent photographs of the family with the car in the background, she scolded him: "What are you doing feeding these girls and not your mother? What is this car, and this radio? A new house. Why are you building a new house in America? You have a house here. Sell everything. Sell the girls, and mail the profits to Mother. Use the money for ship fare. Why are you spending money on photographs of girls? Send me the money you give the photographers so I can send you *my* picture, the face you've forgotten." She did not know that he owned his own camera. His family was one of the first to own a shower, a lawn, a carport, and a car for passengers rather than for hauling.

"You're doing everything backward," his mother wrote. "I'm starving to death. In the enclosed picture, you can see my bones poking through the skin. You must be turning into a demon to treat a mother so. I have suffered all my life; I need to rest now. I'll die happy if you come home. Why don't you do your duty? I order you to come back. It's all those daughters, isn't it? They've turned your head. Leave them. Come back alone. You don't need to save enough money to bring a litter of females. What a waste to bring girls all the way back here to sell anyway. You can find a second wife here too. A Gold Mountain Sojourner attracts ten thousand rich fat women. Sell those girls, apprentice the boy, and use the money for your passage." Of course, though Mad Sao favored his son, there was no question but that, being very American, he would raise and protect his daughters.

"Let me tell you about hunger," wrote his mother. "I am boiling weeds and roots. I am eating flowers and insects and pond scum. All my teeth have fallen out. An army drafted the ox, and soldiers took the pigs and chickens. There are strangers in the orchard eating the fruit in its bud. I tried to chase them away. 'We're hungry. We're hungry,' they kept explaining. The next people through here will gnaw the branches. The sly villagers are hoarding food, begging it, and hiding it. You can't trust the neighbors. They'd do anything. I haven't eaten meat for so long, I might as well have become a nun who's taken a vegetable vow. You'd think I'd be holy by now and see miracles. What I see are the hungry, who wander lost from home and village. They live by swindling and scheming. Two crazed villagers are stealing a Dragon King statue from each other. It goes back and forth and whoever's doorstep it lands on has to pay for a party. There's no goodness and wisdom in hunger. You're starving me. I see you for what you are—an unfaithful son. Oh, what blame you're incurring. All right, don't bring yourself to me. I don't need a son. But send money. Send food. Send food. I may have been exaggerating before, but don't punish me for playing the boy who cried wolf. This time there really is a wolf at the door." He shut his heart and paid his house mortgage. He did nothing for her, or he did plenty and it was not enough.

"Now we're eating potato leaves," she wrote. "We pound rice hulls into paste and eat it. At least send money to bury me." (Sao felt the terror in *bury*, the sound of the dirt packing the nose, plugging the eyes and mouth.) "I've wasted my life waiting, and what do I get for my sacrifices? Food and a fat old age? No. I'm starving to death alone. I hold you responsible. How can you swallow when you know of me?" Some letters were long and some short. "The beggar children who came to the door on your sister's wedding day were the worst-looking beggars in many years," she wrote. "Give them food? Huh. I should have kidnapped them and sold them. Except that people don't buy children anymore, not even boys. There's a baby on the rich family's doorstep every morning. Oh, it's so pathetic. The mother hides behind bushes to watch the rich lady bring the baby inside. There are people eating clay balls and chewing bark. The arbor we sat under is gone, eaten. No more fish in the rivers. Frogs, beetles, all eaten. I am so tired. I can't drive the refugees off our property. They eat the seeds out of the dirt. There'll not be a harvest again."

Other relatives wrote letters about their hunger: "We'd be glad to catch a rat, but they're gone, too," a cousin wrote. "Slugs, worms, bugs, all gone. You think we're dirty and depraved? Anything tastes good fried, but we can't buy oil." "We're chewing glue from hems and shoes," wrote another cousin. "We steal food off graves if people are rich enough to leave some. But who tends the dead anymore?" "Starving takes a long time." "No more dogs and cats. No more birds. No mice. No grasshoppers." "We've burned the outhouse for fuel. Didn't need it anyway. Nothing comes out because nothing goes in. What shall we do? Eat shit and drink piss? But there isn't any coming out." "I can't sleep for the hunger. If we could sleep, we'd dream about food. I catch myself opening cupboards and jars even though I know they're empty. Staring into pots." "I searched under my own children's pillows for crumbs." "Soon I won't be able to concentrate on writing to you. My brain is changing. If only the senses would dull, I wouldn't feel so bad. But I am on the alert for food." "There are no children on some streets." "We know exactly which weeds and berries and mushrooms and toads are poisonous from people eating them and dying." "Fathers leave in the middle of the night, taking no food with them." "The dead are luckier."

When the relatives read and discussed one another's hunger letters, they said, "Perhaps it's more merciful to let them die fast—starve fast rather than slow." "It's kinder either to send a great deal of money or none at all," they said. "Do you think people really go into euphoria when they die of hunger? Like saints fasting?"

"How can you leave me to face famine and war alone?" wrote Mad Sao's mother. "All I think about is you and food. You owe it to me to return. Advise me. Don't trick me. If you're never coming home, tell me. I can kill myself then. Easily stop looking for food and die." "The neighbors heard rumors about food inland to the north," she wrote next. "Others are following an army their sons joined. The villages are moving. Tell me what to do. Some people are walking to the cities. Tin miners are coming through here, heading for the ocean. They spit black. They can't trade their tin or money for food. Rich people are throwing money into the crowds. I've buried the gold. I buried the money and jewels in the garden. We were almost robbed. The bandit used the old trick of sticking a pot, like his head, bulging against the curtain, and when I clubbed it, it clanged. At the alarm he fled. I had nothing to steal anyway." Hearing that money couldn't buy food relieved Mad Sao of feeling so guilty when he did not send money.

"Since everyone is traveling back and forth, I might as well stay put here," wrote his mother. "I'm frightened of these hungry eaters and killer soldiers and contagious lepers. It used to be the lepers and the deformed who hid; now the fat people hide.

"Shall I wait for you? Answer me. How would you like to come home and find an empty house? The door agape. You'll not find me waiting when you get here. It would serve you right. The weather has changed; the world is different. The young aren't feeding the old any more. The aunts aren't feeding me anymore. They're keeping the food for their own children. Some slaves have run away. I'm chasing my slaves away. Free people are offering themselves as soldiers and slaves.

"I'm too old. I don't want to endure anymore. Today I gave my last handful of rice to an old person so dried up, I couldn't tell whether it was man or woman. I'm ready to die." But she wrote again: "The fugitives are begging for burial ground and make a cemetery out of our farm. Let them bury their skinny bodies if only they give me a little funeral food. They ask if Jesus demons have settled nearby; they leave the children with them. If you don't have stories that are equally heart-rending, you have nothing better to do with your money than send it to me. Otherwise, I don't want to hear about your mortgage payment or see photographs of your new car. What do you mean mortgage payment? Why are you buying land there when you have land here?

"If only I could list foods on this paper and chew it up, swallow, and be full. But if I could do that, I could write your name, and you'd be here.

"I keep planning banquets and menus and guests to invite. I smell the food my mother cooked. The smell of puffed rice cookies rises from tombs. The aunts have left me here with the babies. The neighbors took their children with them. If they find food, they can decide then what to do with the children, either feed them or trade them for the food. Some children carry their parents, and some parents carry their children."

Mad Sao wished that his mother would hurry up and die, or that he had time and money enough to pay his mortgage, raise all his children, and also to give his mother plenty.

Before a letter in a white envelope reached us saying that Sao Elder Brother's mother had died, she appeared to him in America. She flew across the ocean and found her way to him. Just when he was about to fall asleep one night, he saw her and sat up with a start, definitely not dreaming. "You have turned me into a hungry ghost," she said. "You did this to me. You enjoyed yourself. You fed your wife and useless daughters, who are not even family, and you left me to starve. What you see before you is the inordinate hunger I had to suffer in my life." She opened her mouth wide, and he turned his face away not to see the depths within.

"Mother," he said. "Mother, how did you find your way across the ocean and here?"

"I am so cold. I followed the heat of your body like a light and fire. I was drawn to the well-fed."

"Here, take this, Mother," he cried, handing her his wallet from the night-stand.

"Too late." she said. "Too late."

With her chasing him, he ran to the kitchen. He opened the refrigerator. He shoved food at her.

"Too late."

Curiously enough, other people did not see her. All they saw was Mad Sao talking to the air, making motions to the air, talking to no voice, listening to someone who moved about, someone very tall or floating near the ceiling. He yelled and argued, talked, sobbed. He lost weight from not eating; insomnia ringed his eyes. That's when people began to call him Mad Sao.

He knew how his grandfather had helped Fourth Grandfather by scolding him on his way. "Go home, Mother!" he was heard to scold, very firm, his face serious and his voice loud. "Go home! Go back to China. Go home to China, where you belong." He went on with this scolding for days and nights, but it did not work. She never left him for a moment.

"I'm hungry," she cried. "I'm hungry." He threw money at her; he threw food at her. The money and food went through her. She wept continually, most disturbingly loud at night; though he pulled the covers over his ears and eyes, he heard her. "Why didn't you come home? Why didn't you send money?"

"I did send money."

"Not enough."

"It's against the law to send money," he told her—a weak excuse. "But even so, I sent it. I'm not a rich man. It isn't easy in this country, either."

"Don't lie to me," she said. She pointed toward the kitchen, where the refrigerator and freezer were filled with food, and at the furniture, the radio, the TV. She pointed with her chin, the way Chinese people point.

"Since you're here, Mother," he tried to bribe her, "you may have all the food I have. Take it. Take it."

She could see her surroundings exactly, but though she could see food, she could not eat it. "It's too late," she mourned, and passed her hand through the footboard of his bed. He drew his feet up. He could not bear it if she should pass her hand through his feet. His wife beside him saw him gesturing and talking, sleepwalking and sleeptalking, and could not calm him.

"I died of starvation," his mother said. She was very thin, her eye sockets hollow like a Caucasian's. "I died of starvation while you ate."

He could not sleep because she kept talking to him. She did not fade with the dawn and the rooster's crowing. She kept a watch on him. She followed him to work. She kept repeating herself. "You didn't come home. You didn't send money."

She said, "I've got things to tell you that I didn't put in letters. I am going to tell them to you now. Did you know that when children starve they grow coarse black hairs all over their bodies? And the heads and feet of starving women suddenly swell up. The skin of my little feet split open, and pus and blood burst out; I saw the muscles and veins underneath.

"One day, there was meat for sale in the market. But after cooking and eating it, the villagers found out what it was—baby meat. The parents who had sold their children regretted it. 'We shouldn't have sold her,' they said. The rich people had bought the babies and resold them to butchers."

"Stop it, Mother," he said to the air. "I can't stand it any more."

Night after night, she haunted him. Day after day. At last one morning he drove to the bank. She sat in the back seat directly behind him. He took a lump of money out of his savings. Then he ran to a travel agency, his mother chasing him down the street, goading him. "Look, Mother," he was heard to say, sounding happier as he showed her the money and papers. "I'll take you home myself. You'll be able to rest. I'll go with you. Escort you. We're going home. I'm going home. I'm going home at last, just as you asked. I'll take you home.

See? Isn't it a wonderful idea I have? Here's a ticket. See all the money I spent on a ticket, Mother? We're going home together." He had bought an ocean-liner ticket for one, so it was evident that he knew she was a ghost. That he easily got his passport proves that he was indeed an American citizen and in good standing with the Immigration and Naturalization Service. It was strange that, at a time when Americans did not enter China, he easily got a visa also. He became much calmer. He did not suddenly scream anymore or cry or throw food and money.

The family told him that there were no such things as ghosts, that he was wasting an enormous amount of savings, that it was dangerous to go to China, that the bandits would hold him hostage, that an army would draft him. That the FBI. would use our interest in China to prove our un-Americanness and deport all of us. The family scolded him for spending a fortune on a dead person. Why hadn't he mailed her the money when she was alive if he was going to spend it anyway? Why hadn't he gone to see her earlier? "Why don't you give the money to some wretch instead of wasting it on a vacation for yourself, eh?" He reminded them of a ghost story about a spirit that refused ghost money but had to have real money. They shook their heads. When my father saw that Mad Sao would not be swayed, he bought two Parker 51 fountain pens for fifty-five dollars, kept one for himself, and told Mad Sao to deliver the other to a most loved relative in China.

Mad Sao packed a small bag, all the time talking: "See, Mother? We're on our way home now. Both of us. Yes, I'm going home too. Finally going home. And I'm taking you home. We're together again, Mother." He hardly heard the live people around him.

All the way up the gangway, he was waving her on. "This way, Mother," he said, leading her by the hand or elbow. "This way, Mother. This way." He gave her his bed and his deck chair. "Are you comfortable, Mother? Yes, Mother." He talked to no other passenger, and did not eat any of the ship's meals, for which he had already paid. He walked the decks day and night. "Yes, Mother, I'm sorry. I am sorry I did that. Yes, I did that, and I'm sorry."

He returned his mother to the village. He went directly to her grave, as if led by her. "Here you are, Mother," he said, and the villagers heard him say it. "You're home now. I've brought you home. I spent passage fare on you. It equals more than the food money I might have sent. Travel is very expensive. Rest, Mother. Eat." He heaped food on her grave. He piled presents beside it. He set real clothes and real shoes on fire. He burned mounds of paper replicas and paper money. He poured wine into the thirsty earth. He planted the blue shrub of longevity, where white carrier pigeons would nest. He bowed his forehead to the ground, knocking it hard in repentance. "You're home, Mother. I'm home, too. I brought you home." He set off firecrackers near her grave, not neglecting one Chinese thing. "Rest now, heh, Mother. Be happy now." He sat by the grave, and drank and ate for the first time since she had made her appearance. He stepped over the fires before extinguishing them. He boarded the very same ship sailing back. He had not spent any time sight-seeing or visiting relatives and old friends except for dropping off the Parker 51. He hurried home to America, where he acted normal again, continuing his American life, and nothing like that ever happened to him again.

5

BEING WHERE WE ARE

Marjorie Sinclair

Once, when Marjorie Sinclair was asked to explain why she writes, she answered the question in a way that shows the thoroughness of her engagement in her creative endeavors. "I have to write. When I don't, the world is warped, awry. When I am writing and things aren't going well, the world is also awry but in a different way. That is part of the long hard struggle of writing—revision—finding the right word and syntax, the right sequence or event, re-reading, tearing up, pasting, wrestling with the word processor, reshaping. You must continually press yourself to probe deeper, to find the core, the very root of the emotion or story. Not to let yourself skim over things, over the human situation. . . . That's all this vital need is: to discover, and in the process of discovery to free yourself. Free yourself, of course, so that you go on being involved."

Sinclair—born in Sioux Falls, South Dakota and educated at Mills College in California—came to Hawai'i in the 1930s. Her interests in international developments in poetry led her to the study of languages—including Chinese, Japanese, and Hawaiian. She taught in the English Department of the University of Hawai'i at Mānoa from 1950 till her recent retirement.

She has published poetry, fiction, translations, and a biography of Nahi'ena'ena, the daughter of King Kamehameha. *The Path of the Ocean*, Sinclair's volume of translations from the Hawaiian, has been much praised by other poets. Michael Ondaatje has called it "a sensual education" and W. S. Merwin has said it "is a wonderfully comprehensive offering of the rich lyrical literature of Polynesia." *The Place Your Body Is*, a collection of Sinclair's own poems, appeared in 1984.

Two of her novels set in Hawai'i in the 1940s, *Kona* and *The Wild Wind*, have been republished in paperback editions and have attracted a wide readership. Her short stories have appeared in numerous journals and have been collected for republication in a number of important anthologies.

The Feather Lei

The notion has been on my mind for a long while. And now with the boys on the mainland making their careers and Brian, part retired and wrapped up in golf, the time has come. The garden is nicely settled down—my own little rain forest (which the neighbors don't like; they think it's a jungle). Hours drift through the house on the trade winds and their feel brings memories I want to put down.

I don't like the words *autobiography* or *memoir:* too self-conscious, too filled with the dust of secrets or the mold of forgotten everyday things. I'm going to call it *notes*—Notes from the Past. Besides, notes can easily slip into a waste-basket if no one likes them. I want to set them down before I forget; it's the tug of the Hawaiian in me. Hawaiian traditions are becoming fragile from the wear of time and tear of constant interpretation. In my mother's girlhood Hawaiians wanted to be like Caucasians. Some were even ashamed of their Hawaiian blood. Mother was not ashamed. She simply didn't feel Hawaiian— nor was she drawn to Hawaiian customs. That was partly because of her father who was English. He taught her to be proud of the English. My grandmother was the first person to make me feel I had Hawaiian blood, that I should be proud of it. The Hawaiian doesn't show in my light hair and blue eyes. But quietly I cherished it and learned all I could of Hawaiian ways from grand-mother. She had an old house full of shadows, corners, hiding places—and the continual fragrance of green foliage and mold. I learned to love pillows that smelled moldy. I loved at night to curl up next to her and listen to the stories she had to tell—many of them ghost stories which she claimed were real. As a child I believed everything she said, so that my mind for a while was a jumble of fantasy and legend, of old facts and bits of folklore. I don't think my mother and father realized how much I began to live in that other world, how it shaped a part of me.

Today is February 11, as good a day as any to start Notes from the Past. I need only pick up my pen (the typewriter will come later) and that ghostly, troubling event of Kapua envelops me. I've never gotten over it, and I still dream of it, sometimes in nightmares. It happened shortly after we had bought our little house on a dead-end street up Nuʻuanu Valley. The boys were away at the university. I planned to spend my days gardening and trying to make our small rain forest on the land. My rampant imagination took wing; long before planting the first sprout I could see what it all was going to look like—an old fading snapshot of Pana'ewa Forest on the Big Island. One of the things that lured me about our place was the remains of an old garden at the end of the street. When I asked our new neighbors about it they said that the house had simply collapsed from termites. No one was there. The family who owned it squabbled among themselves, and so the weeds began to take over the garden. The kids in the neighborhood said there were lots of spooks around the place. "But you know kids," people said. Everyone seemed to like the idea of spooks. I liked the idea, too. It was nice to live next door to such a place. Somehow I never mentioned this bit of neighborhood lore to Brian. He would only laugh.

One day when Brian had gone early to the golf course I decided to explore. The day was bright from the fall of early morning rain. I breathed deeply of the green air from the mountains and walked to the end of the street and onto the stone path which led through the old garden. It curved toward the back of the lot. The steep pali cliffs loomed close—I had not realized how near we were to the mountain flank. The sun was hotter there. I saw many varieties of ti plants, ginger, gardenias and tiare, a mango tree and a soursop, in addition to kukui trees. Everything grew freely and with an energy that was, I thought, startling. It was as if the plants wanted to take over and hide anything human that might have been.

After rounding the curve, I saw the house. It had not collapsed. It was sturdy with lanais around three sides in the old-fashioned way. Curtains hung at the windows and the steps were neatly swept. I could see a chair or two on the lanai and some areca palms. What kind of fantasy did my neighbors have about this house? Had they never looked for themselves? Were they protecting the owners for some reason? Or was it just a story that spread far enough to seem the truth? Looking at the open windows I felt a flush of embarrassment—I was intruding. I scurried back down the curving path.

About a week later I decided to return to see if the house was really there. Perhaps it was only an hallucination brought on by my desire to understand the Hawaiian in me. For there was no doubt in my mind that the house was Hawaiian. It was still there, just as I had seen it. I noticed how much fern had grown through the garden and how much moss was on the tree trunks and old rocks. This time the front door was open. The floor inside shone with wax and was covered with an old Chinese rug. In the dimness I could see heavy koa furniture.

When I was about to turn away, a woman came to the door. We gazed at each other—I felt I had seen her somewhere before. She stepped over the threshold and said her name was Kapua. I told her I lived just down the street.

She invited me to come in and have fruit juice. It struck me as I went in that her house was rather like grandmother's with the old koa and rattan furniture. A tall Chinese vase held several peacock tailfeathers. There was not a speck of dust on the furniture or the floor. She excused herself to go to the kitchen. I sat in the silence and noticed a shelf that held many Hawaiian artifacts—adzes, fishhooks, wooden bowls of different sizes, feather leis, poi pounders. She brought in a tray with two tall glasses, a pitcher and a plate of cookies. "This is fresh liliko'i juice from my back garden," she said. I told her about my sons on the mainland, she told me about a daughter married and living in France. "She's too far away," she sighed. "But that's what happens, we all scatter. The islands no longer contain us." She spoke of her husband who was an invalid. "He never leaves his room. He's rather grumpy." She let a half-smile move across her face.

There was, I had to confess, a certain quality of unreality about her. The accent of her words had echoes of the speech of another period. Her courtesy was somewhat restrained, not the open kind of warmth that Hawaiians of today have. I felt as if I had moved back in time. There was, however, no doubt of her presence. She sat before me, her dark hair combed into a neat bun at the nape of her neck, her blue cotton muumuu somewhat faded from the wash, her hands strong and brown. She wore only a wedding ring. But around her neck was a kukui nut lei with a gold pendant hanging from it. I couldn't tell what the pendant was meant to represent.

Our talk was casual. We settled into the recognition that each of us had Hawaiian blood, and this brought us close in an old-fashioned way. Kapua told me she had twice seen a strange white dog. The last time it came up on her lanai and stared at her. She was convinced its eyes glowed with a yellow fire. And that evening she could see the shape of a dog in the clouds. Laughing at herself, she suggested that it must be a ghost dog. In the old days people knew about him and were frightened. Grandmother, I remember, had told me of a ghost dog in Kona. She said he was some kind of demigod and to watch out for him. I was just a little girl then and I tried to see the dog, but I never did. I told Kapua this and we laughed.

Remembering the days I spent with Kapua, I realize we enjoyed a singular timelessness—hours and days melted together. It rained often and the sound of rain and wind were a part of our companionship. She refused to come to my house, saying she shouldn't leave that unseen grumpy husband. But she urged me to come to her whenever I felt like it. I went often.

I loved everything about her house and garden. They seemed to wrap me in their fragrance, their stillness and isolation. It was as if the two of us, Kapua and I, had a world of our own. I had to admit it was a very small world for Hawaiians. Where was our 'ohana, our extended family? I, as an only child of an only child, had never had an 'ohana. I was always on the edge, not quite belonging somehow, until I married Brian and had the three boys. I wondered if Kapua's life had been a little that way—separated, apart. She, however, never talked of anything in her past except a daughter.

The daughter, Mahea, was a painter living in France. Kapua and her husband scraped together enough money to send her to Paris for the finishing touches of her study of art. There she met her husband. She had not told her parents of the marriage, but simply brought the husband home one day to show him off. Kapua liked him. He was handsome with dark hair and pale skin and he was always gracious to her as an older woman, his mother-in-law. But otherwise he was a complete stranger. And when Mahea was with him she was subtly a different person. She had become—insofar as she could—French: the accent of her speech, her manners, the way she dressed—even the way she thought. Kapua said it was upsetting. Mahea was two persons. Neither was close to her mother and father.

I told Kapua of my sons. They had become mainlanders. Anything Hawaiian about them had long ago vanished. Oh, they still liked poi and lomi salmon and they loved to surf. But beyond that they were young professional men like many others in San Francisco or New York. They were not strangers yet. But they could easily become separated from Brian and me.

We talked sometimes of the frailty of Hawaiian ways, how things these days existed largely in hearsay and very little in day-to-day experience. "We are being swallowed up," Kapua said. "Just like my house. It's being swallowed up by the garden. And one day it will fall down. Even though we struggle to hold on." She paused and looked at the pali cliffs. Her expression suggested she saw a sign or a person. "A good thing I suppose, the past is the past."

I was startled at her words about the house. The neighbors believed it had already collapsed. And I was startled by her passivity, so different from today's Hawaiians fighting for their land, for recognition, for preservation of the old. I had to admit that I too was passive about fighting these issues. Brian always said that things will happen as they will. We can't do much to change the direction of forces long ago set in motion. Whenever he said that, I retreated into myself. I wanted to save whatever I could of Hawaiian things. They were precious. But what did I do?—except plant a miniature rain forest and talk to Kapua and remember my grandmother.

The friendship with Kapua lasted only about a year and a half. Before the end it became a nightmare—that serene beginning in her house and garden. Only a year and a half, which had the weight of a hundred years.

A hundred years in her back garden! Where the liliko'i vines were trained over an arbor, where guava and banana grew. The yellow globes of liliko'i hung down like great ornaments for a festival. The green bunches of banana were like huge green claws of a legendary monster. The guavas fell and cracked, spreading their sweet wild odor through the foliage. We picked fruit together and took it into the house to make jam or jelly, or we put it in bags to give to Kapua's friends. Sometimes we sat in the cool dimness of her living room talking of the past, of how different things were when we were children. Of course, her childhood was closer to the old ways than mine. I cannot forget how on the edge mine was—no shadows in that eccentric geometric house designed by my father, no dark corners or nooks for children to make their own where they could live their imaginary lives. Everything had to be, father said, clear, simple, light-filled. He didn't believe in ghosts or legendary heroes. He wasn't really interested in anything old, in the dust-covered, faintly mysterious objects that people once loved and used.

Kapua and I talked of the food of the old days—always poi and rice for meals, baked bananas and taro, chicken simmered in coconut milk, fish raw or fried. And there were the big round saloon pilots smeared with butter or mayonnaise, a snack for hungry children, and stew with seaweed giving it a pungent or delicate flavor—in Kona I used to walk with grandmother along the shore to gather seaweed, limu as we called it. I used also to pick up shells, glass fishing floats, strange pieces of washed-up coral.

There was a special kind of freedom in our childhood. Mothers and grandmothers then weren't afraid of the sea or the mountains for their children. If a child wanted to swim or climb, he or she could. The land was part of them. The bones of their ancestors were deep in the sand or hidden in the lava rock. People weren't afraid of feeling they could yell at each other in anger, or hold each other in love. Children crawled on many laps, not just mother's. I wonder how much Kapua and I imagined. It doesn't matter. I have it now, here in my head and heart where it lives.

When I told Kapua that Brian and I were planning a trip to Europe, and she heard we were going to Paris, she asked if we would mind carrying a present to Mahea. The day before we left she handed me a round koa box. "Open it," she said. Inside was a beautiful yellow feather lei. "It was my mother's. I want Mahea to have it. Perhaps if it becomes hers she will remember."

Driving in a cab to Mahea's house in Paris I had a feeling of going in circles. Around and around in the same small streets or large ones with boulevards, past the same buildings and parks, until the cab driver finally pulled to the curb and we got out at the number in Kapua's note. I felt slightly dizzy. Brian took my arm to steady me. "Here we are, little one"—he always called me "little one" for he was six feet three. "This is your great adventure for the friend I have never seen."

"You don't really believe in her, do you?"

"I do. And you have the feather lei as proof."

We walked into the central courtyard. Two or three cars were parked in a small space surrounded by a small garden. Two rather spindly trees shaded an area of intense green grass. They cast bluish shadows on the old yellow walls. We rang the concierge's bell. No one answered. A list of residents was posted near the elevator. The names of Mahea and her husband were not there. Brian checked the paper on which Kapua had written the address with information as to how to get there. We were in the right place. We had to be.

A woman came in and went up in the elevator. Brian rang the concierge's bell again. No answer. We wandered out into the street. I remember a sense of heavy disappointment and mystification. We walked into a small bake shop and asked if they knew of a couple with a wife from Hawai'i. They had never heard of them.

Back at the hotel I started a letter to Kapua. It was difficult to write, and I struggled, imagining how I would feel upon receiving such a letter. Then suddenly I realized I had no family name for her. I had no number for the house. A house that the neighbors on our street said didn't exist. But I knew better.

Brian and I decided to try again to find Mahea. Though he had never met Kapua he was curious about the predicament. The second taxi took us to the same apartment with yellow walls, an inner courtyard, the grass and spindly trees. This time when we rang the concierge's bell, she appeared at the door. We asked our question. She looked puzzled and wanted us to repeat the name. No, she had never heard of them. She had been a concierge in the building for many years and no one of that name had ever lived there. I asked if a young woman from Hawai'i had ever lived there. She smiled her first smile, repeating "Hawai'i." She would have remembered that, she said.

After we were back in our cab I said I was sure that somehow Mahea lived there. I could sense it. We just didn't have the correct information about her name. Brian surprised me by agreeing. He said he felt so because of the way the concierge behaved. As if she were protecting someone—bland but at the same time stern except for that one brief smile.

I looked out at the Ko'olau Mountains as our plane settled on the tarmac and felt the usual upsurge of happiness at returning to Hawai'i. Its earth was my earth, the very substance of my bones.

Inside our house I breathed the familiar smells—polished wood, dust, ginger and maile, the mountain wind and the mold. We unpacked and I put the box with the precious lei on my dressing table. I looked out the window toward Kapua's house. The peak of the roof was no longer visible. The trees apparently had grown luxuriantly. A white dog ran out of the ferns. He paused on the street, looked back, then trotted away. A moment of uneasiness came over me.

The following afternoon I put the lei and a small present for Kapua in a paper bag. I started to her house. The curving walk seemed to have more cracks with grass and ferns growing through it. The garden looked as if her yardman hadn't come for a while. At the large curve I stumbled on one of the cracks, through which spiky bamboo was pushing. I fell, cut a knee, scraped my legs. Blood began oozing in small beads. I wiped it with tissues, then sat on the walk until I recovered from the jolt of the fall. In a few minutes I was on my way again. At the end of the curve I couldn't see the house. My heart began thumping and I started to run. There was still no house. The walk ended at steps and a low stone wall, which could have been the foundation. I picked my way through a tangle of plants toward the back garden. A liliko'i vine, heavy with fruit, clambered over everything. The bananas were full of unripe fruit. But no house.

Hysteria rose in me like the sting of a wasp. I called Kapua's name. The stern pali cliffs rose above me. I screamed "Kapua!" The word echoed back. "Kapua."

I returned to the walk and ran out to the street. Blood now streamed from my knee. Twigs and leaves clung to my hair. I continued to scream.

A horrified neighbor came out and took me by the hand. She said something but I couldn't listen. She took me in her arms. I managed to ask where Kapua was, where her house was. She held me close. "But there's no house on that lot. No one lives there."

I broke from her embrace. Numb emptiness swept over me. I said softly, "I fell down. That's all. I was scared."

In my room I lay on the bed and clutched a pillow. Slowly as my mind stopped racing I realized that the bag with the lei was gone.

Almost twenty years have gone by. Kapua, her house and garden are still real. No one can take them away. No one can convince me that I had a spell of some kind of madness. I went back into the overgrown garden and found the bag with the lei. I still have it.

Long ago I gave up trying to understand. I know simply that it happened. Sometimes I take the lei from my dresser drawer and touch the feathers, soft, fragile, yet strong, persisting. The color of them is still as glowing as the moment long ago when they were first plucked from the bird and sewed together. I try to imagine life nearly a hundred years ago. I watch the life around me today. They are two different worlds—how could the earlier one transform itself into this strident, brutal today, clanging with metal and concrete? The feather lei has become my one—my singular—note from the past.

Green Place

I come up from the streets below, ride on roads
turning back on themselves to climb
from the city where traffic beats and beats
angry men drive their cars in and out
pouring anger on men and women
who walk drive sit in their way.
They hate their work convinced
they have no room no space nor hour
for their own and
dread families waiting at dinner
in dimmed houses on darkened lawns.

I come up to this green place.
In early evening the bulbuls call
cardinals whistle at their late feeding
rice birds sweep and plunge in flocks
the old crater below spreads dark shanks
lifts its crested head against the sea sprawling placidly
into horizon into sky.
I go into the house and turn on a lamp
I take out the vegetables for supper.
The house like houses waits
night spreads across the grass.

Octopus

Through low tide
I walked to the small island
along the weedy reef
and saw the octopus
looping and knotting his tentacles
to settle in a shallow pool
waiting for the tide's return.

I stopped near him
his eyes turned he watched
I watched
we waited
he spat at me,
settled things between us.

Farther on I met a fisherman
he asked what I had seen
I said "nothing"
squinting he looked at the sea
and spat in a large arc
toward the tide's return.

Yoshiko Matsuda

Yoshiko Matsuda was born in 1900 in Aki, Kochi-ken, Shikoku, one of the more rural of Japanese islands. As a sensitive teenager, often exposed to the recitation of poetry, her mind often took a poetic turn. Seventy years later she could still remember the feeling that came with the composition of one of her first poems on an autumn day as she walked, listening to the sound of dry leaves crackling beneath her feet. At the age of twenty she joined the Kokoro no Hana tanka club. According to Matsuda, "tanka is feeling from the heart. It is a form that is distinctly Japanese." She believes this delicate traditional form will continue in Hawai'i and Japan, despite the rapid changes that seem to mitigate against the pause and reflection needed for the conception of poems.

Matsuda represents an elder generation of writers in the tanka and haiku genres. Tanka, also called *waka* (Japanese poem), is an ancient form. Haiku developed more recently as a three-line section within the five-line tanka form. Tanka consists of thirty-one *jion* (syllables) written in five lines (5-7-5-7-7). The tanka form already was well established in the fifth century, A.D. The first and most-celebrated tanka anthology, *Manyoshu (Collection of Ten Thousand Leaves)*, was a product of the eighth century.

In 1924 Matsuda married the Reverend Ryugen Matsuda, a Hongwanji Buddhist priest, and emigrated with him to Hawai'i. She lived in Maui, Hilo, and Honolulu, raising her three children, helping in church work in ways expected of a minister's wife, and teaching in Japanese language schools. She wrote poetry wherever she went, joining such clubs as the Hilo Ginu-shisha Tanka Club, the Maui Tanka Club, and the Honolulu Choon-shisha Tanka Club.

In 1957 she studied under and was greatly influenced by the grandmaster tanka poetess Mikiko Nakagawa, the leader of the Odamaki Tanka Society of Tokyo. At the recommendation of Nakagawa, Matsuda established a new tanka club, Odamaki Tanka Kai of Honolulu. Matsuda enthusiastically led and developed this club for thirty-five years.

Matsuda has written thousands of tanka and published them in anthologies such as *Boekifu (Trade Wind)*, *Kinarukao (Yellowish Face)*, *Kurosango (Black Coral)*, and *Sankeika (Trimorphous Flowers)*.

Selected Tanka

(Translated by Jiro Nakano)

Unmei wa	My destiny—
Hone wo gaichi ni	It was the first step
Uzumubeku	Out of the motherland
Sokoku wo ideshi	To bury my bones
Ippo ni arishi	In the foreign land.
Shionari wa	The sound of waves
Waga kyōshū wo	Entices my nostalgia—
Sasou nari	Raging waves
Umare sodachishi	Of Tosa province
Tosa no aranami	Where I was born.
Tekoma no hana	Tekoma flowers
Ki ni michinureba	In full bloom—
Kyōshū mo	Coloring
Usumurasaki ni	My nostalgia
Irodorare yuku	With lavender hue.
Wakamono wo	How heavy is
Yume ni egakishi	This cinerary urn;
Yōfuku ni	Wrapped in a dream
Tsusumishi	Of the young man
Tsubo no omotaki	In a blue suit.
Ito kireshi	Cut its thread,
Noki no fūrin	The wind chime under the eave,
Hisokanari	Remains silent—
Modashite kurasu	I live in solitude
Koto mo hisashiku	long without words.

Torikaeshi	Wrapping
Shiroki shiitsu ni	My past karma
Waga kako wo	In a white sheet,
Tsutsumaru yoru wo	I sleep on at night
Kodoku ni nemuru	In solitude.
Nake nake to	Weep! Weep!
Ware ni notamau	Says nobody in the world
Hito mo nashi	To me in grief.
Sōryo no tsuma no	Ah, how pitiful
Aware naru kana	A priest's wife is!
Kata to to no	Gentle knock?—
Naru ni todoroku	The door sounds unavailing
Omoi sae	Even in my mind,
Munashiku haya	One hundred days
Hyakunichi wo henu	Have already passed.
Imin warera	We, Imin, tired
Ranru no gotoku	Like tattered rags
Tsukaretaru	Yet seeking a citizenship
Yomei kakitatete	By stirring ourselves
Iki semuto shiki	For the remaining life.
Kora no kuni ni	I now decide to die
Ima wa hatenamu	In my children's country
Kika shitsutsu	By naturalization.
Kokoro tsukimete	My thought becomes heavy
Tada kujū ari	With a bitter pain.
Mizu nomite	After drinking,
Tachisaru toki ni	On his departure,
Furimukishi	A cat looks back—
Surudoki neko no	Its piercing stare
Ichibetsu ga ari	Chills my spine.
Tachimachi ni	Instantly, the leaves
Hyōjō katashi	Close and stiffen
Ha wo tojite	Her expression;
Nemu wa futatabi	Mimosa would never
Hirakazarubeshi	Open them again.

Sude ni yo no
Katachi ni nemu wa
Shizumarite
Kokage no benchi
Honoka ni shiroshi

Mimosa already
Is in sleep quietly
As a form of night—
A bench glowing lightly
Under the tree.

Nemu no ki ni
Chikazuki yoru wo
Satoku shiri
Ha wo toji hajimu
Ko no yūkage ni

Knowing cleverly
The night nearing,
Mimosa begins
To close the leaves
In the evening fall.

Kaitei nite
Midori ni ouru
Kurosango
Omoi migataku
Kime ni fure ori

Black coral—
Growing in green
At the sea bottom,
I touch its surface
With deep sorrow.

Yosooi wo
Torite hitori no
Yoru nareba
Igai ni yasashi
Onore no kao mo

Removing my makeup
Alone at night,
In the mirror,
Unexpectedly I gaze.
My gentle face.

Apāto no
Madobe ni yorite
Nakazora ni
Kotoshi owari no
Mangetsu aogu

Leaning out the window
Of my apartment room,
I look up at the sky.
The last full moon
Of this year.

Bōekifū
(Trade Wind)

Phyllis Hoge Thompson

Phyllis Hoge Thompson writes that "the vivid and natural language of poetry expresses with honesty life's truths in a clear verbal music. Deep emotion is not enough. Wisdom, the understanding of experience, however wide and varied, is not enough. Acceptance of the mysterious power of genuine inspiration is not enough. A poet has to discover his or her own language and find out how to handle it—with love, yes, but also with respect. Poets, who understand how dangerous the medium is, learn only by study and long practice how to master it."

Phyllis Hoge Thompson's chief work in Hawai'i, where she joined the University of Hawai'i's Department of English in 1964, was to foster a hospitable milieu for the writing and appreciation of poetry by playing host for eight years to "The Only Established Permanent Floating Poetry Game in Honolulu," an open poetry workshop, which met fortnightly primarily in her home. Later that same year she independently conceived and initiated Haku Mele o Hawai'i, a poets in the schools program. Hawai'i thus became the first or second state in the nation to have such a program. In her classes at UH and in her poets-in-the-schools presentations she encouraged a focus on ordinary, everyday experience as the material for poems and urged the use of natural language, including dialects such as pidgin. Her understanding of the art of poetry derives from the Irish poet Yeats, whose *Dramatic Lyric Poetry* was the subject of her Ph.D. thesis at the University of Wisconsin.

Artichoke and Other Poems, her first collection, was published by University of Hawai'i Press in 1969. Subsequent volumes include *The Creation Frame* (1973), *The Serpent of the White Rose* (1975), *What the Land Gave* (1981), and *The Ghosts of Who We Were* (1986).

The Palms Transplanted

for Tom

The smoky trunks of the palms
curve heavy and tall
on three guy wires
that brace their slant and balance.

They are so shallow rooted
it seems their shafts
cut free of the wires
would fail in the first big wind.

Not so. For years their fronds
will shake in the air
with a sound like water spraying.

Supple as love, the palms
will weather the winds
though they have as little to go on.

Naupaka of the Mountain

Tearing in two the small white flower of the Naupaka,
she tossed the halves away from her, one half to the
mountain, the other to the beach. And she swore she
would not come to her lover until the torn halves
formed a whole flower once again.

Skin prickling, I will not lie down on beaded needles of ironwood
While the breath of a long wind hungers through the branches,
When the wind soughs in the upper branches,
I will not lie down with you.
The wind will talk with the clouds in a clear sky
But you will not come to the mountain.
As the clouds brighten above the paths where the wet seeds spill
Of guava—smell of sweet pink upon dust—
You will not come.
As the clouds are called over green gleaming bamboo
Above the knocking poles,
You will not come to the mountain.
Taut with names I'll rake my face on mountain ironwood bark.
Your arms will not bracket my shoulders,
Your fingers not snag in my hair's tangles
For the sake of a word.

And I will not come to the beach, past the ironwood break
To the cold edges where sea water slides on your ankles
And the salt air licks your ear.
I will not be light in breaking water with you,
Easy diving in images of ourselves
Colliding in the shallows with the backwash.
I will not swim deep with you
Released miraculous as a spear in the silky waters,
Nor wrestle your legs, damp in the stippling sand,
Since I will not come to the beach.

Till the halves of the white naupaka from mountain and beach
Are held together for the sake of a word
You will not come to the mountain.
I will not come to the beach.

The First Heaven

The charitable rain drifting over our valley
Inaudibly in sunlight every afternoon
Is our blessedness made visible. With quiet clemency

The rains of Mānoa move away from the mountain,
Mild and fine, with a cool, milky shining
As of pearl, clouded and luminous as the moon.

Our hairs become hazed with individual glistening
And even our lashes are made wet with the colors
Of the sky's double bow, high overarching.

Such corporeal luster comes upon our hours
That though we know that there are other islands
Somewhere in Paradise, we've chosen these shores

That seem created for us, so our hope corresponds
With the measure of our blessing. Thus contented, wishing
Only for what is ours, we live at peace within the bounds
Of this pacific valley, where the clement rain descends.

Waimānalo

I give this day to heaven.
Nothing prefigured it. It came safe
and suddenly, so without waiting,
that all I could do was stand wild
in the middle of it, allowing myself,
blown, as also the sheeted light was blown
out across wet sand.

This weather had no herald.
An unlikely wind poured down from the wrong side,
so this ocean rose at last
into my reach, cross waters driving
the salt spray of white waves cast
from breakers into the oblique rush of air I was held in
to suffer the sting of sand.

It falls to heaven's keeping
that was hailed in the rage of the lashed ironwoods
rimming the hard sweep of beach.
Sprung from loss, the time is untellable. It brightens
away. Now it's out of my hands.
So breaks the spare joy I was borne to—this day. Blessing,
I tender it. Receive it, heaven.

The Word in the Water at Ka'ena

1.

Where have the voices gone that years ago
Gave us courage to trust,
Though the wind sickle the precipice
And birds scream in the wilderness of air?

Whatever in our lives brought us to this raked ledge
Can drive us into the black folds of water beneath us
Afraid, unless we can find once more the word
Which, under the massed weight of the elements, seems gone.

2.

The sun fails.
Rayed with four hundred golden oars,
It pulls back
Till it leans on the ravenous blue of heaven,
And the ocean floods over its fire.
It sinks forward.
The sounds we are trying to hear are drowned.

3.

Ka'ena: the sea.
Brine of origin stands in these pools
Burning in gold sunfall.
Bright rain has filled them
And what salt has spilled past clefts in coastal rock.

4.

Ka'ena: the hooked wings of the cliff.
They tilt sheer to the stretch of stones and baking dirt
That scrape the bird's wild throat
Tasting of dust.
Against that gray reach of wings,
Banked black rock and red rock rise from the ocean naked
In an ignorant rim.

Bruised by the white waves of years,
They've grown stupid with long standing.
Reared in another age, they stay,
Counter to flight.
The cliff swerves above, pitching down through blue air
To the verge of the sea.
The surf pours forward,
And, under green walls of water, the rocks endure.

5.

At Kaʻena in the night when the birds are still,
And their cries,
And the ocean at low tide pulls down the coastline
As if half asleep,
Sometimes there are strains like songs, voices
Praising the old ways,
Ghosts of those who ran forward to the other world
Exultant,
Chanting on the path as night avalanched behind them
Casting rocks.

They believed the wings of the great bird who brooded on the ocean
When the world began
Would bear them up: they would not become dust and nothing.
They plunged into death's unfathomable water
Trusting the mystery.
The power of their lives still tells us of them.

6.

We are of our own age.
The names we give to things are not the same
As the names they gave.
We may not at first understand.
Yet the sea is as it was. The rocks have not changed.
By faith the living presences remain,
And, far beneath the forward-thundering surf
In the silence the world is founded on,
Abides alone the Everlasting Word.

Blue Ginger: Déjà Vu

for Harriet Gay

Deep as lapis, upon their green stems
Flower these glimmering flames of ginger.
Our gaze keeps swimming in,
Allured to the quiet place where blue lies pooled.
Dark leaves. Whorled dark flowers.
As if we were staring at candles,
We fall silent, turning to blue flowers.

How slowly they open into the glowing mind!
They shine doubled, as if already
Remembered. The shock of peace.
The shade of our lost lives burns into bloom
And returns to us, trembling with immanence.
What can we be sure of, lifted to the soft edge
Of vision? Only the blue fire,
Like ginger, blossoming.

Eric Chock

Through his work as a poet, as a teacher of poetry writing, and as an editor, Eric Chock has done much to open the eyes of people in Hawai'i to the ways poems can serve as means to understanding and opportunities for expression. Chock has long been interested in making intimate connections between literary endeavor and social concern. In a recent statement, he explained the assumptions that underlie his writings. "I believe that the point of view I write from is born of the local culture which developed in Hawai'i. My work often tries to capture some sense of the various cultural influences which affect individual's lives. I believe in the function that poetry performs in reflecting and shaping the people and culture which give it life, which sustain it. I believe that this social function of poetry is part of the give and take between life and art which ideally makes the two indistinguishable, exciting, and mutually beneficial. And I believe that this process is inevitable."

Chock's poems—which have appeared in two collections, *Ten Thousand Wishes* and *Last Days Here*—are usually concerned with Hawai'i scenes and subjects. Many of his poems are addressed directedly toward a presumed listener, often a family member or friend, and speak with understated, yet deeply felt, conviction. The quiet imagery never distracts attention from the direct address but seems carefully selected to enable the poem to expand in the mind during the reading or as the poem is recollected.

As a teacher and editor, Chock has worked for two decades to find avenues for the expression of Hawai'i-based creative writing. His labors as the coordinator and principal teacher in the Hawai'i Poets in the School program from 1973 through the present have enabled him to introduce a great many teachers and students to poetry writing. As an editor, his collaboration with Darrell Lum as cofounder and co-editor of *Bamboo Ridge: The Hawai'i Writers Quarterly* has created a place where Hawai'i-based writing could find an audience. Bamboo Ridge Press has enjoyed remarkable success locally and has also developed a national following; of particular importance are the books the press has published as special issues.

The Mango Tree

"One old Chinese man told me," he said, "that he like to trim his tree so da thing is hollow like one umbrella, and da mangoes all stay hanging underneath. Then you can see where all da mangoes stay, and you know if ripe. If da branches stay growing all over da place, then no can see da mango, and da thing get ripe, and fall on da ground."

And us guys, we no eat mango that fall down. Going get soft spots. And always get plenty, so can be choosy. But sometimes, by the end of mango season when hardly get already, and sometimes the wind blow 'em down, my mother, sometimes she put the fall down kind in the house with the others.

I was thinking about that as I was climbing up the tree. The wind was coming down from the pali, and I gotta lean into the wind every time she blow hard. My feet get the tingles cause sometimes the thing slip when I try for grip the bark with my toes. How long I never go up the tree! I stay scared the branch going broke cause too small for hold me, and when the wind blow, just like being on one see-saw. And when I start sawing that branch he told me for cut, the thing start for jerk, and hard for hold on with my feet. Plus I holding on to one branch over my head with one hand, and the fingers getting all cramp. My legs getting stiff and every few strokes my sawing arm all tired already, so when the wind blow strong again, I rest. I ride the branch just like one wave. One time when I wen' look down I saw him with one big smile on his face. Can tell he trying hard not for laugh.

He getting old but he spend plenty time in that tree. Sometimes he climb up for cut one branch and he stay up for one hour, just looking around, figuring out the shape of the tree, what branches for cut and what not for cut. And from up there can see the whole valley. Can see the trees and the blue mountains. I used to have nightmares that the thing was going erupt and flood us out with lava, and I used to run around looking for my girlfriend so she could go with us in our '50 Dodge when we run away to the ocean. But I never did find her and I got lost. Only could see smoke, and people screaming, and the lava coming down.

The nightmare everytime end the same. I stay trapped on one trail in the mountains, right on one cliff. Me and some guys. The trail was narrow so we walking single file. Some people carrying stuff, and my mother in front of me, she carrying some things wrapped in one cloth. One time she slip, and I grab for her, and she starting to fall and I scream "Oh no!" and then I wake up. And I look out my window at the mango tree and the blue mountains up the valley. The first time I wen' dream this dream I was nine.

Since that time I wen' dream plenty guys falling off the trail. And plenty times I wen' grab for my mother's hand when she start for fall. But I never fall. I still stay lost on the cliff with the other guys. I still alive.

And my father still sitting in the mango tree just like one lookout, watching for me and my mother to come walking out of the mountains. Or maybe he stay listening to the pali wind for the sound one lady make if she fall. Or maybe he just sitting in his mango tree umbrella, rocking like one baby in the breeze, getting ripe where we can see him. And he making sure no more extra branches getting in his way.

Termites

They swarm on summer nights.
They seem to come out of the ground,
out of trees, they fill the air.
They've kept their wings
all their lives
folded on their backs,
but in these insect starbursts
they fly toward whatever shines
in street lights, headlights,
reflections in windows, or eyes.

We turn off the lights inside.
We watch as toads
gather at the porch light
and lick themselves silly.
Lizards haunt the windows,
stalking the winged or wingless bodies.
If the creatures get in
we have candles flaming,
or white bowls of hot water
grandma leaves under a lamp
in a darkened room.
Looking out from the window,
it seems as though they're all bent
on living in our home.

On summer nights, thousands of wings
form feathery wreaths
around each house.
Some of these have made it.
But out in front
under the street light
mother shoots water like a gunner,
picking off stragglers
with the garden hose.

Poem For My Father

I lie dreaming
when my father comes to me and says,
I hope you write a book someday.
He thinks I waste my time,
but outside, he spends hours over stones,
gauging the size and shape a rock will take
to fill a space,
to make a wall of dreams around our home.
In the house he built with his own hands
I wish for the lure that catches all fish
or girls with hair like long moss in the river.
His thoughts are just as far and old
as the lava chips like flint off his hammer,
and he sees the mold of dreams
taking shape in his hands.
His eyes see across orchids on the wall,
into black rock, down to the sea,
and he remembers the harbor full of fish,
orchids in the hair of women thirty years before
he thought of me, this home, these stone walls.
Some rocks fit perfectly, slipping into place
with light taps of his hammer.
He thinks of me inside
and takes a big slice of stone,
and pounds it into the ground
to make the corner of the wall.
I cannot wake until I bring
the fish and the girl home.

Papio

This one's for you, Uncle Bill.
I didn't want to club the life
from its blue and silver skin,
so I killed it by holding it
upside-down by the tail
and singing into the sunset.
It squeaked air three times
in a small dying chicken's voice,
and became a stiff curve
like a wave that had frozen
before the break into foam.
In the tidal pool
we used to stand in
I held the fish and laughed
thinking how you called me
handsome at thirteen.
I slashed the scaled belly,
pulled gills and guts,
and a red flower bloomed
and disappeared with a wave
like the last breath
your body heaved
on a smuggled Lucky Strike and Primo
in a hospital bed.
You wanted your ashes out at sea
but Aunty kept half on the hill.
She can't be swimming the waves at her age
and she wants you still.

Mānoa Cemetary

for Moi Lum Chock, 1975

1

I am late as usual
but no one makes an issue of my coming.
Candles are lit and incense burns
around the stone.
The rituals have begun.
We offer five bowls of food;
bamboo shoots and mushrooms
we've cooked for you today.
And there are five cups of tea
and five of whiskey
to nourish and comfort you
on your journey.
It's been a long year since you left,
and for me, the sense of regret
deepens into mystery.
It is not strange that we miss
your gracious presence,
your good cooking, or good smile;
but as we all take our turns
to bow and pray before your grave,
I begin to wonder who you are.

2

I feel silly
to think I follow custom
pouring you a sip of whiskey
I never saw you drink.
But when I kneel before your stone,
clasp my hands, and bow three times,
I remember how you taught me prayer
before your parents' ashes
stored in earthen bowls
in a sacred room.

They've since been moved
and now they're buried
with a proper stone
just one row up from you.
You know others on this hill.
We give them incense too.

3

It was many years earlier
that an old Hawaiian king
offered a friendly Chinaman
all the land from *Waikīkī* clear up *Mānoa*
to this sacred hill
where we stand or kneel in worship
as our grandparents taught us to do.
The old man refused,
saying, just give me enough
to bury my people.
I wonder if the Chinaman knew
what he was saying?
Even you, two generations before me,
were not born in China
but I think near Hanalei.
So what is it gains a place
among these laborers, merchants, tailors?
The repetition of names
sprawls across the hillside
and I remember once
I thought I saw a baby
in my lover's eyes.
Now I keep an endless pain
regretting great-grandchildren
that were lost. Forgive me.

My First Walk With Ashley

I can't understand any of your gurgling,
but when you raise your arm forward
and stare with raised eyebrows
beyond the opening and closing fingers
of your year-old hand,
I know I should follow that direction.
So with just one finger of mine in your grasp,
you lead me down the back stairs,
past the washing machine with its
audience of orchids and ferns,
and into the front yard.
You squat and smell some purple flowers,
giggling with complete pleasure.
Arm reaching again, we wobble out the driveway
toward the neighboring stream
where you know there are ducks,
one of the three or four words you know
besides mom and dad.
Your feet barely know which way is front,
so I've watched every step
just to make sure you don't fall.
Our path happens like a meditation.
Soon we are bending over the edge of the stone wall
trying to touch the water.
It's close enough.
We do it without having to get on our knees,
just by squatting again.
And the ducks are getting friendly.
You have already touched their wings as lightly
as if your fingers were feathers.
"Ducks," you say.
Now the white one that sits alone
is the one you want.
It runs away.
We pursue but can't get to it.
Once we got close.
It stopped and beat its wings as if
to lift off the ground

and you were in white feather awe,
your soft hands clasped together
as if in prayer,
your face in its light.
You're so young, but already
you know what you like.

Ian MacMillan

Ian MacMillan once said in an interview that the key to the discipline of cre-ative writing is "the way a writer trains himself to think and perceive." Many of MacMillan's best-known works of fiction concern the horrors of World War II. Imagining the unthinkable by rendering it remarkably real and mov-ingly understood has been MacMillan's mission and constant challenge to himself. He sets himself difficult story premises in order to compel his writing to be as good as it can be. He confesses that "I frequently doubt whether a story will work, but I convince myself that it will, push through the doubts and keep at it."

Critics have praised his war novels *Proud Monsters* and *Orbit of Darkness* as "luminous," "ferociously chilling," and "powerfully disturbing." They have been called "dark portraits, yet sublime, ultimately uplifting, in their explora-tion of the means and capacities of the human spirit." Kurt Vonnegut has dubbed MacMillan "the Stephen Crane of World War II."

His short stories have appeared far and wide in many of the most compet-itive journals in America, including *Paris Review* and *Triquarterly*. A collection of his stories, *Light and Power*, was the winner of the Associated Writing Pro-gram's award for fiction.

MacMillan grew up in rural, upstate New York and graduated from the State University at Oneonta. He then pursued graduate work in creative writ-ing at the prestigious University of Iowa Writers Workshop. He has described his coming to Hawai'i to teach as a lucky accident, the result of his happening upon an opportunity to talk with a UH recruiter who was visiting the Univer-sity of Iowa.

The Rock

Calder hits the water with the gleeful vigor of a boy, resisting the shocking cold by churning his legs in a burst of muscular energy. He aims himself at the mysterious, giant rock rising out of the deep water at the mouth of the bay. It is over a mile from shore and halfway there are the crushing breakers which will curl on him with unpredictable ferocity. He has been told more than once that sharks infest the area of the rock, and he has been toying with the idea of cautious approach now for six or seven trips out. Today he has decided that he will make it all the way. He has only been diving four months, but his equipment—fins, mask, snorkel, and spear—all show the satisfying scratches and salt stains of frequent use. He churns along using more force than he needs to because he likes to resist the gentle and powerful motions of the water, likes to challenge its vast, soft bulk.

There is something else—it is the quick and surrealistic, silent pastel brutality of the ocean. Perpetually amazed by it, he regards himself as a humble alien in the last real wilderness, moving in clumsy slow motion in an environment where survival depends on absolute attention. He has been eyeing the rock for months, has been venturing out farther and farther, through the violent and turbulent waves and into the relative calm of the twenty feet of water outside of the reef. He has gone as far as two-thirds of the way without encountering anything odd except very large and dangerous-looking moray eels and some different fish. He is drawn to the rock, trudges along using more energy than he needs to use, enjoying the mummified fear somewhere at the back of his mind thinking, stripped almost naked for it. Stripped down to nothing but a goddamned pathetic bathing suit almost a mile offshore in a place whose only sound is the hum and the ticking of a buzzing confusion of life and me, the humble alien, who trades in gravity for its opposite, goggle-eyed and frightened and enjoying every second.

Calder is a New Yorker in Hawai'i. He got his year here through a few tricky manipulations of influence, losing a casual friend or two and probably gaining back two or three who would turn out to be more valuable than the ones lost. He designs air-conditioning systems, and he was here only three weeks before he settled into his normal, lazy routine, a continuation of what he did in New York, almost nothing in the morning, drink a little too much at lunch, occupy a house a small notch above his means. Until he discovered the water, there was little that interested him here after the initial one-week introduction to what he decided was a corrupted paradise. Not considering the water, here he lived in the moist laziness of a perpetual New York summer without the familiar urban discomforts. Half the secretaries were oriental, half the men you dealt with were oriental, you could not get the New York Times when it was fresh enough to read. In the evening you drank either your own or someone else's Scotch, or you entertained at your house or were entertained at someone else's.

The rilled sand passes under him slowly and he feels like a slow-motion bird, his eyes darting into the corners of his limited field of vision and his legs churning along with more energy than he needs to move at a good pace. He raises his head out into the noisy wind and eyes the enlarging rock. Feels the fear and the eerie hollowness of the unexpected lying out there, jaws open, just beyond the pastel limit of his vision. Thinking, nobody near, so vulnerable, out of yell's reach, close to obliteration without a trace.

Calder is thirty-two and not usually inclined to introspection, but the water and its ticking silence and its pastel madness of life and his own freakish isolation almost a mile out turn his mind into itself with him thinking nearly without words, naked and alone with fear and tense-jawed excitement, you really feel *here*, don't you, really, breathing hard enough to hurt your lungs. He slows down, gasping through the snorkel, through the little death rattle of collected water at the bottom of the U, thinking, I can really breathe—Jesus, I can really. . .

When he discovered the water he stopped smoking. He had smoked all his adult life and quit with the convert's zeal. One could not pay him a hundred dollars to smoke. Once after four days he bought a pack and tried one cigarette, crushed the rest of the pack and cast it into a sewer. He felt ten pounds lighter. His face broke out with pimples as if he were fifteen again and sexual desire bloomed in a sort of innocent lust. His wife accepted the benefits of this change with good-natured amazement. The feeling drove him out of his office on warm afternoons and up to the university cafeteria to sit by the window and watch the braless girls ride by all perky-assed and jiggly and lean on their ten-speed bicycles. Just to watch, because they all seemed so beautiful. He had never realized how beautiful they really were.

Stranger yet than chemical innocence and lust was memory. It was reborn. He could remember with glassy clarity things he had forgotten by the time he was sixteen. Refreshed and weightless in the morning he would shower erect and happy and amazed at his head, and he would go and guzzle half a can of orange juice from the pie-shaped hole in the can, standing with his hand on his hip in the falling coolness of the open refrigerator. He has not been smoking two months now.

Having stopped smoking with his new memory and isolated in the freakish ticking silence and the bluegreen madness of the ocean, he began a kind of brooding consideration of his life and his new obsession with the rock, now closer, the forbidding and barren gray-brown protrusion with the waves crashing against it sending fans of spray fifty feet into the air. In rhythm with the churning of his legs his mind chants the questions to itself, why the water, why the rock at the mouth of the bay? It is not danger itself. It is something else. He has begun to think of it as friction. Resistance. This is what he seeks in the surrealistic madness of the ocean. Resistance. Without it what else is there that you could call life? Somewhere along the line I have negated resistance. And reclaimed it now in the soft but infinitely powerful resistance of water. Chanting, forming the words into the black tube of his snorkel, he thinks, resistance and conflict. I have not felt like this in years. It was a frictionless rise, right up the line, you scratch my back I'll scratch yours. And now, in half-conscious and boyish daydreams he invites the shark, dreads it but secretly hopes for its attack, his thumb gently resting on the crude trigger of his spear. He knows he is defenseless if one comes at him yet he cannot turn back, knows he will push until something comes to him.

He thinks that his memory did it to him. After he stopped smoking, he started recalling the time when he was a boy on a piss-poor farm, his chin like numb putty from the cold, herding the cows from the barn to the watervat, chopping wood trembling with hunger, his hands numbly locked on the axehandle, shivering, still hungry at night, his body tensed up so much that in the morning his stomach muscles would ache. Although those days on that worthless farm were miserable, he remembers them now, with an obsessive clarity, and he feels a funny sentimentality as if somehow those were better days. He thinks of the present with idle contentment, but above that in some loftier recess of his mind there lies a peculiar membrane of disgust.

At home after work he will sometimes sit, drink in hand, in his hip colonial living room and moodily regard the denim-clad crotch of his wife Emma. She will most likely read a magazine, her own drink sweating on the glasstopped table. He loves her. She is strong and attractive and slatternly. It is a kind of sexy laziness. He will sit, sniffing at the vague odor of sweet jungle decay which seems to hang in and around the house. His eyebrows will draw together and he will think: lazy, everything is too lazy. How did we get here? Why do you just sit?

He does not choose to seek excitement in the lights of Waikīkī. Unlike his colleagues, who come to work on Mondays with stories about stewardesses and oriental beachgirls and hookers, Calder finds the attractive depths of moral depravity uninteresting. He has made his slips, but the adventure he would have expected never materialized. His latest was here, on a lunch period—a secretary who would lean over his desk delivering letters and memos, moving in a way which suggested to him a certain substantial mammary heft. It was lunch in her apartment, and after a series of ridiculously obvious mutual suggestions she was naked and hanging on his neck. No conquest. It just—happened, and that was it. And sitting, he can hardly remember it. He can remember with more clarity his first time at sixteen, on wet and dead hay stubble in March at two in the morning, the moon casting his own shadow on the pale body of a girl a year older than him, a girl he had to fight a bigger kid to claim as his. He can remember being cold and bruised, and his shadow moving on her.

At work or at home or at lunch he would sometimes sit and find himself working his knees together and apart together and apart like a boy being denied the shuddering relief of the bathroom. Wrong, something's just—wrong. He would find himself sweating in his air-conditioned office, an air-conditioning system that he himself helped to design. Air conditioning, he thinks, trudging along in the water, slowing down now with deep breaths of satisfaction, air conditioning is the essence of the whole thing. But the water makes him shiver so hard that on the beach after being in for three hours he knows he will sit with the towel around his shoulders and tremble and he will remember again himself a boy trying to talk with a frozen chin, useless putty, remember the terrible itch after warming up leaning against the wood stove above the cherry-hot metal and rotating so as not to overdo one side. He can see the line of his life as forward movement without friction or resistance. How did he come to make so much money when he was not sure that in the last seven or eight years he actually did any work? There is only the nebulous, conglomerate picture of himself behind desk or shoulder to shoulder with the right friends in the apartments or townhouses near Hunter or down the street from. . .

He missed—his spear disappears off into the sand and he tenses himself up. A parrotfish, big. Missed by only an inch or so. He is secretly glad that he missed, because he would have been burdened by the fish and he wants to go to the rock. Outside of that, his freezer has five of them stacked and wrapped in foil, no more than a nuisance to Emma who prefers supermarket fish imported frozen from the Bahamas or California. This has always bothered him because he feels a strong pride about his fishing. Retrieving his spear is a matter of diving down fifteen feet and finding the little trench it made before getting covered by the sand. He grabs the spear out of the sand and slowly ascending, slides it back through the handle and catches its notched rear end in the surgical tubing sling which, attached to the crude handle, makes the primitive rubber tension that provides the spear's thrust. It is held in place by a simple trigger that binds it in the handle, cocked and ready to fire again. He has no use for the new, technological air guns because they make fishing too easy.

He chuckles into the snorkel, thinking of Emma. One night, almost as if inviting a conflict, he told her about the secretary. Fired up on his Scotch at midnight a week ago he talked away about freedom and restriction and about how she was so liberal about things like that and, knowing he should keep his mouth shut because he didn't want to spoil anything, he fell into this almost experimentally pushy interrogation. "Well, suppose I went off now and again and found some girl—" And she, in that wise, blond frankness of hers, said well who am I to tell you what to do? What if I went out and found some. . . He went on with, well, I know how women are supposed to feel about this stuff and. . . Don't worry about me, she said. And he stopped then, thinking, very smart. Build a fence around a pony and he'll jump it and run. Take it away and he'll stay. Very smart.

So he told her, gave her a five-sentence, objective picture of what happened, and then stood there and waited calmly for whatever she had for him. She looked at the floor. "Oh I see, I see what—that's what you're getting at. Well, interesting, interesting." When he walked toward her, across the glass-shiny kitchen floor, she took a little step of her own, as if not aware of his existence but really evading him. So then she was crying to herself, and he cursed himself for letting her know, thought, now you've done it, now you've taken care of it. Six years. No children. How easy it would be for her now to just— the speculations raced through his head, sending a shudder of odd exhilaration through him.

"Only once?"

"Yeah," he said. And she thought about it.

Finally she threw her hands up as if in annoyance and said, "Ah what the hell, it's the twentieth century after all, just be careful, okay?" Then she went off to bed, leaving him standing there in the kitchen looking out the window at the silhouette of the house next door, a carbon copy of his own, squat and comfortable and dark, surrounded by the sweetly decaying plumeria trees.

When he went to bed ten minutes later, apprehensive and cautious, she was hot and lying there in the rumpled bed in her slovenly nakedness and latched onto him and breathed her hot breath on his face and pulled him down on her liquid and softly demanding body. And he looked at her and said, "what— what's the—" and then chuckled to himself in morbid amazement and gave in.

Calder takes very seriously what he is doing, even against the soft and reasonable protests of his wife, who will not go with him to the beach when he plans his excursions. He even enjoys her fear. The last time she went with him, along with some other people from work, they were all worried sick that he would not come back because he was gone for two hours. And Emma said, "It really scares me you know, please don't go out so far . . . you go out so far I can't even see you."

He looks down and nods when she says this, knowing that he will not be able to resist going even farther the next time.

"I just don't understand why," she said. "They don't either," and she poked her thumb over her shoulder. "There's some sort of a—a blindness I don't understand. You say you won't and you do." She held her shoulders up in a sustained shrug.

And he nodded and looked down at the sand. He cannot explain it yet, but is secretly warm inside that she should be afraid. But outside of that there is the gnawing shadow of an understanding suggesting itself—he almost sees something he doesn't like, that in his obsession for the rock there is a certain puerile and egotistical and boyish motivation. There is evidence that he is almost afraid to examine too closely. Once on a short excursion he lost his spear in a cave and foolishly went in after it, knowing that the ocean could decide to drown him in there. Fishing around reef caves was dangerous anyway because one slip, one moment of loss of concentration could mean being badly bruised or even knocked out on the coral, because of the dangerously unpredictable nature of the waves. In the ticking blackness of the cave he retrieved his spear and tried to return to the light and a wave came in and then some strange current, which played with his life for ten seconds while he fought off the powerful impulse to breathe. Finally the current released him and he sprung to the silver surface of the water and exploded coughing into the noisy air, and coughing his throat raw he went right into the beach and sat trembling on his towel, thinking, I almost died there, I almost did not come out.

And later, he had some people over as usual and told them the details of his scrape, not at the moment recognizing that he was romanticizing it somewhat. And Emma, wise, sloppy Emma, said, "See what John Wayne's done to my husband?" Everyone laughed, Calder the loudest, and in the awkward silence that followed he sat in a haze of warm shame, as if Emma had insulted him.

And he thinks, what *has* John Wayne done to me? He deliberately passes up a lobster, sees the black feelers peeking out from under a blob of dead coral. Maybe she is right. Some blindness I don't understand. More evidence: heading for this same rock a few weeks ago he found himself halfway, outside of the crashing breakers, and he felt frightened and happy and looked goggle-eyed at the fish and the sleepy, deadly eels and the rilled sand, thinking, this is far, this is way, way out. Nobody, nobody would—and he turned and saw something off in the distance. He raised his head out into the cold air and saw something protruding from the water and began to back away, muttering with fear into the snorkel. It turned out to be a boy. Local. There was another boy farther off, and when he realized this he moaned, sick of himself, and returned to the beach. Boys. It seemed to prove the dilettantish nature of his adventure. And it was the same day that he looked at the ominous rock off the bay and thought, all right, boys, there, I have to go there.

He slows down and thinks, yes, there is something hokey about this, about me. He is thirty-two, idly resisting the half-conscious impulse to consider himself somebody's Christ. Why? he thinks. All right, so let's find out. He is convinced that the ocean holds for him some personal secret that only making it to the rock will reveal.

There is Martin, too, one of the right friends to have, also from New York. He is the one who said to Calder, "You want St. Johns or Honolulu?" Martin now pokes fun at him, calls him Lloyd Bridges, that guy from the old underwater TV show, or sometimes he says at work: "Ask Jacques Cousteau over there . . ." Calder resents Martin's joking, because he knows that the question of what John Wayne has done to him is important and touchy and personal. Emma, you wise bitch. You who look like a turn-of-the-century New Orleans whore in the morning all hoarse and sexy, you are a wise bitch. How could he explain it to her? Resistance is life, therefore where there is none, then there is no life. The human has purged resistance from his life. What would she say? Aw, up yours honey, come to bed. Those hot, enveloping thighs and the great squash of breast that seems in the process of running off her chest. They seem to negate him.

He stops and puts his head out of the water and scans the mountains, the beautiful dark mountains with their outrageously green peaks in the clouds. He slowly treads water, his jaw quivering with cold. Then he looks at the minute dots of the houses, the crawly feeling at the back of his neck. He is not alert, and in principle, if he were a fish he would be dead. Living in the ocean means for them remaining perpetually alert. Or the shark, living for him means constant movement or suffocation. The eel sits in his hole and waits in perpetual readiness. God. He looks scornfully at the houses nestled under the mountains and shakes his head and snorts, thinks of himself sitting in his hip colonial living room which is decorated to make a social chameleon of him, a place with no bags. He thinks, that is the most indecisive room I have ever seen.

"All right," he says into the snorkel. He looks at the rock, scanning the water near it for the black triangle of a shark's dorsal fin. Only four or five hundred yards. Today's the day. His fear and excitement balance each other out. No one can help him now. He knows he is foolish, that this is not necessary and if Emma knew, she'd probably call the rescue squad. He looks up again, his face whipped by the cold wind, thinking, god it's big. It rises fifty or more feet out of the water, a fractured cube, threatening and monolithic and raw. The water sloshes against it in huge swells and he knows he cannot get too close. He sees also that the water under him is forty or more feet deep, which means he cannot use his spear. In front of him and down the bottom goes, off into the frightening blue distance. He is cold, shivering now, but all the time enjoying it with his tense belly and back and the shudders in the throat and jaw. With the water getting deeper and the rock looming and his eyes darting around in the limit of his vision for the shape of a shark, almost as if it is the shape of proof that he lives at all, thinks okay, Emma, okay, what do you say now? The plot is thickening, honey. We'll move the cameras in when he comes at you.

He thinks, enfolded in the pastel silence of the water with the blue nothingness below him, once you get there what will it mean? Behind this a more threatening thought comes to him, as if he is grimacing at himself in the mirror—he really is hokey, he really is a boy. This is almost too much for him. Trudging along slowly with exhaustion approaching, it is almost as if the excursion is ruined. He is shivering but inside he feels hot with shame. He has had this thought many times before, but today it wells up like a wave in his mind and he cannot easily rid himself of it. He looks up and sees his magnificent rock and now the fear begins to outweigh the excitement. Now the mask hurts his upper lip and the fins are chafing his Achilles tendons and his throat is salt raw as if someone has run a woodrasp down it. Now he is tired and wonders if he should try the last few hundred yards. He looks up and sees that the land jut at the mouth of the bay is actually closer to the rock than his point of entry. He decides he should head for it, the humiliating thought gaining ground in his mind. Another time sonny. Tomorrow maybe. He hangs exhausted in the water and looks down at the blue-gray nothingness of what must be sixty feet of water, hangs blank and tired and thinks, tomorrow Lloydo, tomorrow Jacques. This is enough. He is too far out. Jesus, he thinks, I got to get back in. I really got to get back in. Head for the jut. He will have to go through scary, unfamiliar territory.

But he does not go in. Hanging suspended in the water and now a little angry he thinks, why waste it just because someone implies that you are an irresponsible fool? Nothing to lose out here but doubt, boy. Sullenly biting down on the mouthpiece and disregarding the exhaustion that drags him down he churns on toward the rock, grimly forcing himself on despite the fear which now lies dormant somewhere, shadowed out by his brooding anger at anyone or anything which would influence him not to go as far as he goddamned well pleased.

He is rewarded quickly. Off in the distance, against the soft blue of the ocean, the reef around the rock begins to materialize like a photograph in a chemical solution. The reef is a hundred yards into the ocean around the rock, and it seems alive with fish, and scanning the picture whose clarity increases steadily, Calder sees nothing indicating danger. It is all beauty. It sends a shudder of excitement through him like ponderous electricity. It is incredible—he has never seen anything like this in his life. The yellows and pinks and the fish in schools and the fish alone, going on about their business. It is as if he has crossed a desert and come out into a beautiful town.

He spends ten minutes in a gawking, amazed inspection of part of the reef before he decides to fish for a few minutes. In his excitement he misses the first shot at a large parrotfish in a hole and he stays down, looking into the hole with his body inverted, and grabs for the rear end of his spear, which lies across a crevasse full of little silver fish. He almost has the spear when the spotted eel flashes on his hand. There is no pain, only momentary shock in which Calder even feels the eel's tongue on the palm and sees that its teeth are buried as far as they will go, and in that same, peculiarly objective expanded half-second he sees the little malevolent eye buried in the fat, bulbous head staring back at him sleepily. He jerks his hand out of its mouth so that the teeth painlessly shred the palm and back and he springs off the coralhead already taking water into his throat and he curls up around his shredded hand like a leaf in a fire. He rises to the surface blowing air from the snorkel in a yell and then hangs there waiting for the pain which does not come up beyond a cold and wretched discomfort. Wailing softly with each breath he looks at his hand. The slashes are closed with blood escaping in little billows, like smoke. He gasps his breaths numbed with fear and trembling wretchedly and clasps his hand to his chest, thinking, oh Jesus so far out, and blood escaping, Jesus.

Still without feeling much pain he turns and scans the water again and begins swimming backwards, frightened at the little billows of blood which disperse into the water. No defense, none at all. Get in. He looks up again at the jut of land, and rejecting the hollow fear of what must lie behind him and against his exhaustion he churns with all he has toward the jut. Before going two hundred yards he stops, gasping, cold and giddy and hopelessy tired. Before he can control it, bile scalds his throat and the inside of his nose, and he floats, eyes shut, trying to hold back the dreamy nausea which robs him of balance and strength. In order to keep from throwing up he hangs still, holding his hand against his chest, letting the ocean do to him what it will. For a moment he has a strange feeling, a strong impulse to just hang there forever, just die there enfolded in the water.

He needs to concentrate on something. Floating in aimless exhaustion is terrifying. He looks again at the hand, bringing it off his chest as if it were incredibly fragile. Still, the little billows, the seepage, and a kind of morbid interest in what the eel did makes him gently open one cut. It is even worse than he expects, like razors right into the muscles, all the way in, and the heel of his hand is partially severed, a one-inch chip in the flesh. He chokes with fear again and trudges on cautiously, because of his stomach, half-consciously muttering into the snorkel, Jesus god bad, my god my god, and he is too tired to glance back for the shark he is sure is on its way to finish the job. He can only chuckle with hopeless exhaustion and watch the rilled sand pass under him and curse with his teeth clenched when the ocean gently holds him back with one of its exasperating currents.

It is almost as if he sleeps, trudging along in the blue-green silence, as if he is at peace with his hand and now must simply go home. He has no idea how much time it takes him to make it any distance and he does not care. The fear has crystalized at the back of his head so that whatever feeling it is when some pair of jaws clamp on his neck will make him respond by simply drawing his shoulders up and wincing slightly. For long stretches he swims with his eyes closed, almost not caring if he is going in the right direction. His mind cocoons itself in a half-dream and it is only the growing pain that keeps him aware. Then the powerful breakers wake him up and carry him violently toward the shore so that he must raise his head out to get air. The sea is all foam, tossing him and pushing him and washing over him, all toward the beach, and he lies, his hand clasped to his chest, intent only on getting the air he needs when the ocean will permit it. Before reaching the calm water he has the wind blasted out of him by a high piece of coral that lays open the skin on his ribs. He continues on, a little hopeful because he is inside the reef, and the searing pain of the blow on his ribs wakes him up. And with horribly gradual progress, the bottom comes up to meet him.

On the shore he plows up to dry sand, still holding his hand, and falls back. He is almost too tired to keep going, but the recognition that he has made it to shore gives him a temporary energy and the noise of the land wakes him up and the blood streams from his hand because it is now not held in by the pressure of the water. With his good hand he pulls the fins off holding the bad hand aloft so that the blood runs down his arm over his elbow and toward his armpit. Gasping more air than he needs he is driven by a sullen fear as if something could still chase him, and he begins trotting along the beach toward his car, which is a mile away, and he fights the sand which slows him down.

A man intercepts him bearing a towel, which Calder numbly wraps around his hand, and the man leads him into the bushes saying, "Oh, Jesus . . ." and Calder hardly hears him. It is as if Calder is still in the silent ticking ocean and numbly he follows staring glassy-eyed at his own feet in the sand and then on grass and finally wet and shivering and salty he finds himself sitting in the front seat of the man's car, holding his wrapped hand against his injured side.

The bleeding has almost stopped and blood crusts his wrist and forearm and soaks into the towel. Now he sees that the man is Japanese, old, and keeps glancing at Calder's wrapped hand. Calder looks around, at the ocean, and at the white line streaming into the hood of the car. It is as if he wakes up suddenly. He pulls the towel away and peeks at his hand. It is cupped against his side so that the seeping blood collects in the palm. He is suddenly apprehensive about going home, as if he were a boy who had injured himself doing something he shouldn't have done.

But he snorts angrily at that thought, and turns to the man. "Have you . . . have you ever been out there, by that rock?" His voice crackles, almost as if the question is urgent.

"Not for me," the man says, laughing.

"It's . . . it's beautiful," Calder says. "I've never seen anything like that in my life."

Now he is relaxed, calm, almost content sitting there hunched around his hand, and he thinks, against what reason would tell him to think, if this is the blindness they make it out to be, then I aim to keep it. He takes another look at his cupped hand and at the brilliant little pool of blood in the palm. He holds it as if it is something valuable he has found in the ocean.

John Unterecker

John Unterecker's poetry unites diverse elements. He claimed that his book of poems about the Irish islands refers, in many ways, to the Hawaiian islands and that his poems about dance are, in certain respects, painterly. His comments on the painterly aspects of his poems reveal much about his intensely aesthetic attitude toward his verse. "I think of [my poems] as being laid out on the page almost in the way triangles and circles and squares are laid out in, say, a Cubist painting."

In the first phase of his career Unterecker established a reputation primarily as a scholar. His *A Reader's Guide to W. B. Yeats* still remains an important resource for students of one of our century's greatest poets, and his biography of the American poet Hart Crane was nominated for the National Book Award and has remained a central document of Crane scholarship. Unterecker is also known for his editorial work on a series of studies of modern poets that was published by Columbia University Press.

After Hawai'i lured him away from his position in the English Department at Columbia University and he assumed a similar position at the University of Hawai'i, he increasingly concentrated on poetry writing as his primary activity. His poems appeared in such distinguished publications as *The New Yorker, Shenandoah, Yale Review,* and *The Nation.* His collections of poems include *Dance Sequence* and *Stone.* His enthusiasm for the importance of poetry writing as a vocation, his compelling public readings of his poems, and his wide knowledge of the national literary scene made him an important example and mentor for many of his Hawai'i students and friends.

Waiting

for Maxine Hong Kingston

After the road stops twisting, you arrive at the lookout.
Beyond it, there's an overgrown path, dark even in moonlight, up to the
bare place.
It's not sacred; it's bare.

From far below, headlights startle the landscape, then roar out of sight.

Tonight, when I come to this place, I shall say, *Why here?*
knowing that when I kneel,
it will be to a silence whispering along the palms of both hands.

> There is no throne.
> There are neither gods nor ghosts dangling bare feet in the
>   moonlight.
> My lips shape to a shadow subtler than wafer or wine.

In a place stripped of everything but moonlight and stars,
the extraordinary is as casual
as the pressure of light on bare shoulders.

"Now be quiet," I say to the restless blood in my wrists.
"Hear nothing," I say to the membrane pulsing my ears.
"Touch the silence," I say to strange hands that lift out of darkness.

Volcano

Say that the ground opens up—an earthquake, faults opening;
say that I see you against the horizon, twisting, folding
down: earth: refuge.
(Give us this day.)
Granted no earth to stand on, my voice caught on the wind, flailing—
or that, turning, you speak, out of hearing
(mouth telephoto, talking lips
mouthing)—

There is an ache in things.

The large substance of daytime shatters.

My tomorrow, cold says never, scenery unfolding.

Mouths: "Give us this lava, these openings."

State Symbol

I.

I mourn the nēnē goose, that trivial bird,
whose pattern of retreat tracks clouds.
He is the past.

           Clumsy aristocrat,
gourmet of white strawberry fields,
islander, he lorded it when he could.
(For the waddler in need of home, winded,
lava would do: 'ōhi'a breaking lava toward earth.)
Vagrant, he had luck of the vagrants: ancestral ur-geese
driven on doom's timetable, tiring; then plumes of steam-
driven lava, and on a crumpled field 'Ūhi'a's evolved glade:
white strawberies. It was all nick of time, an island evolving
that precision of broken flight land.
So settlers stumble ashore, already royal, applause of the gods louder
      than storm,

though voted (anywhere, everywhere) bad stock:
"We name you, let this be recorded, least likely (applause) to succeed."
      . . . to succeed (least likely).

II.

Hawai'i's state bird, incompatible, struts off toward clouds,
trying, deposed royalty, to die. He is, of course, protected.
The curious state hatches him out in Honolulu zoo, imports breeding
      stock from English breeding farms.
"Goodbye, goodbye," as off to the wilds go dumb tame chicks,
used to peanuts and popcorn and noise.

III. A Lament: *Goose*

Translator, set this:

> *The unique die quick,*
> *quicker than Model A Fords.*
> *Goodbye, good climb as you go!*

I comb volcanoes for birds.
      But what can I do, hot-footing it through fresh lava flows
toward strawberry islands patched mint?
            "Good luck to you all," I call.
                  Now they are lost in steam:
                  "Good luck, good luck!"

Statistician, keep track:
      Add ten to the hundred-ten;
            count silverswords;
                  nudge counted eggs from counted captive geese.

Oh, translator lend me your skill;
      teach me quick accurate quacks
            that at snowline clouds they might rise.

"Take flight in great storms,"
      I would call,
            calling again and again, like prayer,
                  "Luck give you strawberries whiter than snow, luck

of that other storm,
      or a lucky quick death,
         wings failed,
           geese spattering the sea,
              huge hailstones dropped from the dense violence of
                God."

August 22

Here at the edge of nowhere and the sea
you wind a thread of seaweed on your wrist.

"Now I belong to this place."

Like a coil of sandy hair
it loops the blue pulse of stretched skin.

Salt tides stretch out into the blue salt darkness of the sea.

Inhabitant

Perhaps there are no more apparitions:

There are no figures at the window,
      none on the stairs,
      none rustling through the narrow spaces inside the walls.

Tonight I shall unlock all of the doors and all of the windows.

Even this chair feels empty.

O'ahu: Midday Concert in Orange Air

The guava tree composes catch-as-catch-can harmonies,
leaf xylophones an erratic tune
beneath the ultrasonic zings of peeling bark.
Greyed brown—zing—gives way to a chartreuse hum.
Branch thickens (zing), a little hum of wet chartreuse
while all the listening aphids cluster for a feast,
a shush of scramble,
beneath the whirr of ladybugs descending in a leafy wind.

Today the wind is orange-grey, orange greyed by volcanic smog,
a muffled elegy between the guava and blind mountains.
It is as if thick chords of sunset sift through noontime air:
the singing guava, a greasy hymn of smog,
then absence where the mountain guarded sky.

One must choose on such a day.
I choose the guava, singular melodist,
for yellow guavas bleet "sweet, sweet" in the bad orange light.
Birds also choose the guava.
A crowd of white-eyes choir the undersides of leaves
nibbling wooly aphids into twittering beaks.
Rust-capped Hawaiian finches cheep from leaf to leaf.

And like out-of-tune ukuleles out of Waikīkī,
a trio of bulbuls, sooty as volcanic ash, red-vented as volcanic
        fountainings,
screech bulbul lieder as they smithereen pink gashes in the
yellow fruit.

No doubt it is all a matter of perspective.
On such a day, the foul air brightens everything near. Far is gone.
On such a day, orange air intensifies song.

Morning

The bay is a jumble of wind.
Wind smashes in among the breakers,
a fist smashing them backwards. What jumbled light!

Or that time when we were children,
you bent over the mirror.

Cathy Song

Cathy Song exhorts her poetry students to seek their own voices by paying careful attention to the voices around them. In the introduction to *Sister Stew*, Cathy Song and her co-editor explain that remembered echoes of the voices of family and friends enable us to write about "the moments when we listened, watched, and understood, as if life, like a piece of music, could be apprehended in all its strangeness."

Song's rapid rise to prominence in the national poetry scene shows that she has found a voice that many want to hear. Her Master's thesis for Boston University became her first book, a collection of poems entitled *Picture Bride*, which won her the 1982 Yale Series of Younger Poets Award. Published by Yale University Press in 1983, the book was nominated for the National Book Critics Circle Award. Her second collection, *Frameless Windows, Squares of Light*, was published in 1988 by Norton. Her third book, *School Figures*, appeared in 1994 in the prestigious Pitt Poetry Series published by University of Pittsburgh Press. Song's work has been included in many anthologies, including *The Norton Anthology of Modern Poetry* and *The Heath Anthology of American Literature*. She was co-editor of *Sister Stew: Poems and Fiction by Women* for Bamboo Ridge Press, where she has also served as managing editor.

Since 1987, Song has offered numerous poetry workshops in Hawai'i's public schools under the auspices of the Poets in the Schools Program. She also teaches occasional workshops at the University of Hawai'i at Mānoa.

She lives with her husband and three children in Kaimukī, not far from where she grew up, as she explains in the poem "Square Mile."

Easter: Wahiawā, 1959

I.

The rain stopped for one afternoon.
Father brought out
his movie camera and for a few hours
we were all together
under a thin film
that separated the rain showers
from that part of the earth
like a hammock
held loosely by clothespins.

Grandmother took the opportunity
to hang the laundry
and Mother and my aunts
filed out of the house
in pedal pushers and poodle cuts,
carrying the blue washed eggs.

Grandfather kept the children
penned in on the porch,
clucking at us in his broken English
whenever we tried to peek
around him. There were bread crumbs
stuck to his blue gray whiskers.

I looked from him to the sky,
a membrane of egg whites
straining under the weight
of the storm that threatened
to break.

We burst loose from Grandfather
when the mothers returned
from planting the eggs
around the soggy yard.
He followed us,
walking with stiff but sturdy legs.
We dashed and disappeared
into bushes,
searching for the treasures;
the hard-boiled eggs
which Grandmother had been simmering
in vinegar and blue color all morning.

2.

When Grandfather was a young boy
in Korea,
it was a long walk
to the riverbank,
where, if he were lucky,
a quail egg or two
would gleam from the mud
like gigantic pearls.
He could never eat enough
of them.

It was another long walk
through the sugarcane fields
of Hawai'i,
where he worked for eighteen years,
cutting the sweet stalks
with a machete. His right arm
grew disproportionately large
to the rest of his body.
He could hold three
grandchildren in that arm.

I want to think
that each stalk that fell
brought him closer
to a clearing,
to that palpable field

where from the porch
to the gardenia hedge
that day he was enclosed
by his grandchildren,
scrambling around him,
for whom he could at last buy
cratefuls of oranges,
basketfuls of sky blue eggs.

I found three that afternoon.
By evening, it was raining hard.
Grandfather and I skipped supper.
Instead, we sat on the porch
and I ate what he peeled
and cleaned for me.
The scattering of the delicate
marine-colored shells across his lap
was something like what the ocean gives
the beach after a rain.

Lost Sister

1.

In China,
even the peasants
named their first daughters
Jade—
the stone that in the far fields
could moisten the dry season,
could make men move mountains
for the healing green of the inner hills
glistening like slices of winter melon.

And the daughters were grateful:
they never left home.
To move freely was a luxury
stolen from them at birth.
Instead, they gathered patience,
learning to walk in shoes

the size of teacups,
without breaking—
the arc of their movements
as dormant as the rooted willow,
as redundant as the farmyard hens.
But they traveled far
in surviving,
learning to stretch the family rice,
to quiet the demons,
the noisy stomachs.

2.

There is a sister
across the ocean,
who relinquished her name,
diluting jade green
with the blue of the Pacific.
Rising with a tide of locusts,
she swarmed with others
to inundate another shore.
In America,
there are many roads
and women can stride along with men.

But in another wilderness,
the possibilities,
the loneliness,
can strangulate like jungle vines.
The meager provisions and sentiments
of once belonging—
fermented roots, Mah-Jongg tiles and firecrackers—
set but a flimsy household
in a forest of nightless cities.
A giant snake rattles above,
spewing black clouds into your kitchen.
Dough-faced landlords slip in and out of your keyholes,
making claims you don't understand,
tapping into your communication systems
of laundry lines and restaurant chains.

You find you need China:
your one fragile identification,
a jade link
handcuffed to your wrist.
You remember your mother
who walked for centuries,
footless—
and like her,
you have left no footprints,
but only because
there is an ocean in between,
the unremitting space of your rebellion.

Untouched Photograph of Passenger

His hair is brilliantined.
It is black and shiny
like patent leather.

He cannot be more than twenty:
his cheeks are full,
his face is smooth as a baby's,
though one pockmark
above his right temple
about the size of a rice kernel
is detectable.
His mouth appears to be
curved over something almond shaped.
Perhaps, he is sucking on a sweet plum.

His suit is puckered
at the seams.
The shoulders are too narrow,
fitting badly;
probably stitched in a lamplit tailor shop
hovering in a back alley.
But the necktie adds
the texture of raw silk;
the added touch signifying

that this is meant to be
a serious picture;
the first important photograph
he has ever had taken.
This will document
his passage out
of the deteriorating village.
He will save it
to show his grandchildren.

As if already imagining them,
his eyes are luminous.
He is looking ahead,
beyond the photographer
in the dark room
crouched under the black velvet cloth,
beyond the noisy cluttered streets
pungent with garlic and smoked chestnuts.

Rinsing through his eyes
and dissolving all around him
is sunlight on water.

Chinatown

I.

Chinatowns: they all look alike.
In the heart
of cities. Dead
center: fish eyes
blinking between
red-light & ghetto,
sleazy movie houses
& oily joints.

A network of yellow tumors,
throbbing insect wings.
Lanterns of moths
and other shady characters:
cricket bulbs & roach eggs
hatching in the night.

2.

Grandmother is gambling.
Her teeth rattle: Mah-jongg tiles.

She is the blood bank
we seek
for wobbly supports.

Building
on top of one another,
bamboo chopstick tenements
pile up like noodles.
Fungus mushrooming,
hoarding sunlight
from the neighbors
as if it were rice.

Lemon peels
off the walls so thin,
abalone skins.
Everyone can hear.

3.

First question,
Can it be eaten?
If not, what good
is it, is anything?

Father's hair is gleaming
like black shoe polish.
Chopping pork & prawns,
his fingers emerge
unsliced, all ten intact.

Compact muscles taut,
the burning cigarette
dangling from his mouth,
is the fuse to the dynamite.

Combustible material.
Inflammable.
Igniting each other
when the old men talk
stories on street corners.
Words spark & flare out,
firecrackers popping on sidewalks.
Spitting insults, hurled garbage
exploding into rancid odors:
urine & water chestnuts.

4.

Mother is swollen again.
Puffy & waterlogged.
Sour plums
fermenting in dank cellars.

She sends the children
up for air.
Sip it like tea.

5.

The children are the dumplings
set afloat.
Little boats
bobbing up to surface
in the steamy cauldron.

The rice & the sunlight
have been saved for this:

Wrap the children
in wonton skins,
bright quilted bundles
sewn warm with five spices.

Jade, ginger root,
sesame seed, mother-of-pearl
& ivory.

Light incense to a strong wind.
Blow the children away,
one at a time.

Mother on River Street

1. Lunch

My mother and my aunts
are talking all at once.
It runs in the family,
my father, who has declined
to dine with us at Hale Viet Nam,
says—

the streams of unconsciousness,
he Cantonese soliloquies,
the sideswiping of sentences
from one another.

It does make for a dizzy luncheon.

"Thank God, Lau Gung isn't here,"
says my mother,
leaning back, relaxing,
still referring to my father
in that "psst—better-not-talk,
Lau-Gung-has-just-come-home" way of hers
whenever she is talking stink
about him on the telephone
to one of her sisters.

Lau Gung,
husband in Cantonese—
forty years slapped into two syllables.
Lau Gung,
fish for dinner,
head on the platter.

2. Angel Food Cake

The Baptist Church
saved us,
says my mother,
referring to herself
and her four sisters
who were orphaned young.
We were little lambs.
The Baptists kept us off the streets.
They kept us clothed and busy.
We sang hymns
in our starched and pleated hand-me-downs
and had tea at the gracious
Mānoa homes of old haole ladies
with soft bosoms and light blue hair.
Angel hair.
We were taught to appreciate the finer things.

3. Bad Baby

Your mother was a bad baby,
says my aunt,
my mother's eldest sister.
By the time she was born,
our mother had cancer.
She put your mother in a hammock,
a homemade sling,
and hung it from the ceiling
above her deathbed.
All day long
she rocked your mother
by kicking the hammock with her feet.
One foot,
then the other.
Back and forth,
back and forth.
Your mother—
such a bad baby!—
cried and cried.
But her arms were just too tired.

4. The Scar

My mother has a scar on her chin.
She has had it since she was six years old.
It happened when she fell out of Mrs. Chow's car.
She must have been acting awfully silly
to fall out of a car,
says my aunt
who remembers only that she yelled,
"Sei Mui has fallen out of the car!"
the way Tiki Tiki Tembo
must have wailed when his brother fell into the well.
But my grandmother and Mrs. Chow
were two Cantonese women talking:
sparks flying,
painted eyebrows sharp as scissors twitching,
fingers poking dumplings in the air.
"Sei Mui has fallen out of the car!"
For three blocks they continued to talk
before they braked to a halt—"Huh?"—
and turned to see
Sei Mui running toward them,
chin bleeding,
toothpick arms waving.

5. Fish Wife

It was years before my mother could eat
won bok again,
the white cabbage
her half-brother's wife
fed my mother and her sisters
when they boarded in the unfinished
basement of their half-brother's house.

His mother was their father's
first wife who died in China.

By marrying the dead woman's only son,
Fish Wife took her place.

Save face to the world,
a lacquered smile,
my mother and her sisters knew better.
She kept a stinky house.

First Wife's ghost
appeared every night in Fish Wife's soup,

and while Fish Wife and Half-brother
sucked a tender ginger chicken,

my mother and her sisters
had no say but to swallow
shards of white cabbage.

Mooring

My daughter's long black
hair touches the water

where she sits, waist deep in the warm
bath to receive her baby brother.

I cup the running water,
precious in the summer of drought,

and enter the cool porcelain tub,
my arms weighed with the sturdy

cargo of my infant son.
He lies on his back

and calmly gazes into the faces
of those who love him.

We adore him,
delight in the kernel of toes,

like the youngest corn,
the bracelets of flesh,

the apricot glow of skin.
His sister anoints him with the sweetest soap.

And love passes like this,
cloudless in the face of a thousand years—

for the mother who parts the water
and sends

the baby in the reeds
upstream

to a young girl who waits,
arms and legs

a small harbor.

Tangerines and Rain

The man on the ladder
is the children's grandfather.
The boy and the girl wait for tangerines
to drop like rain into a bucket.

Years of rain have plowed the yard under.
Grass is icing on another child's cake.
Here the damp, red dirt of dog fur
hosts fleas in a desert

marked by the X of watercress and green
onion rising crisp like papyrus
out of the cesspool's oasis.

The man on the ladder
climbs higher into the heart of the tree
and the children are calling

Grandpa. A rustling of leaves is the answer,
a sign of rain and fruit falling
faster than the children can gather.

All summer I hear the soft
shuffling of feet beyond the hedge,
the hedge as tall as my neighbor's tree.

Green and neon globes of orange
muffle afternoon cartoons
like a mouthful of candy.

Gum wrappers litter the tree,
silver-foiled like origami birds
the grandmother folds in the house

for happiness. In the evenings
I hear the boy and sometimes
his sister crying when the father comes home.

This is the summer the mother leaves
for good,
the summer of tangerines and rain

falling under the tree,
in the softest wood of the house,
in the smallest bed.

Rain drifting its way into my yard, my mailbox
where tangerines knock gently,
hesitant as a child's first attempt at a heart.

Square Mile

My son sits in the same classroom
I once sat in, where the instructional

wall clock appears rigged by noon
as if time can't be spent fast enough,

the dull eyelid after lunch and the last
recess bell scuffed by the dry wind gathering

bits of rubbish
into the African tulip and poinciana

trees like confetti
rising from the cracked leather

glove of the baseball field.
My son is covering the same bases,

shouting into the same air
as I pass, honk, and wave on my way

home from the market, climbing
the hill where my mother lived in her brother's house

the last year before her marriage.
The old lawns carry the eye

toward the sea where, gold-tipped
in the sunset, ocean liners

appeared as happiness,
cursive on the horizon, a foreign

cargo of violins and champagne, lily-throated and idle.
They lent their names to these streets:

Lurline, Matsonia, Mariposa.
Saturday nights, money in his pocket

stuffed like feathers in a mattress,
my father climbed this hill, driving

his father's blue Ford, shiny as new shoes.
The long and dusty drive in from the country.

The turns I take he anticipated,
counting each hairpin

turn to reach my mother—
my mother waiting, a butterfly,

pinned to her yellow dress—his heart
racing, taking each curve slow.

Joseph Stanton

Joseph Stanton, an associate professor of arts and humanities at the University of Hawai'i at Mānoa, is widely published as a scholar, poet, and editor. His critical works include studies of such artists and writers as Winslow Homer, Edward Hopper, Chris Van Allsburg, and Richard Howard. Among the numerous journals that have published his poems are *Poetry*, *Poetry East*, and *Harvard Review*, as well as most of Hawai'i's literary magazines. His creative projects include *What the Kite Thinks*, a linked-verse collaboration with Makoto Ooka, Jean Toyama, and Wing Tek Lum. He has long been an activist for the literary arts in Hawai'i and is a past president of the Hawai'i Literary Arts Council.